Pretty
nightmare

new york times bestselling author
ja huss

Pretty nightmare

new york times bestselling author
ja huss

about the Book

INDIE

I have them all now. Just the way I want them.
McKay, the one who loves me deepest.
Adam, the one who protects me fiercely.
Donovan, the one who tells the truth.
They are my friends, they are my lovers, they are my world.
And Maggie belongs to all of us
—no matter who her father is.
This is the family I've always wanted.
This is the family I deserve.
And I will do whatever it takes to keep them.

McKAY

I have a secret that could ruin everything.
But I'm not keeping that secret to hurt her.
Nathan St. James needed to go.

ADAM

I made plan that could ruin everything.
But I did it to save us in the end.
The Company needed to come back.

DONOVAN

I told a lie that could ruin everything.

5

But I didn't tell the lie to them—I told it to myself.
Carter is closer than we think.

There is something truly wrong at Boucher House on the Old Pearl River. Some hidden evil lurking deep inside the woods. Nothing about their blissful life is what it seems. Because just when they think they have it all—he shows up to take it back.

PART ONE
fuel on the fire

This is where you talk about rabbit holes, and falling down into things, and finding tiny bottles of drinks that are not poison, but might as well be.

And then you make a big speech about secrets, and lies, and how the cure for pretty much everything is answers and truth.

Blah.

…

Blah.

…

Blah.

…

Consider all that shit said.

CHAPTER ONE

Indie

I have them all. Just the way I want them.

Donovan is tall and lean. His dark hair is a nice contrast when he stands next to McKay or Adam because they are both blond. Not the same shade— Adam's hair is a little bit lighter. They both have blue eyes, but Donovan's are darker, more hazel than brown. And when I gaze into them it's easy to get lost in the swirls of color. He's tall. All three of them are tall, over six feet. But Donovan has the body of a born athlete. A swimmer, maybe, or a runner. He's filled out a lot since I first met him back when he was fifteen and I was ten. But that's expected. He was still a child even though he didn't act like one. I don't care how high your IQ is, fifteen is still fifteen.

Knowing what I do now, I would not call Donovan a quiet man. But he is quiet compared to McKay. When Donovan is talking his tone is flat and to the point. He's blunt when he has something to say. But he's not inconsiderate. Not at all. Donovan chooses words very carefully before he says them. I think that's left over from his psychiatrist training. But Donovan is the nicest of the three of them. Obviously, Adam is the mean one. He likes it that way. Donovan takes care not to hurt people's feelings. He's not the type of person to yell or insult others. Not that he doesn't get angry, but I get the feeling that Donovan refuses to argue with people because it's not worth his time. He's an opinionated asshole like the rest of the world, he just keeps things to himself.

I think that's because he's been trained to listen to others. But it does make him a hard nut to crack.

McKay's skin tone is slightly more on the brown side than Adam's. McKay tans dark in the summer, like me. His hair gets a shade or two lighter, if he's outside a lot, and he almost always is. McKay is a builder. He can make anything with his hands. He has proved this to me dozens of times over the years.

When Donovan gives me a present it comes wrapped in a fine box with a silky ribbon. I always know that whatever is inside the box, it's going to be sparkly. And it's going to be pricey and come from a store that I've never heard of. But when McKay gives me a gift it's probably not going to be wrapped at all. It's probably too big. Something like a dollhouse, or a swing that hangs from the pavilion ceiling, or a piece of furniture he rescued from the attic and then put his own touches on to make it special. It will have a big bow, but that's about it.

McKay's body is more muscular than Donovan's and if he played a sport it would be something rough. Like football or hockey. Something with a lot of contact and brute force behind the points being earned. And when he talks, even though he doesn't yell very often, his voice carries. It's just loud that way. He's not one to insult people either, but he keeps it in for different reasons than Donovan. McKay doesn't like to be the center of attention. He prefers to have someone's back. Be second in command. He's good at it too. Doesn't need to be given orders to get things done. Just does them naturally.

Adam is as different from them as he is from me. He's hard. Everything about Adam is hard. His blue eyes remind me of cobalt and they don't glint, like McKay's often will. They have a glare in them, a fire inside. A warning too. Don't piss him off, that's what his eyes say.

He's got more tattoos than McKay, who only has a few here and there. But I would not call either of them tattoo enthusiasts. I don't know the stories behind their tats, but I imagine they were things not planned. Heat-of-the-moment artwork. I could be wrong, but they don't talk about them. And I can't even remember the last time either of them came home with a new one. They were mostly all there from the beginning. At least the beginning that started with me.

Adam is the leader. Even during his recovery time, back after his brain injury, he was still in charge. Some people just take command that way and he's one of them. His words are short and clipped. They bark orders. And he will raise his voice in an instant if he thinks you're not paying attention. Adam is a yeller. Sometimes he's a screamer too. If he screams at you, he's pissed off.

But it's when he's quiet that you really gotta look out for Adam. Quiet is a signal that something has gone wrong and his mind doesn't have time for words because he's plotting his actions.

When Adam goes quiet, he's probably thinking about killing people.

His body is hard too—muscular—and he likes to work out. He has a lot of gym equipment in the shed. He likes the bags. Heavy bag. Speed bag. He wraps his hands and kicks things. And he likes to spar with McKay. McKay works out too. It's just part of him. He's always training, but not for the same reasons Adam does. Adam wants to stay hard. Never wants to go soft. McKay just wants to stay sharp. He doesn't like to be caught off guard.

But even though they are so different, they are all the same in some ways.

Mostly when it comes to Maggie. I'm not gonna lie, I'm a little bit jealous that she has captured their love in the same way.

Their love for me was always unequal. Adam loved me when I was in danger. He was a fierce protector. You hurt me, he'll kill you. That was the bottom line. And that's a nice way to be loved. I'm not complaining. McKay loved me like a child. He loved me with his whole heart the way you love something weak and innocent. It's not the same as Adam's protective love, even though it might look that way on the surface. McKay's love was all about preparing me for things. Fights, jobs, danger. That kind of thing. It was a little bit parental. And he is a natural teacher. But Adam's protectiveness was all about ownership. You don't fuck with something that is *his*. And I am his.

Donovan's love for Maggie is more detached. He was that way with me too. He learns from her. Every time she talks he listens, trying to find hidden meaning underneath.

He does that to me too. But Donovan and I are *friends*. Real friends. He never saw me as a child, and I don't think he sees Maggie as a child, either. He saw me as a mind, a collection of unique thoughts and perspectives, and he wanted to know what they were.

So we talked a lot. And not just in the therapy sessions, either. Donovan and I talked about life. I liked to hear about what he was doing when he was away and he liked to talk about it.

When you're Company you can't talk about your life much. But he could tell me anything. He knew I was a vault in that way. That I was never gonna go tell someone what he said. Not even Nathan.

Nathan—even though he's dead—was something quite different than these three men.

Nathan was just… well, the boy next door. That's who he was. He was everything Adam, McKay, and Donovan were, and more. Because he was always there—loving me, and listening to me, and protecting me—and he never asked for anything in return. He never expected me to protect him, and he never expected me to tell him my secrets, and he never asked me to love him.

I just did all those things because that's what you do.

Nathan was… well. It doesn't matter anymore. He's gone.

But Adam, and McKay, and Donovan are still here.

Just the way I want them.

Maggie is here too. And I love her to death. I would do anything for that little girl. But sometimes… I hate to even think this, but sometimes Maggie feels like a secret. Something I should hide away from the world.

I don't understand this feeling very well. I tried to tell myself I'm a mother and that's a mother's job. But that's not it. I did give birth to her, but am I her mother?

No. I don't feel like a mother. She feels more like a friend too. It's almost like I'm her… Donovan. Except she has Donovan too, so I can't be her Donovan.

I feel like her Adam and McKay as well. I want to protect her fiercely and I want to teach her things and make her strong. But again, she already has an Adam and a McKay.

I'm sitting on her bed—my old bed, actually—listening to her brush her teeth in the bathroom down the hall. It's bedtime. She goes to sleep at nine o'clock on the freaking dot every single night.

Just like I did.

McKay cooks her food, and teaches her lessons, and he even bought her a set of throwing knives and has her in martial arts training three times a week because both of those are things you can start young.

This also parallels my training somewhat.

She's very good at both. And we all know that Adam took advantage of the last four years and started training her, even though we don't talk about it.

In fact, almost everything about her life here is just Indie 2.0.

Minus Nathan, of course. I hate that she has no Nathan. It feels like she's missing out on something.

But that can't be helped.

I don't know if I was just too young when I had her. Too immature. Or if it's that I've missed out on so much of her life—more than half of it, to be exact. But I don't feel like she's my daughter. I think mothers spend their pregnancies dreaming of the lives their children will live. What they can give them. How they want to shape them and things like that. And I just didn't do that.

I try to tell myself that it's not my fault—not her fault, for sure, but not my fault either. Because I spent the first trimester of my pregnancy trying to deny it was happening. And I spent the second trying to figure out what was happening with Nathan, trying to keep Adam from killing him, and trying to maintain my relationship with McKay.

The last trimester I fell into a little funk because it was clear that Nathan was not ready for this. Neither was I. And now, looking back, it didn't even matter. He wasn't her father. Or so that card from Carter said a couple weeks ago on Maggie's sixth birthday.

We don't know if Carter is telling the truth. I guess, since he's Donovan's twin brother, we could just do a DNA test using Donovan's blood and see. But Adam says that's risky because, obviously, we have to send that test out somewhere. And his people—which

15

is a whole other topic of conversation—aren't set up to do science like that. So we'd have to send it to a private lab that he has no association with.

Donovan was a hard no on that. So. End of story there.

And it's not like Nathan's even here to push the issue. We're in limbo as far as her father goes.

My point was that I didn't spend my last trimester planning Maggie's life out the way I should've. And even after she was born, I was barely equipped to deal with a baby.

I was good with her. I think. And I do love her. My heart gets tight when I think about her, and I'm pretty sure that's love. But McKay took over because that's what McKay does. And I was… postpartum. I guess that's what we're calling it. That was Donovan's professional opinion.

I'm not sure I completely buy the idea that postpartum depression lasts for two years, but… OK.

It's just… if I were to plan a life for her, I'm not sure I would plan this one.

I love these men. And they love us. But should a six-year-old girl be throwing knives? Even if she's really good at it?

I'm not convinced. I'm just not. I don't know what another life looks like—I just have the one to compare things to—but not all people are like us. I do know that.

"Hell-*looow*!"

I look up and see Maggie standing in front of me with her hands on her hips. Her long, blonde hair is still damp from the bubble bath she took in my old tub just a little while earlier. She's wearing pink bed shorts and a matching tank top. She smells like bubble gum. Kinda looks like it too.

"What?" I ask.

"I was calling your name, Indie. I said it like six times."

"Sorry, I was thinking. Are you ready for bed? Do you want a story tonight?"

She bounces on the mattress past me and then slips under the covers, pulling them up to her chin. It's summer, and it's hot out tonight, but the AC in this room always did work too well. And we keep this house a nice cool sixty-eight degrees almost year-round. "No story tonight. I have things to think about and I don't want to be distracted."

I scrunch up my nose at her. She's forever saying weird shit like this, like she has secret plans going on inside that head of hers. "What things?"

"What I'm gonna do tomorrow, of course."

"What are you gonna do tomorrow? I can't imagine it's any different than what you did today."

She tsks her tongue at me, not liking my statement. "It's Saturday. It's the weekend."

"Hmm." I want to say, *So?* Because again, it's not that she's gonna do anything different. She has no Nathan to make her days special. That really bothers me. "So what are your plans?"

"I'm gonna learn something new. That's always the plan."

"Wouldn't a book help you with that?"

"Your books are stories, Indie. I like the factual books. But before you offer to read me a factual book, just… no thanks. I can do it myself."

She can do it herself. Yes. She can.

17

I smile at her, kiss her on the head, and then get up and walk over to the door. "Good night, Mags. I love you."

"Night, Mama. I love you too."

I flick the light off and close her door, then stand there in the hallway as I listen to the sounds of Old Home.

I'm sleeping with Adam tonight. They won't let me sleep alone because Carter might try to steal me away. We put bars up on Maggie's window the day after that card came. It's got a fire latch or whatever they call it so Maggie can climb out in an emergency. But if she uses it, an alarm will sound on the new security system we now have.

I laugh thinking about all that because Adam was like, "Why the fuck didn't you put bars on this window fourteen years ago, McKay?"

And I knew what he was saying. If my window had bars on it, then a lot of things that happened would not ever have happened.

Including Maggie. Maybe.

If she is Nathan's, then yeah. That would've put an end to Maggie. But if she's not, well. I'm not sure where Carter got a hold of me so we could have sex in the first place, but I'm fairly certain I didn't crawl out my bedroom window to see him.

Adam probably thought this through after his initial outburst and came to the same conclusion.

The stairs squeak and Donovan appears at the end of the hallway. He stops in front of his bedroom door when he sees me. "What's up? Maggie go to bed OK?"

I nod and walk towards him. "Yup. She's in there planning her day tomorrow."

Donovan smiles at me, nods. "OK. So why are you just standing here?"

I huff out a breath that lifts the hair up around my eyes. And when it settles back down I say, "I need a favor."

"What kind of favor?"

"I need you to talk to McKay."

"About?"

"You know. The sex and stuff. I'm tired of bed-hopping. And it's so freaking clear that he and Adam want to be together, it hurts. And if McKay can't come to terms with it, we'll be stuck in this holding pattern for decades before we get to sleep together."

He side-eyes me for a moment. "What about me?"

"What about you?"

"Well… you never asked me if I wanted to share you with McKay and Adam."

Hmm. Donovan and I aren't having sex, but we're definitely skirting the rules on the nights we spend together. His hands will wander. Or my hands will wander. And then… can we help it if we get off on that?

"So you're not gonna do it?"

Donovan grins at me. "Never said that either."

"Gah," I say. "Can you just talk to him? I feel like we're wasting time. Like we're stuck. I don't like it."

He reaches for me. His hands find their way to my body easily and they settle on my hips as he pulls me close. Then he kisses me. It's a nice kiss too. I've kissed Donovan a lot over the years. He and I had a thing going after Maggie was born. McKay caught us once, watched us, but didn't join in. That's how I know we're gonna have to initiate this, otherwise McKay's inability to commit to what he already knows to be true will keep us apart forever. And I'm getting restless.

I pull back from the kiss. "Talk to him, Donovan."

"Fine," he says. "I'll do it tomorrow."

"No. Not tomorrow. Now."

"He and Adam are watching TV in the pavilion. What am I supposed to do? Go down there and interrupt them?"

"I'll tell him you want to talk to him and he should meet you in the kitchen. Then I'll keep Adam occupied. I have questions for him anyway."

Donovan sighs and looks over his shoulder at the stairs. "Fine. But if this goes sideways, it's gonna be your fault."

"Kiss him, Donovan."

"*What?*" Donovan laughs, then pulls me into his room and closes the door so Maggie can't hear us if she's spying. "What the hell are you talking about?"

"Kiss McKay. It'll help him feel better. I'm sure he feels the same way about Adam as Adam feels for him. And I'm sure he's spent the past twenty-five years trying to picture himself kissing the guy. If he just gets it over with, then he can stop thinking so hard about that."

"First of all"—Donovan holds up a finger—"he will punch me in the face."

"He will *not*. McKay is not reactionary like that."

"Are we talking about the same man? Tall guy? Eyes filled with mystery and pent-up hate? Hobbies include training little girls to kill people?"

"You're being stupid. Why are all of you so stupid? And he has no pent-up hate. That's utter bullshit."

"Second"—he holds up a second finger—"I'm one hundred percent certain that Core McKay has spent no time—not a single fucking *moment* of time—wondering how his first kiss with *any* man, let alone Adam, would go down."

"You don't know that."

"Oh, I do know that. Third"—he adds to his finger count—"you really don't see the pent-up hate inside McKay? Or was that just a flippant remark?"

"McKay is not hateful."

"I never said he was hateful. I implied he's got… issues. Long-time lingering issues, Indie. And all of them have to do with Adam and how he came to live with the Boucher family."

I huff, then sigh. "He loves Adam."

"I know he does. But love is complicated, Indie Anna. McKay isn't thinking about kissing Adam."

"Well, he should be. Because those two were meant to be together."

Donovan smiles now. "That I can agree with."

"Then why are you so resistant to my plan?"

"Because it's not a romantic kind of love, Indie. It's something else. They're meant to be together because they don't actually know how to live apart." He stops. Makes a face. "Well. I'm not even sure about that any more. Adam seems to have gotten along just fine without McKay. And while McKay didn't light the fucking world on fire while Adam was missing, he did move on. He's got his workshop now. And his little online store shit."

"Hmm," I hum. "That's not good. They *are* meant to be together. We're all meant to be together. So what's wrong with giving this thing a little push? I'm

21

telling you, McKay has no idea how to approach Adam and tell him these things. You can help him with that. Just get that first kiss over with. That way it won't be awkward when we finally all get together. And that was the plan, right? We're all waiting for McKay to come to some conclusion so we can have sex."

Donovan scratches his neck and shoots me a strained look. "Was that what McKay was thinking when he put us all in timeout? Because that was not my impression, Indie. To me it felt like… he wanted you for himself. But he knows he can't have you like that. So he needed time for you to figure out who you loved most."

"Love most? I love you all. I'm not going to stop loving you, Donovan. Or Adam. Or McKay. This is my point. I want you *all*. And I don't want to take turns. That's not good enough. It's all of us, or none of us."

He just stares at me for a moment.

"I have earned this, Donovan." My voice is soft now. "I have done everything you guys asked me to do and now it's my turn for you all to do something I'm asking for. I deserve this. I deserve this family we've built. I deserve to be surrounded by love. I deserve happiness, Donovan. All I'm asking is that you help me make it happen. Please. We're so close."

"We're not close. Carter is—"

"Forget him. He's got nothing to do with our happiness. This is about us. That's it. All I'm asking you to do is kiss him one time. Make him talk about it. Think about it. I swear to God, Core McKay is thinking about Adam. All the time. He's looking for a way in, Donovan. Not a way out."

Donovan sighs. "Fine. Whatever. But I don't think it's gonna work, Indie. He really might hit me. And he hits hard. He barely likes me. We both know I'm only here because of you. Neither of them would even look at me twice if it wasn't for you."

I scoff. Loudly. Then look him up and down with eyes that say he's crazy. Donovan is a lot of things. He's too smart, too sneaky, and too aloof. He was too skinny as a teenager and a little bit awkward. But he is not invisible. In fact, he is an unmissable-looking man. His dangerous good looks are dark and broody. And every time I look into his eyes, I see lust in there. I don't know what he's been up to all these years in his private life, but I'm absolutely certain that it involved a lot of dirty sex with people of both genders.

He didn't object to kissing McKay because he was a man. He objected because he thinks he'll be rejected. And that's all I really need to know.

So I say, "If they're not looking at you twice, then you're just not trying. If McKay doesn't kiss you back, it's because you didn't flip his switch and turn him on." I reach between his legs and fondle his balls. He breathes out suddenly and his eyes droop a little. "Try a little *harder* to turn him on, Donovan."

CHAPTER TWO

When Adam's father sat me down in his office many years ago and told me this crazy story about zeroes, and negatives, and dead twins, I was only half listening.

Not that fully listening would've helped me understand what the hell was happening. It wouldn't. The things he said to me that day just made no sense and there was nothing I could do to change that.

But I was also distracted. I was thinking about what my own father told me before I was taken away. He said, "Core, there are two ways to go through life and both of them require strength and conviction. You can either listen, follow directions, and be invisible to everyone, including your enemies. Or you can buck, and go your own way, and make everyone *see you*. One is not better than the other. They both have their merits. And you can get where you're going either way, if you're strong enough. But you need to decide early which kind of man you will be. Because once people form an impression of you it rarely changes. So decide, son. Do you want to be invisible? Or do you want to be seen?"

By the time I had landed in Louisiana I had made my choice.

I would be invisible.

And so by the time I got into that office I was picturing ways to make it happen.

I wasn't naïve enough to think my father literally meant invisible, but I was young. So I'm not gonna lie and say that idea never crossed my mind.

I do not hate Adam. Far from it. He is my best friend.

I would die for him, but not for the same reasons he would die for me.

I'm not going to walk away from him. I made my decision back when I was nine and I am nothing if not loyal.

But then Indie came along and everything… shifted.

It's hard to explain. Nothing changed, not really. I was still on Team Adam. One hundred percent. You don't bite the hand that feeds you, especially when the person attached to the hand is loyal, the way Adam is.

But buying up little girls… I don't know. It's not that much different than buying up little boys, I guess. But then again, *everything* about it feels different.

I didn't start up my own team to take over. It wasn't about replacing Adam. It was about helping him. He wasn't the same after Indie's attack in Nathan's cottage. First of all, she fucked him up good and it took nearly six months for him to even be able to think straight for more than an hour or two at a time. Another six before he had enough physical coordination to make me tap out on the mat when we trained.

It's not like he always won in the past when we sparred. But I didn't always win either. We are fairly evenly matched. Hell, we should be. I was chosen to be his equal, his double, his replacement. But when we first started training again after he started getting better, he was… weak. I wanted to stop. I didn't want to do it anymore. I would wake up every morning at dawn and dread the two hours we had put aside for this every fucking day.

It killed me to see him like that. And I was conflicted about Indie too. For the first time ever I wondered, *Is she just… too dangerous? Even for us?*

I guess I was running from it. The idea that Adam would not recover. Because it was very clear to me, right from the moment he woke, that even if he did recover, he would not be the same.

Getting attacked by the dangerous thing you fed, and loved, and cared for—how do you trust anything after that?

And Donovan was in my ear the whole time Adam was in the hospital, telling me, "We need to make a move, McKay. We can't let this Company shit get out of hand just because they think Adam isn't paying attention."

He was right, I guess. But that shit got handled quick without our input, because James Fenici showed up and made a little speech that will burn in my memory for the rest of my days.

His exact words to Donovan and me were, "This is *the* shit show of all shit shows. And I've seen my share of Class A shit shows. I'm gonna let her live, but you two fuckups are gonna stand the hell down, do your fucking jobs, and bend over backwards for Adam when he wakes up so he can resume. His. Duties. I will *not*"—he pointed his fucking finger at our faces and those infamous green eyes of his went feral as they stared us down—"*not* deal with another leadership change. Do you two assholes understand the words that are coming out of my mouth?"

Donovan shut up, I went back to the care and feeding of Indie, Nathan had the good sense to stay the fuck away, and… that was it.

Life went on.

Adam got better.

But I didn't. I was simmerin' with anger.

I can admit that now. Years later. Nine, to be exact.

But back then, I didn't understand what I was feeling. Because Adam never told us he was in charge of anything.

Of course, I realize now, he didn't know either. It took a while to figure that out. Years. Five, to be exact, after Indie went wild and hit him in the head.

Adam didn't know. There was some—I don't know, internal memo maybe?—that Adam was next in line for the throne. Or whatever you want to call it.

He wasn't really. Not by legal succession. That was James. But James was truly out and he was just using Adam to make sure he could keep it that way.

The Company, man.

They will fuck you over every chance they get.

But they come to your rescue too.

That's a very hard road to navigate and I might've taken a few wrong turns.

Adam and I are out in the pavilion watching the sci-fi series we started nearly six years ago but never finished.

Well, I finished it. Without him.

He stops to ask me questions every few minutes. "So she's a Cylon?" He's stretched out on the couch across from me with his legs and arms both crossed. His feet are bare and he's shirtless. It's fucking hot out tonight.

"I'm pretty sure you saw that part. We've known she was a Cylon since season two." I'm also shirtless and stretched out on a couch. Maggie was down here with us until Indie came to take her up to bed. And we were watching cartoons until that happened.

"I think I'd remember if I knew she was a Cylon, McKay."

He's testy about this show for some reason. Maybe because we were into it and it started out as something we did together, but, like everything else, it didn't keep going that way.

"I'm not making a disparaging remark about your fucking memory, Adam. I'm just saying. We're on season three now. You knew that girl was a Cylon."

I'm starting to get testy back. It's too fucking hot out here and I'm just about to stand up and go inside when Indie pushes her way through the mosquito-netting curtains that frame the pavilion and walks over to me.

29

"Donovan wants to talk to you about something. He asked me to tell you because I was on my way out here."

I screw up my mouth at this.

"Why's he wanna talk to McKay?" Adam asks what I'm thinking.

"I dunno," Indie says, shrugging her shoulders as she scoots my legs off the couch and sits down.

Adam's not looking at her. He's pretending to be interested in the alien insurrection drama happening on the TV. "Why didn't he just come out here and talk to him?"

"I don't know, Adam. Why don't you go ask him?" Indie's the kind of girl who will match you mood for mood. She didn't come out here meaning to be short with Adam, but he was short with her first. You get what you give when it comes to Indie.

Adam doesn't even look at her. "I'm watching something."

I stifle a laugh as Indie scowls at him. "He's just being a dick tonight," I tell her. "That's all." Then I stand up and head through the curtains towards the house, grateful that Indie came to save me. Even if it was just to have a stupid conversation with Donovan.

When I get inside, sure as shit, Donovan is waiting for me in the kitchen. He's just closing the fridge door with two bottles of beer in his hand when I walk in.

"What's up?" I ask. "You wanted to talk to me?"

He pops the top on one of the beers and hands it to me. "Yup. It was Indie's idea, actually."

I take the beer. It's nice in the house. The AC is rushing through the vents down by my bare feet and the beer is very cold in my hand. It's kinda perfect actually. And even though I should be concerned that Indie is up to something and she's got Donovan involved, the annoyance that was building outside just slips away when I take that first sip.

Donovan pops the top on his beer too. And his eyes track me as he drinks.

I'm not gonna lie. Those eyes of his have always creeped me out a little bit. They're dark, but not dark. I'm not sure that explains anything. They aren't brown, but they're not green either. Maybe it's just that I'm used to blue eyes around here. We all have them, courtesy of the Company gene pool. Or maybe I have just always been a little mistrustful of Donovan.

He's an Untouchable, like Adam. But it's a whole different kind of Untouchable. The things his family were involved in were some deep-state shit. Genetic engineering. Manchurian candidates. All those little girls in that auction. And the zoo, of course. Hell, that entire island was something right out of that old story, *The Most Dangerous Game*. I've never been there, but just before Adam and his father came up to Alaska and stayed with us, I heard my father telling my brothers about it. I don't remember the specifics, but it had something to do with a hunt.

And to be clear, they weren't talking about hunting the *animals*.

Donovan sets his beer down on the counter and then leans both hands on it, kinda inching forward. I'm on the other side of the island, so we're not that far apart.

Then his eyes unlock with mine and slip down my chest. When they come up, he's smiling at me and I'm

31

JA HUSS

instantly annoyed again. "What the fuck do you want? And why are you looking at me that way?"

"You look pretty good, McKay. For an old guy. I've been meaning to tell you that."

I feel one eyebrow rise up into my forehead. "You called me in here to tell me I look good? And fuck you. I'm not old. Yet. I'm only thirty-five."

"I was just fucking with you. No, but for real." His eyes do that tracking thing again, slipping down, then back up. "I look pretty good too though, right? I mean, I don't work out like you and Adam, it's mostly genetics."

I laugh. I can't help myself. "You look like a strait-laced asshole, that's what you look like. You don't even drink beer so I'm kinda pissed off that you're wasting that bottle right there. We both know you're only drinking it to *bond with me.* Or something. Spit it out. What the fuck do you want?"

"I'm trying to tell you. You're just not listening."

"You're trying to tell me what?"

He smiles at me. It's a weird smile, a little bit creepy like his eyes, and a chill runs up my spine. Then he shrugs. "OK. Forget it. I'm just gonna come out with it because I don't really know how to talk to you, McKay. And pretending to flirt with you—"

I laugh. Like, I'm talking a serious guffaw complete with a backward head throw and closed eyes as I pretend to look up at the ceiling.

"What? It's not *that* funny."

"I'm sorry." And I'm still laughing. "Did you... did you just say you're... *flirting* with me?"

"Laugh all you want, asshole. But she and I?" He points to himself and then towards the front door.

32

"We're gonna fuck tonight. Whether you want us to or not."

"Excuse me?"

"You heard me. We've been skirting around the rules a little for the past few weeks. But she's tired of waiting for you to figure shit out with Adam, so"—he shrugs like this is all just out of his hands—"I'm gonna give you some friendly advice. As you Southerners say. Just kiss the man and get it over with."

"Who?"

"Oh, please. You know who. Adam, for fuck's sake."

I laugh again. "Now, why the hell would I kiss Adam?"

"Because you two have been in love for as long as I've known you. And you can pretend you don't feel that way, McKay. That's fine. It's your life." He sighs. "But Indie's not gonna let you get away with that special little relationship you two have had all these years anymore. She wants us all. At the same time. She made that very clear when she left me in here and went outside to send you in. So I'm just letting you know, I'm done skirting the rules. I'm fucking present. And I'm giving up a lot to be here. I don't want to play by your rules anymore and neither does Indie."

I actually do not know what to say to him. But turns out, I don't have to say anything because he just keeps going.

"Look, we all know Adam has a thing for you. You know it, I know it, Indie knows it. And if one of us confronted him, he'd admit it. But you, McKay? You just push back. On *every*thing. I don't know why you do that, but I have fourteen years of schooling and that

33

means I've earned the right to take an educated guess. And my guess is you hate change, McKay. You hate it. You're all about a fucking routine. You get up at the same time every day. You make the same boring cup of coffee, you read the same bullshit news, and then you go out to the shed and you work on something. That's your routine. And you're gonna do this, without fail, until someone fucks up your good thing."

I point at him. "Fuckin' up my good thing is my example A. I don't want people fuckin' up my good thing. No one wants their good thing fucked up. It takes a long time to get a good thing, Donovan. It's not a gallon of milk. It's not something you just go pick up at the Pearl Springs Market when you run out."

He grins and shakes his head at me. "That's fear talking, McKay."

"So what?" I throw up my hands. "I've never pretended to be fearless. I've never pretended to be anything. I do my fucking job, and I do it well. And so far, that's worked out for me. It's kept me alive, at least."

"What are you talking about?"

I sigh and run my fingers through my hair as I turn away from him.

"OK." Donovan sighs too. "I get it. I mean, it's an educated guess. But I think I've established my credentials in educated guessing. We put a lot of responsibility on you."

I look over my shoulder at him. "That's not what I'm saying. I didn't do any more than you did. Or Adam."

"That's not what I'm saying either. You were responsible for a little girl with a fucked-up mind."

"So were you. And so was Adam."

"But you were responsible for her in ways that we were not. So I get it, McKay. She is something to you that she is not to me."

"She is something to you that she is not to me as well."

"That's fair. But if we were five years younger, I wouldn't be here talking to you about this. I'd just take Indie the way I wanted her and say fuck you both. She and I have been together lots of times, McKay. We practically dated when she was nineteen."

"When did you two really start?"

"When she was seventeen."

"You're an asshole, Donovan."

"I was only twenty-two."

"She was a kid."

"She hasn't been a kid for a very long time, McKay."

"Neither have you."

He sighs. "We're not five years younger anymore. That good thing we had? It's long gone, dude. And if you *really* wanted to keep your current good thing, the one you have right now with that metal art you're doing?" He shrugs big with his hands and shoulders. "Then you'd have stayed in New Orleans."

"I'm not staying in New Orleans when this place is my home."

"Exactly." He points at me. "We're building a new good thing. That's why you're here. But that scares you. Adam's love for you is scary, isn't it? And now that I think about it, it's not just Adam. It's everything. You're afraid of everything. You don't take chances. Ever. You *prepare* for shit. You plan. You study all the possible outcomes, and then you choose one path. Just one. And you go rigid. You plant yourself on that path and you *do not* step out of bounds. If I had a dollar for every time I heard you tell Indie not to take chances on a job, to just follow the fucking plan, I'd be a very rich man."

"You're already a very rich man, dumbass."

He sets his jaw, then kinda juts it out a little as he chews on his lip. His eyes are locked on mine. Not as creepy as usual, but there's definitely something behind them. Then he lets out a long breath and slowly starts to walk around the island.

"What the fuck are you doing?" I ask.

He shakes his head at me and smiles. "I'm gonna show you that this new good thing we're building here, it's not gonna kill you."

I don't move. Just stand there as he makes his way around to my side of the island.

"So I'm gonna help you out a bit, OK?"

"What are you talking about?"

He reaches me. But he doesn't stop. Just comes right up into my personal space. I put both my hands on his bare chest and push him back. It's a hard push too, one that says I mean business. And Donovan might be all muscle, but he's lean, and I've got at least thirty pounds on him. So he takes that step back.

"We're gonna kiss."

"We are not." I laugh.

"We are. Think of it as practice."

"Donovan—"

"McKay? Shut the fuck up. I'm just gonna kiss you and we're gonna get it over with. OK? That way you're prepared. And when you go to kiss Adam—"

"I'm not kissing Adam. I'm not doing anything with Adam."

"When you go to kiss Adam, it'll be part of the plan. And then you don't have to be afraid."

I pause and look at him. "Are you… into dudes?"

He shrugs. "Whatever. You're not just any dude. And look, one day, pretty fucking soon—like tonight maybe—you and I are gonna be in a heated moment with Adam and Indie. She wants it, McKay. Adam wants it. I want it. It's going to happen. So I'm gonna kiss you eventually. And you're gonna kiss me. And I'm gonna touch you. And—"

I guffaw again. I cannot believe I'm having this conversation.

Donovan reaches for my cock.

I stop laughing and push him back.

"Too soon?" He grins. "Noted. But you need to get over this. Because your only other option, McKay? Is to walk out. Like you did the day of Indie's twentieth birthday. But if you do, you should know that Adam won't come after you again. He's in a different place now. We all see it. He's got a new good thing and her name is Maggie. And I'm sure he wants you to be here for it—but if you walk away this time?" Donovan shakes his head. "He'll let you go. You two have been in a relationship for nearly three decades. He's been patient. He's respected you and your beliefs. He did his part and now it's time for you to do yours. Or just move the fuck on. Because Indie doesn't belong to you. She belongs to *us*."

I blow out a long breath of air filled with words I was gonna say back, but can't.

Because he's right. Everything he fucking said was right. I love Adam. I don't know if I'm *in love* with Adam. It might be more along the lines of infatuation. But I can't deny that he and I have something between us. And it wouldn't be very hard to turn it into more.

When I don't say anything, Donovan takes another step towards me.

Then his hands are on my face. His fingers thread up into my hair and he leans forward.

And then he kisses me.

CHAPTER THREE

Adam

Indie gets up from the couch and lingers in the middle of the outdoor living room for a few moments like she's waiting for me to notice her.

"Something on your mind, Indie?"

She walks over to me and sits on my stomach. I laugh. Then give her a shove to make her get up.

She doesn't though. She lies down on me, resting her cheek on my chest. I put my hands behind my head because I suddenly don't know what to do with them and she's always had a talent for making me nervous. "What's going on?"

"Hm. Just thinking about stuff."

"Sounds dangerous."

"It's not." She lifts her head up just a little and smiles. "I have to tell you something."

"OK."

She sighs. "I'm sorry."

I don't need to ask about what. I know what. "That was a long time ago."

"That's not the point. And that's not even what I mean. I am sorry, Adam. But here's the part I never told you. I never told anyone. But. I don't remember it. Time skipped, or something. I can't explain it, or prove it, and I know it sounds crazy, but I don't remember hitting you with that candlestick. It's just… one minute I was standing there watching you—" She stops.

"Watching me beat the fuck out of Nathan?"

"Yeah." She breathes out. "And then the next thing I knew you were on the ground with a huge gash in your head. Blood was spilling out all over the place and I was holding a candlestick. I don't know how it happened. And I tried to tell this to you that one summer we spent all our time gardening. Remember?"

"Of course I remember. I'm the one who told you to plant those damn daphne bushes."

"Yeah." She inhales deeply, then lets it out slowly. "I don't like to think about it."

"Me either. So we don't need to talk about it. I know you didn't mean to kill me."

"I don't know how you can even think that, Adam. Because I tried to kill you again just a few years later. And…" She stops again.

"Indie," I say, bringing my hands down so I can place them on her shoulders. "It's not your fault."

"It is."

I shake her a little. "Listen to me, OK? Because this is important. It's *not* your fault, kid. It's just not. They did things to you, Indie. Terrible, evil things. And they fucked you up long before you showed up in that auction. And by that time, there was nothing any of us could've done to change it."

Her face falls into a deep frown. "Oh." She sounds sad.

"OK, wait. Let me say that again, in a different way. Because that's not really what I meant. They did things to you. They changed you. And then McKay, and Donovan, and I did our best to… take it back and make it right."

"It just wasn't good enough, was it?"

I lift my head up a little to see her better. "It *was* good enough. We're still here, right?"

"Yeah." She doesn't sound convinced.

"We changed you back a little. You're much better now, Indie. You learned a lot of truth over the past few months and you're dealing with it really well."

She nods and sinks a little deeper into my chest.

I want to hug her. I want to hold her and tell her everything's gonna be OK. But she scares me.

And it's not about how dangerous she is. Or if she'll snap one day and succeed in killing me. All of us, really. It's just we're really, really far away from being OK.

"Do you love Maggie more than me?"

I laugh. "Why the hell would you ask me that?"

"Because you act like she's yours."

"You're mine too."

"It's different."

"How?"

She takes yet another deep breath. "I don't know. It just is. The two of you are a team. Everyone sees it."

"Yeah. We are. And I'm real sorry about that, kid. Because I didn't take her away on purpose. I just didn't know what to do once I knew she was gonna recover. McKay thinks I just up and left, but that's not how it happened. I didn't have a phone, or my wallet, or anything. I was still a little fucked up from the drugs.

41

And I was worried. I was very fucking worried. I wasn't thinking about anyone but Maggie. And the day just slipped by without me noticing. Then suddenly it was two days later, and Maggie was out of danger, and I needed to go home. But I didn't come here. I went to the house in the French Quarter. I didn't know what to do. My head had cleared and I didn't know you were gone. If I had known you were gone, I'd have come back for McKay and then Donovan would've eventually shown back up too. And we'd have figured shit out differently."

"But that's not how it went."

"No. That's not how it went. So I just… took her. I didn't know what to do. I just thought it was better if we hid out. So that's what we did."

"Hid out." She sighs. "From me."

I want to take that back and make her feel better about it. But it's true. We *were* hiding from her.

"It wasn't just you I was hiding from, Indie Anna. I didn't know Carter was behind that day. Not right away. I had a list of people it could've been."

"A whole list?" She looks up at me.

"It was a short list. Carter wasn't even on it. It took a while for his name to come up. But I run hundreds of dangerous men, Indie. It's not a big leap to figure one of them was trying to take me out."

She's quiet for a little bit. And I get a little lost in the past, thinking back on those first days. "I was trying to make sense of things, Indie. I was wishing so hard that my father was still around. And then, out of nowhere, it hit me that I had killed him."

"You didn't kill him. I'm pretty sure that was Sasha Cherlin."

"Maybe she did do it. Or someone she was with did it. But I helped her get to that Company resort in Santa Barbara. I put her there. And I only did that for one reason and that was so she could… clean it all up. Do the dirty work. I feel a lot more shame about that than I do about my father dying."

Indie turns her head so she can meet my eyes. "You do?"

I nod. "I do. I don't like who I am most of the time."

She pushes herself up now, bracing her hands flat on my chest so she can look me in the eyes properly. "You're not a bad guy."

"Says you."

"You're not. You saved my life so many times."

"I used you."

"You saved me. You saved me from that snake."

"Shit. There were half a dozen men from all around the world trying to outbid me that night. You were never in any danger from that snake."

"Yeah, but who were they, Adam? Who were all those people who wanted to buy me?"

"I don't know. They were calling in bids. They weren't there in person."

"They would've used me differently, Adam. We both know that. So no. I'm not gonna hate you. Not for any of it. You did save me. It took me a really long time to understand that, but I do now."

"All right. I'm not gonna fight you over that. I know when to pick and choose my battles."

She grins at me and then settles back down on my chest.

This time I hug her. And she slips her hands under my arms until I can feel the tips of her fingers pressing against my shoulder blades.

She sighs. "What do you think they did to me? Before I came here?"

"I don't know. I have no idea who had you before the island. And I've looked, girl. I've looked pretty hard. There's no record of you."

"Do you think Donovan's grandfather knew?"

"Yes. One hundred fucking percent."

"Do you think Donovan knows?"

"He better not. I'll kill that fucker with my bare hands if I find out he's been keeping that secret."

"But wouldn't he have gotten all the files when he inherited the estate?"

I know the answer to this. It's always bothered me too. But I don't want Indie thinking about the past. I just want her focused on the future. So I change the subject. "What did Donovan want with McKay?"

"Oh." She laughs a little, then squirms in my embrace and props her chin on my chest as she smiles at me. "He's gonna flirt with him."

"What?"

"And maybe kiss him. McKay is so... *straight*."

I chuckle. "He really is."

"But that's just because he's... I dunno. A little bit uptight. Don't you think?"

"A *little*?"

"A lot." She laughs again. "So I told Donovan he needed to get McKay used to the fact that he's in this, whether he planned for it or not."

"In... what?"

"Us, you dummy. Me. You. Donovan. And McKay. I'm tired of taking turns in everyone's bed when nothing ever fucking happens. Well." She pauses.

"Well what? Is something happening?"

She shrugs one shoulder. "Donovan and I mess around a little."

"Hmm."

"Are you jealous?"

"No. Of *Donovan*? No."

"It's been months. We're settled in. Things have gone back to normal. We're more normal than ever, if you think about it. It's time to move on. Just... be who we've always known we are."

"What are we?"

"A team." She says this simply. And her voice is a little bit small. It's easy to forget Indie is very young. She's got an old soul, for sure, but twenty-four is practically a child. I think back to when I was twenty-four—we'd had Indie for just one year back then. And I had no idea what I was doing. Of course, at the time I thought I had it all figured out, didn't I?

I bought a girl at a Company auction. With the express intent of using her as a weapon. With the express intent of not using her for sex. With the express intent of never getting another one. Of never turning into my father.

But look where I am right now. I have Indie. I have Maggie.

And that's just where it starts.

I almost laugh. I only hold it in because Indie will ask me what's funny and I'm never gonna admit this shit out loud to anyone, let alone her.

But I turned into him anyway, didn't I?

I am my father's son.

"We're on the same side, Adam," Indie says.

She's so naïve and young. Always has been and always will be. Indie is never going to be normal. She will never grow up.

She will always be that little girl in that cage.

She will always be the little girl who used to climb out her window and creep into the woods.

She will always be the little girl who used to go to church with me.

And now, I take her daughter to church instead.

It's kinda hard to wrap my head around that.

"I'm sleeping with you tonight," she says.

"Yup. It's my night."

Her eyes twinkle a little bit. "We could mess around a little. If you want."

"Uhhh…" I don't know how to answer that. It's not like I'm not attracted to Indie. She's a beautiful creature. Very smart. Very capable. Very sexy. But she's got a big ol' mess of lovely darkness hiding inside her.

Looking at her right now, and thinking about her offer—well, that's like being on your knees, leaning over so you can look down the rabbit hole. You don't know what's down there. Could be an amazing trip of epic proportions. Could be just a pretty little nightmare waiting to happen.

She gets up and extends her hand to me. "Come on. Let's go to bed."

She could be my wife.

I mean, she's never going to be my wife. But she *could be.* I stole her daughter, didn't I? I'm that girl's father now. No way in hell anyone can take that away from me. So Indie could be my wife. We could just…

slip into this. Easily. We have Old Home. We have each other. We have everything we need to grab the good old American Dream. We could have more children if we wanted. And things would turn out differently this time.

I would not turn into my father.

We could start over.

And maybe… just maybe… McKay would join us.

Could McKay ever do that? Will he ever love me the way I love him?

"Stop thinking so hard."

I take Indie's hand and let her pull me to my feet. Then I click off the TV and we walk through the mosquito netting all lit up with fairy lights, and head towards the house.

She holds my hand as we walk, squeezing it a little. It feels natural, but then again, weird.

This girl—woman, now, I suppose—she has been off limits to me for so long. It's really hard to get that out of my head. And sometimes, when I look at Maggie, I see Indie.

It's just… weird.

Indie doesn't lead me to the front porch. She takes me around the side. "Where are we going?"

"To spy on them, of course."

"Ahh, I don't know."

She stops us on the side of the house in front of the office window. "Stop being a baby. Don't you want to be with McKay?"

And this is weird too. Since when do I talk about my feelings with Indie? With anyone, actually?

"You're really trying hard to find an excuse, aren't you?"

"I'm not." It comes out defensive. "Of course I love McKay. Of course I want to be with him."

"So what's the problem?"

I hesitate. She just shakes her head at me and drops my hand. "Fine. Then stay here. I'll spy."

She turns away and continues walking along the side of the house, then looks over her shoulder one last time before she disappears around the corner.

I jog to catch up.

Fuck it.

When I round the corner, Indie has her face pressed against the glass of the family room window. The only lights on inside are the ones under the kitchen cabinets. So it's a low light. A soft glow of yellow But it's more than enough to see them.

Donovan and McKay are kissing.

I exhale and then heat fills me up. And I don't remember breathing, but I exhale again. And then again. My chest rising and falling as emotions flood into my bloodstream.

"It's kinda hot," Indie whispers.

I have to agree. It kinda is. But it's a lot of other things too.

They are both shirtless. And I'm not gonna lie, Donovan is just as nice to look at as McKay.

That's not the only reason it's hot though. This looks like a real fucking kiss. McKay is even kissing him back. And then Donovan's hand slips down McKay's chest, then down his ridiculous sixty-four-pack abs and rests on the waistband of his jeans.

Indie sucks in a little breath of surprise. "Damn. I didn't think they'd… ooohh. Wow."

Donovan is gripping McKay's cock through his jeans. And McKay pulls out of the kiss. I have a moment of hope that he'll push Donovan away. McKay looks down at Donovan's hand as Donovan grips his cock and begins massaging his hand over his groin area.

But McKay doesn't push him away. He closes his eyes and leans back against the counter. Practically giving Donovan permission to do whatever he wants.

"OK." I sigh. "I've seen enough."

I turn and walk back to the front of the house. Indie jogs behind me, catching up by the time we reach the porch. I make a lot of noise coming up the steps and even more when I open the main door.

I can see them in the kitchen pulling apart. McKay disappears out of view before we step into the foyer. But Donovan remains in view, running his fingers through his thick, dark hair as he smiles at us.

I want to punch him in the teeth. Wipe that fucking smile right off his face.

But Indie takes over, grabbing my hand and calling, "We're going to bed. See you two in the morning."

I barely hear what McKay and Donovan say back. The blood is rushing in my head, making it pound. And anyway, Indie is already leading me up the stairs.

She slips right into my room and closes the door behind us, flicking a switch on the wall that controls a small light on one of the bedside tables. She lets out a small giggle.

"What's so fucking funny?"

"Oh, my God. If you could only see your face right now." She giggles again. Points at me. "You're jealous."

"I am not jealous of *Donovan*."

"OK." She shrugs. Then in one swift movement, she has her tank top over her head and is throwing it on the ground at her feet. She stands there in her pretty pink bra as I look at her.

"What are you doing?"

"What's it look like, Adam?" She reaches behind her back to unclasp her bra, and then it's falling on the floor too. She's got a little pile going now.

She saunters over to me, her hips moving seductively. I put up a hand to stop her, but she takes it and places it on the button of her cut-off shorts. And then, without waiting for me to make a decision, she uses my fingers to pop that button.

"You just gonna stand there?" she asks.

"I'm fine with waiting for McKay to—"

"Fuck McKay. He's having a good time with Donovan right now."

"Indie." I sigh.

"Adam," she whispers back, leaning up on her tiptoes to kiss my mouth. "Just stop, OK?" Her words flitter past my lips. "This is happening. We all want it to. We're just not sure how to make it happen. So Donovan and I have taken control. And tonight, you're going to touch me."

She still has my hand and she slips it inside the waistband of her shorts.

I want to stop her, but I can't. Not when I feel the pool of wetness between her legs.

And when she grabs me, the same way Donovan grabbed McKay down in the kitchen, I know what's gonna happen next. It feels very inevitable.

But I force myself to pull away. I'm not a man who gives in to base instincts. I remove my hand from inside her shorts and walk across the room to create some distance between us.

"You're not gonna win this one. You better pick and choose your battles tonight, Adam."

I slip my pants off so I'm bare, except for my boxer briefs. And then I walk over to the little table, flick the light off, and pull the covers back on my bed. Getting in without saying a word.

Indie walks over to her side, quiet in the near darkness. There's a moon out, so I can see the outline of her body as she stands on the side of the bed, then hear the shuffle of her shorts as she drags them down her legs.

She pulls her side of the covers back and slips right in next to me, her body already cool from the AC. Her hand goes to my stomach and rests there. She's waiting for me to say something.

But I don't say anything.

Everything about Indie Anna Accorsi feels *forbidden*.

And, if I'm being honest with myself—and why not, right? It's just me here—everything about her feels *wrong*.

"You wanna know how Donovan and I skirt around the rules?"

"Hmm?"

"I'll show you." Her hand reaches for mine and she places my palm over my cock. I'm not hard, but it

51

would not take much to make that change. Then her hand grips mine until I'm squeezing it. She moves my hand back and forth. And I get what she's doing.

"I'll do all the work," she breathes, turning her body a little so her face is pressed up against my shoulder. "You just get to enjoy it."

"But you're gonna use my hand?"

"That's how we keep it legal. But if you want to say fuck the rules, I'm OK with that too."

My cock begins to fill up and extend and she breathes softly, her breath passing over the curve of my shoulder and hitting my neck.

I close my eyes.

"See," she says, using her other hand to pull my boxer briefs down just enough so that my cock springs out. "It feels good."

It's cheating. But I don't say that. I would like to think I could stop this. I would like to think that this is a decision I'm making. But it's not.

She is totally in control of me.

My breathing becomes ragged and uneven as my heart beats fast. Her hand squeezes mine, making me grip my shaft harder, and then she starts jerking me off.

Or... she makes me jerk myself off.

Her strokes are long and slow. Like she knows exactly what she's doing.

And I'm not gonna lie. There is no point in that. This easiness she has, this knowledge of sex—it bothers me. Because I picture her with other men and I want to *kill them*.

I want to torture them. Slowly. Cut them. Hit them with very blunt objects. Make them suffer and bleed for teaching her how to do these things.

For *daring* to touch one of *my* girls.

"Shhh," she whispers in my ear, leaning into me a little. She kisses my neck again and again. Moving these soft flutters down along my jaw until she reaches my mouth.

I turn my head towards her and kiss her back, repositioning myself so I can lean up on one elbow and grab a fistful of her hair and hold her next to me. I kiss her hard. And she responds by jerking me harder, still using my own hand to do it.

I stop, let go of my cock, turn my whole body sideways, and push her down on the mattress.

"What's wrong?" she asks.

"Not tonight."

"What the fuck? You—"

"Shut up, Indie." Then I grab her hand and slide it down between her legs, pushing her finger inside her thoroughly wet pussy along with mine.

"Ohhh," she moans.

"Yeah. You don't get to control me like that, Indie. Not ever. But if it's cheating sex you want, I'm happy to play along. For now."

It doesn't take much to make her come and that makes me feel a little better.

I don't want to think of Indie out there alone with strange men. I really don't. It sends me into a rage that I'm not sure I can contain.

But the easiness of her climax—the quickness of it—makes me think she's not as experienced as she lets on.

Makes me hope, anyway.

She gushes all over my fingers and then I bring them up to her lips and when she resists me, and doesn't open her mouth to suck them, I feel a *lot* better.

I make her suck them anyway. But I feel better knowing it's not something she's familiar with.

She passes out with her head on my shoulder and her arm draped casually across my stomach.

I don't sleep.

I wait an hour or so and then I get up, go into the bathroom, and jerk off as I imagine that it was me kissing McKay down in the kitchen earlier.

Me grabbing his cock.

Me making him lean back and moan.

And then I come as I picture myself *killing* Donovan.

CHAPTER FOUR

The next morning Adam is already gone from the bedroom when I wake.

The nightmare is still fresh. Too fresh. And my heart is galloping inside my chest, a fast, staccato beat that takes long minutes to settle.

I woke up with full recollection of the dream, but like most nightmares, it fades fast. And then there's nothing left but a general feeling of uneasiness and fear.

And as I linger there in bed, half awake and listening to the sounds in the house, I hear Adam talking to Maggie downstairs.

Last night did not exactly go as planned. But it was close enough.

And anyway, I have a theory I'm working on. Adam isn't going to be with me until he's with McKay. It's not really me he wants. I was just *there* last night.

I am Misha. God, that bothers me. But I am Misha. That's how he sees me. Just someone to take his mind off McKay.

I have plans today though. Lots of them. And none of them have anything to do with Adam. So I stop thinking about Misha. And anyway, she's dead.

I only asked Donovan to kiss McKay because I knew I could make Adam jealous if he saw that. And I know he wants to believe that he's one hundred percent in control, one hundred percent of the time, but he's not.

He can spend the day with McKay for all I care. I'm on a mission to find answers.

I have two journals these days.

This is something no one knows about. I have the one Adam gave me for my last birthday and the one I found in the law library on the third floor.

No one goes up to the third floor. The AC doesn't work right up there and the whole place smells like mold.

I don't know who the lawyer was in Adam's family. I can't picture anyone that high up in rank actually… *working* for a living. A real job, I mean. Because, of course, killing people is work. And whatever Adam's father did, I'm sure that was work too. But I know he wasn't the lawyer in the family because the books on the shelves all date back to the early nineteen hundreds.

Anyway, this is all beside the point and entirely off topic. I went up to the third-floor law library looking for a space to write in the new journal Adam gave me because I still have things to reconcile in my head. I miss my old bedroom. I'm not jealous that it now belongs to Maggie. She needs her own space. And that room was made for a little girl and I'm grown up now.

But I need my own space too. I can't just flutter from room to room, sleeping here and there. It's not right. The law library isn't going to be that space. It's dusty and hot.

So I went over to the other side of Old Home. The side we don't use. There are a lot of bedrooms over there. It's not two floors, though. Only one. This is the original part of the house. I've seen pictures of it before the main part—the big, grand part—was added sometime around the turn of the last century.

It's really just a long hallway with a wall of windows on one side and lots of doors on the other. Kinda like an enclosed breezeway. At the end of that hallway is a big room with a beamed ceiling, a living room with a big stone fireplace and a whole wall of French doors that lead out to the back garden, which has always been neglected. But there's a path out there that leads to the river. Nathan and I used to play on that path all the time.

This part of the house was remodeled with the rest of Old Home just before I came to live here. And it was open for a while back then. There's a TV in there. It's all furnished and everything. Real nice.

But we just never spent no time in there. It was too far away from everything else. So after a year or so Adam just put some white sheets on everything and shut the door to the hallway with the windows and we kinda forgot about it.

But I have now claimed it as my own. It's maybe a little bit big for a private space. But no one else uses it, so fuck it. This wing is mine now.

I need privacy because there are a lot of inconsistencies in my head.

Such as those four missing years when no one knew where I was. That part of my memory never came back. I'm sure Donovan is happy about that because if they did, he'd have to pay a lot more attention to me than he does now. And I get the feeling that Donovan's babysitting days are over. He spends a lot of time in his new Pearl Springs office doing his own thing. I guess he decided he needed his own space too.

Anyway, I'm going back and forth here. Getting things all twisted in typical Indie fashion.

Up in the law library—before I realized that room was not going to be my space and I was going to claim the unused wing on the other side of the house instead—I found an old journal.

It's an empty one and the pages are all yellow and old. But I like that about it. It makes things feel authentic. I started another timeline in that journal. I want the new one, the one Adam gave me, to be about the future. About my dreams and stuff. If I ever have dreams.

But I want the old one to be about the past.

I found a bunch of shit up there, actually. All of them were old things. Dusty. And weird too. I found some World War II medals in cases lined with ratty stained satin. But the weird thing about those, they were not American medals. Not German, either. Thank God. I had a little panic attack at first imagining them to be German and all the things that would come with that. But when I read the words, I recognized them as Dutch. Also strange, because Adam's family is French, not Dutch, but at least they weren't German. And maybe that wasn't so weird, anyway. Adam speaks a lot of languages and Dutch is one of them. There has to be a reason he was taught that language as a boy. So whatever. I just put them back where I found them.

There were some guns too. Ancient rifles that you have to load with powder. And one newer-looking pistol that took me a while to recognize as a tranquilizer gun, like the kind you use on wild animals.

Again, I'm off topic.

The topic is this:

Why, when Indie starts a journal about the past, does the first page always begin with the sentence *Nathan St. James was the boy next door*?

That's my question. Because every time I start a new entry and go thinking about the past, that same sentence is the only thing I'm able to write.

It's like someone has put a magic spell on me. Like I'm an unfortunate princess in a fucking fairytale.

Or… someone has PSYOPSed me. Someone put this particular sentence inside my head and the trigger is me trying to write down anything that happened before the day I was bought in that auction on the island.

The future I can write about, that's just fine. No problem writing about the future. The missing four years aren't affected at all. They are just one hundred percent missing.

I tried it another way too. I bought a digital recorder in the Pearl Springs drugstore. And I tried to start an audio journal.

Same thing happened.

Nathan St. James was the boy next door.

Which would be fine. Because that's actually where the story starts. Mostly.

But I already wrote that fucking story. Word. For. Word. I saw it in the journal McKay found. *Nathan St. James was the boy next door.* That's what it said. Very first line.

I didn't panic when I first figured this out. Because I had the tapes and Donovan didn't take them back after McKay and I listened to them all that night when the truth came out.

Those were me and Donovan talking in our own words. That was my voice. That was his voice. And there was enough information in them to corroborate the story I wrote down in the journal McKay found. Angelica was on those tapes. Wendy was on those tapes. Nathan. Me. Donovan. McKay. Maggie. The jobs. The mistakes.

All of that happened. I have proof.

So why would someone—and let's be clear here, there is only one someone capable of doing this to me—why would they prevent me from accessing anything but the sanctioned story of Indie and Nate?

That's why I want to go backwards. That's the missing piece here. It's Nathan.

Something about him is wrong. I just don't know which part.

Was it the way we met? Was it the way we spent our days? Was it the love? What? Which part is the lie?

There has to be a lie in there somewhere. That's the only way this erasure makes sense.

And I need to know this. I will not die before I get these answers. And this is a tricky thing. Because no one knows when they're gonna die. It might happen today. I could… I dunno. Trip and fall down the fucking porch steps and hit my head so hard, my brain swells up like Adam's did when I hit him with the candlestick. Or hell, someone could hit *me* with a candlestick.

I will not die without figuring out the boy next door.

I refuse.

Because I miss him. And I want him back, even if it's just in a memory. And now that I know someone has fucked up my head about Nathan, I can't trust any of those memories.

Except the one where I kill him, of course. That one seems to be one-hundred-percent accurate.

I try not to think about that too much because I know there's no way to change what happened that day. There is no way to take it back and make him real again.

But it hurts to think about Nathan. And every time I try to write in that journal and his name comes out the end of that pen, it kills me.

It *kills* me.

But no matter how hard I try, I can't go backwards. Not even in my own mind.

And that's just not right.

It needs to be fixed.

I place a small digital recorder on the table in my new living room and wait.

Donovan shoots me a quizzical look. "What's all this?"

Getting him over to this part of the house was a process in patience. Adam and McKay are outside in the pavilion watching TV with Maggie. We had dinner out there, then I asked Donovan to come inside and help me clean up. And after we finished, he was just about to head back outside, and probably leave for Pearl Springs, when I stopped him in the hallway and asked him to come with me. And that's how we got over here.

"This as in"—I cock my head at him—"this room? Or the recorder?"

"What's going on, Indie?"

I huff out a little breath. "Well, this is my new space. Do you like it?"

He looks around the room, takes it all in. "Hmm. It's OK, I guess. Kinda hot in here." He tugs at the collar of his button-down shirt to prove his point.

"I know. I just turned the AC on this afternoon. But it'll get better soon."

"So… why do you need space? And why are we recording this conversation?"

"It's not on yet. But the two go together, actually."

"OK." His eyes narrow down at me. "Do you plan on explaining that?"

I let out another long exhale. "I need more answers, Donovan."

"About what? I gave you all the tapes I have. I didn't hold any back. I'm not going to be Adam's scapegoat. I'm not hiding anything from you."

"Adam's not going to make you the scapegoat. And that doesn't even make any sense. We're all to blame here. You aren't any more responsible for this mess than the rest of us. We all played our part."

"That's how I see it too. And I'm not saying he'll blame me right away, but he'll get around to it eventually. I'm done treating you, Indie. I'm not qualified, I'm not—"

"Stop it. Just stop it. You're the smartest person I've ever met."

"Doubtful."

"It's not about anything we've already covered. It's about... *before*, Donovan. Before Adam and McKay. Before the snake cage. Before all of that. I don't remember much of it. Actually," I amend, "I don't remember any of it."

"Maybe that's a good thing?" He raises an eyebrow at me. "Some things are better left buried."

"I don't believe that and neither do you. We all need the truth eventually."

He shakes his head a little, disagreeing. "I think looking backwards is a bad idea."

"Oh? Then why do you disappear to your office in Pearl Springs every chance you get, hm?" I raise my own eyebrows back at him. "I know what you do there."

He frowns at me. "Is that right?"

I nod. "Yup. You're looking for answers about your past too. I broke in and snooped. Don't worry." I put a hand up to stop his outrage and protest. "I didn't read your files or listen to your tapes. I'm not an asshole. It's just pretty clear that you're looking for answers. You're kind of OCD about labeling shit, Donovan. You should probably stop doing that if you don't want anyone to know what you're up to."

"It's science, Indie. I need accurate records of things. Labeling is an important part of that process."

"Hey, I'm not here to confront you, OK? I'm just saying that we both have missing parts and it's not fair. This isn't normal, Donovan, and you know that. That's all I'm saying. You feel it too and that's why you're searching for answers."

He inhales sharply, then walks over to the window and looks out at the untended garden. He turns back. "Do you know anything about it?"

"About what?"

"My past."

I laugh. "You're asking me, Donovan? I know less than anyone about everything."

He turns to the window again. "Sometimes I feel that way too."

"You do?"

He nods. "Yeah. Shit doesn't add up, Indie."

"What kind of shit?" I'm keenly interested in this. I have never thought much about Donovan's childhood before. None of them, really. Maybe Adam's a little bit because he grew up here at Old Home like me, so we have that in common. But it was all very casual and in the moment. I don't sit around wondering about people other than myself. Which doesn't say much about my capacity for empathy, but what can I do? This was a default setting programmed into me a long time ago.

Donovan turns back and walks over to a dusty, overstuffed chair covered by a white sheet. He takes the sheet off and drops into a heap off to the side, then sinks down into the chair, stretching his long legs out in front of him and sighing deeply. He plays with his lip a little, kinda pinching it between his fingers, looking around randomly.

He exhales again. "Carter," he says. "Mostly."

"I wish I could help you. I'm not just saying that, either. I really do. You helped me a lot over the years, whether you think so or not. And I know I was kind of a bitch to you that night I listened to the tapes with McKay, but I was wrong to yell at you like that. I was wrong to blame you. I've listened to that tape like a hundred times since then and I really do believe you were scared."

His eyes find mine immediately. They are dark, like his hair. He's different than the rest of us in that respect. Not part of the same gene pool, obviously. "I was afraid. I had been for a long time before… everything fell apart."

I hear the words he wanted to say, and didn't. *Before you tried to kill everyone.*

"I knew it was wrong."

"Yeah, but—"

"No." He shakes his head at me. "No. I don't get a pass, Indie. None of us do. I just…" He draws in a deep breath and then blows it out. "I don't understand why I got involved with you and Adam in the first place."

"What do you mean?"

"It was my idea, Indie. I'm the reason Adam bought you at the auction."

65

"I don't believe that."

"Well." He huffs out a laugh. "You don't need to believe it to make it true. I was there when it happened. You were in a cage waiting to be eaten by a snake."

I don't think back on that night much. I don't actually have a lot of feelings about it. Which is telling in a lot of ways.

"I told him to buy you. I practically talked him into it. And I *wanted* to be in it. I offered my services to him. To control you. That's what I told him, Indie. I would use my PSYOPS experience to keep you in line."

I shrug with my hands. "I know that's how it happened. But Adam went to the island all on his own. You didn't make him show up. Plus, it kinda worked. I'm not sure why you're being so hard on yourself now. We know how it turned out. I mean, I could see you having this existential crisis if we were back in the past. Maybe when I was thirteen or something and things were still up in the air. But we're on the other side of it now."

"Are we?"

"Aren't we?"

He shakes his head slowly. "No. That's the problem. We're still in the middle of it, Indie. It's not over."

I sigh long and loud. "I know that. I get it. Carter is still out there and he obviously wants something from me. But listen, I don't care who he is—we're a team of pretty formidable people, Donovan. Whatever his plan is, it's not gonna go off without a hitch."

He grunts a little, but stays silent, again playing with his lip.

"I brought you here because I want you to help me remember things before the island. And to ask you if you found any other files about me."

He stops playing with his lip. "I just told you I handed everything over. I'm not hiding anything."

"But did you look in the records, Donovan? From the island? I know you inherited your grandfather's estate. And I've heard enough of Adam's conversations with McKay to know that you got a lot of money out of that. But your family was in charge of that island for generations. So I was wondering if you came across any other records. Genealogy stuff, you know? Something that could tell me where I came from."

He looks at me thoughtfully. "I don't have access to most of it. It's digital and behind a whole fucking slew of passwords. My grandfather didn't exactly leave me a file with the passwords, ya know? I used to snoop when I was younger. I hacked in a few times." He throws up his hands. "See, this is my problem. I don't know why I did that. Or what I was looking for."

"Maybe you were looking for Carter?"

"But why, Indie? Why would I be looking for him back then? As far as I knew, he was dead. And now, after all that school, I just know way too much to let this go." He points to his head. "The mind is a very powerful organ. We barely understand it. But here's what we do know—it's not reliable. Memories are things we make up, mostly. I mean, if you're not crazy, then a lot of it is real. But it's always tainted. By emotions, or things happening in the background, or just... wishful thinking. But we're not exactly sane, are we? So our minds probably make a lot more mistakes

67

in this regard then most others. So... I don't know what's real anymore. The man I am right now cannot understand what the boy at fifteen was thinking when he agreed to be a part of this. That's why I have the office. I'm doing some self-hypnosis. Trying to dig out the parts that are missing and fill in the blanks. I just need to know why. Why the fuck did I get involved in this? Because all I had to do was just... go to school. Become a doctor. Do what they said."

"Yeah, well." I blow out a breath of air and a piece of hair in front of my face flies up. "Teenagers, Donovan. They're not exactly known for following the rules."

"Understatement of the fucking decade. My point is—the man I am right now? He feels sick about the boy he was. I"—he shakes his head—"I don't like that boy."

"Yeah, well, I'm not exactly in love with the girl I was either. That's my point and why I asked you here. I mean, maybe we can help each other? Ya know? If you help me find my old self, I'll help you find yours."

I smile at him. I'm not the kinda girl who checks herself in the mirror regularly. Or even daily, if I'm being honest. But I can be pretty damn charismatic when I smile.

So he smiles back, appreciating my effort.

I walk over to him and plop down in his lap. His arms fall around me like I'm an old habit and I sink back into his chest and relax. "I like you, Donovan. We've always been friends, right?"

"I guess. I mean, *yes*." He laughs. "You and I are friends. We're not very different, are we? And we're not even that far apart in age. Just five years. Which felt like a lifetime of difference back when you first came here. But it doesn't feel so far away now, does it?"

"Nope. We're peers, right? It's different with us than it is with Adam and McKay. I've always thought of you the way I did Nathan. You know, my *friend*. Not my boss. Even though you were always the one in charge, I never felt like you were demanding things of me. It was always an ask."

"Hmm. That's nice to know. I carry a lot of guilt about you, Indie." He pushes me away a little bit so he can see my face. "I'd just like to say I'm sorry. I shouldn't have—"

"Oh, stop. That's not even true. Who the hell knows who would've bought me if it wasn't you and Adam?"

"Oh, God." He rubs his temple with a fingertip. "As much as I want to tell you not to say that—that I didn't buy you—it's true, isn't it? I did."

"That's not the point I was making. I'm just saying, it could've been a lot worse. I'd probably be dead now if you two didn't buy me that day." We both think about this for a little bit and then I say, "So what do you think? You help me and I'll help you?"

He sighs again, sounding very tired. "What's your plan, then? More therapy?"

"Yeah. I want you to put me under and ask me things. Things about before the island. And then… I don't know. I'll help you any way I can. I'll ask you things, if you want. I can't hypnotize you, obviously. But I can help you figure it out. I don't have any idea what self-hypnosis looks like, but it can't be… reliable. At least I'll keep you honest."

"Is this gonna be a secret? Just between us?"

"It doesn't have to be, if that makes you uncomfortable. We can tell Adam and McKay if—"

"No." He shakes his head. "No. We can tell them about you, if you'd like. But not about me. I don't want them knowing shit before I do. And I can't trust Adam. I love him, don't get me wrong. I'd die for him if it came down to it. Like..." He laughs. "I can't really fight my way out of anything with him. We're not trained the same. But if I could help him in a time of need, I would. No hesitation. McKay too. But this is..."

"Personal," I finish for him.

"Very personal. Carter..." Donovan draws in another very long breath. "If he's alive—and obviously, he is—then we have some shit to sort out. And I don't want Adam or McKay to steal that opportunity away from me. I need to find him and I need that last conversation. He's the one with the answers. If they kill him before I get my chance, well, I'll never be OK, Indie. I can't let that happen. So the deal is, you keep me out of it if you want to tell Adam and McKay what you're up to."

"I can live with that. But I'm not going to tell them. That's why I made my own space over here. We can do me at home and then I'll go into town with you and we'll keep all your stuff separate."

"Hmm. They might start asking questions about that. The town thing."

"Well, we'll have to be smart about it, obviously. I'll tell them I'm working for you. Filing or something."

"Filing." He laughs. "Do people file things anymore?"

"How the fuck should I know? I've never had an actual job."

He laughs again. "How about we just tell them we're spending time together?"

"Like… we're dating?"

I feel him shrug underneath me. "Listen, it's gonna happen sooner or later. Sooner is my guess. We all know that the thing holding this up is them, not us. Right?"

"We saw you last night, by the way. Adam and I were looking in the window when you and McKay were kissing. So it went well?"

"No. It did not go well. He did let me kiss him. And I was pushing it. Gonna take it a little further. But then you and Adam came in the front door and he went all rigid again. Then after you two went upstairs, he pushed me in the chest and told me to back the fuck up and keep my distance."

"Fucking McKay. He's the one holding shit up. If those two would just work it out, we'd all be a lot happier."

"It's not just them, though. It's you and Adam too."

"No. Adam and me are just fine."

"You sure about that?"

"Well… hmm." I think about last night. How he stopped me. Didn't let me get him off, but then got me off instead. "Maybe not."

"You and I have been together lots of times."

I tsk my tongue at him. "I would not call it lots of times, Donovan. It's been like—"

"Eight times, Indie. I'm keeping track. More than you and McKay, that's for sure. But still, McKay and you, that's a done deal. He loves you. You love him. But you've never been with Adam outside that one time."

I make a face and scratch my arm. "I don't know what you're getting at."

"You need to spend time with Adam, too."

"Well, I can't just ignore McKay. He'd get mad."

"My point is, if we say we want time together it's gonna make waves. So you're going to need to make up for that. With them."

"Hmm. Maggie's always with Adam."

"Yeah, well, maybe Mags and McKay need some alone time too? Maybe we should come up with a schedule? Like... divide up our time so no one feels left out. That way when you and I disappear to Pearl Springs no one thinks too hard about it."

"This feels like a plan."

"It is a plan."

"Should we be planning this kind of thing without them?"

"If we're going to figure out where we came from? Then yes. You came to me, remember? I was gonna do this on my own."

"Yeah, OK. That's fine then. I'll ask Adam if he'd like to do something tomorrow. Maybe go into town and order some new things for the garden. That's something that feels normal for us."

"Yeah, good idea. And I'll ask Maggie if she wants to go into New Orleans or something and then offer up McKay as her parent-of-the-day."

"Don't let her pick the zoo, Donovan."

"Fuck the zoo. I'll suggest the aquarium. You got any objections to the aquarium?"

"Nope. Nobody ever put me in a tank. At least I don't think so. Hmm."

"What?"

"I think this is a good plan all the way around. We're all gonna get something out of this."

"Yeah. I think you're right." He sighs. "I actually feel a lot better now. I was in a funk when I came in here. Thanks for that, Indie."

"No problem. I'm glad I helped. For once."

"So when should we get started on your... *therapy*?"

I sit up in his lap and look at him. "Now. McKay and Adam are fishing with Maggie on the duck lake. We should jump right in while we have a chance."

I get up, walk over to the little table, and pick up the digital recorder, a spiral notebook, and a pen. I hand Donovan the pad and pen and then take the recorder with me over to the couch near the windows and sit down. "I want you to start at the island and work backwards. I think I'll make more progress that way. Plus, you were there. So you can corroborate a lot of it. That way we know we're on the right track. No drugs this time, but we might have to use them later, if I don't make progress."

"You've really thought this out."

"I have. I want you to put me under and take me as far back as you can starting with the snake cage."

He stands up and picks up the chair so he can place it near the couch, then sits back down and crosses his legs, getting himself settled into therapist mode.

And I don't know. This feels good. Very familiar. For both of us, I think. This is something we've done together hundreds of times. It feels right.

73

I'm gonna get to the bottom of this thing between Nate and me.

I can feel it.

Like all my truth is just below the surface, ready to come up.

CHAPTER FIVE

INDIE
PRIVATE SESSION #1

DONOVAN: OK, Indie. You know how this starts. So—

INDIE: I get it. I asked you to do this. This is not a medical procedure and this is not medical advice. This is a simple Q&A under hypnosis. I give my full consent and agree that you will not be held responsible for any psychological consequences.

Jesus Christ, Indie.

What? I'm just trying to protect you.

It's just... funny. Thinking back on the very first time we did this and I had to spend like ten minutes explaining things to you.

Yeah, well. Not our first rodeo, is it?

No. OK. So... I think I've got a starting point, so just relax and take a few deep breaths. Clear your mind and feel yourself sink down into the cushions and become heavy.

This is different. You didn't start things this way before.

Ah. I see.

You see what?

We *are* going to do this again. OK. Well... I've learned a thing or two since that last first time. Got some pointers from a friend, actually.

What friend?

Do you really want to spend our time talking about me? Seriously? I'm gonna be honest with you. That was a ploy I used when you were young to make you like me and force a connection. It was a... *technique.*

Hmm. Well, it worked. And our connection has never been forced.

So... should I keep going? Or do you need to chat before we get started?

No, just get on with it.

Relax and let yourself drift. Think about the ocean, Indie. Think about how it smells and how the mist feels on your skin when you're near it. Hear the waves in your head.

. . .

Now picture yourself on an island. It's a tropical island. A very nice white-sand beach. And there are cliffs above you. If you squint you can see a pavilion up there. And you recognize this island. You've been here for six months now. It's your home, for the moment. Tell me where you are.

You didn't count backwards.

Do you want to lead?

No.

Then shut up, Indie. And tell me where you are when you picture this island.

I don't really know where it is, exactly.

No. Forget where it is. This is the island in your memory, OK? It doesn't matter where it is. The only thing that matters is where *you* are. So where are you?

. . . I'm not on the beach. They didn't let us go to the beach much.

OK. Keep going.

I'm near the bunkhouse. That's where we stay.

Describe it.

It's… just a building. A long rectangle. No windows. It's whitewashed concrete. Kinda looks like a bunker. Built to withstand hurricanes. That kind of building.

What do you do there?

Sleep. That's it. They wake us up in the morning and make us… do things.

OK, we can talk about that later. But right now, I just want you to picture yourself there. Feel the island all around you. See in your mind. Tell me what you can feel.

… The air. It's wet. And the sun, it's hot. I'm sticky with sweat.

Can you feel anything else?

I know what the leaves on the trees feels like. Waxy. They're big leaves. And I'm barefoot. I like that about this place. There are a lot of dirt paths and they're smooth. Like someone takes care of them. You can walk a long way before you accidentally step on a rock. So that's nice.

Do you know what day it is?

No. Just a day. Any other day.

Well, that's not true. It's actually a very specific day. It's the day of the auction. Where are you that afternoon of the auction?

In the bunkhouse.

What are you doing?

…. I just took a bath and… now someone is brushing my hair. They're going to put a white ribbon in it so it matches my white dress.

Do you normally wear white dresses?

No. I was wearing shorts and a t-shirt earlier.

That's right. Your shorts were denim and your t-shirt was peach. It said 'Brat' across the front in bold, black letters.

Yeah, it did.

Why do you think that's funny?

Because I was a brat.

Yeah, you were. OK. Now you and I are talking. Do you remember what we were talking about?

Yep. You were telling me to be good and you'd handle things. You were going to make sure I'd be OK. You promised me.

Right. I did. Let's move on. You're in the white dress now. And the sun is starting to drop low on the horizon. They're taking you somewhere. Where are they taking you?

To the Garden of Good and Evil. There's another girl here. Anastasia. She's in the truck with me, but they drop her off first. She screams and kicks. And they smack her. Not on the face though—they smack her on the back of her legs with a twig and it leaves a long, thick welt.

Why is she screaming?

She doesn't like the cage. They didn't tell us why we're being put in cages until they got us out here. So they're explaining the tigers to her and she is frrrr-eak-ing out.

What do you think about that?

I think she's being stupid.

Why?

Because she should know better. I've been here a lot longer than her. But… she's older than me by a few years. She should just know better. They like it when you cry.

Who?

The people here. The grown-ups. They like it when you cry. It's what you're supposed to do. So they think you're with the program when you cry.

Why do you say that?

Because. It's just true. If they say, 'We're gonna put you in a cage with a tiger outside. You'll be just out of reach so it can't maul you to death, but close enough to get snagged by those claws a few times and bleed,' well… that's something you should *cry about. It's normal. So I don't cry when they say that shit to me. And it pisses them off. But that's OK. I kinda live to piss them off.*

Hmm.

What? Why 'hmm?' And you do realize I'm not like… under, *right?*

Let me worry about that.

Why did you say 'hmm?'

I'm making a note about this. We'll talk about it later. But now I want to know what happens next. After you leave Anastasia with the tiger. And by the way, yeah. She should've known better. I didn't like that girl. She whined too much.

Right?

What happened next?

81

Well. It's a long drive out to the snake garden. And it takes a while before I can get out of the truck because the snake is close by. And the cage wasn't really ready because the stupid men in charge of it were afraid of that thing. I mean... what the fuck? I was ten and I wasn't moaning about no snake.

Can you try to stay in one tense, Indie? Either present, or past?

Why's that matter?

It just does. Now. Why weren't you moaning about the snake?

I'm just not afraid of snakes.

Not even thirty-foot-long anacondas? That would absolutely try to swallow you whole?

That's funny.

Why?

Because. If they really wanted me to be eaten by that snake, they'd have fed me to it.

I'm not saying this to be a dick, Indie, but I'm pretty sure everyone wanted to feed you to that snake.

Yeah. That's probably right. But... they couldn't. I knew my worth. Even before you spelled it out to me.

Wait. What are you talking about?

When we were talking. You told me something like, 'Everyone's gonna be bidding on you tonight, Indie. But I'm gonna make sure only one gets to take you home.'

Hmm.

There's that 'hmm' again. What's it mean?

Did I say that?

Yup. You did.

I don't remember.

Well, you did. You told me that all the time.

Hmm.

Stop doing that.

Sorry. OK, moving on.

I'm not sure this is working. I'm not like... out of it enough. This is stuff I already know.

That's not your concern. Trust me, this is the easy part. You should enjoy it while it lasts. Now... let's forget about the snake. We all know how that ends. How about you try to tell me what you did before that day? Do you remember?

Like... the exact day before?

Any day before, as long as you were on the island.

Well, most of the days were just like the other. Same thing, really. Wake up, eat that shit breakfast they served, then they'd take us outside and...

...

And?

... Hmm. Well. I don't know really.

What do you mean? You don't remember?

No. I remember being outside in the jungle. I remember a lot of running. Climbing trees. Stuff like that. But I don't know why I was doing that. Do you?

Mm. Exercise, maybe?

Ha. That's funny. There had to have been a purpose.

Yeah. Let me think for a minute.

...

I don't really remember either. Which is... maybe a little weird.

What were you doing? While all us girls were... running through the jungle?

I don't think we should talk about me in this session. It might confuse things.

How? We could compare notes.

Yeah, that's not a good idea. OK. So. How did you get there, Indie? Do you remember the boat?

How do you know it was a boat? Maybe it was a plane?

It wasn't a plane. I saw the yacht when it arrived.

So you already know.

Jesus fuck. Can you let me lead? Just tell me how you got there.

A boat.

I'm glad you think this is funny.

Sorry. I'll be good. I promise. The boat was small. I came alone. There was just one man with me. That's it.

Who was it? Do you remember?

Wasn't you, that's all I know. Wait. No. Hold on. I do remember. It was Nick.

85

I grab the recorder off the couch and stop it.

Indie sits up and looks at me. "Why'd you do that?"

"Nick? As in… Nick who?"

She laughs at me. "Come on, now. There's only one Nick. Nick Tate."

"How do you know it was him?"

She shrugs. "I've seen him. I mean, I didn't know him then. Well, that can't be right. If he and I were the only ones on the boat, then I did know him. At least a little."

I lean back in the chair and breathe, taking time to think this through.

I didn't plan this session and she's right. She's not under at all. I think I was just going through the motions, not expecting much. I let her slip in and out of her relaxed state when I should've been making her concentrate on being there. In the moment. Trying to get her to turn her past into the present.

Even that's a little weird. I'm not careless with people's minds. Not anymore. I learned my lesson. So this lapse in judgment pisses me off. Even more so because it's her. I know better. I really fucking know better. And I let that happen anyway.

Again.

And then Nick Tate? That was totally unexpected.

"What's going on?" Indie says. "Why are you so freaked out?"

"I don't know. Something about that is wrong, Indie."

"Why do you say that?"

"Because it doesn't make sense." I leave out the part about my lackadaisical attitude about this session, because I need to think about that alone before I admit to it out loud. "Nick was after you. Remember? Adam had that meeting with him the day the Company fell."

"The day I tried to kill him, you mean?"

"Whatever. Nick threatened him. Nick wanted to kill you, Indie."

"Yeah, I know. He got Angelica. Not Wendy, though. Or me."

"So why the fuck would he be dropping you off on the island for the auction when you were ten? Why didn't he just kill you then?"

"I dunno." She laughs and swings her feet over the side of the couch. "Maybe he wanted me to be bought by someone. Or maybe he was just tired of me? I really was a brat back then."

"OK, hold on. Hold on." I close my eyes and think for a moment, trying to recall what exactly I told Adam that night of the auction. "I thought you got dropped off because your house mother was tired of you."

"What's a house mother?"

"You know, those… those *fucking ladies* who run the little girls before they sell them."

She shakes her head at me. "I don't remember a house mother."

I scrub both hands down my face. This isn't right. "Just…" I hold up a hand. "Don't say anything for a minute. I need to think."

She flops back into the couch cushions and blows out some air.

House mothers. I get it. Indie was only ten when she showed up on the island. But I remember plenty of things from when I was ten. And so should she. She would've lived with the house mother her entire life. There would've been other girls there too. Maybe half a dozen from what I remember of that part of the program. So it's just not possible that she doesn't remember a house mother.

"OK, I think we're done for today, Indie."

"Why?"

"Because this could be something we call a transformative moment."

"What's that?"

"It's a moment when you use old information to see things in a new way and it brings understanding."

"I don't get it. What does this have to do with Nick Tate? And I'm definitely not transformed. Nothing about this was helpful. I don't understand anything."

"I don't know about Nick Tate yet. He might not be real. I mean, he's real. Was. Whatever. But he might not be real to you."

"You think I made him up?" Her voice is loud and incredulous.

"I'm not saying that. I'm just saying I can't fathom a reason why Nick Tate would be dropping you off on that island when I was under the impression that your house mother abandoned you there."

"Maybe you got it wrong?"

"Maybe I did. That's entirely possible."

"Why would you be under that impression?"

"I don't know. That's the problem. We have a disconnect here. Remember when I said memories are unreliable?"

"Yeah."

"Well"—I laugh—"there you go. We can't both be right."

"Does it really matter? Maybe you were just jumping to conclusions?"

"Maybe. Or maybe someone told me that lie about your house mother. If so, I need to figure out who said it. There are no coincidences here, Indie. Not when you're born into the Company. Everything comes with a plan. Everything."

"Hm. I see the point. So. Who would want to lie about that?"

"No, that's jumping ahead. First, we need to figure out if it was real on your end. Then we can ask questions like that."

"OK." She huffs out a long sigh.

"But we're done for today. You need to settle before we do another session."

She slaps her legs and stands up. "Fine with me, I guess. Can I have that?" She points to the recorder.

I pick it up and I'm just about to give it to her when I pull my hand back. "Let me keep it for one night. Listen to it again and make some notes. I'll make a report for you."

"Whatever you want, Donovan. You're the psychiatrist."

I cringe at that. "I'm not really a psychiatrist, Indie. But if we're gonna do this, we should do it right. Turn it into a proper case study."

She gives me a weird look. "Number one, you absolutely *are* a psychiatrist. When people learn as much shit about brains as you have, and they have a medical degree to go with it, they are psychiatrists. Even if they're not practicing. And number two—case study? No. I don't want to be your fucking case study."

"It's more credible that way."

"Who will be reading this report that we care if it's credible?"

"Us," I say. "It matters. That's all. It's procedure. We should remain objective. The truth requires it. And if we're only doing this to prove we're fine, if we're just trying to prove that everything's OK and it's really not…" I blow out a long breath. "If we're missing things and we allow ourselves to succumb to cognitive dissonance, then what is the fucking *point*?"

"Well, that's a long, serious sentence there, Donovan. I'm not sure what cognitive whatever is—"

"It's when you see the truth with your own eyes and still you refuse to accept it. That's what it is."

"Oh." She pauses for a moment. "Well, yeah. That's… scary. But—"

"We're doing this my way or we're not doing it at all. I'm not gonna go inside your head again without thinking the whole thing through first and recording the results at the end. I'm not. *I won't fucking do it!*"

Her head juts back in surprise at the tone and volume of my protest. But then she huffs and says, "Fine. I get it. What's the point of investing all this effort into the truth if we're not going to accept it? I agree. We need to figure this out or it's going to follow us. I have way too much recent baggage to let the old stuff get me in the end."

I nod. Sigh. "Yeah."
Her and me both.

CHAPTER SIX

When that card showed up with Carter's signature on Maggie's sixth birthday I was prepared.

I'm not saying I predicted it and I'm not saying it was expected. But I knew something was coming because someone is always coming for you. Always.

I side-eye McKay as we watch TV with Maggie. She likes it out here in the pavilion just like Indie did all those years ago. She took over Indie's bed swing and every now and then I see Indie watching her out of the corner of her eye.

I watch Indie closely. Very. Closely.

And even though she has a right to be jealous—I literally replaced her with her own daughter—I don't think that look on her face when she sees Maggie ride the swing that is rightly *hers* is envy.

I'm not sure what that emotion is yet—Indie has been trained so well, she could be hiding a severe case of raging jealousy and I'd never know it. But I don't get that gut feeling when I look at her. That feeling that says, *She's dangerous. Be careful, Adam. She's dangerous.*

So I'm gonna sit on this for a while and concentrate on other, more immediate, problems.

Not McKay. He's ignoring me today. And that's fine. He can kiss whoever he wants.

No, there are more important things to worry about today than kissing.

Like... things that don't add up about this current holding pattern we're in.

For instance—where the fuck *is* this Carter dude? Like where does he live? What does he do? Who does he run?

Not my men. That's for sure. And that's a lot of eyeballs all over the world if you count them all up. So how does he stay hidden?

This makes me think I've missed something. Something very critical. There are people out there, ex-Company, probably, who do not report to me.

I get a little rage-y when I think about this.

My first reaction is, *How fucking dare they? How fucking dare they work without my permission? Do they even know who I am?*

Which is kinda funny. And says a lot about my ego. But it's also true.

Do they have any fucking idea who I am these days?

Of course they do.

Everyone knows who I am. And I do get it. I'm not the actual Company king or whatever you call it. The next in line of succession would've been James Fenici. He's the real king. But he's not interested in running the leftovers and I am. The only other person who could make a claim above mine would be Harper Tate, James's wife and Nick Tate's twin sister. And if

James isn't gonna run things—and he's not, he's told me so himself—then she sure as shit isn't the one working men behind my back.

So who's left? Who is this Untouchable with a claim in the hierarchy?

Carter is a Couture. Like Donovan. But they are not leaders. That family has never been *in charge*. Not even close. I'm not saying they're insignificant, they hold a very high position in the old Company line of succession. But the Coutures are not above the Bouchers. A lot of Untouchable families would have to be eradicated for a Couture to proclaim himself king.

Not that something as simple as rules would stop Carter. Obviously.

So it's him. He's the one running things. He's got a team. Maybe several teams. Hell, maybe hundreds. I don't really know. I have hundreds, myself. But I didn't inherit the fucking genealogy documents after Gerald Couture killed himself when the CIA raided his island.

Donovan did. Which means… maybe Carter did too.

I should ask Donovan about this. But he's been so removed from the Company for so long, I don't expect a helpful answer. Donovan made it very clear that he was gonna do his own thing after Nick and Sasha took the Company down nine years ago. And he did. He went to LA, started a new life, and began a whole new profession.

I *will* need to talk to him about that, though. Reconstructive surgery only means one thing. He's making doubles for people.

Well. That's probably not true. Yet.

He's been in school this whole time. I don't care how fucking smart you are, you don't just wake up one day and say, *I think I will become a skillful reconstructive surgeon and make copies of people using a knife.*

It takes time. Lots of time.

In fact, Donovan kinda chose to walk away from all that too, didn't he? I mean, if he really wanted to make copies of people, he'd be in LA working hard on making that happen. Not here, kissing Core McKay in the kitchen last night.

Just to be clear, I'm not thinking about McKay. I don't care who he kisses.

Again, I feel like I'm missing something.

Think, Adam. Think. You have lots of things at your disposal. There is an answer to this out there. And it's probably available to you. If you know where to look.

That's the problem. I *don't* know where to look.

I checked all my father's documents after he died. The ones he bequeathed to me and the ones he didn't. I hired a fucking munitions guy to blow open the hidden safe in his office at the New Orleans house. Dude did a damn good job, too. Didn't burn a single thing inside.

And I did find a lot of things in there. Lots of very helpful things. But certainly not everything.

There was enough there to make contact with about forty teams. Which I did. Right on the spot. I called them up and told them to move on. Get on with their life. I was setting them free.

Of course, that's not how it ended up. After Indie tried to kill me that first time, and after I recovered, I got back in touch. A lot of them were already dead or missing. They figured out how to get new names and identities and disappeared.

I didn't think that was strange back then. Only people like me, and McKay, and Indie stick around after the jailer leaves you a get-out-of-jail-free key. Hell, even Donovan moved on. Mostly. He came back regularly. A lot, actually. But he was building something real out in LA. And when Indie went missing, he just slipped into that other life like a cottonmouth sliding into the Old Pearl River.

Never even looked back until Indie reappeared in McKay's driveway.

But there has to be more. And Carter has this information. And if he had access to it, my father had access to it too.

So where could he be hiding secrets after his death?

Could be just about anywhere, I suppose. On some island somewhere. Some house I never knew about. Maybe he had a mistress and she's holding on to the secrets I need? Hell, that shit could be buried at the bottom of the ocean.

This thought exercise is nearly futile. Nearly. But not completely.

Because of course, I am hiding things as well. Lots of things. And while I do tuck them away in nice safe places, none of them have been left with a mistress, or in a secret house, or at the bottom of the ocean. They are somewhere I can get to them. Easily. Quickly. And without much fuss.

And if I died today no one would know about that secret place. Not even Maggie, and I tell her almost everything.

So if I think about where I hide my secrets, and then apply that to my father, who taught me most everything I know, then that means he's hidden these things somewhere personal.

But where?

A place that's not in danger of being sold, that's where. So not some random house with a mistress inside it who might decide she'd like a different life and start over by selling everything.

Not a bank. That's too risky. Even the secret ones.

Not with a trusted friend. When you're the king, or hell, even a couple rungs down from the king, you don't trust people with secrets like that. Not anyone. Not even your Maggie. Not even your McKay.

And my father didn't have a Maggie. That I *know* of. Or a McKay. That I *know* of.

But there must be a place and this place has to be in New Orleans. It has to be. My father was partial to that city. And that old French-Quarter house too. It is his one true home.

But I scoured that house. I spent months—hell, nearly a year—after he died, looking for secret places. And I found plenty of them. But they were mostly hiding money. Or gold. A few files filled with incriminating evidence on people he had been blackmailing over the years, but who were all dead now. Shit like that. Which might have been lucrative secrets at one point in time, but not anymore.

They were not *the* secret.

Not the one I'm looking for.

So now I start there.

What *am* I looking for?

It took me a while to figure this out. And I've changed my mind several times over the years. But the secret I'm looking for has something to do with power.

Not little power, like that blackmailing shit.

Not little power like fifty million dollars in gold.

Power on a grand scale.

Power that upsets the balance of everything we know to be true.

Power that spells out who is actually running this show.

Because while I do have a pretty big ego—it's actually quite massive—I'm am not under any illusion that I run the entire *world*.

And yes, I have been pretty much controlling my own destiny for nearly a decade now—thank you, Nick Tate. I truly owe you one—but everyone has a boss. I just don't know who mine is at the moment.

It feels like we rearranged the power structure several times since I was born. That Santa Barbara incident did it. That FBI shit that went down while I was recovering from Indie's candlestick hit did it too.

James, and Nick, and Sasha were all behind those. The kings and queen of the Company.

And then, of course, Indie going missing—that was another rearrangement as well.

But that was me. When she left I picked things right back up. She freaked me out. I'm not gonna lie. When your little assassin turns on you like that, you circle the fucking wagons and reassess all your life choices. So that rearrangement was me.

But here's the thing that keeps me looking… Indie coming back? That wasn't Nick. He's possibly dead. Maybe not, but if he really did fake his own death, then he's out. For good. You don't put that much effort into an escape plan to just come back and start it all up again.

And it wasn't James. He and I talked about it just before Indie went missing.

And it wasn't Harper. She's stuck to James's hip like glue.

And it wasn't Sasha. Because I found out one little secret no one wanted to tell me about. And that's that Nick Tate had a daughter. A little girl very much like my Maggie. And he dropped that little girl off with Sasha to keep her safe. So Sasha is most definitely out.

Who's left? Who sent Indie back?

Of course it was Carter.

But how the fuck is he pulling these strings? Who is on his secret team? Where the fuck is he and how does he stay hidden?

"It's a goddamned circle."

"What's a circle?"

Oops. Said that out loud.

"What's a circle?" McKay asks again.

I bump my head back in the direction of Maggie so McKay will take a hint and drop it. "Nothing."

My phone buzzes in my pocket and when I take it out and look at the screen, I get that feeling again.

I sigh and get up, then walk away down towards the duck lake without saying a word.

When I'm nearly at the edge, and the phone is buzzing for the sixth time, I press accept.

"What is it?"

"Adam?"

"You know it's me, Wendy. Just fucking spit it out."

She sighs. "I think we have a problem."

"Explain."

"OK." She's a little bit breathless. "We found a girl."

"Hmm. Where?"

"Well, we didn't find her. We saw her. And we don't have her."

"*Where?*" I repeat.

"Savannah."

"Hmm."

"I know."

"Start from the beginning and don't leave anything out."

"Boone was on that job we talked about yesterday. And he was just finishing up when someone hit him on the head."

"Killed him?"

"No," she snaps at me. "Obviously he came back and told me this story."

"Don't get short with me."

"Sorry."

She doesn't sound sorry. "So how's the girl fit in? If he's not dead, he wasn't her hit."

"He was just coming back around when he heard voices. The little girl's and another one too. A man. And he said he couldn't place it, but it was very familiar."

"But what did they want? Boone was just sent to kill someone. He wasn't carrying any secrets."

"They stole the body."

"What?" I kinda laugh about this.

"Yeah, it makes no sense. But Boone swears up and down that this was one of our girls—"

I want to object here. I want to say she could just be any little girl. But very few men take little girls on a hit job. So I just shut up and let her finish.

"—and he recognized the voice of the man. Just couldn't place him. He moaned and they hit him again. He passed out *again*. And then he woke up and everything was cleaned up. The whole room was spotless. No sign of blood, and he checked with the UV light and everything. No sign of anything. Even the carpet under his blood-caked head was clean. Like they picked him up, scrubbed that spot, and set him back down."

I sigh.

"Sorry," she says. "But you need to know. Someone is cutting in on us, Adam. And they're not being shy about it. This is the third time."

"I know."

"Well, we need to do something about this."

"I'm working on it."

"You need to work faster."

"Wendy—"

"Fuck you. Do not tell me anything, Adam Boucher. I'm not your employee. I serve you at my pleasure. And I do that because we're on the winning side. But if some asshole is gonna move in and take that win away, I'm out. You hear me? Out!"

"I said I'm working on it."

She huffs on the other end of the line. "He left a note."

"Way to bury the lede."

"Do you want to hear it or not?"

"That's why I picked up the phone."

"OK." She sighs again. "I don't know what it means, though. It's like… a code or something."

"Will you just read the fucking note to me?"

"It says, 'They pack them in with no regard. They leave no marks and sing no songs. They cover them up and walk away. They did this to you. They did this to me. It ends. It begins. It ends again.'"

It's a goddamned circle.

"What the fuck does that mean, Adam?"

"I don't know."

"Well, who can we ask?"

"I'll get back to you."

I end the call, turn around, and find McKay standing not ten feet away.

His eyes are locked with mine. But then they drift down to the phone in my hand and linger there for a long moment before rising back up to meet my gaze once again.

And he says, "I really need to talk to you."

CHAPTER SEVEN

Adam looks over my shoulder in the direction of the pavilion. "Where's Maggie?"

"Indie came and took her on a walk."

He furrows his brow.

"What?"

Adam sighs, then looks down at his phone, still in his hand, and shoves it in his pocket. "Should they be walking alone?"

"They're just in the garden." I nod my head in that direction. "Look. Right there."

He looks over where Maggie and Indie are walking in the direction of the playset I built after Maggie was born. I admit, I spent a lot of time hurting over the idea that Maggie would not ever get to fully enjoy it.

But she loves that thing now. She plays in it all the time. And she and Indie like to swing together. They have little contests over who can swing higher. And even though it scares me a little to see Maggie flying like that, I like the way they laugh when they're just being kids together.

It's not fair. What Adam did to Indie. She was a good mother, she was just… too young. And troubled.

But we did that to her. When Indie came to live with us Adam and I made a deal that we would protect her first. Above all else. Above ourselves.

I wasn't going to help him unless he promised me we would help her too. And I fully understand that I am a piece of shit for ever agreeing to that deal in the first place. But if we didn't buy her, then someone far, far worse would've.

But Adam… he broke his promise when he took Maggie away.

I get why he did it. I might've done the same thing. And I have done some very questionable things over the years and that's why I need to set things right with Adam now.

But still. It's not fair.

Even though six is still young, and Indie will get her chance with Maggie, she missed things. Things she will never get back. And that's not right.

"Listen." Adam sighs and runs his fingers through his hair. It's a nervous habit we both have, learned from each other at a very young age. "I don't care if you have a thing with Donovan, OK? I'm fine with it."

"What?" I actually laugh. "What the hell are you talking about?"

"I saw you."

"OK."

"You were kissing him."

"And?"

"So I thought you didn't swing that way?"

I narrow my eyes at him. "I do not ever recall saying those words."

"You didn't have to. I came to you. That one day—"

"What one day?"

He points at me. "Fuck you, McKay." Then he turns and starts walking off towards the lake.

I stand there for a minute, watching to see what he does. We're both barefoot and shirtless. It's nearly a hundred degrees out today and not a single cloud in the sky. He's only wearing a pair of cut-off sweats that hang low on his hips and I've got on a pair of cargo shorts stained with the memory of days spent in my workshop.

He stops in front of the skinny gray dock that leads to a section of the lake that is mostly a sparse patch of weedy reeds instead of a proper fishing hole. He looks down the length of it. It's far too skinny for its length. And the only personal memory I have about this dock is the way it sways under my feet as I walk out over the water.

If the water around it was less reedy, we'd have used the dock to set the candle boats afloat on Indie's birthdays. But it's not a good place to launch candle boats. It's not really a good place for anything, actually. Except taking a seat at the end, slipping your feet into the water, and thinking.

And that's exactly what he does now.

For a moment I get lost in time. And that Adam out there is young. We didn't come out here much after I came to live with him. Old Home was a falling-down wreck and Adam's father always did prefer the house in New Orleans.

But a few times we did. And the end of this dock was always his thinking spot.

107

Adam and Indie have a lot in common. They were both very troubled kids. He doesn't ever talk about it, but I was there, so he doesn't need to.

I sigh. This wasn't the conversation I wanted to have with him but I guess it's the one we're having anyway. So I walk down the dock and smile as the gray boards sway under my feet—even more so than in my memory, because I am like seventy pounds heavier these days than I was back then—and I take a seat at the end.

There is not enough room for both of us. Two kids, fine. But even then, we barely fit.

And two grown men? I laugh as I bump him over and he has to scoot to make room with one leg practically hanging off the edge. But it's a fair move. Because I'm half hanging off the edge too.

"Forget I said anything." Adam sighs.

"No." I shake my head. "No, Adam, I'm not gonna forget you said anything. I knew what you were talking about when you said 'that one day'. I was fishing down by the river and you came up and asked if I had ever wondered what it would be like to just give in."

"That's not what I said."

"Close enough."

He turns his head to look at me, his blue eyes catching the sun. His skin is already golden brown from being outside and his hair is lighter than it typically is in the winter.

He reminds me so much of that kid I once knew, even though he hasn't been that kid for decades.

"I *said*," he says, "we could just all *be* together."

We're very close. Just inches apart. All squished together on the end of this dock. "We are together, Adam."

"Don't play with me, McKay. You know what I mean."

"Dude, I love you. You know that."

He huffs and stares off across the lake. "Listen, if you're just gonna let me down easy, go the fuck away." He turns to meet my gaze again. "OK? Just go the fuck away."

"You just took me by surprise, that's all. And back then, the answer was definitely no."

His eyes are locked on mine. "Back then?"

I take a deep breath. Because I only get to have this conversation once. "I have a lot of thoughts and feelings about what you did to Indie when you took Maggie away."

"I was just trying to protect everyone."

"Really, Adam? You're really gonna stick with that?"

"It's the truth."

"Whatever. Just… don't fucking talk. Just let me say what I have to say."

"Hold up." He leans back a little so he can grip my shoulder.

"What?" I shrug his hand off and nearly lose my balance on the edge of the dock.

"If you're just gonna tell me the same shit today as you did all those years ago, then I don't want to hear it."

"You don't get to cheat, Adam."

"What? How am I cheating?"

"You don't get a spoiler before the conversation starts. That's not how this works. You have to listen from beginning to end, just like everyone else. You don't get the answer before the question. You don't get to protect your heart like that. You don't get to cut me off and walk away before I get to say my piece."

"That's not what I meant."

"It *is* what you meant."

He throws up his hands. "Talk then. I'm listening."

I pause, gathering up my thoughts and dialing down my annoyance with him. "Four. Fucking. Years."

He lets out a long breath.

"You were gone four fucking years."

"I'm sorry."

"Just shut up and listen to me. I have spent nearly every day with you since I was nine years old. There were times when we were apart. Few days, maybe a week every now and then. But years, Adam?" I shake my head. "Years? No. We don't just up and disappear on each other for *years*." He turns his head to face me, his mouth opening, but I cut him off. "Don't you dare say sorry."

"Then what am I supposed to fucking say? Huh? What is it you need to hear, McKay?"

"I don't need to hear anything. I'm the one talking. You're the one listening. Why is this so fucking hard for you?"

"Should I answer? Or should I shut the fuck up?"

"Shut the fuck up."

"Fine." He looks the other direction. Over to the bare spot of earth where Nathan St. James used to have a cottage. "I'm shutting up now."

"You know what I think is funny?" He doesn't answer. He knows better now. "I think it's funny that you are *this man* to everyone else but me."

He huffs. "I have no clue what that means."

"No. You wouldn't. Because you can't see yourself the way I see you."

"Is this the part where you tell me I'm a horrible human being?"

"No. This is the part where I tell you…" He turns to look at me. "That you're the kindest person I know."

"Lies," he whispers, his eyes darting back and forth as they search mine. "You're just lying now. Just winding me up. Making me feel better because you're gonna tell me something awful next."

"Why would I tell you something awful? I don't need to tell you awful things. You are fully and acutely aware of more awful things than I could ever imagine. You do very bad things for all the right reasons, Adam."

"Oh, God."

"And I mean that."

"Yeah. I get it. You're fucking pissed off at me for taking Maggie away. For not calling you and telling you the truth. For all those years I stole."

"No. You really don't get it. Because yeah, that was a shitty fucking choice. Really. Fucking. Shitty choice. But that's not why I was mad at you. I was mad because you left me behind. You *fucking dick*. You left me behind and then I had to face the facts that I missed you. And I made a mistake when you came to talk to me on the beach that day when I was fishing. I made a mistake and I should've said yes. Because even though I wasn't sure back then, I was very sure while you were

111

missing that I would rather take a chance on something I didn't really understand with you than be left alone at the end."

He doesn't *want* to smile. But he can't help it. So he looks down at the water to hide it.

"You fucking *dick*."

He laughs.

"It's not funny. I'm not *gay for you*."

He laughs louder.

"I just fucking love you, dude. And that kiss with Donovan last night? It was practice. So that when I kissed you, it wouldn't be awkward."

He's speechless now. But he raises his head up and looks at me. And in this moment, he is *that* Adam. That sad, sad boy who would sit out on this dock all alone and wonder why things had to be this way. Why he was in the middle of it all. Why he was born into this family. This Company. With these people who say they love him, but don't really love him. With these expectations that he be everything he hates about them. And even now, after fighting all these years to not be all the things he hates, he can't escape the story they put him in. He's a kid caught in a cycle. He's a foregone conclusion.

He is Adam Boucher and *nothing* can change that.

"I have always felt sad for you, Adam."

Any happiness he had at my confession falters now. "Why? I have everything. Why would anyone be sad for me?"

"When we first met up at my father's house in Alaska, I saw it immediately."

"You saw what, McKay?"

"You." I shrug with my hands. "I saw you. And it made me so fucking sad that I left my whole family just to make you smile."

"Jesus Christ." He takes in a deep breath and runs his fingers through his hair. "That doesn't make me feel better."

"It's not supposed to. It's not about you, Adam. It's about me. I don't care who your father was or what he thought he was entitled to, the only reason I came home with you was because I chose to. And you can believe that or not. You can tell yourself your father made me. Bought me. That my father sold me. And that's fine. Because that's not false. It's all true. But I *chose* you. And even if I'm the only one who ever believes that, it's still true too. You can't take it away. I chose you."

He's rolling his eyes and shaking his head. And I swear to God, I have not seen him so confused since he was a boy. "So how's this end? Is it over yet?"

"Why are you so anxious to get to the end? Why can't you just enjoy the journey?"

"Because I'm fucking lost here, McKay. You..." He sighs. "You... are so goddamn sure of yourself. You don't go to church, but you have all these ethics. You train little girls to kill, and yet you have this very elaborate bullshit fucking moral code."

"It's not bullshit."

"It *is* bullshit! You don't get to train little killers and hold your head up high!"

"Why not?"

"Because that's not how it's done!"

"If I say that's how it's done, Adam, then that's how it's fucking done."

113

He throws up his hands. "I don't even know what we're talking about now."

"We're talking about us, of course."

He laughs. "We're talking about everything *but* us, McKay."

I reach for him. Place my hand on the back of his neck.

He startles for a moment, then relaxes and looks me in the eyes. "What are you doing?"

"I'm gonna kiss you now. Because I love you and I practiced for this last night and I'm feeling pretty good about it. And I want you to be happy. I think you deserve it. But aside from that, I'm gonna do it because I need it. I need you to know that it's me and you, dude. Forever. No matter what else happens, I'm not going anywhere. I'm not gonna leave you behind because I find a shiny new something."

He frowns. Deeply. "McKay—"

"Don't you dare say you're sorry, Adam. Don't you fucking dare. I don't need the words. I need the actions."

He looks at me. Straight in the eyes. And maybe, for the first time, he *sees* me.

And then it's him leaning forward. Not me.

It's his mouth on mine. Not mine on his.

It's his choice this time. Not his father's.

His kiss is harder than Donovan's was. But Adam has always been harder than Donovan.

And it's better. Because Donovan's kiss was just a kiss.

And this is everything *but* a kiss.

His fingers thread into my hair and he grabs a fistful, holding me next to him, and his tongue is pushing inside my mouth.

And the most surprising thing about kissing a man is… it's not that different.

But then again, everything about kissing Adam is different.

He pulls back first, bumping his forehead against mine. Then both his hands are on my shoulders and he's leaning in to me. Almost hugging me.

So I hug him back.

That's all he was really after. I realize that now. That's all he really wanted from me.

Not the hug.

The connection.

The support.

The love.

The loyalty.

The *truth*.

He's not invincible.

He's not as strong as people think.

He's just a boy on the end of a dock looking for someone to keep him honest.

"Look." Adam sighs. We're all fucking sweaty now. We're too close. There's too much heat surrounding us. The sun is blinding and off in the distance we can hear Indie and Maggie squealing as they play their game on the swings. "I know you don't want to hear it. And… I'm ashamed to admit this, but I'm not sure it's true anyway. So I'm not gonna say it." He lifts his head up and looks at me, his chest rising and falling a little too fast. "But I needed those four years."

"I know you did."

"You don't owe me, McKay."

"I know that too."

"But if you stay, I promise I won't ever do it again."

I nod. "Sounds fair."

"So... now what?"

"I dunno. I'm open to seeing where this"—my phone buzzes in my pocket—"where this is going."

"OK. I have a question."

"Shoot."

He looks across the lake for a moment. My phone buzzes again, but I ignore it. I have special buzzes for the important people and this buzz isn't one of them. So it's probably spam.

"How..." Adam starts, but then he stops. Keeps looking across the lake. Which kinda makes me uncomfortable, because there's nothing over there. Nothin' to see here, people. The cottage is gone. "OK, so how attached are you—"

My phone buzzes again. Like whoever it was hung up and tried again.

"Are you gonna get that?"

"No. Just keep going. It's nobody."

"OK, so how attached are you to Indie?"

"What do you mean?"

He sighs a little. "Is it *her* you want?" He looks over at me.

I think about this for a moment. Because it's not really an easy question to answer.

"It's that complicated, is it?"

"Well," I say, "it is a little. I never wanted to sleep with her, Adam. It wasn't that kind of love. And when

116

she showed up at my house and started pushing, ya know, I gave in. Pretty easily." Adam grins at me. Shrugs. "But it was never that kind of love. I mean, I love her. I would do anything for her. But she's not why I'm here, if that's your question."

"Yeah. It is."

"OK. So that's the answer."

Adam sighs again. "Well, she seems to think—" My phone buzzes again. "Jesus. Just answer it. Then you can block it and it'll leave us alone."

I pull the phone out and it buzzes in my hand as I look at the screen. Then I just… stop. Go still.

"Who is it?"

I hold the phone up so Adam can see.

"Payphone?" He lifts one eyebrow up at me. "Someone's calling you from a payphone." I don't say anything. So Adam says, "Answer it."

I don't answer it. Because I think I know who's on the other end of that call. And I'm not sure—

Adam grabs the phone, tabs accept, presses speaker, and says, "What?" in his mean, I'm-an-asshole voice.

"McKay?"

And a chill runs up my spine when I recognize the voice.

Adam looks at me. Because he recognizes it too.

"McKay?"

"This is Adam. Who is this?"

But all we get are the hang-up beeps.

Adam holds the phone up and glares at me. "What. The actual. Fuck, McKay?"

I run my fingers though my hair. My turn to be unsure of myself.

"I thought you fucking killed him."

"What?" I laugh.

"I knew Indie didn't kill him. I saw him moving around on the ground when I was pulling out to take Maggie to the hospital. So I thought you finished him off."

"Jesus. I'm not that big of an asshole."

Adam gets to his feet and starts shaking his head. "You let him walk away. You actually let that little fucker *walk away*. Core McKay! What the *hell* were you thinking?"

I get up too. And then take a step towards the shore because one of us is gonna fall off this fucking dock if we try to stand shoulder to shoulder.

"Are you gonna answer me?"

"Look, I get it. He's—"

"He's the whole fucking reason she attacked me, McKay."

"That's not true and you know it."

"Really? And you know this how? Because you were there? That little rapist—"

"Oh, come on, Adam."

"—was filling her head up with shit. All these years!"

My phone buzzes again. I snatch it out of Adam's hand and press accept. "McKay."

"McKay?"

"I just said it was me, Nathan. What the fuck do you want?"

"Is Adam still there?"

I don't have it on speaker, but it doesn't matter.

"Yeah, I'm fucking here. Where the hell are you?"

"Nathan." I turn my back to Adam. "Where are you?"

There's traffic noises on the other end of the line. I can hear him breathing. People talking loud. Like he's in a city.

"Nathan!"

But he just hangs up.

Adam snatches the phone, presses call back, and puts it on speaker.

But it just rings, and rings, and rings.

PART TWO
blessing in disguise

Here's the short reprieve.
The calm before the storm.
The stay of execution.
One final deep breath before you go under.

Better take a big one.
Because you're going deep.

CHAPTER EIGHT

FOUR YEARS AGO
OLD HOME
INDIE'S TWENTIETH BIRTHDAY

I just stand there looking at the scene before my eyes.

What. Is. Happening?

Nathan's face is so fucked up from Indie's attack, for a moment I wonder if that's how he dies today. Choking on his own blood.

My head is spinning with confusion because I'm wearing jeans and I'm pretty sure I was naked just a second ago. Donovan is yelling at Adam as Adam struggles to pull on his own pair of jeans under the pavilion. "Take her now! *Now*, Adam! *Now!*"

I don't even know what Donovan's talking about. But he's squeezing my shoulder hard with one hand while the other desperately tries to hold on to Indie.

She is wild. Her eyes have the look of crazy in them as she pulls away from Donovan and rushes back over to Nathan, lying on the ground, face up, his normally blond hair stained scarlet and a long gash in the side of his head that is leaking blood. It pools under him, shining an almost surreal candy-apple color as he coughs and tries to roll on his side.

Indie doesn't allow it. She kicks him in the ribs over and over. And then the face and I swear I hear a snap or a crunch. And I look away.

When I look back, Nathan's body is just still. He's not moaning or trying to roll over anymore. He's just... *blood*.

Donovan lets go of me and scrambles to catch Indie again. He locks her in a bear hug and drags her backwards, towards the house, as she writhes, and screams, and kicks her feet.

I'm so fucked up—I know I'm fucked up. I am at that point of fucked-upness that I'm seeing things almost sober and for a moment I actually want to bitch Indie out for not being able to break free of Donovan's bear hug.

I taught her that move. I know I did.

"McKay!" Donovan is screaming my name as he drags Indie up the porch. "Help me!"

I look at Nathan. But just for a moment. Fuck him. And then I carefully make my way up the porch steps and help Donovan drag Indie inside.

The last thing I see is Adam placing Maggie in his truck. Then the screen door slaps closed and Donovan shoves Indie face down on the dark-wood floors and sits on top of her.

"Here!" He throws something at me.

I feel several hundred seconds behind the action, so I just watch the thing hit me in the chest, then fall to the floor at my bare feet.

"Stick that fucking thing in your leg! Right now, McKay! She *drugged* us! She fucking drugged us!"

Indie is screaming beneath him like a wild animal caught in a steel trap. Gnashing her teeth like she's about to chew off a foot if that's what it takes to escape.

I bend down, manage to pick the syringe up— even though my fingers are tingly and numb—and just look at it.

"Do it!" Donovan is screaming. He's got a syringe too. And I watch him demonstrate. Sort of. He pulls the cap off with his teeth and positions the plunger in his hand. "Sit on her legs, McKay! Help me!"

I sigh. First he wants me to jab myself with a needle. Now he wants me to sit on Indie. But sitting on Indie seems much easier than figuring out how to stick myself with that needle. So I sit on her legs and Donovan scoots his body up so he's got her shoulders pinned to the floor, and then, carefully, he injects something into the bulging vein in her neck.

Indie is growling at him.

And that's how she goes down.

She slips into unconsciousness *growling* at him.

The next thing I know, Donovan is jabbing me in the inner arm with the other needle. But I don't go down. I come up. And everything gets just a little bit clearer.

Donovan snaps his fingers in front of my face. "You there?"

"I'm here," I croak. "I thought you said the leg."

"Fuck the leg. Takes too long. But you're not really equipped to give yourself an intravenous inject— never mind." He shakes his head. "I think we have a dead body in the garden. That's *way* above my paygrade. So can you pretty fuckin' please go take care of Nathan St. James?"

He says all this with a much calmer voice then he did when we're still talking about Indie.

I look at the screen door. I'm still sitting on top of Indie's legs. And I vaguely remember Nathan dying in a pool of blood.

"McKay!" Donovan screams it. Right up next to my fuckin' ear. "Pull your fuckin' shit together! I need to take care of Indie. You need to go take care of that fuckin' body out there."

I nod. Because this is a job I'm good at. Then take a deep breath and feel markedly better than I did just a few seconds ago. I awkwardly get to my feet and as soon as I'm off Indie's legs, Donovan is dragging her down the hallway.

"What the fuck are you doing?"

"This sedative won't last long. I need to get her into the office and give her something else."

"That didn't answer my question, Donovan."

He has stopped dragging Indie and is now hunched over her body and breathing hard, just outside Adam's office. His gaze meets mine with a glare you don't often find in Donovan's eyes. "You do your job, I'll do mine."

And then he continues his job and I watch Indie's legs disappear inside the office.

A moment later, the door slams.

I consider if the dead body can wait. I should go see what Donovan is doing to Indie.

But a dead body in this heat?

That's probably not good.

I turn to the screen door and walk through it.

Nathan isn't dead.

He's moaning and writhing face down on the pea-pebbled garden path, a short trail of blood behind him, like he was trying to crawl away.

I stand over him. My head is clearer now than it was inside, but I would not call my thinking sharp. So I just consider him for a moment.

And then I wonder aloud. "What the fuck just happened?"

Nathan attempts to lift up his head, maybe prodded to do so by the sound of my voice. Gets it an inch or so above the pathway. Enough for me to see all the pea-pebbles stuck to the blood on his face.

But I can't see his eyes.

She fucked. Him. *Up*.

"Help me." I bend down to Nathan and he says it again. "Help me, McKay."

"I think… actually… I'm supposed to finish you off, Nathan." These words come out cold. I'm talking arctic. And for a moment I don't even recognize my own voice.

I feel like Adam in that moment.

127

And then I blink and reach for Nathan. I pull him up so he's sitting and consider my options.

They're not good ones. Not ones I'd even consider if I wasn't in the middle of an out-of-control situation. But I only have two. So I'm gonna spell it out the best way I can, in my present situation.

"Look at me, Nathan."

He can't, of course. He has not reached a point in this—event?—to open his eyes. But he goes through the motions and his head tilts up in my direction.

"I'm gonna let you live, boy. But we're gonna come to a little agreement right now. You hear me?"

He nods, then chokes and begins coughing, blood spilling out of his mouth. Probably swallowed it. You can only swallow so much before you get sick and it comes back up. There are plenty of monsters living in the Louisiana woods, but none of us are vampires.

"You're supposed to be dead. I think. But... lucky you, I guess. You're not. And"—I sigh and look up at the sky—"I don't know. I don't really feel like killing anyone right now."

He hangs his head and spits out more blood between his legs. "She would never forgive you if you did." His words come out weak and low and also, a little bit gurgled, on account of all the blood in his mouth.

"Did you see what just happened here?"

He wipes the blood from his eyes. Doesn't help much. Just smears it around, mostly. But I manage to see a sliver of silver blue in the one eye that isn't completely swollen shut. "I saw it."

For a moment I'm confused because I had forgotten what he walked into. He saw more than Indie kicking his ass from the ass-*kickee* perspective.

He saw us.

What we were doing in the pavilion. What we had been doing all day.

And how that all started in the kitchen.

I turn away from him and start walking down the path.

She tried to *kill* us.

"McKay!" He coughs. "Where are you going?"

I don't answer him. Just continue walking towards the house. I go inside and when I walk past Adam's office to get to the kitchen, I can hear Donovan talking in a low, calm voice on the other side of the door.

But I don't stop to listen or go in and ask him what's up. I just continue to the back of the house where the kitchen is and stop in front of the cupcakes and empty champagne bottles.

I know she drugged the mimosas. I think I knew that before Nathan even left with Maggie this morning. But I am truly stunned to notice the little bits of—what are those things?—in the frosting of the cupcakes.

I pick one up, swipe my finger through it, and then I get that feeling in my gut. That feeling that says something has gone terribly wrong while I wasn't looking.

Daphne berries.

That's when everything truly comes back to me. Why Adam was in the truck with Maggie.

She ate the berries.

That's what sent Indie into a frenzy. It wasn't Nathan catching us having sex. It was just… *her*. Indie. Reacting. Or overreacting, as per usual.

She didn't just try to kill *us*. She tried to kill her daughter too.

I pick up the cake plate where she had arranged the cupcakes in a neat circle and I dump the whole fucking thing into the trash.

When I go back outside Nathan has managed to get to his feet and is limping through the garden in the direction of his cottage. Which is a pretty impressive accomplishment, all things considering.

He's tougher than he lets on, that's for sure.

I jog after him. My head is straighter, but not wholly well. So I have to stop and bend over when I get dizzy.

But Nathan isn't moving very fast either. And he waits for me to catch up before he even gets halfway to the little path that cuts through the trees.

He bends over, the palms of his hands braced on his knees to keep himself from falling forward. "Whatever you're gonna do, do it then. I'm fucking done with you people."

"You *people*?"

"Company." He spits on the ground and then looks up at me without straightening his body. His face is turning into a purple fucking mess right before my eyes.

"What do you know about it?"

He laughs. Well, tries to. Then forces himself to stand back up so he can glare at me through that one half-good eye. "I know what I was told."

"And who told you? Your grandfather?"

"Did you think someone who was not Company would just be given a little house next to the Boucher family?"

I knew this. Have known it since—well, always. I am well aware of who the Bouchers are. I understand them better than anyone. Probably better than they understand themselves. It's hard to see what's right in front of you sometimes. You need to take a few steps back to get a clear picture. And even though Adam and I hardly ever talked about Nathan and his grandfather, we didn't have to.

This big revelation of Nathan's right now? It has been an unsaid fact since the day he showed up back when he was still too young to even go to kindergarten.

Nathan spits again, this time off to the side. "So if he wants me dead? Fuck it. He's always wanted me dead."

I frown at him. "Who?"

"Who the hell do you think? Adam, of course."

"Look." I shake my head and sigh. "We haven't liked you in a *long* time. But we never sat around plotting your fucking demise, Nathan. It's just not like that. We don't have time to hand out fucks to people like you."

He chuckles a little. And I can tell it hurts him. It's quite probable that Indie broke a few ribs when she was spinning out of control. "I guess we'll have to agree to disagree about that, McKay."

"Whatever. I'm not interested in your cryptic secrets. I've got enough of my own."

"I bet you do."

"I'm not gonna kill you."

131

He sneers at me. "I'm so over it. And besides, Indie will come back around. She always does. And when that happens, she'll ask about me. She *always does*. And trust me on this, McKay. Doesn't matter what she *thinks* I did to her. Or even what I actually *did* do to her. She loves me. And if she ever finds out you were the one to end it, she would never forgive you."

"You don't need to threaten me to save your life, Nathan. I already told you I wasn't gonna kill you."

"They're not threats. They're just facts."

"Believe it or not, I don't actually have an issue with you." I narrow my eyes at him. "At least I didn't. Up until now."

Nathan says nothing to that.

And it's a good thing too. Because I hear it in my voice. That growl. The very same one that Indie just used on Donovan when he dragged her into the house.

It's not unique to her.

We all have it.

"But now," I say, looking over in the direction of his cottage, "now you're gonna sell me that land." I nod my head towards it. "And you're gonna disappear. For good, Nathan. I don't care where you go, ya just can't stay here."

"Why? Because I might mess up his little plan? I might actually save Indie and Maggie instead of feeding them to the wolves? How fucking dumb are you?"

"How fuckin' dumb am I?" I point to my chest, then shake my head. "I was just thinking the same thing about you."

He looks back at the mansion and spits on the ground one more time. Like he's trying to get the bad taste of Old Home out of his mouth. Then his one open eye finds mine. "Fuck you, McKay."

I picture how I might kill Nathan St. James. Right here, standing on the edge of the garden, in full view of Old Home. Where Donovan might see. Or hell, maybe even Indie.

I put all the moves together the way I might on a job. When I'm in a rush and... you know, don't want to drag the fucking process out. When I want to be efficient instead of psychotic.

But I cut off that imagery and tuck the plan away somewhere safe. Because he's right.

The risk of Indie ever blaming me for Nathan's death is low. Very low. Hell, she's so damn impressionable, one short conversation—phrased just the right way—would be enough to convince her that she did, in fact, finish him off. And that would be the end of it.

But I'm tired. And still drugged. I feel better, but not a hundred percent. Nathan St. James won't go easy. He will fight. He has a savage side to him. Always has. He will fight until his last fucking breath. And even then, he'll use whatever residual chemical and neural reactions he has left inside his body to strike a final blow.

I know this because he is me.

He is Adam.

He is *us*.

"Here's how this is gonna go down, Nathan. You are gonna leave here today and you are never gonna come back. I'm gonna make sure there's nothing for you to come back to. Hear me?"

"As if there was ever anything here for me but Indie. And Donovan took her away from me a long time ago."

I chew on that for a moment, trying to make all the words fit together in some sensible way.

"But I would just like to go on record…" Nathan's eyes blaze with hate and anger.

Fuckin' A. All this time I thought it was us who hated him, but this look right here? This says something else. *He* was the one who hated *us*.

"I would just like to make it clear that I *left*, OK? I left her when she told me I had to."

"What the fuck are you talking about?"

"I didn't leave her behind when I went to school because Adam threatened me. If you guys think I'm afraid of you—" He laughs. It devolves into a cough pretty quick. But I get the general idea that he feels this to be a joke. "I'm not afraid of you. You know why I'm not afraid of you, Core McKay?"

"I'm not in the mood to guess. Or have this conversation, to be honest. But if this is something you need to get off your chest before you leave and never see my face again, then"—I pan my arms wide—"by all means, tell me more."

He pauses. Makes a decent attempt at a smile. His one open eye might even be twinkling a little. "Because you taught me everything I know."

I let out a long breath. He's not wrong. I did train this fucking kid. And thinking back on it now, it was even my idea. He's tough. And his martial arts skills are better than mine. Not as sure a shot as Indie. Or me, probably. But he can shoot. Not that it matters. Not that any of this matters. He has no gun now. He would fight, and he'd fight hard, but he wouldn't win. Not in this condition.

But in another condition, one where he is not bleeding from the head and mouth, one where both of his eyes are open and he doesn't have several broken ribs…

Then maybe. He's in his prime. I'm on the other side of mine.

So. Maybe.

Maybe killing him is the better option?

If Adam were here, he'd do it.

"I left because Indie begged me to, McKay. She was waking up. She was remembering things." He shakes his head. "Every day she would tell me something new while she was living at the cottage with me. Every fucking day it was something else you fuckers did to her."

Something happens to me when he says these words. It doesn't happen often. And it's almost always just before something real bad is about to go down. I feel a rush of adrenaline. Not in my blood, like is typical. My heart doesn't speed up at all. That's not what this feels like. It's in the muscles. In my arms. In my legs. It feels like I just did two hundred bench presses and every bit of stored energy in my body has been used up in an instant. It only takes a second or two. And then my arms and legs get tingly and numb.

And I feel… *weak*.

"She wanted me to take Magnolia with me. Bet you didn't know that, did you?"

"What—"

"You're so fucking stupid, McKay. You're his little fucking... what? What are you to him? Do you even know?"

I don't answer. I figure the question was rhetorical. But there is a part of me that wants to answer. I just don't know how.

"He used you, McKay. Just like he used Indie. She *told* me things. Maybe not everything, but she *told* me things. I know who you are." He whispers this. "I know what you guys do."

I laugh it off. "What do you want? A fuckin' medal?"

He huffs, nods his head. "It's all a joke to you guys, isn't it? That little girl you stole. Those jobs you made her do. All that killing. The way Donovan warped her mind."

"What the fuck do you know about it?"

"I know who I am, at least. Can you say the same? Can Indie? Adam?"

This little fucking prick really does want to die today. Maybe I should just give him his wish?

"Do you even know who my grandfather was, McKay?"

I shrug. "No one special. Just like you."

"You sure about that?" He eyes me with what might be a grin. I wish his face wasn't so fucked up. I'd be able to read it better. But it's all contorted and swollen and my mind is still spinning.

Shit just went *down*. Indie is psycho. Donovan is doing... whatever the fuck he does to her mind, right this very moment. And Adam is driving drugged to... where? A hospital? I don't know how serious eating daphne berries is. Maggie was screaming for sure. But

I can't fit all the consequences together. Can't predict what might happen next without all the information. And now Nathan St. James is here telling me—

"My grandfather was second in command to Admiral Tate up until that shit went down in Santa Barbara. You ever hear of a man called *Tate*, McKay?"

This, I decide, is a loaded fucking question. Because of course I have heard of a man named Tate. Two of them, to be exact. "So what? Admiral Tate wasn't ever in charge. That psycho bitch Francesca Fenici was."

"Mm-hmm. She had an affair. Who do you think she had that affair with?"

I chew on this for a minute.

"Ding, ding, ding." He says this weak and slow. And I wonder if he's been playing this conversation out in his head his whole life. Dreaming of the day when he could spill his secrets. And how he might surprise the person he's spilling them to.

But should I care if Nathan St. James is part Fenici?

Maybe.

"You have no idea what's been happening in this world while Adam's had you here."

"And you do?"

"I know as much as Adam does. I know way more than you do. And your friend, Donovan?" He shakes his head. "Do you have *any* idea what kind of monster that man is?"

"Donovan?" I have to laugh.

"You ever hear of cognitive dissonance, McKay?"

"What?"

"It's when the truth is right in front of your fucking face and your mind is so blown, you can't *see* it. But the truth always comes out. No matter how hard you fight it, it always comes out. And I'm gonna give you a little friendly warning here, OK? Because you were always good to me." He straightens up. Lifts up his chin, even. And his one good eye bores into mine. "There's a reckoning coming, McKay. I hope you're ready for it."

"Listen," I say, forcing a laugh. "I don't have time for this shit. But I'll tell you what. I'll give you a little head start before I set you loose in the big wide world, OK? But I don't actually hate you, Nathan. And all I really want to do is go back inside, figure what the fuck just happened—"

"She happened, McKay. He *triggered* her."

The next obvious question is—who? But I can't even go there. I'm not playing this boy's game. "Nathan, if you really are Company—"

"If?"

"Shut the fuck up now! You hear me?" I lean forward and scream it at him and he takes a step back. So I continue. "If you really *are* Company, then you know there's only one path for you in life. And it just so happens that I got a little side hustle going."

He nearly guffaws even though that laugh has to hurt like hell. "You?"

"What is this surprise I hear in your voice? Never mind who you are, do have any idea who *I* am, Nathan?"

"Yeah." He spits blood again. "Mr. Rule-Follower. Mr. Up-and-Up. Mr. I-Have-Ethics. You're not gonna offer me anything good. But whatever. Let's hear your deal. Not like I have much choice now. Fuckers. My grandfather warned me over and over again that my love for Indie would be my downfall."

I can't even take this bullshit, so I just ignore that last part. "You know that saying? The one that goes, 'We're all in this together?'"

He stares at me.

"Well, we're not. In this together, I mean. It's one hundred percent every man for himself. And maybe I don't know where you come from, Nathan, but I'm gonna take a wild guess and say it's probably closer to where I come from than you may think. So what if that psycho Fenici bitch had an affair with some high-ranking Tate man? That makes you special? That don't make you special. That makes you a bastard. The way I see it, that lands you a few rungs down the ladder from me."

"Says the boy who was sold to the Bouchers at age *nine*. Did you even question it?"

"Do you want to hear the fuckin' offer or don't you?" And that *growl* is back.

It disturbs me. Possibly more than it disturbs Nathan. Because it doesn't come out often and this is twice now. Twice in the span of minutes.

He takes a breath, probably considers saying something smart-assy back to me, then thinks better of it. Because he hasn't ever seen this side of me. He hasn't seen any side of me, actually. Few people have. I keep the real me hidden well away from anyone's prying eyes.

But Nathan senses it. And when he speaks next, he whispers. "Fine. Let's hear it."

"You're still gonna sell me that land. We're done with you. It's over."

"Like I fucking care. Selling it is the whole reason I'm even in town."

"Good. That's the easy part then. And then you will disappear. For good this time. Indie isn't gonna come looking for you again. And you're not gonna go looking for her."

"You better make a damn good offer on that cottage, Core McKay. Because that's the only way I'll sell out."

"Oh, the offer will be generous, don't you worry. I'll set you up just fine. But let's be clear here, OK? Let's be honest. A sellout is a sellout. Doesn't matter how high the offer is."

"What. Is. The job?"

"It's not a job, per se. It's a life."

I expect a quick quip back from Nathan St. James. But he's cautious now. Or maybe he's just wounded and he suddenly realizes all this talking has cost him, because he looks like shit. At any rate, he takes his time to consider his words. Finally, he says, "Do I have to answer to you?"

Of *course* that's his first question. God forbid this boy have to take orders from *me*. "No. I'm a silent partner in this particular endeavor."

I expect a comeback to that. Something along the lines of, *Haven't you always been the silent partner? Wasn't that why you were bred in the first place? Just a replacement.* Not even *the* replacement, either. Because I had those older brothers. I was the backup's backup's backup. Not sure that makes sense. But it encompasses the general idea.

Nathan chews on this last bit of information. "Will I answer to Adam?"

"No."

"Donovan?"

"Listen to me. Because my head is pounding like a motherfucker right now. I've got a team working on a project, and I'm down a grunt at the moment. You can have the job if the boys can trust you. How that shakes out is not up to me. Like I said, I run them, but I don't get involved. So if they kill you because you piss them off with your wild mouth, Nathan, that's on you."

He sighs as he rolls this around in his mind so he can see it from all angles.

But he can't see it from all angles. Even if he had all the pertinent information, which he doesn't.

He can't see it because he blew out his knee. No more football for this boy. He could go back to college with the money I pay him for the cottage and the land, but he's in way too deep now. He's seen way too much. And I don't mean that in a threatening way.

He's absolutely right about one thing. I can't kill him. Somehow, some way, Indie would find out. And then I'd lose her. And why the fuck would I put up with ten years of all the shit we've been through if I were just gonna let her slip through my fingers after I lost my cool in a critical moment?

That's not gonna happen.

Nathan is Company. He might not be an integral part of it, but his grandfather raised him up knowing where he came from. And once you understand that there is a group of super-elite assholes running this world and then you find out you're *one of them*—no matter how low your rung on that ladder—that shit *consumes* you.

He wants in.

I can take a good guess and figure his grandfather tried to shelter him from the Company life. Hell, I'm pretty sure my father, and Adam's father, and every Company son's fucking father had that same idea at one point right after their baby boys were born.

But it never works, does it?

I was sold to the Boucher family.

Adam was trained. Only half finished, but it doesn't matter.

Donovan took the bait whole. Hook, line, and sinker.

I could list every single Company man I know of as an example. Nick Tate wanted out too. Look where that got him. James Fenici turned down his little-girl promise, Harper Tate. But he came after her more than a decade later and took her back.

Power is a *sickness* and we're *all* infected.

Nathan sighs. It's a resigned sigh. And his words are low and filled with resignation when they come out. "Will I have to kill people, McKay?"

"Only if they get in the way, Nathan."

It's not the answer he wanted. But it's the same one my father gave me when I asked him that very question. And it's the truth. That's the only thing that matters now.

"Does Adam know about this?"

I look over my shoulder at the mansion. No real reason. Adam's not there. But he'll be back. And if he ever figures out what I've been doing in the years since his head injury, he won't be happy. "No," I tell Nathan, and then I look him in the eyes. "He doesn't know. And it needs to stay that way."

Nathan leans up against a tree, exhausted, the adrenaline of the fight and flight gone now. He's hurt. Probably badly hurt. And he's got to be wondering, at least on some level, what Indie's intentions were when she did this to him.

Did she *really* want him dead?

I wish I had an answer. If I did, I'd tell him yes or no definitively. Just so he could deal with it and move on.

We all know Indie is insane. That she is gone, and probably has been for several years, at least. That she isn't going to make it much further.

I'm on her side. Even Adam is on her side. Donovan…I can't tell. But I don't think he matters. She never relied on him for much. He's just not reliable.

But Nathan St. James has been the one thing she had going for her that other girls in her situation would not have had. He has been her constant for ten years and now that is about to be over.

Even if he stayed, even if she comes back from this… *breakdown,* it's over now. There is no way Nathan will ever trust her again. Not after this beating.

I see the look in Adam's eyes when he watches Indie. There's still love there, but it's tempered with a healthy dose of caution, not to mention a Plan B, should he ever need it.

If Nathan ever sees her again—and I'm gonna do my best to avoid that—he will have that very same look in his eyes.

It's one thing to suspect someone you love is insane and this cannot be changed, no matter how you try, and hope, and pray. But it's something else altogether to be kicked in the face with the truth.

Or hit over the head with it.

When I reach into the front pocket of my jeans, I am surprised to find my phone. Because it's been a totally what-the-fuck kind of day and finding a thing you need, in the moment that you need it, is akin to a miracle in my eyes right now. But here it is, so I press a contact and turn my back to Nathan, who has slumped down to the ground in exhaustion.

"I have a pickup," I tell the man who answers. I give him Nathan's address and end the call.

"Stay here," I tell Nathan. "I'll pack up some things from your cottage and then I'll take you down the driveway to wait for them to collect you. Is there anything special you want me to grab? Photos? Old family recipes?"

He laughs and then coughs and spits out blood. "Recipes, McKay?"

"I dunno what the fuck is dear to you, Nate. Do you want to keep anything or not? Because I'm gonna flatten that cottage to the ground and wipe you off the map. Two weeks from now there will be no evidence that a boy called Nathan St. James grew up there or that the cottage ever existed."

"What will you tell Indie?" I see the pain in his eyes when the words come out. It's a real question. But he's not asking it as a threat. As a way to stop me. He's asking it because he cares about her.

"I'm gonna tell her you died." I look back at the house. "I'm gonna tell all of them you died so they don't have to lie to her too. Just me. Just in case that matters one day."

Nathan thinks about this for a moment. "You're gonna tell her…" His one eyes squints down until it's nearly closed. "You're gonna tell her she killed me, McKay?" I nod, but he is shaking his head at the same time. "No," he says softly. "Please don't tell her that. Make up something else. Anything else. Just don't let her eat that guilt. It will kill her, McKay."

I start pacing in front of him, unsure now, because he's probably right. "It's my only option here. I'm not gonna tell her I did it. Or Adam. Or Donovan. It has to be her, Nathan. That's the only way that makes sense. That's the only way she'll believe it without seeing a body. So do you want anything from your house or not? Because we need to make this happen."

He repositions himself so he can see his home and then spends several long moments considering my question.

"If you don't want anything," I tell him softly, "you don't have to take it with you. We'll have everything you'll need when you get where you're going. And if it makes this decision any easier, Nate, I didn't take anything when I left, either."

I think he might cry right now. If he could. If his face wasn't a swollen mess.

But it is a mess and he can't.

"I guess I'll leave it," he whispers.

"Wise choice. And here's a little tip for you. Since we're on the same side now and I'm invested in your success. Don't keep the evidence, Nathan. None of it. Ever. And that includes all the feelings inside you too. I cannot even tell you how many men have gone down

145

because they needed to hold on to the evidence like a prize."

His look is pure confusion. But that's OK.

There's no way he can understand the full meaning of my warning right now.

But he will soon.

The distant sound of a screen door slapping drags our attention back to the mansion. We find Donovan standing on the porch, flat hand up to his eyes like a visor, as he scouts for me.

Our eyes meet, even though I'm a good hundred yards away and across the garden.

Donovan doesn't call out or try to get me a message. He can't see Nathan, since he's still sitting on the ground, propped up against the tree. He simply walks over to his car, gets in, and drives away.

"Where the fuck is he going?"

"I don't know," I tell Nate.

Nathan is trying to get to his feet, but I walk over and place a hand on his shoulder, pushing him back down. "Did he take Indie, McKay?"

"No. And sit your ass there. Don't move. Donovan sent me out here to dispose of your body. He thinks you're dead. I'd like to keep it that way."

"Why do you take orders from him?"

I glare down at Nathan. "I don't take orders from Donovan. No one takes orders from Donovan. Not even Indie takes orders from Donovan."

He huffs and whispers, "Whatever."

I consider Nathan's earlier words about Donovan as I watch his car disappear through the Old Home gate and turn left, in the direction of New Orleans, and not Pearl Springs. *Do you have any idea what kind of monster that man is?* But then my phone buzzes in my pocket and I turn my attention to things I can control. I answer it with a curt, "Yeah," then listen to the voice on the line as I stare at the mansion. Indie is still in there. Donovan left her. Why? "We're ready," I tell the voice on the phone. "And you can pull down the driveway. No one will see you."

I end the call, then help Nathan to his feet. The car arrives long before I get him back to the cottage. But my men wait patiently, inside the car, until we're upon them. Then both the front doors open at the same time.

Beck is closest on the driver's side, so he grips Nathan with one meaty hand on his upper arm and then Moore is there, opening the door to the back seat. They're shoving him in without ceremony when Nate places a hand on the edge of the roof, resisting. "Where are they taking me?"

"Just go with it, Nathan. You don't have any choice now. The deal has been made."

Moore pries Nathan's grip loose from the edge of the roof, places a hand on his head, and pushes him inside the car.

Beck slams the door and then turns to me as Moore walks around to the passenger side and slips into the back seat next to Nathan. "What's the plan with this one?"

"Same," I tell him. "Same as always. Get him ready. He's not up to par, but he's close. I know what he's capable of, so don't go easy. Full ride for this one."

"Got it," Beck says, sloppily saluting me with a finger. "Talk soon."

147

I don't wait for them to pull away before I start walking back to the house. I don't even look back.

Indie. That's all I'm thinking about now.

Then I huff out a laugh. Because she is all I've thought about for the last ten fucking years.

I do it for you, Indie. Everything. It's all for you.

The minute I walk through the screen door and enter the foyer I feel it.

I can't describe the feeling. But it's there.

I walk down the hallway towards Adam's office. But the moment I see that the door is open, I know she's not in there.

Still, it's good practice to check. There is a recording device on the desk that I recognize as Donovan's outdated mini-tape player. But there is no tape inside. Just the empty machine with the cartridge door left open.

The couch on the long end of the office is empty. But even if I didn't know Indie was in here with Donovan, I would know. I can feel her phantom presence and smell the lingering scent of her shampoo.

I retreat to the front stairs and take them two at a time. This time the door I approach is closed. But I can feel a whoosh of wind coming from under the door as I stand in front of it with bare feet.

I open the door and the curtains on the far window billow out from the wind.

The screen is gone and so is Indie.

I take a deep breath and force myself to remain calm as I walk over to the window and peek out towards the woods. A rush of panic fills my chest. Tightens it. Like a vice on my heart. And then the questions come rolling in, unbidden.

148

How long did Donovan have her in the office?

When did he bring her up here?

How long was she alone after he left her?

Did she see me and Nathan?

Did she see the car over at the cottage?

Is she gone? Or is this just a stunt? A normal, Indie stunt?

Donovan's voice is coming through my phone before I even realize I've called him. "Hello?"

"Where is she?"

"In her room. Why?"

"She's not here, Donovan."

"What do you mean?"

"I mean I just came upstairs and her screen has been pushed out and her window is open. She's. Not. *Here*, Donovan. Where the fuck is she?"

"You saw me leave, McKay. I left her up in her room."

"Awake or asleep?"

"She was awake when I took her up. But I gave her a sedative. A very strong sedative."

"Then how did this happen?"

"How does anything ever happen with Indie?"

And again, Nathan's words come back to me. *Do you have any idea what kind of monster that man is?*

No, I decide. I don't.

There are several blank, silent seconds where I get lost for millions of years and then return to a world where nothing has changed, but everything is different.

"Just let her go, McKay. You can't help her anymore. We all know she's out of control and her disappearance a few weeks ago is just the beginning. She's not yours, ya know."

"I know," I hear myself say. Because it's true. She belongs to all of us.

And I don't mean that the way it comes off, either. All three of us—hell, four, if you include Nathan—we're responsible for what she is. It wasn't Adam's rules that drove her crazy. It wasn't my overprotection, or Donovan picking her brain. And it certainly wasn't Nathan's enabling.

It was all of it.

It was all of us who did this to her.

We can't even blame the trainers who came before us anymore. It's so far past that now.

"I gotta go."

"Wait," I say. "What about Adam? What about Maggie?"

"I don't know, McKay. It's… it's probably not gonna be good."

"What the fuck do you mean? What the fuck does that mean?"

"I did a finger swipe of Maggie's mouth before I handed her over to Adam and there were at least a dozen chewed-up berries in there. They are…" He pauses. "They're highly toxic."

"Did you call Adam?"

"He didn't pick up."

"So how do we get a hold of him? Is he in Pearl Springs?"

"I couldn't tell you. But I have to go."

"What the fuck do you mean you have to go, Donovan? Indie is missing. She just…" And I have to pause here and ask myself, *Do I want Donovan to know that Nathan is alive?* I quickly decide no. "She just *killed* Nathan, Donovan."

"She tried to kill *us* too, McKay. And you don't need to be a genius to see that she is *done*. This shit is *over*. Move on. Let her go. Maybe she'll never come back. That's the best-case scenario. But I have a life and I've worked damn hard for it. I'm not going to throw it all away over some crazy little girl I took a fucking interest in back when I was fifteen. Not anymore. I'm out."

"What do you mean, *out*? There is no *out*."

"There is. And if you were smart, you'd be out too, McKay. It's *over*."

He doesn't hang up on me. I can hear the sound of his car on the highway in the background. But he doesn't say anything else after that.

He leaves that final decision up to me.

So eventually it just… ends.

CHAPTER NINE

I just stare at McKay as the last of his story fades away.

"Say something, Adam."

We're still standing on the skinny lake dock. The sun is beating down on my bare shoulders. Has been this entire time. And I can feel my skin starting to burn.

"Fucking say something."

"I don't know what to say." It's true. He got me. I knew McKay was keeping something from me, but I really fucking thought he killed that little fuck. Was counting on it, actually.

"This is why I came outside to talk to you."

"This?" I ask. "Meaning Nathan?"

"Mmm… no. Not Nathan."

"Oh." I say it softly. "You're running people, McKay?"

He nods.

"Ever since Indie hit me?"

He nods again.

"How many?"

"Well." He sighs. "None anymore. They all died." He shakes his head. "Obviously they are not all dead."

"Shit." I sit back down on the dock and McKay joins me. We are much too big for this. When we were boys it was a much better fit. Though this was always my spot the few times we came out here together. Was my spot long before McKay came to live with me. "Why do you think he's calling you?" I look over at McKay, search his blue eyes. Smile at him a little because he's frowning. "I'm not mad, if that's what you're thinking. I don't care if you were running people. In fact, it would be a relief if you still had teams out there. Because someone *is* running people, McKay. And even if you were doing some shitty, dirty things with those men, I'd feel better knowing it was you."

"It's not me, Adam. They were dead a long time ago."

"And Nathan?"

"I was under the impression he died with my two best men. Beck and Moore."

"Beck and Moore, huh?"

"You know them?"

"No. Heard of them. Been a while, though. We were still kids when I knew them."

"Hmm. I didn't know them until after your accident."

"Did they come to you?"

"No. I was trying to get in touch with James Fenici. Everyone thought Nick Tate was dead, so he was the only one I thought I could trust."

"Hold on." I place a hand on his arm. "What do you mean… everyone *thought* Nick Tate was dead?"

"You know. Fucking doubles and shit. When the Company prince dies a very public death—at the end of Sasha Cherlin's gun, no less"—he shrugs—"well, that's pretty fucking convenient, don't you think?"

I nod. I do think. I met his double negative down in Daphne, Alabama. So I had a lot of suspicions. But I didn't have any proof.

"Anyway, the rumors were all over the place. Fucking leftovers kept calling me looking for you. And I didn't want to spell it out that Indie went crazy, so I just kinda…" He eyes me, unsure if he should say the rest.

"It's OK. I'm not mad that you took over, all right? Those were our men anyway."

"Right. So. They were all asking for you. Obviously. You're next in line, if there was a line. And I went looking for James."

"Did you tell him what Indie did?"

"No. Fuck that. I don't trust him that much. I mean, he did a lot for us. Everyone who got left behind. But he's not my partner. You are."

I bump him with my shoulder. "Thanks."

"No problem. So James came and read Donovan and me the riot act—"

"Hold on. Donovan was in on this too?"

"Yeah. Of course. I mean not really. He knew about it, but he wasn't running anything. He was taking care of Indie."

"Continue."

"So James came that one time, barked a bunch of fucking orders, then he left us to it. The guys came to me. And I tried to get in touch with James again a few times. But he had disappeared." McKay shrugs.

"I think he was on the ocean back then."

"Yeah, I heard that too. So about a week later, Moore and Beck showed up. Said James sent them—"

"Whoa, whoa, whoa. So *they* came to *you?*"

"Hmm. I guess. Yeah. They said James sent them. I just assumed that was correct at the time."

"Why would you assume that?"

McKay rubs his hands on the top of his shorts. "Felt right."

"Felt right?"

"Don't judge me. I do the best I can, OK?"

"Fine. Whatever. Keep going."

"So they showed up about a week later, telling me that James sent them and I was under orders to finance some things as a favor to him."

"For James?"

"Yup."

"That makes no sense. He was out."

"Maybe? But I had orders, so I followed them. I'm not you, Adam. I'm not Untouchable."

"Why didn't you tell me this?"

"They told me not to."

"What kind of things were you doing?"

"Mostly recruitment shit. I just paid the bills. They did it all."

"A training camp?"

"Pretty much."

"And you didn't think this was weird?"

"Weird?" McKay laughs. "As compared to *what?*"

"Fine. I get it. OK. Fast-forward to Nate after Indie tried to kill him." It occurs to me in this moment that Nathan St. James and I have something in common. I shake that thought off and continue. "So then... how did Nathan die? Or not die, as it were." I side-eye him and McKay smiles. But it's an uncomfortable smile.

"Everyone got taken out at the same time at some party in Savannah about six months after Indie's twentieth birthday."

"That doesn't sound familiar at all."

"Right." McKay chuckles. "Santa Barbara all over again. It's a fucking circle." A chill runs up my spine when he says that. "It was all over the news. They even blasted names. All my fucking new men. Dead."

"When was this?"

"About... maybe six months after Indie disappeared? I'm surprised you didn't hear about it."

"We were on the water."

"That doesn't sound familiar at all, either."

I point at McKay. "True. So... six months? He only lasted six months."

"He lasted four years, Adam. Obviously."

"Do you think someone got to him? And the others? Just took over?"

McKay shrugs. "Well, that makes sense *now*. But back *then*, I dunno. I was still reeling from everything that happened. I thought Maggie was dead. Indie was gone. Donovan wouldn't answer my calls. Just fucking disappeared for almost a year before I talked to him again."

"Where'd he go?"

"LA, I assume. But that's only part of it. The other part is—"

"Hey."

McKay and I both turn to find Maggie walking up the dock. "What are you guys doing?"

"Nothing, little peach." I ruffle her head when she stands next to me. "Just talking."

"Can I sit with you?"

"Sure, baby."

She climbs in my lap and I scoot back so she can sit between my legs and put her feet down in the water. She splashes for a moment. Then she looks over at McKay. "Don't stop on my account."

He salutes her. "I'm afraid we're done."

"I missed all the good stuff again?" Maggie whines a little, but it's not real. "Indie asked me—"

"Do not call her that," I chastise. "She is your mama. You will call her Mama."

"Fine. Mama asked me to come ask you boys if you want to go out to eat because Donovan is gone—"

"Where'd he go?" I interrupt.

"Town?" Maggie shrugs. "I dunno. Where does he ever go?"

"Town," McKay and I both say.

"Right. So. I want pizza." She tugs on my arm and makes fish lips at me. "Can we get pizza?"

"I'll take some pizza," McKay says. "But I'm gonna go shower real quick." He gets to his feet. "I'll meet you in the house."

"OK," Maggie says, smiling at McKay's back as he walks down the dock. We're silent until he's out of sight. Then she says, "So… I've been thinking."

"About?"

"You know that problem we have?"

"Which one?"

"The things your father left behind."

"Oh, fuck! I totally forgot!"

"What?"

"Fuckin' Wendy called me. Right before McKay came out. She said—fuck, what did she say? Some riddle, Mags. She had a riddle for me."

"Oh. I love riddles. What kind of riddle?"

"I know you do. I was just gonna go find you and see if you could help me figure it out when I got sidetracked."

She tsks her tongue at me. "Well, what is it?"

"Let me text her and get the verbatim. Hold on." I text Wendy.

"OK, while we wait for that, I had an idea."

"About the missing secrets?"

"Yup."

"The suspense is killing me, peach. Spit it out."

"OK. So the problem is that they have to be hidden somewhere close."

"Yup. They have to be."

"They're probably here, Adam."

"Why you gotta do that?"

"Do what?"

"Call me Adam?"

She shrugs. "You are Adam. Daddy feels so… childish." She wrinkles her nose.

"Well, you are a child."

"Am I?" She tips her head way back to look at me. "Am I really?"

"Just get on with it."

"I think there're here. They have to be here."

"I looked here, Peach. Every fucking where."

"There ain't no other places though."

"Don't say ain't. Please? We already sound hick enough. But there is the house in New Orleans."

"You said you looked there too."

"I know. But it was a while back now. Maybe I missed something?"

"Maybe you missed something here?"

"Point." She's just about to open her mouth to say something when my phone dings a text. "OK, here it is. It was a note." I eyeball her. "And don't ask me where it came from. You don't need to know. It said, 'They pack them in with no regard. They leave no marks and sing no songs. They cover them up and walk away. They did this to you. They did this to me. It ends. It begins. It ends again.' What do you think of that?"

"Say it again."

I repeat it.

"Hmm. 'They pack them in. They cover them up. They leave no marks and sing no songs.'"

"Where do people usually sing songs?"

"A church?"

"Church. Maybe. Fuck. If I have to dig up the fucking church we used to go to in New Orleans, I'm gonna—"

"No, no, no! Wait! I got it! It's not a church, it's a cemetery!"

And that, my friends, is how it's done.

I hug her. "I love you so much."

"Love you too, Adam."

I laugh and then get up and pull her to her feet. "Let's get some pizza. We're gonna need it. We have a big night ahead of us."

CHAPTER TEN

Indie

Nathan St. James was the boy next door.

Those words follow me around like a half-starved stray kitten, mewing and whining like it's trying to get my attention. And I know it's wrong to turn your back on something so small and helpless, but if I could make it go away, I would.

I would do terrible things to make it disappear.

But I can't. Can't do that with thoughts. They linger. Even if you manage to banish them for a while, they linger. And then, when you're not expecting it, they come back and start begging for attention again.

I have tried my best to sort through the past several years. Not just the four I've been missing, but the long-ago ones too. Before Adam bought me. Before McKay took care of me. Before Donovan helped me cope. Before Maggie.

And of course, before Nathan too.

I don't want to admit I miss him, but I do. I loved that boy so hard. And thinking about what I did to him—it's eating me up inside.

I've been trying to ignore his voice in my head, but he was such a big part of my life. Even after he moved away to college. And every time I picture his face I am filled with regrets. I'll find myself wandering around the swamp when everyone is busy so they can't take too much notice of me. I don't go far. I don't go into the river town, for instance. They won't let me do that. I stay close. Mostly I sit somewhere in the woods, or maybe I'll climb up into the little fake treehouse at the top of Maggie's playset in the garden. Just anywhere I can see the dirt patch across the duck lake where Nathan's cottage used to be and no one will take too much notice.

Because I'm *dwelling*.

And I like to pretend it's still there.

I pretend to open the door and go inside. And then I pretend to walk up the stairs and plan the words I will say to Nathan to make him smile. I pretend we're still carefree children, even though that might not have been real.

I question it. I question everything about memories these days. But I plan a day for us anyway. Like the ones I wrote about in the journal McKay found. Swamping, and fishing, and boating, and just generally traipsing around being children. I always plan a trip to the meadow where he used to make little flower crowns for me in the summer and twig crowns for me in the winter.

I pretend we're ordering ice cream in the drug store up the river. And we sit in the cool air condition and lick our cones, smiling at each other.

If all that stuff in my journal was true, then I had a pretty great childhood. Even though I know that's not true. Even if all that stuff I wrote is accurate, my childhood can't ever be considered great.

I want to embrace all those entries as truth. I really do. Some days I just force myself to believe in them. But then other days I see how some of it doesn't add up.

For instance, I noticed something about my writing where I talked about Nathan. He didn't say much in that journal. It was mostly just me doing the talking. But that's not how it was in real life. I would not call Nathan a quiet boy. He was definitely a conversation-starter.

Like when we first met on the river bank he talked a lot. I mostly just listened. And watched him. Everything about him felt right. I knew he was good from the first moment I saw him.

In this memory he was in the sunshine and that's how I got his eye color all mixed up, I guess. They were already pale, but the sun turned the silver-blue into a muted gold. The river water was slapping against his knees because he was standing in it holding his fishing pole, his boat nearby on the sand.

And he was talking. He didn't use my name at first, because it took me a little while to tell him that secret. I think he knew it, though. It took me a little while to realize that too, but looking back on it now, I'm pretty sure he already knew who I was.

Anyway. When I first came out of the trees, he was pulling the boat up the sand and I think I scared him. Because he stopped and stared at me, and then said, "Jesus Christ. Where the hell did you come from?"

Normally I would not show myself like that, but I had had *a day*, if you know what I mean. I was a little out of sorts. So I said, "The island." Because that was the truth. I still felt a part of that place and the reality of Old Home hadn't quite set in yet. There was a disconnect there. Between who I was in that moment and who I would become tomorrow.

Because tomorrow I wouldn't *be* from the island anymore. I'd be from Old Home. And even though I was young, I think I knew this instinctively. So I said, "The island," because that would be the last time it would be true. He would know me as the girl next door after that.

I don't recall all his words that day, obviously. But there was a lot of talk about islands. And that's how we decided that the land around Old Home was almost like an island—the river on two sides, because it curved around the property, and the duck lake.

But he started talking about things right away. Running in the woods. The jungle, he called it. I remember that. Because I knew about jungles, and the swamp didn't really qualify. So I recall thinking about that a little more than I should've and missed parts of the conversation.

But anyway, my point is that Nathan was a talker.

He was charming too. Like McKay. Always grinnin'. Always ready with a smile. Always ready with ideas too. He was full of big ideas. I would not call myself an idea person. I'm not imaginative that way. I mostly try to keep myself rooted in reality. Whenever possible, that is.

Nathan though, he was always about what's not possible. He liked to talk about fantasy things. Like... we had games and stuff. Very complicated games we'd play in the woods and on the river. His little fishing boat was a pirate ship and we'd be looking for treasure. Or sometimes it was a yacht and we'd be looking for food. He'd make me do the imagining because I was bad at it. He was always able to conjure up realistic descriptions of just about anything. Not just birds and moss on the trees, but clothes. He would imagine whole outfits for me. Pretty ones, too. Or weapons. He would make weapons out of sticks and stones and we would practice using them. He could spear a fish with a stick. He didn't need a line to catch a fish. And he always had a slingshot in his pocket. This was before McKay really started teaching me things, so it was in those first few weeks.

Nathan and I, we just fell in to each other that way. Like we had been friends before in another lifetime.

But there is no denying that we grew apart as we got older. I could feel it happening. And part of that new distance was about Adam, of course. And McKay too, but mostly Adam.

I was Nathan's at first. For a lot of years, even though I lived with the men, it was me and my boy.

I have been thinking back on that recently, wondering, *When did it change? Was there a moment?*

There was. It was after the first kiss. When that first kiss happened, we were tight. Still peas and carrots back then.

But it was definitely before we had sex in the tree house.

That was when we were seventeen, so four years between the kiss and the sex.

And boy, did a lot happen in those four years.

There were two big things keeping Nathan and I apart in that time. My jobs—because I was working a lot in those years—and his school. Because of course, he had to go into town and be this other boy nearly every day.

So he had his secret life and I had mine.

That's what changed us.

A wise person once told me that you had better be very sure you want the truth before you ask for it.

Is this a Dear Diary moment?

Isn't that how girls start their journals in the movies? Do they really do that in real life? Dear Diary. Who is Diary? Why not address your pathetic inner ramblings to the actual person you are rambling them to? Which is yourself.

Dear Stupid Indie who lived in the past, I have advice I think you should consider.

Period. New line.

You have been fucked over by ruthless men since you were born.

Period. New line.

Well, that's a lie. You don't really know that for sure. Because you can't remember anything before you came here with McKay and Donovan a few months ago. But you're good at deducing. Critical thinking, contrary to what the people closest to you might think, is actually a skill you possess. You should take that skill out every once in a while and dust it off. Put it to some practical use.

Period. New line.

But you wanna hear the really fucked-up part, Indie? Do you? Are you ready for it? Because it's super fucked up!

You have a record of what happened to you before that day you came home a few months ago. And... *and*... it's in your own fucking handwriting!

Is that convenient or what?

I mean, you lose your memory and then poof. This journal shows up out of nowhere—in the hands of McKay, no less—proclaiming to hold all your dearest secrets and fondest memories.

That journal. Right over there. You wrote it all down. How much you loved this place. How much you loved Nathan.

Who? Oh, yeah. That kid who lived next door and made firefly jars for you. It lit up this super-romantic fort in the woods, which he created with his bare hands—like he was McKay fuckin' Junior or something—so he could give you your first kiss.

Yeah, that journal. That bullshit, lying piece-of-such-and-such journal that, when contrasted to the tapes—oh, yeah. There are recordings, Indie! In your own *voice*, no less! Telling Donovan all about the most fucked-up moment in your life!

Anyway. My point was, when you contrast the journal to the tapes there is a very clear discordance. I'm talking *major*, San Andreas faultline cracks in this fucking story, OK?

One piece of crucial evidence detailing your forgotten past is convenient. I can *maybe* buy the journal in my own handwriting.

Twice, though? And on tape, no less? Um, I was gonna say that's a really big coincidence, but nah. I'm gonna have to go with suspicious for the second one.

I'm just waiting for the video to show up. Where's that hiding, I wonder? Who's gonna come home with that? Which of these men are gonna point to it and say, "See, Indie. You're fucking crazy. This here movie of your life proves it?"

And it's gonna be in like 4K Ultra or something. I'm talking details like you're living it in real life.

And it's gonna come from Adam. It's got to be Adam. He's the only one left who didn't come home with evidence.

Oh! That's not even true!

He came home with my *daughter*!

My. Fucking. Daughter!

I throw the journal across my new living room. It sails right over the second couch and falls with a *thunk* onto the slate floor.

My heart is racing. The adrenaline coursing through my body feels good the way a drug does. It's a friend to me. It keeps me on my toes. Keeps my eyes peeled and my hearing sharp.

It has saved my life, if Donovan's tapes are to be believed, on many an occasion.

But not this occasion. Right now, it feels more like... *panic*. More like a complete and total unraveling of Dear Indie's psyche.

I take a deep breath, hold it just the way Donovan taught me, then let it out in a burst of laughter. It's the crazy kind of laughter. Like… picture insane-asylum inmate type of laughter.

Maniacal, maybe?

That might be a tad over the top. But only a tad.

I'm fuckin' losing it.

Because using a relaxation technique provided by Donovan feels a little bit like… that stupid girl in a horror movie who says, "I'm gonna go check it out," when she hears a weird noise in the attic. She's probably a babysitter. Home with the kids. It's super dark outside, probably past midnight, and she's the butt of everyone's joke. So it's maybe a prank. But of course—I stop to laugh here—an inmate, a psycho inmate from the nearby insane asylum, just escaped that afternoon and he's on the loose.

You know, I get it. It sounds stupid. All those coincidences leading up to the dark attic. Kids begging her not to investigate. They're on the ball. They know what's up. Hell, these days they've whipped out their cell phones to TikTok the whole thing. It's gonna go viral tomorrow.

Take a deep breath, Indie.

As I was saying. It sounds like a really low-budget horror movie.

But this shit is real. This level of stupidity is an actual fact.

I know. I'm that girl walking up those creaky stairs with a half-dead flashlight asking, "Is anyone there?"

Yeah, you clueless bitch! The fuckin' boogeyman is up there. Turn around. Grab those kids. Run to the neighbors—oh, I forgot. No. The neighbors live far,

far away. Miles away! Except for that boy called Nathan who lives just across the duck lake. But he's dead and the house was torn down. So no. Can't run. Gotta just suck it up and go up in the attic and ask that stupid question.

"Is anybody there?"

Of course someone's there! That's the whole point of the movie! Or journal in your own handwriting. Or tape in your own voice.

Correction. Someone is not there. Someone is fucking *here*.

There's nowhere left to run, Dear Indie.

The only thing left to do is fight.

Dear Indie,

Let's try this again. Without the insanity, please and thank you.

Adam gave me this new journal for my twenty-fourth birthday. We didn't have the big traditional celebration. McKay wanted to, but I told him no.

It just didn't feel right.

It won't ever feel right again.

But I did get presents. Well, a present from all of them, including this journal. Donovan wanted to "switch things up" so he offered to cook breakfast. Obviously not something he does. That's McKay's job. But that was the point. He said sometimes traditions become ruts and wouldn't we like to try to get out of our rut?

No one objected and the thought of seeing Donovan wear an apron made me smile.

It still makes me smile. But I'll get to that part.

So Donovan said he would cook and McKay should do something that Adam usually did. And then Adam should do something Donovan usually did.

Adam always bought me a dress but McKay didn't buy me a dress. That was too close to the real tradition and none of them were very excited about reliving the last time I put on one of Adam's special dresses.

But McKay figured he only owed me something beautiful and beautiful was a thing he could do. We only made this decision the week before my birthday. That was the deadline for when McKay had to order the cake and he needed to know what our plans were. So he didn't have a whole lot of time to come up with the pretty, but that never stopped McKay before.

He made me a carpet of flowers.

I was sleeping with Adam the night before. We were all doing this weird turn-taking thing with where I sleep each night because McKay insisted that we 'cool things down before they got too hot'.

I respect him for that. For respecting *me* like that. But who in their right mind wants to cool things down when you are in this kind of unique situation?

Not me. But whatever.

Anyway. I woke up the morning of my birthday. Adam was in the shower and I was doing my best trying to picture that. This whole cool-down idea is not easy when the men surrounding you look like Adam, and McKay, and Donovan. And picturing him fifteen feet away—naked and wet, inside a shower? Yeah. I needed to get the fuck out of that room.

171

So I threw open the door and took one step, and when my feet hit the soft petals I stopped and looked down.

There was a path of rose petals—white, and yellow, and pink—leading down the stairs.

And I swear to whatever the hell is running things from above, I will never forget how those soft, soft petals felt under the tired soles of my feet.

They were like... being lost in a forest without water. All dried up and weary. And then suddenly you come upon a clearing with a waterfall and the mist hits you and your whole body is refreshed.

That's what it felt like to walk on his path of petals.

He didn't skimp, either. It was a thick path. A cushion. And my weary feet—well, they had never felt so refreshed in all their days.

McKay was waiting for me at the bottom of the stairs, shirtless, arms crossed, face all asmirked as he watched me walk down to him.

I could hear Donovan in the kitchen banging things around. And I could also hear Maggie talking to him while he did that. Also the sound of Adam's shower running through the pipes. So it was just McKay and me.

I expected the path of petals to lead me to the kitchen. To breakfast. To Donovan and Maggie. But it didn't. It stopped at McKay's feet. Right there in the foyer. And there was a kind of curve to the end of the path because McKay was leaning against the archway that divided the hallway to the dining room about halfway between the kitchen and the front door.

No real rhyme or reason to the location he picked. We had never had a special moment in that particular place. But it was a spot where he could watch me come down the stairs. Like a girl in a movie who descends for her first date, or whatever.

He wanted to see me before I saw him.

He had several seconds on me because I was still fixated on the feeling of silky pastel petals and I cherished every step. I didn't see him until I turned the corner on the landing near the bottom and then…

It takes my breath away just thinking about that moment.

Because then… he was *all* I saw.

The sound of Adam's shower went away. Maggie's and Donovan's voices went quiet and the banging stopped. And at first I thought, *Well, they were all in on it and now they're watching too.*

But that wasn't the case. No one was watching. It was just us.

McKay waited for me to travel the entire path. I could tell he was nervous by the way he was breathing. But he didn't move or say one word until I ran out of petals to step on and I had to look up to meet his blue-eyed gaze.

That's when all the breath ran out of me. That's when my heart stopped beating. And that's when he took my face in both of his hands and leaned down and kissed me on the lips.

Just a very soft kiss. Not a kiss good night, or a kiss of passion, or a kiss hello or goodbye.

Just a kiss. That's it.

I closed my eyes and went still like my breath and my heart.

173

And when he pulled back and I opened them back up, he pressed his forehead to mine and whispered, "The end."

I get what most people would think about those words. That something is over. And that is true. And he did mean it that way. But when you are standing at the end of a pathway of rose petals and there is this man—a glorious, beautiful man who can kill you and save you in the same breath—and he is waiting for you with something soft and slow…

No. That's not what he meant.

He meant this is the *beginning*. Because that's what happens when you get to the end of something. It doesn't matter if it's a road, or a story, or a goal—when you get to the end of it you start over.

Then he hugged me and just held me. For a long time, I think. And eventually the bustle of Old Home came back. Donovan and Maggie were laughing in the kitchen as they banged things around. Adam came downstairs, his upper body bare and still wet from the shower, his old jeans hanging off his hips and his scuffed boots in his hand, and he just stopped and looked at us. Cocked his head a little and said, "What the fuck is this?"

Such a typical Adam question.

McKay didn't say nothing. So I said, "My dress."

Donovan and Maggie appeared in the archway that separated the hallway from the kitchen and Maggie squealed with delight at the sight of the rose petals and started dancing in them. Spinning and spinning with her arms out so that the petals under her feet were a little whirlwind.

And that was the end of the moment.

For a second I thought, *Well, it was a nice present. But it's over now. And that's OK.* Because petals on the ground were always meant to be a sign that something was over.

It wasn't until late that night, when I was lying in bed with McKay's arms around me as I stared out his window and found a few stars through the branches of the pecan tree thick with leaves, that I ran the whole day through in my head.

That's when I realized it would never be over.

Because my present wasn't the path of petals that led down the stairs into the foyer.

My present was the man waiting for me at the end.

Donovan made a goat-cheese quiche for my birthday breakfast, which makes me laugh even now as I write this. Because that is *so* Donovan and so *not* McKay. Maggie had set the dining room table with Adam's family china and there were crystal wine glasses filled with sparkling cider that projected little dots of amber onto the walls and the ceiling and made us all look like we were adrift in someone's bokeh-enhanced photograph.

We ate in there like a family and even though nothing about my birthday breakfast felt familiar, everything about it felt *right*.

It felt like we had always been this way. It felt like we defied time and logic. Like there was no world outside the gates of our little Garden of Eden and no matter who forced their way in, they couldn't touch us.

It was perfect.

We spent the day fishing and didn't go anywhere near the pavilion or the duck lake. We have a little boat house on the Old Pearl River. It's really more of a rickety gray-wood dock with a green and white striped canopy held up by rusty metal poles that have seen better days.

We took a trip downriver and just kept going, something we had never done before. For most of my years at Old Home the boats we had were in drydock. And they were nothing special to look at. Or very big. Just fishing boats anyone who lived along this river would have. Large enough for all of us to sit, but there was no cabin or anything. But Adam had arranged for the boat to be put in the water and even though this was a brand-new tradition, it felt so right. We didn't come back until after the sun set.

We made it all the way down to Grand Isle in the Gulf of Mexico and then we all passed out on the beach in the sun and took naps.

We are maybe getting old.

It was a great day.

And I didn't even realize that Adam hadn't said anything about his present. He was supposed to be Donovan in this scenario and I'm not sure Donovan would've planned a boat trip. But later that night, when

McKay was putting bubbles in Maggie's tub and Donovan was downstairs on a phone call with someone in California, Adam came into McKay's room and handed me a finely wrapped gift.

I was sitting in the chair near the window with my legs pulled up to my chest just thinking about the day. I had been dreading it for obvious reasons. But they all came through. It felt like a mixture of forgiveness and love all wrapped up into one bright moment of sunshine.

He sat on the bed and his fingertips were busy playing with the gift in his hands. Like he was worrying over it.

I turned in the chair and smiled at his nervousness. It didn't make sense, this uneasiness. It's not an emotion Adam pays much attention to. Even when I carefully pulled the pretty paper off the journal, I didn't get it. Not until I opened it up and saw that on every tenth page, he had written something for me.

"Don't look ahead," he whispered as I paged through it. "It wasn't meant to be read that way. Just... let it come as it comes, Indie. It's better that way."

Then he stood up and leaned over to kiss my forehead. And he lingered there in my space for a moment. Like he was taking time to enjoy me.

And then he pulled back and walked out.

I didn't page ahead. I wanted to honor his request. But I did read the first entry.

It said, "Truth is precious. Treat it with respect. Because even though all truth is better than lies, it can hurt you, Indie. And the last thing I want it to do is hurt you."

My breath got caught somewhere between my heart and my head for a little while after that. And I knew this journal was so much more than just a journal.

Just like that day was so much more than just a day.

Side note for Dear Indie. That was much better. Keep going. You've got this.

I write in this book every single night now. That's not how I did the journals of my past. Those were for coping. That's why Donovan used to give them to me. So I could write down the things I couldn't say. But we had a stipulation that when they were all filled up, we had to sit down and read them together and talk it out. It was all part of keeping me intact and sane.

And then we would burn them.

I'm not going to go on a tangent and say this is convenient or suspicious. Even though it's both.

It's just a fact, Dear Indie. That's all. I wrote in the journals. We discussed the journals. And then we burned the journals.

Period. New line.

This journal will not be burned at the end. There isn't a chance in hell of that. But Adam is right. Truth needs to be treated with respect. So I don't write anything about the old days in here. There are no sentences about jobs, or regrets, or mistakes.

This is a book of hope. It's a book about slow days and easy nights. It's book about me, and us, and this place. It's a story of three men and two little girls. And how things change over time, and get better, or worse, and then no matter what happens, they go on.

I hope it has a happy ending. I want more than anything to get to the last page of this journal and make the very last words in this book be that they lived happily ever after.

But I'm not stupid. I understand how fairytales work.

You have to live a *million* disappointments.

Crush a *billion* evil dragons.

Face a *trillion* moments of crisis.

And even then, there is *no* promise.

CHAPTER ELEVEN

FOUR YEARS AGO
TEN SLEEP, WYOMING

From the view at the end of her long driveway Anabelle Avery's log cabin appears minimalistic. Just four walls, a small porch with two Adirondack chairs slightly angled towards each other, and white curtains billowing through the one window on the front side.

This is a relief.

When she told me that she opened up a spiritual healing center in Wyoming on a twenty-eight-thousand-acre lot of land I pictured... I don't know. A *lodge*, I guess. Something with a massive wood-beamed drive-through portico out front and a door that leads to a well-staffed lobby.

But this? This is nice. Quaint.

Which is normal for Ana. She is—and I'm not being disparaging in any way when I use these words

181

to describe her, they are just part of her charm—she is earthy. And soft.

You know the type. Likes those floaty gauze shirts and long chiffon skirts. Keeps pink crystals in her pockets in case she needs *grounding*. And wears flowers in her long, light brown hair.

Kind of… *boho*.

But she is not stupid, or flighty, or gullible. Anabelle is the first girl I met after I moved to LA when the Company fell five years ago. I was just switching over to reconstructive surgery and she was finishing up her PhD in cognitive neuroscience. It was one of those burn-too-bright relationships because she left right after successfully defending her thesis in the spring quarter of my first year to open up her *healing center*.

She is rich as rich comes. I'm talking old, East Coast money. Not Company. That was the first thing I checked. My family was in charge of the care and feeding of the Company pedigree book, which I inherited after my grandfather's suicide when everything fell apart.

So unless she's using a fake name—always a possibility, but highly unlikely in this case—Ana Avery is the real deal.

And I love her.

Not *love* love, though we did a lot of fucking back in the day. It's a different kind of love. Maybe like the love McKay has for Indie, minus the whole training her to kill thing.

She is six years older than me but she makes me feel ten years older than her when we're together.

I don't know if that's a good thing or not. But I don't mind it. I went through life as the kid who didn't really belong anywhere. Too smart, too young, too weird, too rich, too secretive.

I was too much of everything to just about everybody. Except Ana.

In Ana's eyes, I was just right.

She might be the only person on this godforsaken planet I trust with my whole heart.

Not trust to keep me alive in a sticky situation. That would be McKay.

Not trust to implement big ideas on a grand scale. That would be Adam.

Not trust to challenge my worldview. That would be Indie.

But trust with my heart and my feelings. Trust with the truth.

And that's why I'm here. I need some truth right now.

Because somewhere along the way I took a wrong turn and got lost. And I have an idea of how I might get back on track, but I would like a trusted advisor before I move forward.

Yesterday's incident with Indie—what she did to Nathan, what she tried to do to us… that was too much.

It was the last straw for me. A fucking wake-up call. *Pay attention, Donovan. Things are happening here, right in front of your fucking face, and you're missing them.*

And it's so much easier to miss things. So much easier to ignore all those warning bells ringing in your head and red flags waving in front of your face.

Because if I admit the bells are ringing and the flags are waving... well, then I'd have to *do* something about it.

I can't ignore it anymore. I have to do something about it.

I have known for a long time now that what we were doing with Indie was wrong. And I tried to get out. I kept my distance, I lived my life, I moved on. But they—she, and Adam, and McKay—they aren't the kind of people you just walk away from. I don't have any words to explain that feeling or my connection to them, but I was always the outsider there. I was the one only ever half in. The one only half there. The missing one.

I don't even know if I like Adam. McKay, he's... whatever. I tolerate him, I guess. And I *do* like Indie. She feels a lot like a best friend (with occasional benefits). A childhood friend, I guess.

Because wasn't that what she was to me? My childhood friend?

I don't care what the IQ tests say, a fifteen-year-old genius is still nothing but a kid.

I was a fucking teenager when I got involved with this program. And I cannot, for the life of me, make sense of that.

I'm not ready to admit that I'm not invested in these people. In Adam, and McKay, and Indie. Because they are a huge part of my life. And you don't just throw that away because you're having a crisis of conscience. I know McKay and Adam love Indie. And we were all in the room when we came up with the plan to keep her alive and try to give her as normal a life as we could.

But I have to face facts here—the whole thing was *in*-fucking-*sane*.

I feel bad for leaving McKay to clean up the Indie mess. Especially after he called me and said she was missing. Again.

But I had this compulsion after I left her upstairs—all sweaty with leftover rage and drugged out of her fucking mind—I just needed to get the fuck out of there and clear my head. Stop breathing the air there. That place is like a drug. It's hell dressed up like the garden of Eden. And to be perfectly honest, I didn't stay away so much in the early years because I was obsessed with school. Fuck school. I never gave a shit about school. All that was just a job. Something I was ordered to do.

I stayed away because... that *place*.

Old Home.

I mean, I'm just gonna be honest here. The people inside that house are a good enough reason to keep your distance. But there's more to it than that.

The swamp and the woods.

The snakes and the gardens.

The way things creak in that place. And the way they don't.

All of it unsettles me.

Every time Adam called me back, I had this overwhelming compulsion to get the fuck out of there as fast as I could. And when I pulled away, I had this equally overwhelming feeling that my entire life with them was nothing *but* an overwhelming compulsion that I had no control over from the beginning.

185

I'm not an impulsive man. At all. I'm methodical. I am contemplative. I am rational, and steady, and objective.

So what the actual fuck was I thinking? Who was I at fifteen that today, at twenty-nine, I can't recognize that kid?

Was it life on the island that warped me? Seeing those girls in cages? The excitement of the auction and the forbidden nature of the *events* that took place there? What? What *was it*?

I don't know. All of it, maybe?

And here's the real problem: I can't go to an outsider and ask these questions. If Ana knew what I've been up to for the last ten years, she would quickly diagnose me as a psychopath. And that would not be a casual diagnosis, either. It would be legit. This woman has as much training as I do. She's not a medical doctor, but a PhD in cognitive neuroscience is no fucking joke.

It doesn't even matter what she thinks. I understand I'm a psychopath. I have to be. There is just no other explanation for the decisions I've made. And yeah, I could just point to Adam and McKay and say, "So are they." But it's not the same. They don't know better and I do.

There has to be something wrong with me. There *has* to be.

Of course, it's pretty common for most psychopaths to feel normal. And I do. Most of the time. I don't *feel* like a psychopath. I can point to hundreds of things in my day-to-day life that are completely normal.

I chuckle under my breath as I pull forward, listening to the tires of my Jeep crunch on her gravel driveway as I approach the cabin. Because that's part of the problem.

I feel *so fucking normal* and that *has* to be a sign of disease. Doesn't it?

Ana pulls the white curtains aside to peek out the window. But I only get a glimpse of her. Two seconds later she's throwing open the raw-wood front door to her little cabin and walking through it to greet me with a wide, honest smile.

She waits for me on the porch with her hands on her hips looking like a dream in a light-green chiffon dress with tiny straps that show off her bronze shoulders.

I step out of the Jeep with a grin I couldn't hold in if I wanted to. And I don't want to.

After everything that happened yesterday, I need this.

I need *her.*

She opens her arms to me as I approach the porch stairs. "My Donny. How are you?"

"Donny." I laugh. She is the only person who can get away with calling me *Donny.* "Forget about me. How are you?" I pull her into a hug when I reach the top step and just hold her for a moment.

But she pushes back almost immediately and holds me at arm's length. "What's wrong?"

I sigh. "Nothing now."

"Stop it. I'm not going to listen to lies, Donovan Couture. A man from my past does not travel seventeen hundred miles from New Orleans to Ten Sleep on a whim because nothing is wrong." She looks me up and down for a moment. "And I can feel the stress coming off you like heat."

"Well." I take a moment to gather my thoughts by running my fingers through my dark hair. "I'm not here for *that*. You know." I wave my hand at her cabin. "Your facilities. Which are sparse, by the way. But I like it."

She looks at me funny for a moment. "Oh. No. This is your cabin, sweetie. I thought you might need some privacy. I live on the other side of this hill in the lodge. That's where the guests stay. We'll take a look at it later. After you tell me why you're *really* here."

"As I was saying, I didn't come for your healing. I just need some advice. You know. Colleague to colleague."

She raises one eyebrow at me. "You came all this way to ask me an academic question?"

"Yeah."

"That must be some question, Donovan."

"It is."

"OK. Well." She looks over her shoulder. "Let's go inside and have a chat then." Then her wide smile is back and she hooks her hand around my arm and leads me inside.

It's a typical cabin. Comfy couch and chairs. Raw-wood end tables. Small kitchen with knotty-pine cupboards and wide-planked floors. Very chic, and yet simple at the same time.

She makes tea and I sit on the couch and watch, wondering why I didn't pursue her more. Why I ever let her leave. Why I didn't chase her down and keep her a part of my life forever.

Her tea is a production. Tea pot, little cups sitting on pretty saucers. Flowers on the tray when she sets it down on the table in front of me. And the whole place smells like jasmine and... I don't know. Something sweet. Sugar, maybe.

I wait patiently for her to serve the tea. She is a slow woman. A woman who will not be rushed for any reason, and if you understand anything about her at all, you don't want to rush her.

You just want to settle in and enjoy it.

The slow life.

I could get used to it.

She made me an offer. "Come with me," she said. "Let's do this together. I know you don't really want to be a doctor. I can feel these things, Donny. Just come with me."

But I walked away and now, for the life of me, I can't understand why I did that. It's the same feeling I get when I think about Indie and why I convinced Adam to buy her and then shape her into the pretty little nightmare she is today.

But this isn't about Indie. It's about me. So I push her out of my thoughts and try to concentrate on the best way to phrase what I need to ask Ana.

Finally, Ana settles in the chair across from the couch and we both take a sip of our tea and then set the cups down, the fine china clinking in that old-fashioned, alluring and seductive way that fine china does.

"What's on your mind?"

I take a deep breath and spit it out. "How..." Well. Not quite spit it out.

"Go on, go on."

189

"Have you ever done any self-hypnosis?"

She raises that eyebrow at me again. "Like… the power of positive thinking kind of self-hypnosis?"

"No. The other kind."

"Hmm." She looks up at the ceiling, thinking. "Yes. I'm pretty sure I did." Then she laughs. "But I was a little bit high on peyote at the time."

I laugh too. She makes me *want* to laugh. She is a good thing. Something I didn't… ruin.

"OK. I'm getting serious now. The answer is yes. And yes, I was on peyote. But I had a fantastic guide."

"So you had someone there with you?"

"Yes. Of course." She says this like it's a given and for a moment I second-guess my decision to come here. "But listen…" She pauses and leans forward. "If you're looking for the self-guided kind, I'm not going to talk you out of it. You are a genius of a man, Donovan. If this is what you think you need, then who am I to caution you?"

"Well… you're Ana. And if it's a bad idea, I'd like to hear it from you."

She slows us down again—on purpose, maybe. Or maybe not—and takes another sip of her tea. She doesn't set her cup down this time. Just holds the cup and saucer in her hand. "What are you looking for, Donovan?"

"I don't know yet."

"But something. There must be something. Or you wouldn't be here."

"Fair enough." I wipe my hands on my jeans. They're sweaty. "I've made some decisions over the years and I don't really understand why."

"Hmm."

190

"I just want to like… go back, ya know? And figure it out."

"You have regrets?"

"I think so. But it's more than that."

"I could help you—"

"No." I cut her off and her head juts back a little. She's not quite startled—women like Ana don't startle easily—but she's definitely taken by surprise. "It's not that I don't trust you. You know I trust you, right? It's just… it's very personal."

"OK. So you're looking for a technique?"

"Yes." The word comes out rushed and filled with relief. "A technique. Because, as I'm sure you're aware, this is kinda"—I bob my head back and forth and suck some air—"unscientific."

"I wouldn't call it unscientific, Donovan. It's just outside the realm of typical."

Like her healing center.

"Exactly. This is my point. The information I have access to, on how to do this in a… *scientific way*, well, it's sparse. At best. I need something I can *track*."

"You're going to record the sessions? Video them?"

"Both. Probably."

"Hmmm. This is very interesting."

"How so?"

"Well, you're a psychiatrist."

"Not really."

"Stop it. You are a medical doctor who specializes in the art of minds, Donovan. And you did a PhD in psychoanalysis."

"I never finished."

191

She waves a hand in the air. "Neither here nor there."

"Ana, I'm not saying all this to… be *propped up*." If she raises that eyebrow any higher it's going to disappear into her hair. "I am quite aware of my limitations."

"Well. I'm not *propping you up*. So you can let that go. I don't feed egos. Not even for friends. I'm telling you that a psychiatrist—which you are, like it or not—performing analysis on himself…" She shrugs and throws up her hands. "It's not recommended."

"I understand that. And again, I'm *not* a psychiatrist. I'm a reconstructive surgeon."

"So this is self-help?"

I see where she's going. Anabelle Avery is the most ethical person I have ever met. She dots the i's and crosses the t's. And then she dots the t's and crosses the i's just to be double sure she's walking the line. She is not going to teach me self-hypnosis if I'm going to hurt myself in the process.

But. If I tell her that I'm looking for some techniques to aspire to a higher realm of… what's the word she used to use? *Enlightenment*. Yeah. She would be on board with that.

So I say, "That's right. Self-help."

"OK." She pauses for a moment to smile at me from behind her cup as she takes another sip of tea. Then she lowers the cup, her smile gone. "But I get to do a baseline."

"Fine."

"Because you said you wanted to know if it was a bad idea. So we do a full session. One on one. And I get to record it."

"OK."

"*Really?*" She cocks her head at me.

"I'm fine with it. And I trust you. Whatever you need to feel comfortable with this. I just need... some truth, Ana. So say what you need to say."

"But you're going to do whatever you're going to do in the end, aren't you?"

I don't answer. I don't need to.

"OK, then. But we should do it in my office." She stands up and smiles wide at me, then extends her hand. "Are you up for a hike?"

A hike. You gotta fucking love her. And I do.

So I take her hand and let her take me on a hike.

PRESENT DAY

The first thing I did when I decided to leave my partnership in LA and move back to Old Home after Indie returned from her four-year hiatus was to rent an office space in Pearl Springs. It's on the second floor over the printing shop on Main Street. Close enough that I could come here regularly, but still have the privacy I was used to.

I'm not hiding anything from Adam and McKay. If they wanted my secrets, they would have them. But so far, neither of them has taken much interest in my frequent trips into Pearl Springs.

The office is large—much larger than I need—and smells like old books. Not the good kind of old books, either, if that is even a thing, but the musty, moldy smell of ink and paper that's been hoarded over decades.

But it's only seven hundred dollars a month and that includes utilities and internet, so… fuck it.

There are seven rooms up here. Three of them feel more like large closets than the private offices they might've been at some point. One is a bathroom with a shower. Handy. One is an open space that was probably a reception area. And then there are two larger offices. The partners worked there, I suppose. This used to be a law firm.

But I only use the main reception area and one of the large closets. I pulled up the old carpet and refinished the floors before I moved in, then added some haughty leather couches with nail-head trim and a matching set of wingback chairs by the long wall of windows.

I sometimes sleep here. I like this place even though it's not that private. The walls are thin—I can hear everyone downstairs in the print shop—but they close at four-thirty Monday through Friday, and I mostly work here in the evenings. So it's fine.

But the main reason I need this space is so I can continue my sessions.

I spent three days with Ana up in Wyoming during my first visit four years ago. The 'office' she took me to that first day was a small ledge at the top of a nearby plateau with views of a river valley down below and her healing center off to the west.

I lost my breath up there, it was that beautiful.

Her healing center though… it's huge. Everything I had imagined it would be on the drive up and then discarded when I saw the small cabin.

I wanted to resent it. And I had a few thoughts about her being a sellout. But I am the last person to judge anyone who sells out.

Anyway, it's a very nice place. Has a very spa-like feel to it.

We didn't do the session on the plateau. We just sat there in silence for a little while. I'm the kind of man who is comfortable in silence. I've been alone my whole life.

Well, most of it. Anyway. Carter was there in the beginning.

Wasn't he?

This is part of my problem. I remember having a brother. A twin brother. He *was* there. But memories are unreliable. This is what Ana and I talked about once the initial silence was over.

Memories. The memory. It was mostly an academic conversation about anatomy that called up—ironically—memories of med school.

But the take-home message we both agreed on was that it's all very unreliable.

Not comforting, but what can you do?

We didn't do our session until the morning of the third day. And by that time, she had talked me down from the idea that I could do this all myself and I let her hypnotize me with a specific set of questions.

They were not the questions I needed answers to. The baseline, as it's called. This was her idea and it made sense scientifically. She needed to get a general starting point. But we recorded it. That was the important part. This is how I learned her technique for putting someone under. My own technique was severely lacking, I was not too proud to admit after I saw how she did it. And I felt so bad for how I had mishandled Indie all these years that I nearly fell into a crushing depression when I got back to LA.

Nearly? That's a lie. I took two months off and pretty much started talking to myself. It wasn't the rambling of an insane man. It was more… functional. List-making. Talking things through. Planning. But it wasn't how I had planned on returning home.

McKay called a few more times, mostly asking about Indie. Filling me in on his attempts to find her. I never heard from Adam at all.

I was never important enough for Adam to call me. If it didn't involve Indie making a catastrophic mistake, he couldn't be bothered with me.

Eventually I went on to finish my residency and then I started formulating my plan to tackle my memory issues. And specifically why I cannot recall a clear reason for taking such an interest in Indie.

But I've had some success in that area, at least.

When I put myself under it's not really under, it's just a very deep relaxed state. A freeing state where my mind is allowed to wander and thoughts pop up almost at random. Visions too. I can even hear people when I'm in this state.

It's not a dream, but a precursor to a dream. In science, we call this hypnagogia. It's an intermediary state of consciousness people experience just prior to falling asleep and consists of visual and auditory sensations. It's quite helpful for problem-solving. Although the difficulty of inducing it for a long enough period to study, and the fact that, like sleep, it induces amnesia, makes it a little unreliable.

Some people never experience hypnagogia, or don't remember it. But I have always had bouts of extremely vivid visions and sounds as I was falling asleep. Stress can bring it on as well. And it's been known to be helpful working things out. Some very smart and famous people have reported solving big problems while in a hypnagogic state.

Ana was the one who turned me on to this. Prior to seeing her out at the healing center I hadn't thought about it much. It was brushed over in my neuroscience classes in school. One or two paragraphs in a text. A single multiple-choice question on an exam. That's about it.

It's not very helpful in a therapeutic situation. It doesn't last long enough and again, the memory of it is unreliable.

In Ana's world this state is used for lucid dreaming.

I was skeptical at first. But after I left and went home to LA, I practiced. It was surprisingly enlightening. I videotaped every session, even though the video was mostly me just lying there, and hooked myself up to an EEG and did an audio-only recording too, trying to keep it all scientific.

It's not very scientific.

But I had a timer set to wake me. A loud bell that would jolt me. And then I would talk it out. Say everything I could remember.

On a scale of one to five, I would rate this therapy a one and a half. But I persisted. Because even small steps forward can be helpful. I remember that much from all that PSYOPS training.

Also, I kind of enjoyed it. The lucid dreams were interesting. I'd see people sometimes. Doing very random things, like riding a bike in a circle. And they talked too. That was creepy, but also cool. Most of it is meaningless. But it was a little bit like... spying on strangers. I understand that these people I saw weren't real, but... fuck it. I wasn't consciously making them up. So they were a little bit real.

Anyway, I'm gonna ask Indie to watch me. That's the trade, I think. I'll do her sessions and she can just watch mine. I have the videos, so I'm not expecting much. But Ana was right. The reason my progress has been so slow is because I don't have anyone helping me.

Tomorrow night. That's when we'll start.

My phone rings. It's Indie. "What's up?"

"Where are you? In town?"

"Yup. At the office. Why?"

"We're all heading in for pizza. Wanna meet us?"

"Sure."

"OK, we're on our way."

"Oh, hey, Indie. Wait. So tomorrow?"

"What about it?"

"I think we should start. I have a plan. For you and for me."

"What is it?"

"Are you alone?"

"Yeah. Why?"

"I just don't want Adam and McKay to know what we're doing. You didn't tell them, right?"

"No. It's our thing. Nothing to do with them."

"Good. OK. Just checking. I don't want Adam prying. It's… you know."

"Personal."

"Right."

"I get it. So we'll be there about forty minutes. Bring your appetite."

I can hear her smile on the phone before she ends the call.

She seems to be in a good place right now. And there's a part of me that wants to leave well enough alone. Just… give her time to enjoy this new stability.

But this is a chance to learn all her secrets.

And there's no way I'm walking back from that.

CHAPTER TWELVE

I think about Adam the whole drive into Pearl Springs. We take his truck, so he drives. Maggie wants to sit in front, so Indie and I sit in the back. She's stretched out on the seat with her feet in my lap. If this were the time before, I'd be harping on her to put her fucking seatbelt on.

But she's not a little girl anymore. And if she wants to stretch out and put her feet in my lap, fuck it.

Pick and choose your battles, right?

I play with one of her toes as she and Maggie have a conversation about frogs. Which makes me smile. And when I lean to the side a little, I can see Adam smiling too. Every few miles he checks me in the mirror. Habit? Maybe. Or maybe he's thinking about our talk this afternoon.

So… this is happening.

I don't really know what to expect. Indie is supposed to sleep with me tonight. She doesn't know that Adam and I have come to an understanding, so if we're gonna get things started tonight, the offer will have to come from me or Adam.

201

It's a wait-and-see game, I guess.

Pizza in town is nothing special, really. But it's refreshing to be out and all together.

Still here.

Still alive.

Still mostly sane.

Donovan meets us out front of the little Italian restaurant. Pearl Springs only has four eateries—this place, a fast-food taco place, a Subway connected to the gas station, and a place that is only open for brunch on Sundays.

We all slip into a large half-circle booth and it's not quite big enough for three grown men, a small woman, and a child. Our elbows are all touching. But it feels good.

Adam and I sit on the outside. Maggie sits next to Adam like she's attached to his hip. Indie sits next to me, like she's attached to mine. And poor Donovan is stuck in the middle.

He's in a good mood tonight. Joking and laughing with Mags. Teasing her the way he does with ridiculous statements and helping her do the word search on the kids' menu using a broken red crayon.

We feel like… a family.

Indie gets in on their joking. And I lean back against the booth and look across the table to find Adam grinning at me.

I lift my chin up at him. "What?"

202

"Nothing."

I wait for him to say something about our talk this afternoon. But he doesn't mention it. Probably because Maggie is here.

He looks happy. Or maybe that's not the right word.

He looks satisfied.

And that's kinda how I feel too.

After we're done eating, he asks Maggie if she wants to ride home with Donovan. And she jumps at this.

"I'll ride with you too," Indie offers. Then she squeezes my thigh under the table. Like she's in on some secret plan.

And it does feel like a plan. Because now Adam and I have forty minutes to ourselves on the ride home.

I expect him to bring up what happened this afternoon. And he does. But it's not the part I was thinking about.

Because he asks, "What are you gonna do about Nathan?"

"What do you mean?"

"Are you gonna tell Indie?"

"Fuck, no." I just stare at him. "Why? You think I should tell Indie?"

He shrugs as he pulls onto the highway. "Secrets, McKay. You should know better."

"This is not the time to tell her. Trust me. She's in a good place now."

"Yeah. She is. But the longer you go—"

"It's too late. The time to tell her he was alive was four months ago when we listened to those tapes together."

"Yeah," Adam says. "I don't understand that. Why did you lie?"

"I thought he was dead."

"McKay. She thinks she *killed* him. Indie thinks she killed her best friend in a fit of PSYOPS rage. You knew that wasn't true. That's the lie that's gonna get you in the end."

"I know."

"And he's not dead."

"I know."

"So what if he shows up here?"

"He won't."

"You don't know that." He's quiet for a few moments. But then he glances over at me. "If you're gonna keep this lie going, then we need to find him. Threaten him, or pay him off, or…" Adam shrugs.

"Or what?"

"Kill him."

"You're not serious."

His eyes dart over to me again, then return to the road. "Are you trying to tell me that thought didn't cross your mind this afternoon?"

I draw in a deep breath. "Maybe."

Adam laughs. "Asshole. Don't try to make me feel like a psychopath."

"But then I came to my senses because—"

"Listen. We either have to tell her or we have to take care of it, McKay. Those are the options. I don't really fucking care either way. But we need to figure it out."

"You *should* care."

"Why?"

"Because he's back now. And that means…" I pause, unsure if I really want to go there.

"That means what?"

"Maggie is not your child, Adam."

"She's not his, either."

"You don't know that. We get some stupid birthday card from Carter Couture telling us he's Maggie's father, and we're what? Just supposed to believe it? Maggie looks just like Nathan."

"Bullshit. Maggie looks just like Indie."

"Yeah, I thought that too. Until I got a phone call today from her other maybe-daddy."

Adam side-eyes me. "He's not her father."

"You can't prove that. But he sure as fuck can prove *you're* not her father. All it takes is one DNA test."

"Fuck you, man. She is my kid."

"She's not your kid, Adam. You took her when she was two years old. She feels like your kid because you're all she's had."

"So you're what? Holding a grudge about that?"

"I thought I explained this."

"I thought you did too. But obviously, you left a few things out."

"Look, I get it. You love this little girl. If anyone understands that, it's me, Adam. Because I feel the same way about Indie."

205

"Gross. Do not compare your relationship with Indie to my relationship with Maggie. It's totally different. Trust me on this, if nothing else. I will not be sleeping with my daughter when she comes of age."

"What the fuck, Adam? You're an asshole."

He huffs a little air. Stays quiet.

"Maggie does look like Indie. But she looks like me too. And you. And Nathan. And you know why she looks like all of us, Adam?"

"I don't need a lecture on the Zero Program genetics, thank you."

"Well, Maggie sure the fuck doesn't look like Donovan. Does she? Not a single fucking thing about Maggie reminds me of Donovan. So the logical conclusion is—"

"The logical conclusion has been settled." He glances at me. "She's ours."

"Fine." I throw up my hands. "She's ours."

"You know, for a man who just said he's not interested in making Nathan St. James really dead, you're sure making a good case for it."

"If I was gonna kill that boy, I'd have done it four years ago when I had the chance."

"Why didn't you?"

"Because he wasn't even that hurt. His face was fucked up and I'm pretty sure she broke a few ribs, but he was walking and talking. I wasn't gonna kill Indie's best friend in the spirit of finishing him off."

"If he comes back, you have as much to lose as me."

"Of course I do. I love both of them just as much as you do."

He's shaking his head no. "I'm not giving up Maggie. I'll share her." He glances at me. "I would love for you to be close to her the way I am. But I'm not giving her up. I don't care what the fucking DNA test says. She's mine."

I sigh and give up. "OK."

"It's not OK. We need to find Nathan and get ahead of this."

"Be my guest."

"I'm not doing it alone, McKay. It's your secret. Not mine. So what town were you running this little side operation out of? And who's left that we can talk to?"

"Savannah."

"The same place where you thought all your people were taken out at a party?"

"Correct."

"Why Savannah?"

I lean my elbow on the edge of the door where it meets the window and look out. There's not really anything to see. The moon is full, but this stretch of highway is just trees.

"Why Savannah, McKay?"

I blow out some air. "Because…"

He waits. But not very long. "Because *what*?"

"Nick."

"Nick? Nick? Nick as in—"

"Yup."

I glance over at him. He's not looking at me. He's squinting his eyes, focusing on the road ahead. But I've known this man nearly my entire life. I can see the wheels spinning in his head.

"Hold on. Give me this timeline again. When did you start up this little side job?"

"Right after Indie attacked you. During your recovery."

"You said that was James this afternoon. You said James sent Beck and Moore—"

"Right. But then I was gonna tell you this part and Maggie came up to the dock."

"And you couldn't pull me aside and fill me in on the rest?"

"I'm filling you in now."

"Because I'm practically dragging it out of you. So when did Nick come up?"

"A week later. When I first started paying the bills for that training camp."

"That's who really sent Beck and Moore."

"Yes."

He works his jaw. Practically growls out the words. "So you *knew*. You knew he was alive. Jesus fucking Christ. Anybody else alive that I need to know about?"

"Are you telling me you didn't know?"

"I suspected. Like most intelligent people. But no. It was never confirmed to me. In fact, I saw Vincent Fenici in the Maldives about eighteen months ago. I even asked him—"

"Wait." I rub my temple with my finger, a fucking headache starting up. "Who the fuck is *Vincent?*"

"James's twin."

"Wow." I shake my head, tab the little button on the door, and roll the window down. Because I need air. "Do I have a twin?"

"Not that I know of, why?"

"Because everyone but me seems to have one floating out there in the ether."

"Well, you're not Untouchable. So no. There is no other McKay out there. My point is, I specifically asked Vincent if he had heard anything about Nick being alive. And he said no. But you"—he glances over at me—"you *knew*. James told you. Why?"

"I just told you. I was running—"

"Under James's orders."

I hesitate.

"That's what you told me this afternoon, McKay."

"No. For fuck's sake, Adam. What's wrong with you? I just said Beck and Moore showed up and I assumed they were from James."

"Jesus. You're leaving things out on purpose. Aren't you?"

"I just told you it was Nick, didn't I?"

"Five hours late by my standards."

"Anyway. Beck and Moore ended up being there on the orders of Nick. So I did what I was told because you could barely walk back then and shit needed to get done."

"Do you know where Nick is now?"

"No. I haven't heard from him since Beck, Moore, and Nathan were presumed dead."

"That was nearly four years ago. This whole thing started *nine* years ago, McKay."

"I am aware."

"So you're telling me you've been in contact with Nick Tate for nine. Fucking. *Years?*"

"It's not like that, Adam. Jesus. After the massacre at the Savannah party, Nick just… disappeared."

209

"It *is* like that! Don't you understand? Nick Tate is the missing fucking link. You could've told me this earlier, McKay. I could've had people on this already. Now Nathan is calling you, and Carter is out there, planning who knows what, and we're all sitting here like a bunch of fucking ducks. Waiting for the shit show to come to us!"

He turns into the driveway of Old Home and I press the button on the gate clicker attached to the driver's side visor.

Two minutes later we're parked, he's getting out of the truck, Donovan is pulling up behind us, and of all the ways I thought we might be spending tonight, Adam walking away pissed at me wasn't one of them.

Maggie and Donovan follow Adam into the house, but Indie comes up to me and hooks her arm around mine. "What are you doing?"

I run my fingers through my hair. "Nothing."

She smiles up at me. "It's our night, McKay."

"Yeah. It is, I guess."

"What's that mean?"

"Nothing, Indie. Sorry. Adam and I just had a disagreement. That's all."

Indie sighs. "You two need to work this out. We're all waiting on you."

She starts to leave, but I grab her arm and pull her back. "Indie?"

She turns back to me. "What?"

"You don't think of me like a... like a father. Do you?"

She side-eyes me. "That's a loaded question."

"Not really."

"Yes, it is. Because…"

"Because what?" My heart thumps inside my chest. Because I know what she's gonna say.

"Well." She shrugs. "You were the closest thing I ever had to a parent."

I nod at her. Say nothing.

She stares into my eyes. "It's not weird though."

"Isn't it?"

She yanks her arm out of my grip. "Fuck you, McKay."

And then she walks off and leaves me standing in the driveway all alone.

CHAPTER THIRTEEN

Someone had to die.

That's how stories like this go.

But the only thing I really care about is that it wasn't me. And won't be. Not anytime soon. Maybe not ever.

Everyone dies. But it seems like everything in this world has a hack these days.

Why not death?

The summer heat in New Orleans is something I've come to terms with, but I would not say I like it. I didn't know any better growing up. I thought this was just what summer felt like. It was hot, and sticky, and uncomfortable for everyone.

Also true for most places. But summer here feels like an invisible force is trying to suffocate you from the inside out. That's another familiar feeling for me.

The light from the lantern wobbles, obscuring my view of the dirt below my feet. Then it disappears altogether.

"Dammit, Magnolia. I gave you *one* job. Can you keep the fucking light still?"

"Sorry." She peeks her head over the side of the hole I'm digging, smiling like being out at four in the morning while her father digs a hole in Holt Cemetery is no particular big deal.

I both hate and love that at the same time. Everything about her is complicated in that way. I love that she's so smart. A little genius. Raising her has been the greatest pleasure of my life even though how I've done it has been questionable.

And let's face it. I'm not winning any Father of the Year awards right now.

Especially in McKay's mind.

"I was swatting mosquitoes," she says, sighing. "There's blood on my calf. I took a hit. But I'll live."

I look up into Maggie's blue, blue eyes. They sparkle a sea-green color with the amber glow from the lantern light she's holding for me. She smiles at me with a grin that says, *I know I'm adorable.*

"Just keep the light steady. The sooner I get done, the sooner we go home."

"We're gonna miss breakfast. They're gonna know we were gone."

I love her accent. It's soft and barely there. But it *is* there. She didn't pick it up here. She's barely spent any time in Louisiana after I took her away. And we've only been back a few short months.

So she picked it up from me. And I like that because she didn't inherit anything else of mine.

I forgot I had an accent, to be honest. People do that. Sometimes one never even knows they have one until they are told. But that's like the chicken and the egg in a way. Which one of us has the accent? The one who notices or the one who doesn't?

214

This might not be a deep philosophical question, but it's worth some casual consideration while I dig up this grave.

"How much deeper can it be?" Maggie yawns. "I'm tired."

"I figure this is deep enough, to be honest." I pause my digging and lean on my shovel. Wipe the sweat from my brow. "But there's nothing here."

Maggie doesn't respond. Just rolls over on her back and sighs, making sure that the lantern is still shining down on my work area. "Why do we need this body again?"

"I don't need the body, Maggie. That's gross. I just need what's inside the coffin."

"Isn't that the same thing?"

I shrug even though she can't see me. "One comes with the other, I suppose. But no. It's not the same."

She rolls back over again. The light disappears, then it's back, and she's hanging her head down into the gravesite. "He was your twin brother?"

I nod.

"But he died at birth?"

"Near enough. I was told he lived a day or two."

"And your mama died too?"

"Correct."

"Well, Adam." She sighs again and pouts her lips at me. "That's all very sad."

I shoot her a dirty look for calling me Adam, but don't say nothin'. She knows I hate it. And telling her again, for the hundredth and first time, isn't gonna change her mind about using that name in situations that call for it.

And this, she must feel, is a situation that calls for it.

I did drag her out of bed at midnight, drive her two and a half hours down to New Orleans, and make her carry a pickax and a lantern over here to Holt Cemetery. And for the past hour and a half she's been tasked with holding the light steady as I dig up my twin brother's grave.

She is my partner in crime.

Has been since the very beginning.

It's all kinds of wrong. I really do understand that. But I'm really just trying to do what's best for her. And sure, some people might argue that having your six-year-old help you dig up a grave in the middle of the night is borderline child abuse, but if we find what we're looking for these secrets will keep her alive one day.

God. I'm getting really good at rationalizing.

"I'm sorry, peachface. Maybe we should just go home?"

"No. No. No." She gets up on her knees and lowers the lantern down into the hole. It's deep. Past my waist. "We're already here." She swings the lantern around, searching for signs of a coffin. Then she looks over her shoulder. "There's a headstone right there that says Aiden Boucher. It has to be close. Right?"

"You would think." But this gravesite has always bothered me. Why here? We have a family mausoleum not far from Old Home. But this is where poor Aiden got dumped. It never did make sense, but I stopped trying to figure my father out long before I helped him get killed.

"Do they bury babies six feet deep too?"

"It's got nothing to do with how big someone is, Mags. And it's not actually six feet. The depth of a grave varies by locality. But deeper is better because it keeps the animals away."

She wrinkles her nose. "That's gross, Adam. It's inside a coffin, anyway. Animals don't have thumbs. They can't unlatch a coffin or open a lid. Seems stupid to go so deep."

"Listen, a shallow grave comes with all kinds of consequences. So if, at some point in your life, you find yourself digging a grave and figure you can take a short cut and only go two feet"—I point at her—"you'd better think again, princess."

She chuckles. "I'm not gonna be digging no graves."

"We're digging a grave right now."

"*You.* Not *me.*" She wrestles with the front pocket on her bib overalls and then pulls out her phone. "It's nearly five, Adam. Hurry. You know how much I hate lying to McKay."

I sigh and take another stab at the dirt with my shovel. Throw the dirt over my shoulder so I can stab at it again. "What's the difference if we get home at seven or nine? It's the same fuckin' lie."

"I know. But this is gonna be a hard one."

I pause my digging to point at her. "A test of your skill."

"Dig. Or I'm gonna jump down there and do it myself and you can hold the stupid light."

I tsk my tongue at her. "You just told me you weren't gonna be digging no graves."

"Why are you so impossible?"

"I learned from the best."

217

She grins and the light from the lantern makes her look like a spook. "From me?"

She's hopeful. She's a good kid. A very, *very* good kid. So very, *very* smart. I had her intelligence tested last year and the woman took me aside afterward and told me she was gifted. A genius. IQ of a hundred and forty-nine.

No surprise there. She's not as smart as Donovan—his IQ is somewhere in the high one-sixties, I believe. But she is Company. And related to him.

Maybe. Maybe not. I hate that McKay brought up Nathan yesterday. He is not Maggie's father. I would rather it be Carter than Nathan.

But who her real father is isn't even the point.

Company kids are not born. We are bred.

Even McKay has an IQ of one thirty-two. And he's considered slightly above average for a Company kid. I'm just a bit higher in points. Mine was clocked at one forty back when my father had me tested. Respectable enough, for an Untouchable, but not standout special as far as my father was concerned.

That testing woman wanted to put Magnolia into a program for little geniuses. But that was in Germany and we were only visiting, so it was easy to say no.

But now we're settling in. And even though I know that Maggie will get a proper education homeschooling with me, McKay, and Donovan, sometimes I get this urge to slip her into a more typical life.

It's a dangerous urge. Because people will take notice of Maggie if she becomes part of regular society.

They will, at the very least, become curious. Possibly obsessed.

Little Company girls like her just have this… *draw* to them.

"Sure," I tell Maggie, finally answering her question. "I learned it from you."

"Now you're just lying to me. Who did you learn it from? Indie?"

"Did we or did we not just have this talk, hmm?"

She tsks her tongue. "Mama. Fine."

She does not think of Indie as her mother. But I'm doing my best to fix that. I really am.

I don't answer Maggie's last question. Just stab the shovel at the dirt. And when it hits something that is not dirt, and makes that sound everyone who has ever watched a treasure-hunt movie recognizes, I look at her and smile.

That smile is partly about being thankful that she won't be asking any more questions about Indie, but also because we finally found our prize.

"That's it," Maggie says. She jumps down into the hole with me, then reaches for the light and lowers it to where my shovel is still in the dirt.

It takes another ten minutes to remove enough dirt around the tiny marble coffin before we can see the edge of the heavy lid.

"Jump back up now," I say, pointing at the ground above her head. "I need some room."

"You just don't want me to see it."

"Neither here nor there. I can't lift the lid off if you're crowding me."

She sighs heavily, always frustrated when we're in the middle of some important job and she gets sent to the sidelines. But she doesn't argue. Just places her foot in my palm when I offer a leg up, and climbs out of the hole. But she hangs her head over the side and lowers the lantern as far as she can.

Not for my benefit, but hers.

She wants to see.

The lid is heavy marble. The coffin is more like a sarcophagus in that nature. But it is small and after I get the tips of my fingers into the groove, it comes off easily.

I set it aside and reach for the lantern, taking it from Maggie and lowering it over the open coffin.

"That's not a body."

"No," I say, crouching down and reaching for the stack of folders and yellow envelopes encased in plastic. "It's not."

"You knew, didn't you?"

I nod, but don't say anything. I didn't know that my twin brother, Aiden, wouldn't be in here. But I did know there was something more than him inside, if he was. This was the last place these things could possibly be.

"So that's what you were looking for?"

"I dunno. But it's something, anyway. Here." I hand the plastic packet to Maggie. "Hold on to it. I'm coming back up."

I slide the lid back on the coffin, then toss the shovel over the side and climb out of the hole. I sit down and dangle my legs into the grave. Maggie sits next to me with the lantern, eager to learn new secrets.

"Are we gonna look at them now?" She glances up at me with a stoic expression, all business.

I nod. "Yup. Right now."

She rubs her hands together. "OK." I can hear the satisfaction in her voice.

Did I turn her into an inquisitive kid who lives for secrets? Or is this just who she is?

I guess I'll never know.

Because she loves a good secret. Getting one, keeping one—doesn't even matter. She is my little vault.

But I have been training her. I started back when she was two. First, she needed to learn how to swim. That's kind of important when you live on a yacht. Then I taught her to catch fish. Later, she learned to rock-climb. I had a climbing wall built in the yacht gym. It wasn't high, but when you're three years old, high is relative.

Then I took her hiking, and camping, and taught her McKay skills. How to track things. How to build a fire. How to find her way in seven different forests in five different countries.

She learned to cartwheel and then front and back flips. And when I had to go to Europe for six months just before she turned five, I put her into dance and ice skating classes.

She's athletic and graceful. Strong, but still a little on the willowy side. Like her mother.

She hasn't learned to shoot yet. But it's coming up soon. McKay has an old .22 rifle left over from Indie's childhood days that will be perfect to start on this fall.

No archery. But I did try that out with her last year. She's just not physically able to draw the bow back yet.

And fine. My girl is never going to be an Olympic gymnast, or a professional ballerina, or world-class skater or swimmer. But knowing these things will keep her alive one day. They give her poise, and balance, and teach her determination. They will prepare her for the serious training that comes next.

Because I *will* train her.

Not because she's my weapon, the way Indie was. But because there is no way to change who and what she is.

Either she learns to fight back or someone will kill her.

There is always someone out there hunting these girls. Including me. That's why Wendy was so freaked out when she called me yesterday. There is a new one on the loose. One we didn't know about. And if there's one, there's more. And this little girl, who we will now be hunting, has a man like me back at home base. A man like me who taught her things to keep her alive. To slip away when the Company men come for her.

"Open it up."

"Be patient," I say. "This packet is old. We need to be careful. Hold the light a little closer."

She does that. And I peel the plastic cover open and remove the first yellow envelope.

I already suspect what's in this one. I can just tell by the weight of it.

But Maggie audibly gasps when I pull out four straps of hundred-dollar bills. "Wow. How much is that?"

I flip through them and decide. "Ten thousand each." I toss one of the strips into her lap. "You keep that one for now. Keep it close until we get home." Then I toss her another. "And you can give this one to the guard out front when we leave."

She makes a little huff of noise, but doesn't get excited or go crazy. Just stuffs the straps into the bib pocket of her overalls.

They are old bills, not the colorful ones that circulate these days. Which means they will need to be laundered. But that's to be expected. We deal in gold anyway.

Maggie has had her own stash of money since she turned five. There are always some low-value bills in that stash, just in case. But she's got a debit card from a Cayman Island bank with her name on it, a bag of American Gold Eagle coins, and a memorized phone number she can call to access her trust, if those options are not enough and I'm not around.

I won't always be around. It takes a lot of effort to live to old age in this business. Gerald Couture was probably the oldest Company man I've ever known. I'm trying to prepare her for that inevitability.

"What's in the next one?" Maggie is ready to move on. Money isn't exciting. Money is just money.

I pull out the next envelope and open it up. Inside is a small stack of passports held together with a rubber band, three birth certificates, a deed to a house I have never heard of, and an envelope with the name 'Nick Tate' scrawled across it in my father's handwriting.

Fucking Nick Tate. Why the hell is he suddenly popping up everywhere all of a sudden?

"Huh." Maggie is reaching for the envelope.

I snatch it away before she can grab it. "Not for you."

"But it says Nick on it. I want to know what's in there."

"None of your business, little girl."

She tsks her tongue in frustration. "Then show me something I can see."

I hand her the birth certificates. "Here. Read them to me."

She huffs, but this time it's satisfaction. She opens it up. Squints at the small typed letters. "OK. Number one is... Mallory Match-it." She looks up at me. "Hmm. Who's that?"

"It's pronounced Machette. Like machete. No clue." Which is not entirely true. I mean, I don't personally know Mallory Machette. But the Machettes are an old family in the Company. Scientists, mostly. "What's that birth year say?"

"Whoa. It says eighteen seventy-five."

"What's the next one say?"

"This one is for... Neek-klos Zzzzabo. I don't know how to say that." She hands me the paper and shines the light on it.

"Sab-oh," I say, sounding it out. "Nikos Szabó. The z is silent."

"Let me guess. You don't know him either."

"I know the surname. But they're all dead now." The birth year on this one was in nineteen twenty-six.

"OK, then. This one is... oh, it's an easy one." Then she laughs. "Here, you do it."

I take the stack and read the last one. "Ameci. Sidonia Ameci."

"What kind of names are these?"

"Old World ones."

"Whatever. They're weird. Who are the passports for? Not Americans, obviously. They are not blue."

I bop her on the head with one. "You're a smart girl. But American passports weren't always blue. Red

224

was the color of the first booklet cover and they were green for a while too." I open the first passport and find that it matches Mallory Machette. "Hmm."

"What?"

"Mallory's. But the year is off. I mean, obviously, even though this passport is green, it's still modern. Issued in nineteen forty-nine. And if Mallory was born in eighteen-seventy-five then—" I shuffle through the papers that were stuffed in the plastic and come up with a death certificate for Mallory. "Yup. She died in nineteen eighteen."

"Then they're fake identities."

"Jesus Christ, Maggie. You know way too much about this shit."

"It's your fault." She's right about that. "But I'm right. Aren't I?"

I open the other two passports and find they match the other two birth certificates, and then find two death certificates for Mallory and Sidonia, but no Nikos. Which might be odd. "Hmm. Three random fake identities and a bundle of money that isn't a whole lot, considering. I mean, what can you really do with forty thousand dollars? Not much."

Maggie shrugs and swings the lantern. She's not impressed with our booty. Paperwork is boring. And forty grand isn't enough to impress her, either. Hell, we're gonna give ten of it to the fucking cemetery guard to keep his trap shut when we leave.

I can't say I disagree, but paperwork often leads to answers to questions you didn't know you had. Except... "Why did my father hide them in this coffin?" I whisper. Mostly to myself.

"And where the hell is your brother?"

225

I don't say anything about her swear word. I let it slip every now and then when we're into something deep. And anyway, it's a good question.

"Maybe he's not dead?"

"He better be fuckin' dead," I say. "Because someone has to die. That's how these stories go."

It takes a good hour to fill the hole back in. And by the time we're done, we're filthy.

"No way is McKay not gonna say something when we pull into Old Home looking like a pair of midnight gravediggers."

I turn left on Burgundy and then ease the truck up to a tall, wrought-iron gate. "Let me worry about that."

"What's this place?"

"You've been here before."

"When?"

"Oh…" I think back a little. "You were probably four the last time we stopped by."

"Hmm. I think I'd remember that. Four was only two years ago. And this place is… nice." She leans forward in her seat and looks up at the tallness of the compact French Quarter mansion I grew up in. "Nothing like that cemetery. Why did your father bury your brother in that place, anyway? It's"—she wrinkles her nose—"not right."

She probably didn't notice that Holt Cemetery was wrecked when we entered it because it was the middle of the night. But there was no way to miss the fact that

226

the old resting place for local New Orleans indigents was in complete disarray when we left in the glow of a morning dawn.

"I guess we'd have to ask him to know for sure." That's the standard answer I made up back in my teens when I was still trying to piece together my life. The Boucher family mausoleum is located just west of Old Home, on a mostly untouched piece of wild land about halfway between the property and Pearl Springs.

"Hmm. Well. Neither here nor there, I suppose. He wasn't buried there." Maggie wipes a hand across her nose as I get out of the truck and open the wrought-iron gate. This mansion has been here for nearly two hundred years and even though driveways in this part of the French Quarter are nearly unheard of, we have one.

I get back in and ease the truck up the driveway, put it in park, and then turn the engine off. "OK. Let's go. We're gonna clean up here and then head home." I check the time on my phone. "It's only six-forty-five. We'll be fine if we play it right."

She looks down at herself, then at me. "We look like gravediggers."

"Not for long." I reach behind me and grab a garment bag. "By the time we leave here we'll look like we're heading home from church."

"Oh." Mags laughs, points at me. "That's good. You're so clever."

"I do my best."

We get out and walk around the truck to the front of the house. It's a stately white Greek Revival mansion that is three stories tall and has really over-the-top columns and a two-sided porch. Very traditional

227

French Quarter architecture with tall, skinny, floor-to-ceiling windows facing the street. You can't see the top floor from the street, because it's set back. And the bottom floor is more like a garden level. But the fucking place is imposing. Especially when you're six. I know. I lived here when I was six.

"Wow." Maggie is in awe even though Boucher Manor is less than one third the size of Boucher House back on the Old Pearl River. "This is so special."

"I guess." I never saw it that way. I have been in love with Old Home for as long as I can remember. This house couldn't hold a candle to it if it wanted to. It's too close to the street, too close to the houses on either side, and every time I walk through the front door that outside feeling of claustrophobia closes in on me and becomes something akin to suffocating.

It's not even like I have bad memories of this house. McKay and I had some fun times here. Schooling in the back room much the way Indie schooled in the back room of Old Home. And we ran these streets like hellions. We knew every alley. Every secret patch of grass hidden away from the prying eyes of tourists. We were a first-name basis with every local eatery bus boy. And we did have us some fun.

Hell, our old bedrooms are just the way we left them when we moved out fourteen years ago. And this city is filled with dark magic, which was alluring to little boys like us.

Little girls too. Because Maggie is transfixed as we walk up the porch steps and I punch in the code to unlock the door.

The lock releases with a beep and we enter a tall foyer. This part of the house is deceiving, because the foyer ceilings are seventeen feet tall. But it's a small foyer. And if you choose to go towards the back of the house, that open-air feeling disappears immediately.

It's not even like the ceilings are low. They aren't. They are nine feet, at least. But everything is narrow. You can practically *feel* the houses next door and the street out in front. Even when you're in the back yard, which is its own separate lot of prime New Orleans real estate, you can feel this city sucking the air out of the sky. Like it can't breathe. Like it needs fuel.

It's the complete opposite of how Old Home feels.

I nod my head to the stairs and that's the way we go.

There are four bedrooms and three bathrooms on the second floor, which makes this house sound big. But the rooms are tiny. The square footage is just a little over twenty-five hundred square feet, total. Old Home, by contrast, is nearly triple that.

Most of the space at Old Home is unused. We stick to the rooms we love most. But nothing about the property surrounding Old Home, or the house itself, is suffocating.

It feels like freedom when I'm out there.

Here? This place? It feels like a prison. All that wrought-iron out front—and trust me, there is *a lot* of it—they feel like bars keeping you in instead of a pretty, decorative gate keeping others out.

I stop at the first room, McKay's old bedroom, and then unzip the garment bag and pull out her white dress. "Go in there and take a two-minute shower. Two minutes. Ya hear?" She nods. But I am not holding out hope that she actually listens. It just feels necessary to make the demand. "In the bathroom there is a cupboard. Inside the cupboard are towels and little bottles of shampoo and tiny bars of soap. Use them to wash up. Dry your hair. Put on the dress. And then come downstairs."

I hear the back door open below us and Maggie looks up at me, panicked.

"Just the caretaker. No need to worry. I'll be downstairs talking to him by the time you're finished. Put your money in here." I take a little pink purse out of the garment bag and hand it to her. "Bring me the brush when you're done and I'll do your hair. Hear me?"

She looks down the stairs for a moment, then back at me. "I hear ya."

"Good." I hand her the dress and she disappears inside McKay's old bedroom.

I let out a long sigh as I continue down the hallway to the next room. My room.

It's exactly how I left it at age twenty-two, when McKay and I finally decided that the renovation at Old Home was well enough along to move up there for good.

No little-boy things in here. No trophies on display in the built-in shelves. No certificates of achievement tacked to the walls. No baseball bats or other sporting equipment propped up in corners. That was all put away long before we moved out.

But there are still a few remnants of my childhood about.

Framed pictures of McKay and me in Fiji. We went there once a year, every year, until my father died.

And then I guess we figured we'd had enough of Fiji. Because we never went back.

There's an old jacket hanging on the back of the desk chair. And a pad of paper on the desk with the note 'call the plumber' written on it in faded blue ink.

There are also four high-end cameras on the desk. I was into photography for a while back in my teens and my equipment was too dear to just shove it in a box in the attic.

But the duvet is new. Never seen it before, actually. And the rugs as well.

And when I open the closet, it's empty.

I knew that. But I had an urge to check. My men use this place often. Sometimes the new ones need a place to stay while they wait for their first-job payout and I'll send them here. Other times they just need a little safehouse to wait out some heat. They're not supposed to stay in this room. Or McKay's room, either. But I don't check up on them, so it's not like I would know if they decided to make themselves at home.

I don't like coming here. It reminds me of my father. And I'm not saying I hated the man, but I'm not saying that I regret getting him killed either. It was just convenient to come here and clean up after last night's job.

But the minute I strip off my filthy clothes and step into the too-narrow shower I just want to finish and leave. Leave it all behind me.

I felt that way when I took off with baby Magnolia four years ago too. I just needed some space. Not space from Old Home. I missed that house every moment of every day Maggie and I were on the run. But from McKay, and Donovan, and even Indie.

There are so many complicated strings tying us together I just needed some time to make sense of it.

I wash up quickly, truly taking a two-minute shower. And then I get out, wrap a towel around my waist, and sit on the edge of the bed. Listening for Andrik's movements downstairs.

He's quiet. Waiting me out.

So I listen for Maggie too. The house is old and even though the plumbing has been updated, it's got a sound all of its own. You can hear the pipes when they are in use like they are living things.

My thoughts drift back to Indie, even though that's not where I want them to be.

Every time I thought of her after Maggie and I took off, I burned inside. And then I would look at little Mags—her light blonde hair just like her mother's, and her blue eyes that were only slightly like her mother's—and I would get this urge to do something to Indie.

To get *even* with her.

Nothing about that feeling was good. I don't hate Indie. I don't even blame her. But every time I think back on that day and how Maggie was screaming in the truck on the way to the hospital… I lose my mind all over again.

Maggie was shrieking. And her mouth was bleeding. And my head was foggy and confused. And I didn't know what I was doing, really. I was on autopilot. Donovan said, "Take her to the hospital." So that's what I did.

It was just… a very bad day and I won't ever forget that fear I had. That Maggie would die. She could've too. Daphne berries are so toxic. We were just lucky that the Pearl Springs doctors knew their limitations and got us a Life Flight into New Orleans.

But if I was going to kill Indie, I'd have done it years ago. Because I knew. I knew she was sick. I knew she was never gonna be right in the head.

McKay loves her, though. She is the love of his life. And if I had hurt her—in any way—he and I would be over.

Not that we ever got anything started, but we're not done yet. It could still happen.

Core McKay's bedroom is one door away.

He has always been just one door away. Even back at Old Home we sleep separated by less than twenty feet.

So close. Just… never close enough.

Sitting here on the bed in the summer heat has both dried me off and made me sticky at the same time. I walk over to the switch for the AC unit and flick it on, then stand underneath and let it cool me off for a few moments.

The pipes tell me that Maggie is still in the shower. So there's no real rush to get dressed. But I need to go down and talk to Andrik before I leave.

So I put on my church clothes. I don't wear a suit. Not in the fucking summer. I wear a white linen long-sleeve button-down shirt that's loose enough to look elegant, but not oversized. I leave the shirt unbuttoned as I pull my tan trousers and then run my fingers through my short blond hair to tame it up a little.

I don't bother looking in the mirror, just head down the hallway, rapping on McKay's door to let Maggie know she needs to hurry up as I pass, and then descend the stairs and find Andrik sitting at the marble counter in the kitchen. He's dressed in some old ripped jeans with no shirt.

If he were working for me personally, I'd have to say something about that. But fuck it. If I didn't have to dress like this right now, I sure as hell wouldn't have a shirt on either.

Andrik Kalchik stands up and bows his head a little. Just enough. Never too much. I kinda like that about Andrik. "You need something today, boss?" His hair is so blond it appears white when it's not buzzed so close to his head. And his eyes are so blue, they remind me of high-quality sterling silver—he *looks* Slavic. Hell, his name is the dead giveaway. But he has been practicing his American English for almost a decade now and he's always proud when people ask him if he's American. Especially after he tells them his name, which is so obviously *not* American.

He's not American. I picked Andrik up in Romania about twelve years ago. He was just a gangly fifteen-year-old boy back then. But he's a man now. Broad shoulders. A tattoo across his upper chest that says LOYAL in black Old English letters. Like he's a gangbanger.

But he's not a gangbanger, either.

He's just the caretaker of this old French Quarter mansion. He keeps the new boys in line while they stay here and he plays backup for the ones who have heat and need a friend. He's good with a gun and even better with a knife. You do not fuck with a man who looks like Andrik. Even when he's smiling at you, he looks more like a high-ranking alpha wolf than a good-natured nobody.

No. Andrik wasn't born into this world to be some nobody. So I was surprised when he seemed to be content with this job here. In fact, I was a little disappointed in that revelation.

But he doesn't give me any trouble at all. And he's saved more than a dozen men when I had to call him in to help them clean things up.

So. Whatever. Maybe he likes the semi-quiet life. He could make a lot more money if he were out in the field running his own team. But I like to let the boys dictate their own path if I can. And Andrik seems to have settled here.

"I'm stopping by to clean up," I say. "Maggie's upstairs." His eyes drift up towards the ceiling, then back down to me. "We'll be out of your hair in a few minutes."

He nods, rubs his hand unconsciously across the nearly nonexistent buzz of hair on his head, like he took that comment literally. "Well, I'm glad you're here. Because I've been meaning to talk to you."

"Oh?"

He opens his mouth to continue, but his eyes drift over my shoulder and I turn to see Maggie walking towards us wearing her white church dress and holding a brush in her hand.

"Hair time. As requested." She thrusts the brush at me, then hoists herself up into the chair at the marble counter where Andrik was just sitting and twirls in the seat so I can have easy access to her hair.

"We can talk later," Andrik says.

I start brushing Maggie's hair. It's still a little wet. "I told you to dry it, Magnolia."

"I did dry it."

"It's still wet. And that means it will be wet when you take it out of the braid later."

"No one's gonna notice."

"Don't sell him short," I say, cautioning her not to underestimate McKay. "He will notice. McKay understands how hair-braiding works."

Andrik laughs unexpectedly. I would not call him friendly with McKay. But everyone in my organization knows of him.

I point the brush at Andrik and make the same caution. "You either. Keep talking, Andrik. She's fine."

He looks at Maggie, then shrugs. "OK. Well…" He sighs. "Nick Tate."

My eyebrows go up.

Andrik nods his head at Maggie. "You want me to continue?"

Maggie snorts. "Hell, yes. Keep talking, Andrik."

"It's fine." I sigh. "Spit it out."

"We've been hearing rumors for a couple weeks now."

"What kind of rumors?"

"That he's not dead."

"Anything else?"

"Isn't that enough?"

"Is there anything *else*, Andrik?"

"No. Not specifically. Just that he's been around. And…" He rubs his head again. "How can he be around if he's fuckin' dead?" Andrik glances at Maggie. "Pardon my French, little lady."

Maggie doesn't say anything back. Not because she doesn't want to. But I snag her hair with the brush in that same moment and she turns to chastise me with an angry look.

I ignore her and start a French braid high on the top of her head. "Let me deal with those rumors. If anyone else starts talking about Nicholas Tate you will politely remind them that I don't pay them to speculate."

Andrik nods. "You got it, boss. Anything else I can help you with today?"

"Yeah. Find me a rubber band for this hair."

"No," Maggie says, pointing her finger at Andrik. "Not a rubber band. They snag. Please find Adam a proper hair tie."

Andrik's face scrunches up and I imagine he's wondering what the fuck a proper hair tie is. Because he has no clue about braids. His past experience hasn't included the specifics of caring for little girl assassins.

I leave the braid untethered. "Never mind, Andrik. We've probably got one in the truck somewhere. I'll catch up with you in a day or two. I have some things I want to talk over. But not today." Then I slap Maggie on the leg. "Let's go."

I'm just closing Maggie's door and walking around to the driver's side of the truck when my phone buzzes. Wendy. "Talk to me."

She blows out a long sigh on the other end of the phone. "Nathan called."

My heart skips. And Maggie is watching me from inside the truck because I have stopped in front of it to take this call. "What did he want?"

"He wants to meet you and McKay in Savannah tomorrow morning."

"Why?"

"That he did not say. I've got details. You gonna go?"

"Probably. I'll have to talk to McKay first."

"I would not stand him up. If he's calling—"

"Hey, why aren't you surprised that he's alive?"

"What do you mean?"

"He was dead."

"He was never dead."

"Wendy—"

"Adam." She practically snarls my name. "I don't owe you explanations, OK? When I agreed to work for you I made it very clear that I had a private life and you were not invited into it."

"And Nathan is part of your private life?"

"Do you want to hear the rest?"

"Fine. Talk."

"OK, so several months ago I got word of a woman who was killed out in Wyoming—"

"What's this have to do with Nathan?" Maggie is making to get out of the truck to listen to my convo, so I put up a hand and shoot her mean eyes. She pouts and crosses her arms as she flings herself back into the seat.

"Nothing. This is something else."

"Do you have anything else on Nathan?"

"No. I'm trying to tell you about a woman who was killed up in Wyoming."

"Why do I care about this woman?"

"Because I'm telling you to care, that's why."

I say nothing for a few seconds and Wendy, ever the patient little killer, waits me out. "Fine. Tell me about this fucking woman."

"She wasn't Company, but her death got on our radar anyway."

"So why are you just telling me this now?"

"Jesus Christ. Never mind. I'll text you the details about Nathan."

She hangs up on me and I just stare at the phone for a moment. Then the horn honks and makes me jump. And when I look through the windshield I see Maggie smiling at me.

The ride home is quiet. Maggie sleeps almost the whole way, only waking up when we get to the little town of Snake River where our church is. We don't stop at church. We get donuts. This is what we usually do on Sundays. And we have a little time to kill, actually, since McKay won't be expecting us home until nearly eleven. So we go inside and I have a coffee and bear claw and Maggie gets her usual too—one of those pink frosted donuts that make my teeth hurt just looking at them and an apple juice.

She's still a little kid in some ways. Not many. But this is one of them.

Even though we've only been back in Louisiana for a few months we're locals here. The donut people remember me from days gone by when this was Indie sitting next to me instead of Maggie.

239

I see all the questions in their eyes. They want to ask who this girl is. This girl who's just like the other one I used to bring in here.

I don't think they ever assumed Indie was my daughter. We're too close in age. But they probably thought she was my sister.

At any rate, all this careful planning goes completely unnoticed when we arrive back at Old Home. We catch a glimpse of McKay working on something in the back of the shed where he keeps his tools now, suited up in one of those welder suits that make me sweat just thinking about the heat coming from the torch in his hand. And Indie isn't around.

Donovan left last night to… I dunno. Whatever the fuck he does when he leaves. So he was never part of the return-home plan.

But neither McKay nor Indie bother to greet us as we cautiously get out of the truck and look around, ready to tell all the lies.

We shrug and ease back into our normal routine. "Go change," I tell her. "And put the donuts in the kitchen. I'll go see what McKay's doing."

She skips off without comment. Then I remember the money in her purse, but she's already too far away to call out instructions on that regard. So I let it go and turn towards the shed.

I find McKay in the back of the huge outbuilding we call the shed, where we saw him when we pulled up, totally engrossed in his project. Which is some kind of metal sculpture.

It takes him almost a whole minute to notice me, which is disappointing in a couple of ways. But I don't want to think about that shit right now.

Finally, he sees me and he dials the torch down and lifts the faceplate of his welding helmet up to smile. "You're back."

"Yup." I keep it simple, unsure if he knew we left in the middle of the night or not. It was his night to watch Indie, so she slept in his bed last night. And I know he likes those nights. Not that I suspect they are getting up to any funny business. It was McKay's idea to keep things platonic with Indie until we sort out whatever the fuck it is we're doing with her.

"How was church?" He asks this same question every time Maggie and I come home. Hell, he asked this same question every time Indie and I came home too.

I let that sink in for a moment. The entirety of it. The length of time that we've been doing this.

Has there ever been a time when we weren't in charge of the care and feeding of a little girl?

CHAPTER FOURTEEN

I put my welding helmet aside and take off my gloves. "I'm glad you're here."

"Why's that?" Adam leans against a long wooden workbench, folding his arms across his chest. He seems to be in a good mood.

"Because I wanted to apologize. About the conversation we had in the truck last night."

Adam just shrugs. "She's mine, McKay."

"I know," I say simply. "I get it."

"Look, I'm sorry too."

"What are you sorry about?"

"Comparing Indie to Maggie. She's not your daughter. It's not even close to the same thing."

I want to agree with him, but I can't. Not really. Because this is the reason I never wanted this kind of relationship with Indie.

Well, that's a lie right there. I have wanted it. "She's just…" But I throw up my hands. "I dunno. I do love her like that. I'm not gonna lie. But it does feel wrong. And you saying it so plainly…" I sigh.

Adam uncrosses his arms and walks over to me. We stand, eye to eye, just a few inches apart. "It's all in your head, McKay." He taps me on the head while he says this. "It's a construct."

"Yeah. I get it. There is no blood relation between us. At least I don't think so."

Adam chuckles.

"It's not funny. Maybe there is? We could be brothers. We'd never know, Adam. They hide that shit from us."

"I think Donovan would know. And he would tell us that. Besides, I'm sure my father knew. We're not related. We look alike, but you are the spitting image of your brothers and father."

"Were," I correct him.

"Yeah." His guard drops down a few notches. Then he takes a deep breath. "Did you ever regret leaving home, McKay? Is that why you were never interested in me?"

I think about this, but don't say anything.

Adam's eyes search mine. "I mean, I would understand if this was the case. If your father had come to my house and paid my father to take me away, I'd probably resent you too."

"I don't resent you, Adam. It's not that."

His eyebrows go up. "But it is *something*?"

"I'm just… into girls. Ya know?"

"Right. Indie."

"Yeah. Among others."

"You have others right now?"

"No."

He nods his head a little. "You want others? Besides Indie?"

"Listen," I say. "I love you. We can do this. But I don't know if this…" I pan my hands wide. "If this is all there is, ya know? I can't say that for certain."

"So you see yourself walking away at some point?"

I laugh at this. "Adam, if I could walk away from you, I'd have done it over a decade ago. I'm not going anywhere."

"Then what are you saying? Yesterday was a mistake?"

"We kissed. So what? It's not a big deal."

He frowns. Breathes. Takes his time. "It's a big deal to me, Core. And I'm gonna say something right now and you can do whatever you want with it. OK?"

I'm stuck on the way he used my real name. It echoes in my head. I can count on one hand the number of times he's called me Core without saying McKay at the end.

"OK?" he asks again.

"I'm listening."

"I'm sorry I left. I knew it was a mistake on day one. But I was afraid."

"Of Indie?"

He nods and presses his lips together in a tight line. "She has never attacked you. It's not as easy to get over as you think. So I just… poured myself into my work. And while I was doing that I had to admit that somewhere along the way, I turned into my fucking father. I bought a girl. And I swore I'd never do that. I swore I'd break this fucking cycle. And maybe I could talk myself into believing that before I left with Maggie. But now I have two girls, Core. And a packet filled with secrets I'm not sure I really want to know about. Maggie and I didn't go to church. I woke her up in the middle of the night so she could help me dig up the grave of my dead brother."

"What?" My heart is beating so fast as I process this. "I thought we were talking about kissing?"

He laughs, smiles. His eyes brighten. "Trust me, I'd much rather be talking about kissing."

"What the hell—OK." I grab my hair and shake my head. "What the fuck?"

"This is my point." He takes a deep breath. "I'm losing, McKay. I always find a way to justify the means to the end. And it's not gonna stop. Not unless I do something new. Not unless I break free of this cycle I'm part of. And you..." He sighs. "You have always been my something new. You're my way out. I can't explain that, but I know it. I have known it since the first moment I saw you at your family compound up in Alaska. I wanted you. I fucking love you. You, Core." He shakes his head. "You are all there is for me. And I know that's not a good enough reason for you to stick it out and see where this goes, and what I'm doing to you right now is borderline emotional blackmail. I have no right to ask you to help me, but I'm gonna ask you to do it anyway."

I open my mouth to reply, but he puts up a hand.

"Hold on. I'm not quite done yet. I was wrong to take Maggie. I was wrong not to come home. I was wrong to leave you all alone. Especially since I *wasn't* alone. It was selfish, and childish, and it was all done in fear. Taking Maggie was easy, Core." He swallows. Hard. "That's the real Adam, right there. The real Adam *takes* things. The real Adam takes little kids to use for his own purposes. Just like his father." He

246

pauses, his eyes locked with mine. "And I don't want to be that Adam anymore. I don't—"

I reach up and hold his face in my hands, startling him into silence. I can practically feel his heart beating inside his chest as I stare into his blue eyes.

And then I push him backwards until he bumps up against my workbench and can't get away from me. "Listen to me. And I mean *really* listen to me. You are not your father."

"I am, McKay. I'm doing it, ya know? I'm doing it just like they planned. And all this time I thought I was breaking free. But look at me—*really* look at me—and look around you, McKay. You have been trapped in this fucking life since you were nine. I've had a hold of Donovan since he was fifteen."

"Please. Donovan does whatever he wants. You didn't force him to stay here."

"You don't think so? Yeah, he walks away. But he always comes back, doesn't he? Why do you think he comes back?"

"Because of Indie."

"Huh. The same reason you stay too. How convenient."

"It's not just Indie," I say. "It's all of us. We built something here—"

"We built the Company here. We *are* the next generation of the Company. We broke it. And then we all built it back up. Even you. None of us got out. We're all still here. Keeping it going. And did you ever wonder if this is just how it was supposed to be? I mean, maybe in thirty years our grandkids take us out. They rebel too, thinking they can change things. But they won't. And we didn't. We just reinvented it, McKay. That's all."

"Are you done now?"

He nods.

"Good." I lean forward and erase the few inches that separate us. And I kiss him.

It's a slow kiss this time, softer than the one we shared yesterday. His mouth opens and my tongue slips inside. His hand comes up behind my neck to keep me from pulling away.

But I'm not pulling away.

I reach down, grab his shirt, and rip it open.

He pulls back and laughs when the buttons go flying. "What the fuck—" But my hand is on his chest and he stops abruptly.

"I'm not going anywhere," I say, letting my hand slide down over his hard abs. He looks down at it like he can't believe this is happening. And I yank his belt open, pop the button on his pants, and slip it inside. His cock is growing when I grab it. It fills up my palm.

His eyes come up to meet mine, lots of questions in those eyes. "I thought you liked girls."

"I do. But I like you too."

"Are you sure, McKay? Because—"

"If I wasn't, I wouldn't be doing it, Adam." I pull his cock out and start slowly jerking him off, my hand sliding up and down his shaft.

"Fuck," he says, leaning against the workbench. Placing both hands flat on the surface like he needs to hold himself up.

I manage a crooked smile. "Don't think too hard."

"I think that was supposed to be my line."

"Yeah, well, if I waited for you, it might take twenty-five more years before we got this far."

His smile falls a little. "I don't want to pressure you—"

"Shut up, Adam."

"Right."

I take a step forward until my chest is right up against his, my hand still jerking on his dick. He reaches for me, but I shake my head and stare into his eyes. "Don't. This is all you right now. Just enjoy it."

His eyelids get heavy and start to close. But then he opens them again.

"Close them. I don't mind."

I can tell he's confused. Or conflicted, maybe.

"Don't worry. It's not gonna change nothing."

"That's what I'm afraid of. That I'll get this one little taste and then you'll change your mind."

"You wanna stop now? And never know?"

He shakes his head. "No."

I lean in and kiss him again—"Good"—and whisper past his lips. "Then just close your eyes and let me handle things for once." I keep kissing him, grinding my hips against his as I move my hand up and down his cock. He moans into my mouth. "This is just a little taste right now."

Adam chuckles. "Jesus fucking Christ, McKay. Are you trying to fucking kill me today? Or just make me question reality?"

"I have to admit"—I pull out of this kiss and squeeze his cock a little harder, making him growl out a moan—"I'm a little surprised you're not reveling in this right now."

"I just can't fucking believe it."

249

I let go of his cock and force my hand deeper into his pants so I can grab his balls. "That's fear talking again. Just let it go."

He stares at me with half-mast eyes, looking a little bit helpless, and then his hand reaches for the zipper of my coveralls. I think he's waiting for me to stop him. And I consider it. Not because I don't want him to touch me, but because this isn't about me right now.

But I fear he will mistake that for rejection. I don't stop him. Just fondle his balls and then take my hand back up to grip his shaft.

I don't have on a shirt underneath the coveralls. So he finds my bare chest immediately, slipping his hand down the inside of my coveralls, under the waistband of my shorts. "Commando?" he says, grinning as he finds my dick. I'm already hard. I was hard all morning thinking about him. Planning how I might take this to the next level. I figured it would be make-up sex. Kinda hard and heated. Since we fought last night.

But slow is better.

"Now you know my last secret," I say, pushing myself against him. "But I gotta say. You're fucking turning me on right now." I pause, breathing heavy as I enjoy his skill with my cock. Like he knows just what to do. "And you think this is gonna be some epic marathon—"

He laughs. Loud.

"Fuck you, asshole."

He kisses me. "Go ahead, McKay," he whispers past my lips. "You can come all over my hand. Any time you're ready. Because I'm about to fucking spill mine into yours right fucking—" His cock jerks beneath my palm. And then I feel the warm wetness against my knuckles as they slide up and down his lower stomach.

He grips me hard. And then the tip of his thumb rubs across the head of my dick and I lean into him, out foreheads bumping as he jerks me faster. Harder. And then I can't hold it in any longer. I groan and grit my teeth as I explode into the palm of his hand.

We stay like that for a few moments, holding each other's cocks, breathing heavy, sweat running down my back. And even though I fully intended for this to happen today, I didn't have any idea it would feel like this.

This good.

This perfect.

"Fuck," he says, kissing me hard. "I want to do it again. Right now."

But I hear Indie's voice outside. And then Maggie.

And we pull apart. I grab a rag off the bench, throw it to him, then use another to clean myself up.

"Rain check?" I say, smiling at him.

"Yeah." He throws the rag into the bin I use for ones that need laundering and then tucks his dick away, watching me as I do the same. "That's the reason I came in here."

"Really?"

"Shut up. You wanna take a trip to Savannah with me?" He looks over his shoulder, making sure no one is coming into the workshop. "Because I got a message from Wendy."

"Wendy? Why does that name sound familiar?"

"Little assassin girl? Indie's friend. Sorta. Worked with Chek?"

"Oh, yeah. She works for you?"

"Yeah, ever since Chek died. I kinda took her in."

"Hmm. You do realize you've got yourself three girls now?"

"Does she count?"

"Do you think she counts?"

"Point. Anyway. Nathan called her."

"No. Fucking. Shit. Way to bury the lede."

"Is that a complaint?"

"Nah." I chuckle. "So what'd he have to say? Are we gonna have to kill this boy?"

Adam looks over his shoulder again. "I don't know yet. He wants to meet me in Savannah tomorrow morning. So we're going. We'll listen to him, but if that fucker threatens me, or Indie, or thinks he's gonna come here and mess up our good thing, then—"

"Yeah. I get it."

"I need to make some travel arrangements. We'll take the jet."

"There you are! I've been looking for you two." We both turn to see Indie, who has a weird look on her face. "What's going on here?" She points her finger back and forth between us.

"Just making plans for a quick trip." Adam turns to me. "I've got a few other things to take care of. But we're leaving this afternoon. We'll stay the night there."

"Gotcha."

Adam has his back to Indie when he says this and his gaze lingers on mine for an extra second, giving me enough time to replay what just happened over in my head real quick. Then he turns and walks over to Indie, stopping to kiss her on the lips.

She pulls away a little. But then she kisses him back, laughing. "What's going on?"

Adam smacks her ass, then walks off. "Ask McKay. He'll tell you."

CHAPTER FIFTEEN

The story McKay tells in his workshop wasn't what I was expecting.

"You two," I say, "just—"

"Yup."

"Hmm. How you feel about that?"

McKay nods his head and smiles. Maybe even blushes.

"Are you serious?"

"Why?"

"Because I—" I have to pause, catch my breath a little. "I have hoped for this. But"—I blow out a long breath of air—"I never thought it would happen. So what about me? And Donovan? Is this—"

"I think so. If that's what everyone wants. Is that what you want, Indie?"

His voice is low. And I can hear the doubts in it. I nod at him. "That's what I want. I've wanted it for so long, I almost gave up hope. But what is this trip? Why do you have to go now? I want us to be together tonight."

255

"It's just… business. We have to take care of something."

I don't know why, but I get the feeling he's lying. "Just business?"

McKay shrugs. "I mean, we're gonna be in a hotel room tonight, so—"

I slap him on the arm, laughing. "I'm not talking about your sex plans, McKay!"

"Oh. No. It's just business then."

I raise one eyebrow at him. "Everything's fine?"

"Everything's perfect. But I gotta put this shit away. I'll be inside in a little bit."

"You just want to daydream, don't you?"

"Maybe."

I cover my mouth to hide my grin. Then I reach for his shoulders, lean up on my tiptoes, and kiss his mouth. "Thank you," I say, whispering it past his lips.

"It's my pleasure." He grins at me. "So why'd you come out here?"

I did have a reason. I saw Adam and Maggie come home from church. I was standing up in Adam's room, looking out the window. And I saw him stash something in the truck. He and Maggie had a small conversation before getting out. It looked… suspicious. But maybe I was imagining things? So I don't want to say anything now to spoil McKay's good mood. "Just saw Adam come in here. Figured I'd join the party."

"I don't think we're quite to the 'join the party' stage yet."

"Jesus. Are you fucking horny or what? I didn't mean sex, McKay."

"Oh." He looks a little embarrassed.

"Never mind. I'll see you when you come inside. OK?"

"I'll be in soon."

I kiss him one more time. "I'm really happy you two worked it out. I knew we'd get here eventually."

"Yeah. I guess I did too."

Then I turn and walk out.

I stop at the truck, then look at the house. Don't see anyone watching, so I snoop. Looking for the thing I thought I saw Adam stash.

Nothing though.

So I go inside and walk straight to his office. And sure enough, he's in there. So whatever it was he came home with today, he put it in here.

"What are you doing?"

Adam is crouched down in front of the bottom drawer of an antique filing cabinet. He pushes the drawer in, then stands up before looking at me. "Nothing."

"Hmm. Nothing, huh? That's not what McKay told me."

Adam raises one eyebrow. "He told you?"

"He did. And I'm so happy!" I clap my hands.

"Why are you happy?"

I whirl around to find Maggie right behind me. I blush. Even though I wasn't involved in the kinky fuckery that just happened in McKay's workshop. "Nothing."

Maggie makes a pouty face. "Is this a secret? I hate secrets."

"It's not a secret, Mags."

I look at Adam, just as curious about what he'll say as Maggie is.

257

"McKay and I—"

"Adam!"

"What?" He looks at me. "It's no big deal." He directs his attention back to Maggie. "McKay and I are going on a short trip." I breathe a sigh of relief. Adam scowls at me, shooting me a look that says, *I'm not fucking crazy.* "Just one night. We'll be back tomorrow. So you're gonna stay with Donovan and Indie." He looks at me. "You guys can handle that, right?"

"Handle what?" Donovan has joined the party.

"They're going on a trip," Maggie says.

"Where to?"

"It's not important," Adam says.

Donovan looks uncomfortable. "Is this a good idea? I mean—"

"You'll be fine, Donovan," Adam says. "Indie will protect you."

I laugh. Hook my arm into Donovan's. "It's good actually. We can spend more time together."

"Can we get pizza again?" Maggie claps.

"No," McKay says, coming up behind us. "I was gonna make spaghetti and meatballs tonight. But Donovan knows how to make that, don't you Donovan?"

"I do." Donovan looks proud of himself.

Then we all look at each other and get quiet.

But it's a nice quiet.

It's a very nice quiet.

Everything is coming together. Just the way I wanted.

It feels natural.

And inevitable.

The afternoon passes quickly. Adam spends most of it in his office while Maggie hangs out with McKay as he packs a bag. Donovan disappears to make phone calls. And I sit on Maggie's bed and watch her through the open door. McKay's bedroom isn't right across from mine—well, it's not my bedroom, is it? It's Maggie's. Anyway, it's a little bit catty-corner. So I can't see everything. Just a little sliver.

Maggie is on McKay's bed brushing the hair of a doll that used to be mine.

I guess I never thought about it before, but everything she has now used to belong to me.

She got a few new things for her birthday, and once Christmas gets here, she'll get a few more. But she and Adam showed back up at Old Home with nothing. I don't even know where they were.

Adam has explained. Mentioned a few countries. The yacht. The ocean. The islands. But no real details.

I'm not sure how I feel about that.

In fact, I'm not sure how I feel about any of it. Not her. Not Adam, either. Separately, I love them both to pieces. But together I feel something else trying to creep in.

I know it's jealousy. And little bit of hate, maybe. A touch of rage every now and then.

Because she is my daughter, but she rarely feels like my daughter anymore.

259

I try to cling to the memories of when she was small. Back when she was all mine. When she was a new baby she needed me so much. Not even McKay could take my place because I nursed her. So for about six months it was truly just her and I.

But then I didn't want to do it anymore. And even though both McKay and Adam wanted me to keep going, Donovan was on my side and he's a doctor, so I won. He said my mental health was more important than nursing.

I don't recall being crazy back then, but clearly I was.

I should be writing this in my journal, but I'm tired of writing in that journal. Sometimes I feel like all the journaling I do is counterproductive. Like, should a person dwell so much on her faults? No one else journals. Maggie doesn't have to journal.

Maybe Dear Indie needs to get a life? She's been living vicariously through me for a long time now.

I linger on the bed, even after McKay finishes packing and goes downstairs with Maggie. Then Adam comes upstairs and packs too. I can't see his room from any vantage point in mine. So I just sit on my old bed and stare out my window.

How many times have I looked out that window when I was growing up?

Even if the cottage was still there, I wouldn't be able to see it from the bed. All I see is the tip-tops of trees and some sky. But even if the cottage was still there, I would not want to look at it.

I miss him.

My boy next door.

I feel the tears fall down my cheeks even before I realize I'm crying.

"Indie?"

I wipe the tears and turn my head to find Adam standing in my doorway.

"Are you OK?"

"Yeah." I nod my head to emphasize this. "I'm fine. Really. I'm just thinking about…" I don't need to say who so I stop.

Adam walks over to my bed—*this is not your bed, Indie*—and sits down. I turn on my stomach and look up at him. "I miss my room, too. I miss my life. And sometimes I think… I don't like to admit this, but sometimes I think… it would've been better if I had never gotten pregnant."

He opens his mouth to say something, then thinks better of it.

"I love her. I do. And I would do anything for her."

He swipes a stray piece of hair out of my eyes. "I know you would."

"But you were right to take her from me."

"Indie—"

"No, listen. I was crazy. I understand that now."

"And that understanding is the exact reason why you need to be in her life. You are her mother."

I shrug. "And you're her father. Now, anyway. I mean, who knows who her father is?" I hold my breath for a moment, letting the reality of that sink in. "If I was one of those teen moms who slept with a whole bunch of boys, and that's why I didn't know who the father was, well." I sigh. "I think I'd be OK with that. It would be better than the truth."

261

He sighs too. Like he has something to say about this. But again he holds his tongue.

"I know what you're thinking."

"What am I thinking?"

"You're thinking, 'Please, God. Please don't let her lose her mind again.'" We stare at each other, "You don't have to worry. I know I'm being silly right now. But I feel a lot better. I'm not angry with you. I'm really not angry about anything. But here's the thing, Adam. Whenever I let the anger go, then the sadness creeps in. And while I do hate being angry, I hate being sad even more. Every time I get mad, it's only because I'm sad."

"I think that's pretty normal, Indie."

"I think so too. But they are both bad for me. I want to be happy. How do I get to happy?"

"Is it so bad right now?"

"No. It's good. I think it's gonna get better. But it's hard to be here. It's hard to look out that window and see nothing across the lake. It's hard to wake up in this house and know he's not here. And I did that. I have no one else to blame but myself."

Adam lets out a long breath. "Indie—"

"No. You don't need to say anything. I'm fine. I really am. Donovan and I are pretty close now. He's my new best friend, I think."

"Good." Adam forces a smile.

"But I'm…" I suddenly can't talk. And my lips are all bunched up. And my eyes are tearing up, and there's a lump in my throat, and—

He leans down and kisses me. Right on the cheek. Right where the tears are. And when he pulls back his lips are wet with them. "Listen to me." He pets my hair, plays with it. "You're my number one, you know that? My number one. My very first."

"Your very first crazy girl?"

He smiles and so do I. Then he nods. "My very first crazy girl. My last crazy girl, too. There is no other girl on this stupid planet like you. And you"—he takes my cheeks in his hands and leans his face down into mine—"you are loved, Indie. You are loved so hard, and so much. You *own* me. That's how much I love you. And Maggie, she's not mine. She's yours. I'll be here. Always be here. For both of you. But listen to me, she is *yours*."

I wipe my tears and sniff, look up at him, and whisper, "Can I ask you for one last crazy favor, Adam? Before I go all sane and shit?"

He grins. "Anything you need."

"Can we just pretend that Nathan is her real father? Like the birth certificate says? And forget about that other guy?"

He nods at me. But doesn't say anything at first. Then he takes a deep breath and stands up. "We can do that. I've gotta get going. But you call me if you need anything. You hear?"

"I hear."

"And I'll be back tomorrow. And when we get back, Indie?" He pauses. "I promise you, I'll bring you home a whole bunch of happy."

I smile and chuckle a little. "I will hold you to that."

He leans down, kisses my cheek one more time, and then grabs his bag in the hallway and disappears.

The next thing I know I'm waking up to the smell of dinner and Donovan in my room—*this is not your room, Indie*—banging on the window.

"What are you doing?"

"Oh, good. You're awake. I'm checking the fucking locks on all the windows."

"Why?"

"*Why?*" He imitates my Southern drawl. "Because I don't even know how to fucking shoot. I can't do fancy kicks, or throw knives. I'm really uncomfortable being here alone with you two. In charge of everything and shit."

I laugh. I can't help it.

"It's not funny. Anything could happen."

"You're scared?" I sit up and swing my legs over the side of the bed.

He stares at me. Points his finger at me. "Don't laugh at me."

"I'm not."

"I was in school this whole time. I didn't grow up like you guys. I feel very ill-equipped here."

"Just put the alarm on."

"I already did that. And reprogrammed a new master code. So if anyone tries to leave"—he points at me—"I'll know. You can get out with your regular code, but unless you have the master, it will beep. All over the house."

"Number one, I know this. I know how it works. The whole fucking system was put in so I can't escape.

Number two, I'm not going anywhere. Where the hell am I gonna go?"

"I'm not afraid you're gonna leave, Indie."

"Oh." I pause. "Ohhhhhh. Carter."

"This would be a good opportunity, wouldn't it? I'm home alone with both of you. Adam and McKay are far away."

"Jesus, Donovan. Calm down."

"I can't." He paces the room, grabbing at his hair. "I can't calm down. I'm worried, Indie. And I don't understand why they left. Why?" He stops in the middle of the room. "Why the fuck would they leave me in charge?"

"Dude. You're freaking out right now. We're gonna be fine. If that asshole shows up, I'll fucking kill him. I would not even blink."

"So you're protecting me now?"

I chuckle. "Tell me, please, that this is not all about some alpha-male complex."

"If it were just me and you?" He points to his chest. "I would be OK with it. But I'm in charge of keeping *Maggie* safe. I'm not sure I'm up to it, Indie."

I get to my feet and walk over to him. Gently grab his arm. "Donovan. You need to calm down. We're locked in. We have a shit-ton of weapons if we need them. And I'm a crazy assassin. We're OK. I promise."

He stares at me. Says nothing.

"Is that dinner I smell?"

"Yeah. Maggie's setting the table."

"Then let's eat. OK? We'll eat, put her to bed, and then I think it's time for you to have your session. I owe you. We did me and now it's your turn."

265

"Yeah," he says, scrubbing his unshaven face with both hands. "Yeah. OK." He exhales. Like he was holding his breath.

"We can do it here. We don't even have to go to the other side of the house, if you want to stay close to Maggie. We'll do it in your room. OK?"

He nods. And boy, I've never seen Donovan this strung out. But he smiles at me and I get the feeling my words have made a difference.

For once, it's *me* talking *him* back into sanity.

And huh. What do ya know?

So that's how you find happy.

CHAPTER SIXTEEN

PRIVATE SESSION #58

INDIE: OK, Donovan. I don't know what I'm doing. So give me some guidelines.

DONOVAN: It's just relaxation stuff. That's pretty much it. When I'm alone, I use this recorder. It's like one of those... mmm. What do you call them? Fuckin' crunchy people use them? Healing... center... people?

What the actual fuck are you talking about?

Self-guided meditation. That's it. It's like that. Only it's me. Listen. You have knowledge, you have power, you are the master of your own future—

Why the hell are you talking in that stupid accent?

It's not stupid. It's just... American. And I don't know. I just wanted it to sound... you know. Not like me.

If you say so. And that's all I do? Just say stupid stuff like that?

I wrote you a script.

Oh. Why didn't you just say so?

...

Does that work?

It's your party, Donovan. I'll read whatever you want. OK. So we're ready? Flip that bitch on and let's get this show on the road.

We're already recording.

Perfect. OK then. Lie back, Donovan. And clear your mind—

Will you be serious?

What? You got to change your voice. That's my sexy, I'm-a-therapist voice.

Just use your regular voice, please.

Fine. Lie back, Donovan. And clear your mind of all the pollution. Pollution? I'm not crazy about your word choice there.

Indie?

What?

Are you going to take this seriously? Or should we just forget it?

Lie back, Donovan. And clear your mind of all the pollution. Picture yourself on a sunny beach. Feel the sand underneath you. Feel the wind blowing across your wet body. Relax. Deep breath in. Deep breath out.

… (deep breathing)

How do you feel?

Not terrible.

Hmm. … OK. … OK. Got it. Feel the mist off the sea. Hear the blowing of the leaves in the jungle—Oh, God. Donovan. I don't know about this.

What?

I'm picturing this fucking jungle. I'm on this beach. I don't know if I can do this.

What do you mean?

I think it's like fucking with my head, or something. I don't want to be on that beach. I was OK until the jungle part.

Indie. We are literally two minutes into this.

I'm just saying. This is making me feel weird.

Weird how?

… (deep breathing) Is this your grandfather's island?

No. No. God. I wouldn't do that to you. It's my home island.

…

Why, Indie?

I don't want to picture any tropical islands.

It's me picturing, not you.

But I have to say the words. I feel like I'm going on this trip with you. And I'm not sure I can do any islands. This was the Caribbean?

Yeah.

Then no. We need a new guide… thingy. You need to make a new script. Let's be in the mountains. I'm pretty OK with mountains.

OK, forget it.

I get up and turn off the recorder, then toss it onto the bed. It bounces and then disappears over the side and lands on the floor with a *thunk*.

"Jesus, Donovan. I'm sorry. But I… I… I just—"

"Never mind. It's fine." I rub my temples with two fingers on both sides. "I didn't really think this was going to work."

Indie gets up from the chair and sits next to me on the bed. Puts her arm around me. "I'm sorry. Let's do it again. I'll try harder."

"No. You're right. Hell, this whole treatment I've been giving myself for the past four years is probably stupid, anyway."

"Whoa. You've been doing this for four years?"

"Yeah. After… that day, you know—"

"Um. Yup. I get it."

"—well, I went up to Wyoming. I have a friend there who runs a healing center. A huge ranch with all this spa stuff. And she's all new age-y." I point my finger at Indie. "But not stupid. None of it is stupid. She's got a PhD in cognitive neuroscience. So it's got science behind it. Anyway, I went there and that's how I came up with this treatment plan for self-guided hypnosis."

"Nice." She sighs. "I could use a spa-like healing center. We should go together."

"It's closed."

"What? Fucking A. I always miss the good shit. Why'd she close it down?"

"She didn't. She died in a car accident a few months ago . And then the place just kinda… fell apart. It closed down a few weeks after I came back here with you guys."

"Bummer."

"Yeah. I liked her. She was a pretty great woman."

"It's kinda weird though."

"Which part?"

"You started talking about her in the present tense. Like she was still alive."

I sigh. And it's a long, tired sigh. "Yeah. I miss her."

Indie leans in to me. "Sorry, Donovan. Oh. But hey! I know a secret. Do you want to do something sneaky with me?"

"Sneaky?"

"When Adam came home this morning from church, I caught him hiding something in his office. I wasn't gonna get you involved, but fuck it. You look like you need a little pick-me-up. And you're the only partner in crime I have left these days."

I side-eye her. "We're *not* partners in crime."

"We are now. If Nathan was here, I'd make him come on this little adventure. But he's not. So you're all I've got left." She stands up, takes my hand and half-heartedly tugs on it. "Come on. Let's go snoop."

She leads me downstairs and then drops my hand once we're inside Adam's office. "It's in there." She points to the bottom drawer of an antique wooden filing cabinet. "It's got a key lock."

"I don't have the key."

"That thing is like a hundred years old. How hard can it be to pick?"

"I'm not picking Adam's lock, Indie. If it's important, he'll show us."

"Oh, really?" She narrows her eyes at me. "I would call all those hundreds of tapes of my therapy with you important, and you never let me listen to them. Even when I asked."

"That was different. You were a child."

"Well, I'm not a child anymore. And I want to know what's in there."

She goes for the drawer, but I hook my arm around her waist and pull her back. "No. We're not doing this."

She tilts her head up to me, smiles. "We are doing this. I'm tired of secrets. And so are you. That's why you've spent the last four years trying to tease them out of your brain."

"My brain isn't keeping secrets."

"No?" She taps my head. "And anyway. I'm bored." She leans up and kisses me. "So if we're not going to be partners in crime, then we're gonna be partners some other way."

I picture a whole night of Indie in this mood. I'm very familiar with it. And when she was a child it would manifest in various trouble-making ways. But as an adult, it's morphed into flirting.

"I can read your mind, Donovan Couture."

"I wish. Then you could tell me one way or the other if I'm insane."

"What?" Her head juts back in surprise. "You're the sanest person I know."

"Fine. Break into the drawer."

"Yay!" She claps, cracks her knuckles. "OK. Just give me one second." Then she goes over to Adam's desk, finds a paperclip in the top drawer, and goes back over to the drawer and bends down.

"Paperclip?"

"Like I said, this lock is a hundred years old. It's a very simple mechanism." Her little tongue darts out as she squints one eye and twists the thin piece of metal inside the lock. Then something clicks and she looks up at me with a smile. "Bingo."

She pulls the drawer open, takes out a dirty plastic packet, and then gets up and dumps it all out on the desk. She's already fishing straps of money out of the first yellow envelope inside by the time I walk over there.

"Money," I say dryly. "How interesting."

"Yeah, that's pretty boring. It's old too." She squints at the printing date, then loses interest and goes for the second envelope. She spills this all out as well. "Hmm. Passports and papers." She shuffles through them. "Standard fake identity stuff? What do you think?"

I pick up one of the passports and matching certificates. Birth and death. "Yeah. But…" I pick up a second set. Then the third.

"What?"

"Hmm. Interesting people."

"How so?"

"We have a Machette. We have a Szabó. And an Ameci."

"Who are they?"

"Well, the Machettes are an old inner circle family. Very Company. The Szabós are an old worker-class family. Slaves, really. And the Amecis—they got out fifty years ago."

"Out? How's that happen?"

"Um… yeah. It was a big fucking deal."

"So why does Adam have these?"

"No idea. It's probably not even important." I pick up the plastic the folders were in and study it. "Looks very old. And it's dirty. Might've been buried."

"A mystery," Indie whispers. "I love it."

"It's not a mystery," I say, putting everything back the way we found it. Then I take it over to the open drawer and toss it in, kicking it closed with my foot. "It's got nothing to do with us, so who cares."

"Really?" She sounds disappointed. "Why are you so boring, Donovan? If Nathan was here, we'd make this into an adventure."

"Well, Nathan's not here. Is he?"

Her face flushes red and she narrows her eyes at me. "Asshole."

I pull her towards me. "I didn't mean anything by that. I'm sorry. I'm just… I feel like… unsettled. Or something. And I'm taking it out on you. It's not fair."

"Whatever." She pushes me off her. "It's fine."

"Come on, it's nearly eleven. We should go to bed. We'll do something adventurous tomorrow. Maggie will love it." I lead her out of the office, flick the light off, and then take her towards the stairs.

"What could we do? There's no adventure around here anymore. It died. Just like Nathan."

"There's plenty of adventure left in your life, Indie. I promise. We'll find it together. Tomorrow."

I'm used to having Indie next to me in bed now. And it didn't take me very long, after I moved back here, to realize that I miss her when she's sleeping with Adam or McKay. She's been a part of my life for so long, this shouldn't take me by surprise. But it does. Because things are changing now. She's not a child anymore. Maybe she was never a child? Maybe all those things McKay did to give her a normal childhood were just an illusion. Maybe none of us in this house were ever children?

I certainly didn't have a normal childhood. It wasn't filled with physical training, like Indie's. It was all academic stuff. And drugs. They gave me a lot of drugs when I was little.

In fact, when I look back on my early years, this is what I remember most. I was always in some kind of emotional crisis. Always in therapy. And when I wasn't, I was journaling. That's probably why my first inclination when I have a problem is to write it down. Or find some way to document it. Turn it into something scientific instead of something emotional.

My body relaxes as I ponder this in the dark. Indie's breathing has already evened out and the house around us is quiet. I can just barely make out the chorus of crickets over the low hum of the AC. And my mind relaxes into the hypnagogic state I'm so familiar with. It usually starts with a geometric pattern inside a tunnel. It's a very fast-moving animation of falling into a vortex.

Sometimes the geometric pattern inside the tunnel is a small checkered pattern. Sometimes it's triangles, arranged so that all sides are connected to another triangle, the way hexagons are arranged in a beehive. And then, sometimes, but not often, the tunnel morphs into a blinking pattern. If I don't fall asleep, or become too aware, then it might turn into moving pictures. Like I'm watching a movie. Sometimes it has sound. Sometimes not.

But it's always repeating.

I empty my mind and wait and soon, the fast-moving tunnel appears. It's not triangles or squares but lines. And I'm *whooshing* though this tunnel at a very high rate of speed as it curves and bends. The lines are fluorescent green and yellow.

And then they stop.

I'm standing in a forest. Not a musty, woody forest, like the one surrounding Old Home. But a jungle. Like the ones that take me back to my childhood.

All the vegetation on the floor of the jungle has large, broad leaves that collect the water and funnel it down to the roots and enable the plant to catch stray bits of sunshine that barely filter through the tall canopy of trees above.

My feet are bare and the ground is soft dirt. It's dark down here but when I look up, past the tall trunks

277

of the kapok trees, I see that the sky beyond is blue. So not night.

Someone runs by, breathing hard and making the plants rustle. But by the time I look in that direction, all I catch is the trailing blonde hair of a little girl.

"Wait!" I call. I run after her. My legs are longer, because I'm the oldest one out here. "Wait! Sheltee!"

"Shut up!" she yells. And she doesn't slow.

"Sheltee!" I'm catching up with her, reaching for her thin t-shirt so I can grab it and make her stop.

She looks over her shoulder with wild eyes. "Shut up! Shut up! Shut up!"

I grab a hold and pull, yanking her backwards. She falls on top of me and we land on a bush crawling with ants.

"Leave me alone! Don't touch me!"

And then I hear them laughing behind us. Sheltee screams and I cup a hand over her mouth out of instinct.

"You shut up," I whisper. "Or I'll let them find you. Understand?"

She looks up at me with wide blue eyes filled with fear. But she nods.

"Get down," I whisper. "And come over here."

She crawls with me and we hunker down under the cover of the large, dark green leaves of a miconia shrub, the scaly leaves scratching our bare arms.

They have dogs. I can hear them baying off in the distance. But none of them are close.

"Just stay still," I tell her. "We'll be OK. I promise."

She doesn't nod this time. Because she doesn't believe me.

The men are quiet as they stalk near us. But I know they're talking with hand signals.

A pair of boots comes into view and Sheltee's chest hitches as she tries to gasp past my palm, still cupped tightly over her mouth.

The boots keep walking. And I'm just about to breathe a sigh of relief when another pair appears. Closer this time. And they stop. Listening.

My heart is calm but Sheltee's is beating so hard, I swear everything in this forest can hear it.

She scrambles, trying to get away, but I hold her tight as the boots turn towards us.

And then she grabs my hand over her mouth, rips it free, and *screams*.

CHAPTER SEVENTEEN

The hotel isn't a hotel. It's an elaborate Georgian Revival mansion in the Landmark District right on Forsyth Park. Owned by the Boucher estate, Adam informs me, when we pull the rental up to the front gate and a teenage boy opens the door of the car. Adam tosses the keys to him so he can park it, and we grab our bags from the back and head up the stately brick walkway towards the porch.

"You stay here a lot?"

"No. Not for a long time. We rent it out for shit mostly. It's wedding season, but this weekend's wedding party checked out already and no one's due to arrive until Wednesday. So it's all ours."

The inside is so ornately Southern, it almost makes you want to gag on the history. This is what Old Home looked like, though mostly in disrepair, before the reno and modernization just before Indie came to live with us.

People greet us, Adam makes pleasantries to the staff, then he points to the stairs and we go up. I follow him down the long hallway and he opens a door, panning his hand wide for me to enter first.

I lift an eyebrow at him. "One room then?"

He flicks a switch on the wall and everything lights up. "McKay, you can stay in any room you want. We have eleven of them."

"I'm joking, dickface." I push past him, toss my bag on the floor near a wingback chair, and decide… I am not *this* Southern. There's a canopy bed—because of course there's a canopy bed—and lots of little side tables with ruffle tablecloths that pool on the floor around them. There are two chandeliers, more crystal lamps than I can count, and framed oil paintings hanging on the walls depicting uptight white men with hunting dogs at their feet.

There's also a seating area with two small white velvet, sorta half-circle couches with fringe along the bottom and an intricate polished-wood Queen Anne coffee table that looks like it got thrown out of the palace for trying too hard. On top of the table is a tea set.

"Wow," I say, spinning in place.

"Shut the fuck up. You can stay somewhere else if you want."

I chuckle. "I meant it like, 'Wow, this is lovely!'"

"Fuck you. I'm not into this style, either. Obviously."

I walk over and punch him in the arm. "I'm just fucking with you. It's just… I feel like we're on an episode of *Bed and Breakfast Travel Dates*. The gay version. I'm just waiting for the cat to appear. Those places always have some weird, creepy cat lurking about." I actually look for it. It's gotta be here somewhere.

He laughs, but walks off carrying his bag over to one of the stupid-ugly couches. "Never heard of that show."

"*Right.*"

"Like I said—"

"I'm not staying in another room." Then I bounce on the bed, cross my legs, put my hands behind my back, and smile up at him. "I'm looking forward to this."

"You are?"

"Mm-hmm. It's our first date." Then I guffaw. I can't help it.

"Why are you being an asshole? I didn't plan this as some kind of romantic getaway, McKay. It's just a place we own. That's all."

"We?" I point to myself. "I one hundred percent do not own this place."

"Try again. Your name's on the fucking deed, dumbass."

"What?"

"McKay, are you fucking serious? Your name is on everything. If I died, I wasn't gonna leave you hanging."

"I have more money than I could ever spend. I don't need your shit."

"And more homes than you could ever sleep in too. And it's not about need. It's about keeping things in the family."

"Hmm." I have to admit, that's kinda cool of him. He sighs and sinks into a ridiculous wing-back chair that reminds me of Donovan. "I wonder what Donovan and Indie are up to?"

He stares at me for a minute, then shrugs. "Call them and find out."

"Nah. I'm sure Donovan feels safe with Indie there to protect him."

This makes Adam laugh. "He was kinda worried, wasn't he?"

"Yeah. He's a fuckin' wuss."

"I get it though," Adam says, busy with the task of kicking off his boot. "Carter could see this as an opportunity. Maybe we should call?"

"I'll text him." I pull out my phone and send the text.

Adam kicks off his second boot, then leans back in the chair. "You're taking this all pretty well."

"All what?" My phone dings a reply, and I scan the message. "They're fine."

"Us," Adam says.

I shrug. "We've always been an us, Adam. It's not really any different."

"You don't think so?"

"You're the one who wanted this. Why are you so insecure?"

"I'm not insecure. It's just… this *is* different."

"You're still my best friend. I don't love you any different. I'm not looking to change you. Whatever you've been doing in your private time, keep doing it."

"Oh, I see. So you can keep on doing what you're doing."

"If I want to fuck a girl, I'm gonna. If that's what you're asking."

He tilts his head at me. "Do you fuck a lot of girls, McKay? Because you've never brought one home."

"I don't bring anyone home. And neither do you. But you sure as shit did fuck Misha's brains out for nearly a decade, didn't you?"

"Were you jealous?"

"Of Misha? That traitor? She got what she had coming."

"I killed her. James Fenici told me to." He shrugs. "But she wasn't the kind of woman you bring home, even if I didn't kill her."

"That's my point. You're home, Adam. Donovan is home. Indie and Maggie are home. Everyone else stays outside those gates. That's been an unsaid agreement between us since the beginning. And that's not gonna change."

He's quiet for a moment.

"So do you have a problem with me keeping things the same?"

"I can't actually think of a single time I recall seeing you with a girl, McKay."

"Exactly."

He shrugs. "That's fine with me, then."

I sit up, take off my shirt, then kick my boots off too. Adam watches me the whole time, his eyes lingering on my chest and abs. "You wish you had these abs." I joke with him.

"Every fucking day." He grins at me. Then he stands up, takes off his shirt too. Eyes almost never leaving mine. And he walks over to the bed. He pauses for a moment. Maybe wondering if I'll come up with some excuse to stop him from doing what's coming next.

285

But I don't.

There's only one reason we're sharing a room tonight.

He leans one knee on the edge of the bed, then straddles my legs, his hands braced on either side of my head, his hips pressing into mine. His cock is hard and mine responds in kind when he rests the full weight of his lower body on me.

His blue eyes are locked on me, his jaw a little tense as he leans down. Our lips touch and my hands come out from behind my head to grab the thick muscles of his shoulders.

His mouth feels familiar now. And our tongues seek each other out as I slide my fingers into his hair and grab it. The kiss turns harder and more urgent. And then his upper body drops lower and we're pressed together, his hips grinding against mine.

When we break apart, he rolls off to the side and unbuckles my belt. Still watching me for… something. A sign of resistance, maybe.

But I don't resist. And just as he finishes tugging on my zipper I'm already dragging my jeans down my legs. He pops the button on his jeans too. And then, just a few moments later, we're lying naked next to each other. His hand on my cock, pumping it in his fist. And my hand reaching under his balls to cup them. Squeezing gently, the way I squeeze my own when I'm jerking myself off.

I don't know how far we're gonna go.

I don't know what this looks like tomorrow.

I don't know anything.

And when he leans his head down to take my cock in his mouth, I stop worrying about it.

CHAPTER EIGHTEEN

"Donovan!" I shake him awake.

He opens his eyes to find me peering down at him with worry.

"Jesus fucking Christ," I whisper, not wanting to wake up Maggie down the hall. "You punched me!"

"What?"

"I think you were having a bad dream. Or maybe I was having a bad dream?"

"Fuck," he says, sitting up. "I *was* having a dream." He looks over at the window, then glances at the clock. It's still very early. Just past five.

"I was having a dream too." I'm still breathing hard from the memory of it. "Fucking forest. I hate that dream."

"Forest?" Donovan is still confused. "I was in a forest too."

"It was that hypnosis. I know it. It brought back memories."

"What kind of memories?"

287

I shake my head. "Running. I was running. Like…
full on, heart-pumping running. For my life, or
something."

"Was someone chasing you?" His eyes dart back
and forth as he looks at me. Like there's something
hidden behind them.

I squint my eyes, thinking. Then I shrug. "I dunno.
It's fading now. Fucking forest."

"What kind of forest was it? Like the one here?
Or—"

"No. Tropical. A jungle. What kind of forest were
you in?"

"Same."

I flop back on the bed, so close to him our
shoulders are touching. "That's weird, don't you
think?"

"Maybe?"

I prop myself up on one elbow so I can see him.
"Maybe? You don't think it's weird that we have the
same dream on the same night?"

"Was it the same? We don't know. Maybe it was
just the imagery from the relaxation tape?"

Relaxation tape? Is he for real?

"Was there a beach?" he asks.

"No. It was just a forest."

"So it can't be the tape. Just a coincidence."

"Not likely."

He shrugs. "Bad dream. That's all. I've had plenty
of them over the years. Just like this, in fact. So for
sure, it wasn't the tape. I've listened to that dozens and
dozens of times."

I sigh.

He pulls me towards him, wrapping his arms around me. "You're safe. You're fine, Indie."

He says these words softly. Like he needs to be careful with me. And it helps. Donovan has always been helpful in stressful situations. But I can't get the feeling of that dream out of my mind.

My heart was pounding. Fear. That I know for sure. It was filled with fear.

Hmm. "Someone was there with me."

"Where?"

"In the dream."

"Hmm. There was someone in my dream too. Was it a little girl? Mine was a little girl."

I scrunch up my face, trying to remember. "I don't know. It's all fuzzy now. The only thing left is the lingering feelings, ya know?"

We're quiet for a little bit. But I can tell by Donovan's breathing that he's not drifting off to sleep. "What are you thinking about?"

"The dream," he says. "The little girl. She reminded me of you."

"Me? Why?"

"She looked like you."

"Hmm. She was a little killer?"

"Maybe?"

"Do you think she was real? Or just…a dream girl?"

"Not sure. She had a name though."

"What was it?"

"I don't remember. Something weird."

"Weird how? Like Indie Anna?" I giggle. I can't help it.

"Yeah. But no. It was one word, I think. Fuck, why can't I remember?"

"Stupid dreams. What is the point of dreams, anyway?"

"They're emotional manifestations of unresolved problems in real life."

"Right. It was kinda rhetorical. But OK. That is such a *you* answer."

He turns his head to look at me. "Sorry. Medical school just comes rushing back at the most inappropriate moments."

I yawn. "It's almost dawn. Should we just get up?"

"Fuck that."

I lean my head on his chest and listen to his heartbeats. They're still very fast. "Having trouble letting go?"

"Huh?"

"Your heart is racing."

"Oh. Yeah. I'm just… it was a weird dream, Indie. It felt so… real. More like a memory."

"Hmm. Maybe we should try the"—I make air quotes—"'relaxation tape' again. Hey, I have an idea!"

"Hm?"

"We should do it together this time. Both of us. Make a new sequence. In your weird American voice. Only this time, we're in that forest. Because we were both there, right?"

"Maybe."

"Maybe we were on the same island? Not the snake island. The other island. What was your island called where you grew up? And how have I never asked you this before?"

He turns his head to look at me. "You didn't pay any attention to me when you were little. You were too anxious to go outside with Nathan."

"Yeah." I flop back into my pillow. "But what was it called?"

"Banyan Key. Because we had those strangler fig trees everywhere."

"Strangler figs. What the hell is a strangler fig?"

"It's a parasitic tree that wraps around the trunks of other trees and eventually kills them."

"Eww. Like a snake. Snake Island. I've been there."

"Yeah, you have."

"No. Not the auction island. Snake Island. That was a real place they used to take us. That's what we called it, anyway. Because all the trees looked like they were being strangled by snakes."

"Hmm."

"You're doing that again."

"Doing what?"

"Going 'hmm, hmm, hmm.' I hate that. Just tell me what you're thinking."

"We might've been on the same island, Indie. I'm sure there are banyan trees on a whole bunch of islands. They're an invasive species, after all. But... another Company island that had so many your made-up name for it was Snake Island? I'm not sure that's a coincidence."

"Especially after our twin dreams."

"Yeah."

"So? You wanna do it? Or not?"

"Make a new tape? Go for a little mind journey?"

"You did promise me an adventure today. And obviously Carter didn't come try to kill us in our sleep, so you're really on the hook for something adventurous."

"I did promise that." He sighs. "OK. I have another digital recorder right here." He opens up his bedside table drawer and pulls it out. "I'll make a new tape and we can listen to it together while the other one records. Can't hurt, right?"

I go check on Maggie. Can never be too sure. And Donovan starts making the new guide tape.

Maggie is fine. She's snoring like a buzzsaw and all her floppy arms and legs are tangled in the covers.

She reminds me of long-ago days when I used to be all floppy arms and legs too.

I blow her a kiss, then creep back down the hallway to Donovan's room and close the door behind me.

He's just finishing up the tape. And it's weird to hear a traditional American accent coming from his normally Caribbean-British mouth. It makes him look different too. For some reason I can't quite explain.

I remain quiet while he adds a few more prompts. And then he stops the recorder and rewinds to the beginning. "Ready?"

"I'm ready."

We both lie down on the bed. Hands on our stomachs. Staring up at the ceiling.

CHAPTER NINETEEN

Donovan

"Hold on." I swing my legs out of bed. "I just thought of something." I pull my medical bag out of the closet and open it up, looking for the small vial of clear liquid. I hold it up to the hazy pre-dawn light filtering in through the window and check the level.

"What's that?"

I look down in my bag and grab two syringes and two tourniquets, and then go back to the bed and take Indie's arm.

"What is that?" she repeats, but doesn't resist when I tie off her arm and snap the veins in the crook of her elbow.

"Brevital. It's a short-acting sedative. And I'm going to give you a very small dose. You're gonna feel it in seconds and it will only last about five minutes. But this will be enough to get us into the proper relaxation state. Your head will be a little foggy as you wake up. Just lean into it. Relax. Don't panic or think about anything but the voice. I'll set the recorder to start at the five-and-a-half-minute mark so we're awake enough to hear it. I've given you this lots of times, so I know how you'll react. It's safe."

She shrugs. "I'm not worried."

I load two syringes, mine with a little more than Indie's since I'm a lot heavier than she is. But not as much as the typical anesthesia dose. Then I tie off my own arm. I want us to go under as close together as I can get it. And this shit is so fast-acting, with such a short duration, I'll have to move quick.

Then I set the digital recorder to play in five and a half minutes, and wait for her to give me a nod of permission.

God. Is it weird that I've been sedating her for so long, and so often, that we have an unspoken consent procedure?

I definitely think it is.

I push the drug into Indie's veins, then snap off her tourniquet and watch her as it hits her bloodstream. It takes about thirty seconds for the drug to make it to her heart, then a couple more to get up to her brain. Her eyes flutter and she exhales a long breath, her head rolling to the side.

I'm already pushing my own dose in. And the second I snap the tourniquet off, I can already feel it.

I barely have time to set the needles down on the bedside table before I'm sinking down too.

And then... darkness.

SESSION #1
INDIE AND DONOVAN
DREAM THERAPY

VOICE: Where are you?

Where am I?
I look around. A tall, thick canopy of trees. Just like my dream.

Describe your dream.

It's dark. Not the dark of the understory in the daytime. But real, proper darkness. I can just barely make out a bit of moon between the leaves above my head. It's full.

Can you see anything else?

I turn around, listening for something. I'm not sure what, I just know that I should be listening. But there's no one there.

Can you see anything else?

Yes. I see… kids. Other kids. My age. We're all in a group but I'm standing apart from them a little bit. Oh… there's that girl. She has a weird name. But I can't remember it. She's crying and this is upsetting to me. I really want her to stop crying.

Why? Is she scaring you?

295

No.

Then why do you care if she cries?

Because this is what they want. And if she gives them what they want, she will make them happy. And then she'll disappear.

Where do you think she will go?

Someplace bad.

How do you know that? Maybe she's being taken someplace nice.

No. That's not what happens. That's what they tell me. They tell all of them that. But it's a lie. Nothing good happens when kids come here. And even worse things happen when they take them away.

I think you're just imagining that, Donovan. There's nothing going on here. This island is a paradise. You have a very advanced imagination. You're a genius. And sometimes geniuses have… issues. That's all. Just a small issue distinguishing between real and imaginary. This is all imaginary. These kids aren't even here. And neither are you. You're lying down on a bed inside a big old house on the Old Pearl River.

I don't believe you. I think you're lying. I think you've always been lying.

Why would I lie to you? That doesn't even make sense. This island is fun. You get to run in the woods.

I don't like the running.

But you always win. You're a very good runner, Donovan. Unlike Carter.

What?

…

What did you just say?

…

Hello?

…

Answer me, you piece of fucking shit voice!

"Donovan!"

Where is he? Where is he? Answer me!

"*Donovan!* For fuck's sake!"

A hard slap across my face makes me jolt awake. I sit up out of instinct and just... pant. Barely able to catch my breath.

"Jesus. You scared me!"

"What?" I turn and find Indie on her knees, her body twisted so she can see my face.

"You fucking scared me! You weren't breathing."

I take a deep breath. "Seems to be working fine."

"No shit, you dumbass! I punched you in the chest. That made you gasp. And then when you didn't open your eyes, I slapped your face."

"Really?" I look around again, the drug wearing off quickly. "Wait. How are you so awake? We just went down."

"Didn't you just hear me? I woke up. You *didn't.*"

"That's crazy. I feel fine."

"Oh, my God." She slaps herself on her forehead. "I'm never doing this with you again. I think you had a bad reaction, Donovan. I think you almost died."

I laugh. "It's pretty hard to kill someone with the dose I gave us. It wasn't even close enough to knock us straight out. It was just a sedation. Oh!" I turn and grab the recorder. "What did we say?"

"I didn't listen to it."

I study the recorder. "But it's not on. Someone turned it off."

"Or"—Indie is still mad. I think I really did scare her—"you didn't turn it on."

"Of course I turned it on. That was the whole point of doing this." I sigh. "Well, do you remember anything? Did you answer any of the questions?"

"No. It didn't ask me anything. I was in like a dream state, and it was a forest. Just like my nightmare. But I didn't hear any questions."

"Dammit. How did I fuck this up so bad? And I heard questions. They weren't exactly the ones I recorded though."

"That's because it didn't play."

"What are you guys doing?"

We both look over at the door where Maggie is standing in her bed shorts and t-shirt.

Indie gets up off the bed and walks over to her, turning her around by the shoulders and marching her into the hallway. "Come on, let's get breakfast. Donovan promised we could do something adventurous today and I have big plans that you're going to love. You coming, Donovan?"

I nod, then catch myself. "Yes. I'll be right down."

Right after I listen to this tape.

Because I *know* it recorded.

I *know* I turned it on.

And I *was* answering questions.

Questions no one was *asking*.

CHAPTER TWENTY

McKay is already in the shower when I wake up. It's barely dawn, and even though I need to have this meeting with Nathan, it suddenly feels like a very bad idea.

Especially when Core McKay is naked in the shower just a few feet away.

Huh. It occurs to me that almost exactly twenty-four hours ago I was sitting in the New Orleans house, in another one of my bedrooms, lamenting over the fact that McKay was always so close, just never close enough.

And now everything has changed.

We're gonna go home. We're gonna put Indie between us. Probably Donovan too, but whatever. And then we can really begin the process of starting over.

It feels like such a dream. Something wholly unattainable.

And yet here I am.

So why am I sitting here on the bed?

I get up, still naked from last night, and walk into the bathroom. It's steamy, but I can see the outline of McKay's body through the shower glass. He's got his back to me. Washing his hair.

I pull open the shower door and step inside, and he whirls, like he's gonna attack.

"What? Did you forget you're in love with me?"

He grins at me. "Fuck you."

"Yeah. One of these days we'll get there."

We didn't get that far last night. It was too overwhelming. Too exciting. Too much of nearly everything.

McKay moves over and pans his hands to the rain shower falling from the ceiling. I step under it and close my eyes to get wet.

When I open them, he's leaning against the tile wall, jerking off, a sly, lazy grin smeared across his face. My hand reaches down and starts tugging on my half-erect cock. Our eyes are locked and then I step towards him and take his other hand and place it over mine. He grips and begins to pump our hands up and down my shaft.

"Did Indie teach you that?" He nods to his hand on my cock. "That's her cheat."

"Yeah. She got me. Just a couple days ago. You?"

"Fuck that. I know all her tricks. I don't fall for any of them."

"Whatever. You were sleeping with her the day she showed up at your workshop."

He shrugs. "That was my decision. Not hers." He stands up, takes my hand, and places it over his. And I start guiding him. Long, slow strokes. Then I lean in and kiss him.

But it's a short kiss. And this is gonna be a short interlude.

Everything about us is still way too overwhelming. Way too exciting. We're too much of everything to care about making it last. Because that's how beginnings are. They feel like they will last forever and you have all the time in the world to do those other things. Beginnings are about living in the moment. Seizing the fucking day and smelling those goddamn roses.

I come in his hand first. I don't even care that it took like two minutes. I don't care. Because there's more where this came from. And then I lean against him, pushing into his chest and pinning him against the tiled wall. I reach down and cup his balls with my newly unoccupied hand while the other one picks up the pace and strokes him harder. Faster.

I lean into his neck and whisper, "If you ever fuck another girl, Core McKay, you had better invite me along."

He laughs. And I probably just fucked up his moment, but I don't care. I'm dead serious.

"Shut up and jerk me off, Adam. We have business today."

"Say, 'I agree, Adam.'"

"Or what?" He tips his chin up, challenging me. But it's not a real challenge.

I don't really have a threat ready. So I make one up on the fly. "I'll take away your tools."

He laughs again.

"I'll have someone hack into your stupid Etsy store and change all the prices."

"You're a dumbass." Then he points at me. "Do not fuck with my Etsy store."

I grin. "Say, 'I agree, Adam.'"

"There are no girls. It was a precautionary loophole."

"Say, 'I agree, Adam.'"

"Fine. Whatever. I agree, Adam."

"Good." I turn my body and lean against the wall next to him. He turns with me, never letting go of my cock.

And then he's pressing his body into mine. One working my dick while the other tugs on my balls like he knows just what to do. "If I find a nice girl with a dirty mouth and sense of adventure, I'll be sure to let you know and invite you in. Happy now?"

I nod and close my eyes. Smiling.

And then I come in his hand.

The meeting place is in Forsyth Park. The only detail Wendy gave was to meet at the fountain at eight forty-five. It's right across the street from the mansion, but we head out a little early. And even though the sun is still low, and mostly hidden by the large Southern live oaks the park is famous for, it's nearly ninety degrees.

McKay and I walk with purpose down the wide asphalt walkway lined with trees that leads to the fountain. Our eyes wandering. Looking for the boy who caused us so much worry and stress over the years.

There is no way to mistake the blond man leaning up against a huge oak tree just west of the fountain.

He's wearing a pair of desert camo pants, a tight mustard-yellow shirt, and mirrored sunglasses, which he removes to see us better as we approach.

And there… are his eyes. Those piercing, spooky fucking eyes. In the sun they are so blue, they're nearly silver. Like ice. But in the shade—Indie's description in the journal McKay found was dead on. The color of almond shells in the shade. Which is almost like no color at all when you think about it. And she saw that in him.

McKay and I are both wearing boots, even though it's way too hot. They thud on the asphalt, then go quiet as we veer off and step onto the grass to head in his direction.

I don't take my eyes off him as we approach. He's not a boy anymore. That boy is long gone. And the first thing I want to call out, before we even reach him, is… *What have you seen? Where have you been? What have you done?*

Because it is immediately clear he has seen, and been, and done a whole helluva lot.

This man is *grown*. Lean, but broad in the shoulders. Not as muscular as he was the last time I saw him, but the tight t-shirt shows off every single abdominal muscle. His mouth is a tight slash across his face. Neither friendly, nor mean. And his arms are covered in tattoos.

McKay and I stop about six feet short. McKay says, "Nathan."

But Nathan's eyes are on me when he nods his greeting.

"So why are we here?" I ask. Because I don't like this. I don't like it one bit. Nathan St. James is a man with secrets. And I have enough secrets of my own, thank you. I'm not really interested in his.

He looks around with a critical eye. "Anyone else come with you?"

The accent is the only thing that feels the same. It's thick. Very *hick*. His grandfather never bothered to tamp it down the way my father did.

"No," McKay says. "It's just us."

But Nathan isn't satisfied. Because he continues to scan the area as he talks. "I need to see Indie."

"That's not gonna happen." It comes out of my mouth so quick, Nathan's brows go up as his eyes track to mine. "It's not even up for discussion."

"I don't think you understand—"

"Oh, I understand plenty. You need to stay the fuck away from my Indie. Forever. She's in a good place right now—"

"Fuck!" Nathan's laugh takes McKay and I both back a step. That's how loud it is. "Good place? Have you lost your goddamned mind? Do you have any idea where she was the past four years?"

My heart skips. "Do you?"

"Were you with her?" McKay asks, taking a few steps forward, like he might start choking Nathan out any second now.

I grab his arm and pull him back. Because I get the feeling that Nathan St. James can turn violent on a dime if the occasion calls for it.

"No, I wasn't with her. But I've seen things, you guys. I'm not here to cause trouble. I'm just here to help Indie. She needs—"

"You don't get a say in what she needs," McKay interjects.

"Why?" Nathan growls it. "Because I walked away?" He narrows his eyes at McKay. "I didn't walk away. You *chased* me. I'm the one—"

"What the fuck do you want?" One minute into this little meeting and I've had enough.

"I need to talk to her. There are things we have to discuss."

"We're here." McKay pans his hands wide. "Let's discuss."

Nathan is shaking his head before McKay even finishes. "No. This is between me and her."

"Then I guess you're shit out of luck," I say. "Because if you step one foot onto Old Home property, we're gonna make damn sure you'll never do it again."

"I'm already dead, Adam. Your threats don't scare me."

"Obviously you are not dead, Nathan. Because you are standing right here in my fucking face."

"Well, here's a threat that should scare *you*." He glares at me. And I know what's coming before he even says it. "Magnolia Accorsi is *my* child. My *legal* child. That's *my* name on that birth certificate, not yours."

"Well," McKay says, keeping his cool—and I am very thankful for that because I'm about to lose mine—"we've heard otherwise, Nathan. So if you wanna make this into a big deal, we can. But it's not gonna make Indie love you again."

"Again? She never stopped loving me. I was the one who was there. I was the one who saved her. I was—"

He falls on his ass because I punch him in the face. And then I grab that stupid yellow t-shirt of his and wad it up in my fist, dragging him back onto his feet. I push him up against the thick, trunk of the old oak tree. And I lean into my threats, my words coming out like venom. "You did *not* save her. I did. I'm the one who saved her. I'm the one who took her out of that cage. I'm the one who gave her a home."

But Nathan doesn't even flinch. Even though his lip is bleeding and his cheek is red. He just glares at me. "Yeah." He wipes the blood away from his mouth. "You saved her all right. You took her out of the Garden of Eden and straight through the gates of Hell. You don't know anything, Adam Boucher. Nothing. You think you're so powerful? Did you ever ask yourself *why* it felt so *easy*, Adam?"

"Easy?" I laugh. "Nothing about my life has been easy."

"Everything about your life has been easy. It was planned this way. You really don't get it, do you? He planned this. He planned it all from the very beginning. You're like a little fucking puppet on a string. So goddamned predictable. Nick and James take out the Company and what do you do? Build it right back up. Did you ever ask yourself why, Adam? Why the fuck would you *do that?*"

McKay pries my clenched fist off Nathan's t-shirt and starts pulling me backwards. "Come on. We should go. People are starting to notice us."

"Who?" I say as McKay pulls me backwards. "Who was it?"

Nathan spits blood at me. And it's got both distance and aim, because it lands just short of my boot. "You really don't know, do you?" He smiles then, a little 'gotcha' smile. "Let me talk to Indie and

I'll tell you. But not down there. Not at Old Home. You bring her somewhere else. Anywhere else but there."

"Fuck that," McKay says. "And fuck you, Nathan. I should've finished you off when I had the chance."

"Yeah," he says, tilting his chin up and sliding his mirrored sunglasses back onto his face. "You really should've."

"Stay away from her," I call, walking backwards, never taking my eyes off Nathan. "You stay the fuck away, Nathan. Or you'll be sorry you ever came back from the dead."

He doesn't say anything back. Just spits on the ground and tracks me with his eyes until I turn my back and follow McKay onto the asphalt path towards the mansion.

PART THREE
in the same boat

Or... maybe we're just flying the same false flag?

CHAPTER TWENTY-ONE

Indie Anna Accorsi was never just the girl next door. She was the saddest girl in the world.

Up until the moment I first met her I didn't understand much about sadness. I certainly couldn't smell it. I didn't realize sadness had a scent until that first moment when I saw her in the woods.

That's when I noticed that sadness had a scent and it smelled like this girl.

I was surprised at the time. Not that sadness had a smell, but that it didn't smell like something awful. It smelled like the forest a little bit. Like mud and the thick, humid air that hovers on the edge of the trees. But that smell had been lingering alongside me for as long as I could remember and so Indie Anna's sadness always felt a little bit like home.

But there was more to it than that when it came to Indie because she hadn't been in the woods long enough for it to be made of just one thing. Her sadness was made of two things.

The woods and the *secrets* the woods kept.

That's why she ran away from Adam and McKay that first day I saw her standing on the edge of the trees alongside the Old Pearl River. She even told me that. Those words came out of her mouth not ten minutes into our new friendship. I asked her what she thought she was doin' in the swamp all alone. Because it was clear she had no fear of anyone or anything and there are plenty of things in this swamp to be afraid of. I just wanted to make sure she was aware of that.

And she said, "I had to drop off some secrets before I started my new life."

That's it. That's all she said that first day. I had no idea what she was talking about back then. And I mostly ignored her answer. Just cooked and fed her some fish on the beach because she looked weary. Like she'd just gotten home from a long journey. Then I took her back to my house and hid her in the thick trees while I went inside and fed my grandfather his dinner. And while I was in the kitchen with my grandfather, I thought about how it had been a long, long time since I thought about the smell of sadness.

And now here it was. Back again. Clinging to this girl who should not be here, but was.

Her sadness smelled like faraway islands and little girls wrapped up in snakes. It smelled like a dark summer night and a winter rain on a gray day. And every once in a while, her sadness smelled like bloody knives and slit wrists.

But if that was all there was to Indie Anna Accorsi, it wouldn't have gone on this long. No one would've paid any attention to her. She would've been just another little girl with blonde hair and blue eyes. Just another little girl wearing a loose white dress inside a cage. Just another little girl no one would remember tomorrow.

But that's not all there is to Indie. She is also lit-up fireflies in an old mason jar. And squishy mud between toes in a misty summer morning. She is little weedy flowers in an August meadow, and a burst of happiness when you need it most.

Everyone sees it.

Everyone.

I knew some things about what had happened to her before she came to live at Old Home. And my grandfather told me plenty of stories about what Adam and McKay got up to in the world. All those stories came with warnings at the end. *Stay away from them. Don't go over there. Don't be seen.*

He didn't mean *seen* as in don't let them see me. By the time Indie came they had already seen me a couple dozen times at least.

He meant... *see me.* Through me, past me, inside me.

The real me.

Because I had one thing going for me that Indie never did.

I remembered everything.

So I knew things. But it wasn't just the life Indie lived before she came to Old Home that made her smell like sadness. It was everything that came after too.

It took me a long time to figure that out. I was only ten and I had been sheltered from the outside world for years by that time. I went to school in Pearl Springs. I had friends. I was planning on playing football that summer. I was on a local team and had even gone to some practices. But when Indie stepped out of the woods smelling like a swamp full of secrets, I quit the football. Didn't go back to it for another four years because her appearance swept me up and knocked me down.

Life before Indie was one thing and life after her was another. And never did the two lives ever meet again.

Not even now. Even though I've been calling the past several years "life after Indie".

She changed me. At least I thought she did.

But looking back now, I can see that she didn't really change me.

She just… revealed me.

She uncovered me.

And from that day on—even up to and including this day right here—nothing about who I was or where I thought I came from would ever make sense again.

FORTY-EIGHT HOURS AGO

I stare at the payphone after I end the call with McKay, wondering if I should just leave well enough alone. Wondering if Indie is better off without me. Wondering if this new little girl who is so obviously hunting me will make these decisions for me.

Then I walk back to the motel and go inside. Don't flip on the lights. Don't sit down. Just stand there in the middle of the room and try not to spin out of control.

The answer to the first question is probably yes.

The answer to the second question is a definite no.

As far as the third one goes, I can't see the future. If that little girl really wants me dead, there's probably nothing I can do about it. So I'm gonna take that as it comes. She will make her intentions known when she's good and ready.

A vehicle pulls up directly outside the motel room so I walk over to the window and swipe the curtain aside.

Beck and Moore are facing each other in the front cab of a truck having some kind of heated conversation—which is most likely about something inconsequential because that's just how they act.

Beck is a big white guy with steel-gray eyes and a nearly shaved head of golden fuzz who is way more muscle than brain. I'm not calling him stupid because I don't care how big you are, you don't get this far in this line of work by being stupid. He's just more front-line defense than he is back-end planning.

Moore is an equally huge black dude from Detroit who picked up my Southern accent and ran with it. At first, he was just making fun of me because my roots run deep. But he's been doing that for four years and now I can't picture him talking any other way. He's my tech guy. You give that man a computer and he will fuck a whole lotta shit up with the tips of his fingers.

They continue their argument in the truck so I let the curtain slide back in place and go back to thinking about Indie.

We spent weeks running around in the swamp when Adam first brought her back to Old Home. I hid with her during the day and I took her home at night. She would climb up a tree, and walk along the roof of my grandfather's cottage, and then slide her little slip of a body into my attic window. She slept on the floor those three weeks we were hiding from Adam and McKay. I offered her my bed but she said no. She told me...

I have to stop in the here and now and swallow hard as I think back on this moment. Because she said it so casually.

But she told me... "I always sleep on the floor. It's fine for me. But you're probably used to sleeping in a bed, so it wouldn't be right to take a good thing away from you just to make myself comfortable." She had a different kind of accent back then. I don't know what it was. Maybe it was just regular. I can't remember it very well now. I just recall thinking, *She's not from around here.*

That's how it started. My internal musing about her accent, or lack thereof, and where she might be from. That was the loose thread that, when tugged on with the slightest pressure, started to unravel everything I thought I knew to be true.

That first night she took the blanket and pillow I offered her, went into the corner, and curled up like she was both a lost little kitten and a fierce, wild lioness at the very same time.

She didn't have any trouble falling asleep. She snored a little, breathing deep at times. She even moaned now and again and kicked her feet like she was dreaming.

318

I didn't sleep the whole night. Not one second of it.

I spent every moment of that night trying to imagine where this little golden-haired girl with bright blue eyes came from that she never had a bed before. I pictured caves. Because I was a child with a sense of adventure. I thought myself a boy akin to Tom Sawyer or Huckleberry Finn. A boy who craved, and looked for, and oftentimes found—with a little imagination—adventurous things right in front of him almost every second of the day.

So I didn't picture scary caves. I didn't have the… the right… *mindset*, I guess, to think up awful living conditions for other children.

Oh, to be young like that again. To be *that* innocent.

The kids in Pearl Springs were not rich. Not by any means. In fact, knowing what I do now about that town and the people in it, I would definitely call almost all of them poor and underprivileged. But they had homes. And families. They had bedrooms and food to eat. They had clothes to wear to school and clothes to play in after they got home.

And in that respect, all those kids were a lot like me. I know now that I had privilege that others in my school did not. But I didn't know it back then. I don't really understand my privilege right now because it's not all that easy to… to *quantify*, I guess.

I have things others do not. Things like a bloodline and a last name that guarantee me a certain place in the world. Of course, that's the Company world and not the one everyone else lives in, but I get it. Certain things are guaranteed to me.

319

Like McKay saving my life after Indie tried to kill me.

So I didn't picture Indie's life before me filled with mind-control assholes who doled out a special kind of punishment when she didn't obey her orders.

I didn't picture her running in the woods, panting so hard, she was on the verge of hyperventilating.

I didn't picture her being yanked backwards by her long, golden hair until she fell to the ground.

I didn't picture what came after that, either.

I pictured Indie Anna's life before me as one long, grand adventure instead. I was enamored with her from the very first second. And when she started telling me about tropical islands, and jungles filled with snakes big enough to eat a man alive, I fell into her face first.

She was no Becky Thatcher, that's for sure. She was so much better than any girl I had ever read about in a story. But sometimes she was exactly like a storybook girl. She would wear pretty dresses, and she lived in that mansion across the duck lake. And she went to school at home. She didn't have a mother or a father, but two men took care of her like she was a treasure chest overflowing with jewels and gold.

And the idea of her never having a bed to sleep in—the idea that she had spent her whole life sleeping on a floor... well. I had to figure that out. Because even though it felt foreign, it felt familiar too. After a while, anyway. Not that first day. But maybe a couple weeks later. By the time Indie had agreed, with some prodding from Donovan, to leave the woods and go home I was caught in the net. Struggling to connect the dots of memories that were starting to pop back up in my dreams.

It would take me years to understand what her life was really like before she came to Old Home to live with Adam and McKay. Five years on and I was still trying to piece it all together.

I would not call Indie a liar. She wasn't a liar. Because to be a liar you have to tell untruths on purpose. And she *never* did that.

She only told lies she thought were truths.

The door beeps, then opens. Beck comes in first, still arguing with Moore about whatever the fuck. He throws the truck key down on the dresser. "You're so full of shit, Moore."

Moore kicks the door closed with his foot and slumps down in the nearest chair facing a small table. "I'm telling you, if you make her gargle with lemon juice, cures that shit right up."

I cross the room and take a seat at the small desk in the corner. "I don't even want to know what you guys are talking about. Did you get it?"

I'm talking to Moore so he looks at me and nods with a sly grin. "What do you think? Have I ever come back empty-handed?"

"Plenty of times."

He points his meaty finger at me. "None of which count. Circumstances beyond my control are considered acts of God. Not even insurance policies cover those." He reaches into his jacket, produces a thick envelope, and slaps it down on the table. "What's this?" He makes a mocking surprise face. "Looks like peaches, motherfucker."

Beck laughs into the mini-fridge as he grabs a bottle of beer.

"What does that even mean?" I ask.

Moore blows on his fingernails. "Means I got the job done, son. Passports, IDs, and birth certificates. Order fulfilled."

I walk over and pick them up, studying the passports the longest for the telltale hologram that declares them to be legit. "Damn, Moore. These are perfect."

"All I did was pick them up. You're the one in debt to that chick now." He throws a strap of cash down on the table. "She said to tell you to keep this. She did this as a favor. But there's no such thing as favors."

Beck nods his head, agreeing, as he takes a sip of his beer and then flops down on one of the beds. "Not in this business, there ain't."

"Did she say anything else?"

Beck looks at me. "She said to tell you…" He squints his eyes like he's thinking.

"She said to tell me what?"

"Something about… ice cream? You owe her now and she wants a…"

"A strawberry shortcake," Moore says, flicking the TV on with the remote.

"Yeah." Beck snaps his fingers. "That's it. A strawberry shortcake."

"Hmm." I consider this.

"What's it mean?" Moore is mostly focused on the TV, but is still shooting me a sideways glance.

"Don't ask me," I lie. I pick up the cash and shove it and the documents into the safe. "I'm going out. I have a few calls to make and—"

"Don't do it," Moore says as I lock up the safe. "Calling him now, after we've made up our minds, is just gonna get him all riled up again."

"Agreed," Beck says. "I want to get the fuck out of here. I hate this state, I hate this weather, I hate the way people talk—"

"Hey," Moore objects.

"I swear to God," Beck continues, "I have an unnatural urge to kill every little blonde girl who looks in my general direction. Little fuckers creep me out."

"I know." I sigh. "But I owe him. We *all* owe him." Moore snorts, but doesn't look at me. "I'll be back in thirty."

Neither of them says anything as I walk out the door.

I don't take Beck's truck. I just walk. Outside it's hot and humid. That's why Beck hates it here. He's not from the South, he's from one of those little states up in New England. Maybe… Rhode Island? Not sure. But he hates the South with a passion. Can't take the weather.

But I like Savannah. If I wasn't running from a little blonde assassin and directly involved in the biggest global conspiracy in human history, I might even think of settling here. It reminds me a lot of Louisiana. Kinda makes my heart ache for times gone by.

The Thunderbird Inn is one of those throwbacks from the Fifties. All kinds of post-modern accents littering the place. But that's not why I chose it for a temporary home base. It's in the middle of things. Lots of traffic and people all around. And a pay phone located just half a block up Oglethorpe. Which I make use of often. It's hard to find a payphone these days.

I jaywalk across the street, pass the Family Dollar store, and head into a shitty strip-mall parking lot. The pay phone is located on the western edge of the last shop and by the time I reach it sweat is running down the middle of my back.

Two quarters slide down into the belly of it and I press the contact number from memory.

It rings, a low, throaty kinda buzzing that is both comforting and familiar.

He picks up on the fifth ring. "Yeah."

"So listen," I say, turning as much as the short phone cord will allow to study the people around me, automatically scanning for creepy little girls with golden hair and blue eyes. "I got what I needed and we're out of here tonight."

"There's been a change of plans."

"No, Nick. There hasn't. We're done. We did our time, we did our jobs, and we're taking the fucking paycheck and getting the hell out before it's too late."

"I found another nest."

My stomach falls. That feeling when you're at the top of one of those dead-drop amusement park rides. "No. You're fucking lying. I took care of them. All of them."

"This one's new."

"How is that possible?"

"I just discovered it. And you're not that far away. I need you to—"

"No. No, fuck that. I'm not doing it. Get someone else."

"There is no one else. You, and Beck, and Moore are the only team working on this. You know that."

"Fuck you, Nick. This wasn't part of our deal. I've got one of them after me right now and—"

"This is my whole point. You didn't finish the job."

"She's not one of them. She's different."

"Does it matter?"

"Yeah, it fucking matters. You know damn well the only reason I agreed to work for you was because I was trying to save Indie."

"You don't think you owe *Wendy* anything?"

"According to her, I don't. Since she just gave me the documents for free."

Nick is silent at this revelation. Then he whispers, "Did she ask about me?"

"No. Beck and Moore said it was a quick exchange and she just gave us the payment back."

He pauses again and I sigh. Nick and I are friends because we understand each other. We have a connection. A shared experience that binds us. "She had to have said *something*."

Jesus Christ. It's like he's not even hearing me. "All I know is that Wendy gave them a message to pass along to me. I owe her now, I guess. It's not even true, but we can work that out later."

"That's it?"

"That's it. I swear to God. I would tell you if there was anything else. You know I would."

Nick sighs on the other end of the line. It's a sad sigh. One I'm also familiar with. I've heard Adam and McKay use that same sigh with Indie over the years. Hell, I've used that same sigh with Indie over the years.

325

"This nest I found? They're all *her*, Nathan."

"Bullshit." I shake my head, refusing to believe it.

"Same genetics, same—"

"That's not possible."

"And yet there is a house in Vicksburg, Mississippi with a set of triplets."

"I've got it all ready, Nick." I whisper this as I lean my head against the phone. "All I need is a ride down to Pearl Springs and then it's a straight shot into Mexico. I can take it from there, OK? Please. Do not fuck it up for me now."

"I need to talk to Wendy, Nathan."

"I understand. And once I get Indie away from Old Home, I promise, I will go back for Wendy. This is all in the plan. OK? Nothing has changed. She's not in any danger."

"She *works* for them. She has no idea who they are."

"Things have changed. They're getting suspicious. They know something is up. They can feel it." I turn back around to face the phone and clench my teeth as I whisper, "Which is exactly why we need to do this now. If we wait any longer then Carter—"

"If you leave now, you'll save Indie. But Carter will get Wendy instead." Nick pauses for a moment.

I turn and scan the parking lot again. Because I feel it now. I feel the off-ness of this day. "Not if you get him first." I say the words absentmindedly as I scan the streets for that little girl.

She's here. I know she's here.

"That's exactly why I need you, Nathan. Your exit strategy is on hold. I'm texting you the address. I want you in Vicksburg by tonight and I want it taken care of.

Then I will send the jet. And *then* you can leave. I have a truck for you to pick up. Texting the location now."

The call drops and my cell phone buzzes an incoming text in the same moment. How did he even get this number? I bought this new cell at the gas station *last night*.

I slam the payphone into the cradle—"Fuck!"— then pace the little walkway under the thin awning that provides mere inches of shade from the hot summer sun above me.

Back and forth and back and forth. Always looking for people out of place.

You're being paranoid, Nate. This life is finally getting to you. You're gonna start seeing things, and hearing things, and none of it will be real. You're gonna slip right into the insanity, just like all the others.

I pick the phone back up, slide two more quarters down the slot, and take a risk.

She answers on the first ring. But all I hear is breathing.

"Wendy?" I say tentatively.

Silence.

"Something's wrong. I need—"

She hangs up.

I slam the phone back down again. "Fuck!"

I spend the next ten minutes pacing in front of the phone. Always on the lookout for those shadow people my grandfather first told me about as a kid.

He knew what Indie was the very first moment he opened the front door to answer a soft knock and saw her standing there. I remember him telling me, way back when I was eleven or twelve, that she was not really a girl. I didn't believe him. Of course she was a girl. She looked just like a girl to me.

That was back before I started remembering things so I didn't think much of it.

But then Adam came over not long after that. I was chopping wood and my grandfather was too sick to get out of bed. And Adam told me the same thing, just... not as plainly as my grandfather had.

She is not an ordinary girl, Adam had said.

He was trying to tell me she would not be *my* girl.

But it was too late by then. She was already mine. And had been mine since the very first time I saw her in the woods. It just took everyone else a little longer than me to figure that out. Because none of them were there when I *first* met Indie.

None of them except—

The deep, rumbling *waahh-waahh-waahh* of a siren blares from somewhere down the street to my right and then a firetruck goes racing by.

I take a deep breath and try to think about what comes next.

I need Indie. I'm not leaving her behind again. I made dozens of promises to that girl on thousands of days when we were growing up. I promised her I would keep her safe. I promised her I would keep her sane. I promised her that we'd be friends forever.

And where are we now?

Right back where we started from, from what I can tell.

Running in the woods. Running for our lives. Running away from the *men*.

An ambulance siren screams from another direction and I tilt my head a little trying to see around the dollar store.

Fuck.

Fuck.

Fuck!

I run. I run hard and fast. But when I come around the side of the Family Dollar building, I stop dead in my tracks.

The Thunderbird Inn parking lot is filled with police cruisers and fire trucks. And just as all this registers, I see the ambulance skid to a stop near the lobby entrance.

Our hotel door is wide open. Dozens of cops are crowding around it.

And for a moment I can't move. I lose every survival instinct I ever had and I freeze there. Picturing what that little girl did to Beck and Moore.

And then I turn around.

And I run.

RIGHT NOW

I watch McKay and Adam walk away. Follow them with my eyes as they pass the fountain and head back towards the Boucher mansion across from the park.

I want to call out and stop them. Tell them everything. And I almost do. But my phone buzzes in my pocket and I fish it out and press accept. "Yeah."

"What happened?"

I sigh. Rub that spot right between my eyes with two fingers. "They threatened me. Blah, blah, blah—"

"What happened about *Wendy*?"

"I didn't even get that far, Nick. They just... 'We're gonna kill you, you stay away.' Same old shit."

I can feel Nick's anger on the other end of the phone. It comes through like heat. "I gave you one question to ask them. One. Did you ask them anything?"

"I asked about Indie."

"But not Wendy. Did you at least *warn* them?"

"They are not going to believe me. I don't understand why you don't just call up Adam and tell him the truth. He'd listen to you."

"You know goddamn why I can't do that. I'm dead, Nathan."

I practically guffaw. "Please. Everyone knows you're alive."

"They *think* I'm alive. What they know is another story. I don't understand why Wendy will get you papers and passports, but not agree to meet you face to face."

"Because Wendy is fucking smart. She smells it, Nick. She can sniff out betrayal like a bloodhound looking for dead bodies. And she knows what you're doing. OK? You need to lie low—"

"Fuck that."

"Listen," I say. And now I'm growling. "I lost two friends this week because of you. Two very good friends. And she'll go get Indie next. If McKay and Adam are here in Savannah, then that means Indie is at home with—"

"You get me Wendy. I'll get you Indie."

And then he hangs up.

"Fuck!" I want to throw my phone. But people are looking at me now. They saw that confrontation with Adam and hell, fuckin' cops are probably on the way. So I check my anger, shove my phone in my pocket, and decide that if no one is gonna help me save Indie from those sadistic bastards down on the Old Pearl River, then I'll just have to do it myself.

CHAPTER TWENTY-TWO

I halfheartedly log the sound of Indie and Maggie down in the kitchen for a few minutes, trying to process what's happening. The sun is fully up now and when I look at the clock, it's after nine.

I close my eyes and shake my head.

No. No, this isn't happening.

Indie was right about the tape. The questions I recorded didn't play. Or maybe I forgot to press record? That would be a logical explanation.

But then I saw the empty Brevital bottle on the floor.

Empty Brevital bottle.

It was three-quarters full when I took it out of my bag. And there is no way I used three-quarters of a bottle of Brevital. We'd be dead.

That's when I saw the injection marks on my arm. Not one. *Seven.*

Seven injections.
Seven doses.

This would not only explain how a three-quarter bottle of Brevital could turn into an empty bottle, it also explains the time difference.

Did she try to kill me?

And did it record? So she erased the tape?

I did not want to go there. I did not want to fall down into that fucking rabbit hole again. So I pushed it away.

But then I got this urge. This feeling. That I should fast-forward that tape and see if there's anything on there.

And there was.

Me. Talking.

Me answering questions that were never asked. A lot of imagery about running through a forest.

Then there was a pause. And some shuffling. And then I heard Indie.

"Oh, shit. Oh, shit. Donovan?"

But she must've found the recorder still on. Maybe I was holding it?

Because it clicked off and that was the end of that.

"Donovan!"

"What?" I call back.

"Breakfast is ready. Are you coming down or what?"

I get up, leave my room, and stand at the top of the stairs. Indie is looking up at me, smiling. "I made waffles."

"Frozen?" I ask, letting the uneasiness fall away.

"Fuck you. Come on. They're getting cold."

"Oh… Indie?"

"Hmm?" She turns back to me.

"Did we… fall asleep?"

"Yeah. I guess so." She chuckles out her words. "We're not very good at this, are we? But anyway. I don't want to think about that stuff right now. Maggie's excited about our adventure day. And McKay called."

"When?"

"Just a few minutes ago. Checking up on us."

"What'd you tell him?"

She shrugs. "We're fine, right? So that's what I told him."

"When are they coming home?"

"He said this afternoon. So let's hurry. I have a great idea for an adventure and if they get home before we leave, they'll spoil it."

A shiver runs up my spine for some unknown reason.

"Are you coming?"

I nod, then start down the stairs. Indie turns and goes back into the kitchen.

The house is unusually quiet when McKay and Adam leave.

But I like this quiet. I actually need it.

Ever since Carter's card showed up on Maggie's birthday my mind has been anything but quiet.

Adam took it all in stride. He handled that revelation so well, I get the feeling he knew. Like he'd been waiting for this card and so when it finally showed up, he was more relieved than surprised.

Adam knows more than he's saying, that's all I know.

McKay immediately went to over-protective mode. He didn't take his eyes off Maggie and Indie for three days. Finally, Indie told him to back off and stop hovering.

He *was* hovering. He knew he was hovering. But that's just how McKay is.

His offer to leave Old Home and go with Adam on this trip was a surprise. Not an altogether unpleasant one, either. I find McKay's hovering borders on suffocating most of the time.

The idea of being here alone with Indie and Maggie is a little bit exciting and a little bit terrifying.

Exciting because I can't help it, I covet Indie. We have always been close. She's closer to me, in some ways, than she is McKay. I know I wasn't there most of the time during her formative years, but I was her sounding board. She told me all her secrets. Willingly. I didn't need to listen to tapes or sneak peeks into her journal. Not that I ever caught McKay reading her journal when she was younger, but I have always suspected he did.

But it is also slightly terrifying to be here with the girls by myself too. I am not usually home alone with Indie. And I don't think it's because they didn't trust me. I was just never that reliable. Always going here and there. Back and forth. My visits were sporadic. Sometimes short, sometimes long. Never any pattern to them.

Have I *ever* been home alone with Indie and Maggie?

No.

I'm trying to recollect another instance where Indie and I had a whole night together alone, and, disturbingly, the only other time this has happened was when she showed up at my house when she was missing those four years.

I'm sure there were times in years back when I happened to be the only one here with her. There had to be times. But they were short times. Not a whole day. Certainly never a whole night. McKay probably went to the store. Adam was probably on some kind of Company mission.

I might not recollect these times exactly, but there's something else I do remember about them.

Indie's attention wasn't on *me*. It was on Nathan St. James.

If she was bugging me, back in the day, I would send her outside. "Go play with Nate," I would say. And she would disappear into the woods and that would be that.

It occurs to me now that we were very naïve with her. *Go play outside.* Really? In the fucking swamp? Forget the snakes. We focus on them because snakes are just a part of who Indie is. But it's the gators we should've been worried about. There are gators everywhere around here.

She could've been eaten alive. Hundreds of times.

We were, for all intents and purposes, terrible parents.

But she's still here, so…

Downstairs I take a seat at the island and start eating my waffles. They didn't come from a box. But they didn't come from Indie, either. Maggie is the one spooning batter into the waffle iron.

337

I look over at Indie and find her smirking at me. She shrugs. "She likes to cook. Why should I stop her?"

I take another bit of waffle and chew. "So what's the big adventure plan for today?"

"Oh. Yeah. So... Maggie hasn't been up the river yet. You know, for ice cream? I want to take her."

"Take her upriver...?"

"To the river town."

I shake my head. "Does this town have a name?"

Indie crinkles her nose and shrugs. "I don't know. We just call it the river town."

I recall the river town. She has mentioned it during various sessions over the years. But I never did get a name. "Well, how are we supposed to drive there if we don't know which town it is?"

"We don't *drive*, Donovan. We boat."

"Oh." I feel slow today. Off kilter, for some reason. "Yeah, yeah, yeah. OK. I get it. A boat. Right. OK. Fine. We can boat up to the river town to get your swampy ice cream. Even though I'm pretty sure McKay has ice cream in the freezer."

"The ice cream isn't the point, Donovan. The point is the *trip*."

Adam has a bunch of boats. Most of them are small rowboats. But there is one slightly bigger fishing boat with an outboard motor and a twenty-footer that we took to the Gulf for Indie's birthday.

I expect her to head towards that one, but Indie looks at the small fishing boat with longing.

And then I remember something else about boats around here. She's looking at it like that because that's not our boat. It's Nathan's.

"I think we might be driving," I tell her.

But Indie walks over to the boat and starts pushing it through the sand towards the river. "Help me, Mags," she calls over her shoulder.

They are both wearing cut-off denim shorts and tank tops. Sneakers on their feet. And for a moment I get lost in them. They are so alike, Maggie could be Indie.

Except Indie was never that young when she lived here.

When Indie was six she was… in training.

Her file never stated outright where she came from, but kids like her all come from the same place. Give or take an island here or there. They all come from the training centers.

Nick Tate's training center. Before he died. If he's dead.

Or… possibly… Carter's training center. Before he died. If he's dead. Which he isn't, if that birthday card is to be believed.

Of course, that place is gone now. The jungle probably overtook it. I'm fairly certain the CIA and local authorities in the Caribbean never did find those. And all the people who might've had that information are probably dead now. So it's a thing of the past.

I watch the girls get the boat in the water. Then Indie jumps into it, lowers the motor, and pulls on the cord like this boat is an old friend.

To everyone's delight—and surprise—the fucking thing actually turns over. Doesn't even sputter.

Indie beams a smile at me. "Come on. Let's go." She helps Maggie in and points to the little seat near the bow. "That's your seat, Mags. That's where I used to sit when I was a girl."

She's still a girl.

She just doesn't know it.

I get in, almost tipping the little boat, and sit on the bench seat in the middle, letting Indie take care of the driving. Even if I didn't trust her to navigate, I would still let her. Because while I am fairly good at barking directions to the crew on the various Company yachts I've been on, I've never actually learned to sail myself.

Not that navigating this little fishing boat is rocket science. Or sailing for that matter. But Indie has a plan in her mind for this day, so I drop the reins and give her room to run.

Let her take me along for the ride.

Besides, I'm still dwelling on what happened this morning. And the trip upriver is long, and the motor is too loud to actually talk. So the three of us just sit and take in the beauty of the Old Pearl River as it meanders its way north.

We boat for what feels like hours. Even Maggie starts looking over her shoulder at me, wondering where the hell we're going.

Finally, I turn to Indie. "Where the hell is this place?"

"What?" she yells over the sound of the motor. I make a slicing motion across my throat and she cuts the engine. "What?"

"Where is this town, Indie?"

"It's up here somewhere."

I look around.

"There's nothing here," Maggie says.

And she's right. There is literally nothing out here. I'm not familiar with the town on the river. I can't say I even like this part of Louisiana. I prefer New Orleans. But honestly, I prefer LA. I'm not a nature boy like Nathan was. After growing up on an island and relocating to Durham, North Carolina for med school at Duke, I decided, once and for all, I was a spoiled city brat and I'm not even embarrassed to admit that.

But from what I've seen of this trip so far, there is no town upriver.

Like. None. No towns at *all*.

I look at Indie and begin to worry. She's got a confused look on her face.

Maggie looks at me. "Maybe we should go back?"

"Yes. I agree."

"But…" Indie is still looking around. "It has to be here, Donovan. Towns don't just disappear."

No, Indie. They don't.

That town didn't exist any place other than your mind.

By the time we make it back to our shabby little boat house, my phone is buzzing with messages from McKay and Adam, wondering where the fuck we are.

I jump out of the boat and call McKay as Indie and Maggie drag the boat up onto the sand.

"Hey," I say, when Adam picks up. "We're out back on the river. Went for a little boat ride."

"Shit, we've been calling you for like two hours. McKay has his gun out. He was about to go hunt you down."

"Sorry, out of range."

"Everything OK?"

I pause. Then sigh.

"What happened?"

I look over my shoulder and find Indie staring at me, a nervous look on her face. "Nothing. We can talk about it later. Why don't you guys come down here? Wear trunks. Let's beach."

Indie smiles at this idea.

"Let's *beach*?" Adam asks.

"I think I just need a day off, ya know?"

"Dude, I so get it."

"What happened with you two? Get what you were looking for?"

"Yeah. Let's beach. We can talk all this shit out later."

"Fine with me." I end the call and try to force the day's events out of my mind. Try and stop them from making sense.

Because there is only one way these puzzle pieces fit together.

Insanity.

CHAPTER TWENTY-THREE

The truck Nick left me is parked in a garage four blocks away. I head there, because what choice do I have? All that work getting a hold of those passports, gone. I don't even have the cash that Wendy gave back.

It's a ten-hour drive to Vicksburg, Mississippi. But Pearl Springs is only three hours south of there.

I could make it to Vicksburg by seven tonight. Do the job. That's maybe an hour. If it all goes well I could be at Old Home by midnight.

It might be too late. It feels late, anyway. It feels like I'm way behind. I should've never counted on anyone else to save Indie.

They all say they want to save her. Even Adam and McKay. And I almost believe them. But they can't.

Because saving her means they have to walk away.

And they can't let her go. Just like Nick can't let Wendy go.

And now that fucker is trying to take my daughter.

McKay told me something that day Indie almost killed me. He said, *We're not all in this together. It's every man for himself.*

343

And he was right. When it really comes down to it, it's just every man for himself.

Back then I couldn't imagine doing all this on my own. I needed the team. I needed Beck and Moore to have my back and I need Nick to keep an eye on everything while we were busy.

But they're gone. So where the fuck was Nick when this little girl got my friends?

He's using me.

I've known this since the day he faked our deaths and slipped us out of McKay's pocket and into his.

I don't know the full story of Nick and Wendy. She never mentioned his name at all when we were kids. And she won't talk about him now. But whatever it is, it's strong.

And he won't let her go.

Not without a fight.

The address Nick gave me reveals a rustic—but modern—farmhouse with forest-green wood siding and a long, pitched, tin roof that hangs over an open porch held up with thick, raw-wood beams. There is a main section and two small wings off to the side that curve forward slightly, giving the overall impression of a semi-circle.

There are lights on inside. And when I sneak around the perimeter, peering into windows, I see one of the girls Nick was referring to and have to swallow down the bile that threatens to come up.

She *is* Indie.

She is the *spitting fucking image*. And if I didn't know better, I'd call her name. I'd go inside. I'd tell her all my plans and make all my apologies.

But I *do* know better.

They make doubles. Triples. Hell, who knows how many they make these days. It used to be you had to propagate the Company by natural means. But now? Now they just inseminate a teenager and have her pop out twins. Triplets. Whatever they need. Whole *litters* of Company girls are made these days.

I've seen it so many times over the past four years. In so many parts of the world. And a lot of them did look like Indie. But they have a template for them, don't they? They all kinda look alike. The Wendys of the world aren't much different than the Indies, or the Angelicas, or the *Harpers*.

She's the same age as Indie too. Or close enough. Not a teenager. Twenties, at least.

This gives me pause.

I can take one Indie. If I'm prepared. But three of them? Nick said triplets. Three girls like Indie against me?

Nope.

I'm not gonna do it. Fuck that shit. I didn't make it this far, come this close to walking away still alive, just to let one of these freak copies kill me now.

And it's getting late. I need to get to Old Home. That's where the real job is.

I'm just about to walk away, Nick be damned, when a scream echoes inside the house. A bloodcurdling scream that stops me in my tracks. And when I peer back through the window, I catch the tail end of Indie-twin running towards the east side of the house.

I run around, peeking into windows, trying to see where she's going. But it's not until I get all the way to the far side of the east wing that I find all the commotion.

She's sitting on the edge of a bunk built into the side of a wood-paneled wall. It's a large room with two overstuffed couches and two matching chairs arranged into a seating area in the center. There are four bunks built into the wall, two on each side of a set of built-in wooden stairs that gives access to the top bunks.

It's a beautiful room. A beautiful house, from what I can see by peeking in the windows. Very rustic. Fitting for the area, which is a thick, hardwood forest nestled up against the Big Black River.

Everything about this place is custom. Including the three children Indie-twin is comforting.

Three little girls. Triplets. Long blonde hair. Frightened blue eyes.

They are crowded into Indie-twin's lap. And she pets their hair and kisses their heads, comforting them.

Nightmares. We all have them.

But there's something different about these little girls. Something just a little bit… *off*.

They aren't Indie. They are only about four. So I don't know. Maybe that's what Indie looked like when she was four.

Nick lied.

The woman might be Indie. Probably is.

But the little triplets are… Maggie.

They are *Maggie*.

I back away, stumble over a tree root and fall to the ground, then scramble back, into a shadow and under the cover of a shrub, just as the woman comes to the window and peers out.

She grabs the curtains, closes them, and then she's gone.

I'm on my feet, running hard through the woods, trying to get back to the truck—and that's when the memories come rushing in.

CHAPTER TWENTY-FOUR

It's a nice day on the beach even though I can tell Adam, Donovan, and I are all thinking about everything else that's happening to us.

Not that Donovan knows about Nathan. That's not a short conversation because first we have to explain that Nathan isn't dead. And I don't know what's on his mind, because that must be another long twisted road to navigate.

And this day needs to stay simple.

So we beach.

Just thinking the words make me smile.

Because even though we're all thinking about serious shit, Maggie and Indie make the most of their beach day. I'd forgotten how much of a nature girl Indie was as a child. Maggie isn't as rugged as her mother, but she tries hard. And she listens to Indie when she points out things Maggie needs to know. Like the snakes slithering along on top of the water. Or the gators hiding behind the reeds.

We don't let them swim, even though Indie proudly informs us that she and Nathan used to swim down here nearly every day the summer she turned fifteen.

I look at Adam and see the panic on his face. But then he relaxes.

Indie at fifteen—she was in her prime. I feel sorry for any gator that crossed her back then.

It's a nice slow day that makes Nathan St. James seem far, far away even though Indie brings his name up nearly a dozen times over the course of the afternoon.

Part tense. All of them.

And that's where he needs to stay.

Tomorrow we will tell Donovan. And then… I don't know.

I know Adam is worried about Nathan's threat. He talked about it the whole ride home on the jet. Planned out seventy-five ways to kill that boy. But it's all talk. At least for today.

Eventually the sun is hidden behind the trees to the west and we pack up, hungry for dinner.

We barbecue in the pavilion—steaks and corn on the cob—and eat out there too, with the TV blaring cartoons for Maggie as she and Indie lie on their swing and Adam, sitting in a nearby chair, pushes it with his toe every few minutes to make it sway.

Even Donovan relaxes, lying down on the couch opposite the one I prefer with his hands behind his head, pretending to watch cartoons with the rest of us.

Around eight-thirty Indie and Maggie go inside so Maggie can take a bath before bed. Donovan and I start cleaning up the mess we made. Adam wanders inside after the girls, but when we go inside with the dishes, he's in his office with the door closed. Talking on the phone.

"So where did you guys go?" Donovan asks this as I pile our dishes into the sink. They can wait until tomorrow.

"I think we're gonna have a little meeting about it tonight. But I'm pretty sure it can wait until tomorrow like the dishes."

Donovan nods, but stays silent.

"You got something on your mind?"

"Yes. So—"

"Hey!"

We both turn to see Indie walking into the kitchen. "What are you guys talking about? Sharing secrets?"

I see Donovan wince out of the corner of my eye. But Indie has her back to him, looking out the window at the back patio where the pool is.

She tsks her tongue. "I miss the river. We're forever fooling around in that pool. There's nothing cool to see in a pool."

"Yeah." I agree. "Today was fun. We all needed this day."

Especially me. Because once she finds out I lied to her about Nathan, she's gonna hate me. I just know it.

Donovan slaps the countertop. "I'm going to go wash up."

"Well, I'm gonna show McKay my secret room."

I side-eye her. "What secret room?"

She takes my hand. Winks. Smiles. "Come with me, and you'll see." She starts dragging me out of the kitchen and into the long foyer hallway, but instead of heading towards the stairs, she makes a right and we cross the living room. "Join us when you're done, Donovan," she calls over her shoulder. "We'll wait for you. And tell Adam too."

"What's going on?"

She opens the door to the breezeway that leads to the unused part of the mansion and is tugging me through and down the breezeway before she answers. "You, that's what. You and Adam. Did you have a nice romantic getaway?"

I laugh. Loud. "Is that what you think happened last night?"

"Wasn't it?" She stops as we enter the large living room and spreads her hands wide. "Ta-da!"

"What's all this?"

"My secret room. I needed a place for myself since Maggie stole my space."

"Well, shit. I didn't know you felt that way about Maggie taking your room. Why didn't you say something?"

"There was no point. She needed that room. And we only have four bedrooms up there. Unless one of us wanted to go up to the third floor, there was nothing to discuss. And I didn't want to be on the third floor. Do you?"

I picture the musty, hot third floor, trying to imagine it as a bedroom. "Fuck that."

She shrugs. "So I decided to take this side of the house. Now sit. And tell me everything that happened last night."

"What makes you think something happened?"

"Well, if it didn't, your time is up. Because we're doing this tonight, McKay. *All of us.*"

Then she places two hands on my bare chest and pushes me backwards until the back of my knees bump up against the couch. Forcing me to sit.

She climbs into my lap, straddling my legs, and then whips her tank over her head and throws it off to the side. I stare at her face as she takes both my hands and brings them up to her breasts. I can feel her heart beating fast in her chest.

She leans in close, her lips fluttering against mine. "Did you kiss him?" she whispers.

"Yeah."

"Did you like it?"

I nod, then kiss her. She responds. And we tangle our tongues together for a moment.

"Did you do anything else?"

I picture what Adam and I did last night. His lips sealed around my cock as I stared down at him. "He sucked my dick," I say, whispering it. "And before you ask"—I yank her bra down, fondle her breasts—"yes, I liked it."

She leans in to my ear. Nips my earlobe and sends a shudder through my body. "Good. Because we're gonna do it together tonight."

And then she scoots back in my lap and stands up. Releases the clasp of her bra and lets it drop to the floor. Then she slides her shorts and panties over her hips and those drop to the floor too.

She pulls me to my feet and kneels, popping the button on my shorts and dragging them down until my cock springs out. I sit back down and she eases forward between my legs. Her hand already working the shaft of my dick. Her mouth slowly descending onto the tip of my cock. Her lips puckered and her eyes locked with mine.

I put my hand on her head and push her down.

CHAPTER TWENTY-FIVE

Wendy has been ignoring my calls all day. I need to know how Nathan got a hold of her, if she's been in contact with him this whole time, and if she's heard from him since we walked away from the meeting this morning.

I think I know the answers to one of these questions. She has definitely been in contact with him.

I glance down at the bottom drawer of the antique filing cabinet, remembering the packet of secrets I found in my dead brother's grave.

Well, not his grave, obviously.

I'm just opening the drawer to look at the whole thing again—this time in better light—when a soft knock on my office door stops me.

"What?"

"Can I come in?" Donovan peeks his head in without waiting for my permission.

"What's up?"

His eyes dart down to the drawer, slightly ajar, then dart back up to me. "I know you said we'd talk about it tomorrow but—"

"Hey." I put up a hand to stop him, then reach down and grab the plastic packet with the envelopes. "I found this. I think these things belonged to my father. Can you tell me more about these three families?"

Donovan studies the packet in my hand for a few seconds longer than I think is necessary, then reaches for them. "OK." He empties the contents of all the envelopes onto my desk, then pulls one of the chairs forward so he can see it properly. "Machette. They're second-tier. Touchable, but if you wanna kill one of them you better have a good reason. Szabó. Absolute nobodies. And Ameci. Not Company."

"What are you? A fuckin' walking genealogy record?"

"That's what you asked for."

"How do you know all this? I mean, off the top of your head?"

Donovan shrugs with his hands. "Lucky, I guess. So listen—"

"You have to know more. You *have* to. There needs to be a reason that I found these documents in my dead brother's coffin."

"What?"

I walk over to the door, check for eavesdroppers, then close it up. "I know my father was hiding shit. And I have been looking for something like this ever since he died when I was eighteen. Someone sent me a clue the other day."

"Who?"

"Well, Wendy was the one—"

"Wendy? Wendy, as in Wendy—"

"Yes."

"Damn. That girl is still around?"

"Never mind that. She came into the possession of a note for me. And it was like a riddle. A riddle that Maggie, correctly, deduced meant something was buried in a cemetery. So we went out—Maggie and I—and dug it up."

"What the fuck are you talking about? You made Maggie help you rob a grave?"

"We weren't robbing it."

"You just told me—"

"It's my fucking brother. If I want something inside his coffin, I'm gonna go take it."

"Graverobber!"

I sigh. "I'm tired, Donovan. I've had a fuckin' day, OK?"

"You've had a day? I've had a fuckin' day!"

"Details, Donovan. I need details. Do you have any on these people, or not?"

He looks at me for a moment like he's got something on his mind. But his problems can wait. Something is definitely happening. Like… right now. Under my feet or over my head. I can't see it, or hear it, but I sure as fuck can feel it.

"I feel like I'm missing something, Donovan. And whatever it is, it's very important. No one knew I had this obsession with my father's missing secrets. No one except Maggie. And I know she didn't tell anyone. So why does this message show up on the very day that McKay gets a call from someone who should be dead and—"

"Who?"

"That's a whole other conversation, OK? Just… do you *know* anything?"

357

He sighs. Picks up the passports and papers again. Shuffles through the death certificates. "Well, I guess they might have a connection. On first glance, no. They're in totally different classes, genetically speaking. Ameci was a family we used when we needed new blood, but didn't want to add a new family to the roster. We just used them as breeders with the Tate men. But that was a long time ago. This Sidonia, though, she was second generation. So she technically *was* Company. Full blood. Through and through. But she had red hair, so they didn't want to use her for the program and just left her alone."

"All this off the top of your head? What kind of freak are you?"

He looks up at me, hurt.

"Donovan, I'm fucking kidding."

He frowns at me for a few extra seconds, then says, "Oh." But the frown remains.

"Sorry, dude. I didn't think... you're not a freak. OK? Anything else?"

"Szabó." He squints his eyes. Like he's thinking. "I'm not sure about this one. I know the name, of course. But they were workers. I'm fairly certain that no one ever used them for breeding stock. They worked—" He pauses, kinda stares off into nothingness.

"They worked where?"

"Snake Island." He picks up Mallory's passport. Studies her picture. "They ran..."

"They ran *what*, Donovan?"

"The hunts. They were huntmasters."

"Huntmasters for...?"

"Hunts."

"Obviously, Donovan. Jesus Christ. What's going on—"

"She was the foundation mare."

"What?"

He holds the Mallory passport out. "Sorry. That's a little breeder inside joke. Kinda tasteless, I do admit. But... Mallory Machette. She was the very first *zero*."

I grab the passport and study her picture again. "She's not blonde, though. She's got dark hair. She can't be a zero."

"No. They bred in the blonde hair and blue eyes over several generations using Tate men."

"Huh." I have to admit, it's a little bit fascinating. Also... more than a little bit sick. "So why did my father have this shit? And why hide it in an empty grave? And why did someone want me to find it *now*? And where the fuck is my *dead brother?*"

Donovan stares at me for a few moments. "Someone's playing with you."

"Who?"

"Please, Adam. We both know who."

"But why is Carter all up in my business lately? I mean, what the actual fuck is he *doing*?"

Donovan's eyes go blank for a second. And they stay that way for more seconds than I am comfortable with. "Donovan?"

He blinks and looks at me. "What?"

"OK. Listen." I sigh and run my fingers through my hair. "I think we've all had a long day. I'm ready to turn in. Who is Indie sleeping with tonight? I've lost track."

"Everyone."

"What?"

"She's waiting for us on the other side of the house. I saw her take McKay that way."

I look at the door, not understanding anything in this moment. "The other side of the house?"

"Come on, I'll show you."

I follow him into the living room and immediately spy the open door that leads to the side of the mansion we never use.

We're only halfway down the breezeway leading into the great room when I hear McKay and Indie.

And then there they are. McKay, sitting on the couch with Indie kneeling between his knees. Her head in his lap. Bobbing—

"Fuck," McKay moans, grabbing her hair with both hands.

"What the hell is going on?"

Indie doesn't turn. McKay barely opens his eyes. Donovan is already crossing the room, unbuttoning his pants as he walks. He stops and drops them to the floor, then starts fisting his cock as he watches Indie and McKay.

Indie stops and peeks over her shoulder at me. "Don't forget to close the door on your way in."

I shut the door without thinking, then cautiously walk towards them.

There are a thousand reasons why we should not do this tonight, and only one why we should.

Any logical person with half a brain could predict what will come of this, even if they didn't have the history we have between us. Three men—even three men like us, totally devoted to this girl since she was a child—is never gonna work.

And is it ironic or just a bad omen that I'm the only one thinking rationally about it?

Donovan is sitting next to McKay on the couch now, rubbing his leg, leaning in to him. I watch them kiss with a sort of… indescribable detachment. But then Donovan stops and looks at me. The hesitation he was displaying in my office just two minutes ago is gone now. "Come on," he says. "This is how it's supposed to be."

Is it? Is it really?

It's not jealousy, either. I'm not jealous of either of them being with Indie. I'm not even jealous of Donovan and McKay being together because I know he would pick me over Donovan any day of the week. And I'm not even disagreeing. We knew from day one we'd end up here. It was inevitable.

But it's just… something feels so *wrong* about this right now.

The timing?

The room?

The people?

I'm not sure.

Indie scoots over and then she's kneeling in front of Donovan. I catch McKay's eye as he gets to his feet and walks towards me. Naked. His long, hard dick swinging between his legs. A grin on his face. He pushes me, two hands on my shoulders, hard enough to force me to take a step back.

"Did she drug you?" I ask it because… I don't know. We had our first kiss a day and a half ago. We spent our first night together last night. And now, we're here?

"No." McKay laughs. He pushes me again and I run out of room. And then McKay's hands press flat against the wall on either side of my head. Boxing me in. He leans into me, pressing his bare chest up against mine.

He kisses me. But I hesitate. I'm just so certain that there's something going on here that I'm missing, I can't shake the feeling.

"I thought you wanted this?" McKay whispers.

"I do."

"Then what's the problem?"

"Is Indie—"

"She's fine. We're all fine."

"McKay, we need to talk about what happened today." I say it quietly so Indie can't hear us. "If she—"

"Shut up, Adam. It's late. We're all here. Finally, on the same page. We've got time for that tomorrow."

"But do you agree, you think she should know?"

"She will." He pulls back and looks me in the eye. "I promise. We'll tell her. But not tonight. We've earned this moment. We put in fourteen long years, Adam. We've been through everything together and we're still here. We made it. Why can't we enjoy it for just one night?"

"Are you guys gonna have your own private party over there?"

I look over McKay's shoulder at Indie. She's smiling at me. She was always a pretty girl, but tonight she looks downright beautiful, her face and shoulders kissed by the sun she got on the river today, her blonde hair bleached a little lighter than it normally is in the winter. And she looks happy. It's been so long since I've seen Indie truly happy. Years. Maybe… never?

"Well?" McKay is impatient.

I've always wanted her to be happy. I did try my best, it was just never enough. But I can make her happy tonight. Give her this control over us. Let her know I love her, because I do. I really do love this girl. She was my first. The very first girl I ever cared this much for. The only one, until Maggie came, who filled my thoughts even when she wasn't around.

I made a lot of mistakes. I don't deny it. Pretty much everything I did with her, to her, for her—it was wrong on many levels.

But it saved her. Nathan St. James was wrong this morning. He wasn't the one who saved her, I was.

I was.

I look at McKay and nod. "OK."

And then he kisses me. It's longer this time. Harder. More urgent and erotic.

After all these years, after all that indecision. Here he is. Giving me exactly what I asked for.

I push him off me. His head juts back in surprise. But I just grin at him. "Are we gonna stand over here and be antisocial? Or are we gonna join them?"

McKay chuckles. "Let's go."

He follows me over to Donovan and Indie, but when I make to sit down, he grabs the belt loop of my shorts and slips his hand inside.

I draw in a quick hiss of breath as his hand wraps around my growing cock and begins to pump it. Gripping it hard as he kisses me. I pop the button on my shorts and drag the zipper down to give him better access, then let them drop to the floor.

He pulls back for just a moment. Our eyes meet and then I'm all in.

Fuck it. If we get one perfect night, I'm not gonna waste it.

I grab his hand and place it on my cock the way I did this morning.

Jesus Christ. Was that just this morning?

He takes my hand and does the same. So we are jerking each other off.

Then Donovan is next to us. He takes my other hand and places it over his, which is tugging on his cock.

A circle jerk.

Indie slips under McKay's arm and positions herself in the center, watching our hands on our cocks. Her face lifts up, looking at each of us in turn, and she smiles. "I don't even know what to do," she whispers.

But Donovan does. He grabs her hair. Not hard. And he doesn't tug. But he guides her towards him. I shoot a look over at McKay and find a look on his face that is something between fascination and lust.

He catches my eye and nods. Then he's reaching for me. Leaning in to me. Kissing me. Donovan lets go of his cock, so I let go too. And then he's walking backwards, Indie following him on her knees, until he reaches the couch and sits down.

McKay and I watch as Indie takes Donovan's cock in her hand and begins to slowly stroke him. I walk over to the couch and take a seat on the far side, my body angled so I can watch Indie as she takes his cock deep into her mouth. McKay sits between us, slumped down into the cushions, but his eyes are on me.

"Indie," I say. Her eyes dart to mine. "Come here." I beckon her with two fingers and she stands up and positions herself in front of me. But I shake my head and point to McKay's lap.

Indie glances at Donovan, then McKay. And then she does as she's told and straddles McKay's lap and begins stroking his cock. I reach between her legs and find her pussy wet. She sucks in a long breath of air when my fingertips hit her clit.

Donovan is standing now. Then he kneels behind Indie and places the palm of his hand between her shoulders and pushes her down onto McKay's chest. And then he traces two fingers down her spine, his eyes locked on me now, and slips them between her ass cheeks.

They push against mine, not fighting over who gets to finger her, but... sharing. He chuckles a little. Very at ease with what's happening here. And I take a moment to wonder how many times he's done this.

But then McKay's hand reaches over for my cock and begins to jerk and tug on me. "Put me inside her," he says, his voice low and throaty, his desire clear.

Indie lifts up her hips and Donovan's fingers back off as I grip McKay's cock tight and place it at her entrance.

She sinks down on him, moaning. And I know we've done this before. Once. But I barely remember it. The drugs were thick. Acting like a hazy curtain hiding reality. This time everything is 4K Ultra clear and I know I won't be losing any time or forgetting any moments of this night.

Indie begins to rock and writhe in McKay's lap, kissing his mouth with such tenderness, I get lost in it for a moment.

Donovan bends down again. He spreads Indie's ass cheeks and licks her, pressing his finger against her asshole. And for a moment my heart beats too fast, because I know what he's going to do.

"Donovan," I say, objecting.

But he puts a single finger up to his lips and says, "Shh. She's OK." And then he's pressing the tip of his cock against the tight pucker.

Indie gasps, her hand reaching for my shoulder and gripping it tight. So tight her fingernails dig into my skin and I'm just about ready to object again when her face relaxes and I realize Donovan is inside her.

She thrusts her hips back, asking Donovan to take her deeper, and suddenly McKay is moaning. Slinking down further into the couch so he's almost horizontal. And then he wraps both his arms around her and holds her as close to his chest as he possibly can.

They move together like one. And I angle myself into the corner a little more, trying to take it all in. Trying to see everything at once.

Because. *Fuck.* That's hot.

Indie is looking into McKay's eyes. She's kissing him, but it's an afterthought. Like she just needs to do something with her mouth.

I stand up, then step up onto the couch and straddle the back, inching forward until my cock is right next to McKay's cheek. Indie smiles up at me and takes my cock in her hand, guiding it towards her mouth like this is exactly what she needs.

Donovan begins to pound her hard from behind. So with each thrust her mouth slips a little further down my shaft.

And then I meet McKay's eyes and all my reservations disappear. I need him. I have always needed him, but right now, I can't imagine living without this man. He is my best friend. He is my conscience. He is the one who has always had my back. And now he is my lover.

I place my hand on McKay's head, gripping his hair tight in my fist. And then, without any more prodding from me, two things happen at the same time. Indie lets my cock slip out from between her lips and McKay turns his head. And then his mouth is there. And the moment I slide inside him, and feel his tongue press against my shaft while his lips seal around my head—I feel like all the mysteries of the universe are revealed. All the answers are in front of me. And every single one of them begins and ends with Core McKay.

I inch forward on the back of the couch. Get as close to McKay as I possibly can. I hold his head in my hands. Hugging him. Desperately wanting him to understand how deep this love goes. Indie presses her forehead against his cheek, so close I can feel her ragged, panting breaths. Her hand comes up to cup my balls and then she gasps a little.

I look down and realize that McKay is fingering her clit as she glides her hips across his lower abdomen. Donovan leans over, grabs her tits with both hands, and then... I don't know. I can't articulate anything.

We become something other.

Something more.

367

Something new.

Indie's back arches, and Donovan grabs her hair, pulling her head back so he can lean over and kiss her mouth.

She pants hard. And then she goes still and I know she's close.

McKay moans, maybe feeling her pussy contracting around him. And this moan creates a vibration against my cock, and then I'm moaning and pushing McKay's head down.

Indie squeals and stiffens. Donovan slaps her ass with his free hand, still yanking on her hair. And it cracks into the still quiet of the room.

McKay grabs Indie's breasts and squeezes them and then… everything happens at once.

Donovan pulls out and spills his release all over Indie's ass.

McKay looks up towards the ceiling and closes his eyes. I pull my cock out of his mouth and he grits his teeth as he spills himself inside Indie.

Indie presses her head against McKay's chest, muttering, "Fuck. Holy shit. Holy fuck," in a sexy whisper as her whole body quivers.

And then I pump my dick a few times and explode all over her back.

CHAPTER TWENTY-SIX

TWENTY YEARS AGO

I can hear them all in the woods.

Small feet. Some running. Some not.

Loud voices. Some crying. Some not.

Some acting their age. Some not.

Those who do act their age will die tonight. Not right away. There is a ritual to perform. But they will be dead by morning.

So you hide first, Nathan. You hide in the river and let all the others run.

You do not cry.

You do not scream.

And you do. Not. Watch.

These are all my grandfather's words. But he has repeated them so many times over the last week, they are stuck in my head with nowhere to go. They echo around inside me.

He made me practice that. Every day, at least twice. Because before he came to the island to visit me, I only knew how to count to twenty. But it's not that hard. He said, "Numbers have a pattern. And you just follow the pattern. Everything has a pattern. And if you know what it is, you will always win, Nathan. This is a cheat. And I'm sorry to say this, son, but you were born into a world where the only way to win is to *cheat*. I'm here to help you cheat."

So I ran right to the river. Just like he told me.

Then I got in. Got cold. Started shivering. And I listened.

"You wait there," he said. "You wait there and do not leave the river. You're gonna get very cold, Nathan. Your body will go numb. But cold and numb is better than dead every day of the week." Then he took my face in both hands and stared into my eyes. His are blue, almost silver, like mine. And he said, "I'm counting on you. I need you to *live*, do you hear me?"

And I nodded yes.

So that's what I'm doing. I'm waiting. I'm cold and numb already and I've only been here for a few minutes.

I listen to lots of things.

The little kids screaming and crying.

The hunters, with their heavy boots, chasing them. Making them cry harder.

A few cracks of rifles.

"Darts," my grandfather said. "They're just darts. The killing will come later."

I hear all that. Plus the chattering of my own teeth.

And then I hear something else.

"*Fuck. You!*"

I peek my head up, my whole body shaking so hard from cold that this new air feels hot across my chest.

It's not a man cursing. It's a little girl.

I get up out of the water and run up the muddy embankment. She's blonde, but we're all blond. So I shouldn't know which little girl she is.

But I *do* know.

She's standing in the middle of a well-worn dirt path. Her white dress is filthy, but there's a moon out, so it still looks pretty.

"Indie!" I whisper-hiss. "What are you doing?"

She looks at me, her face contorted in a fit of childhood anger. "Fuck them! I'm *not* running! I'm *not* afraid!"

She's wiry and small even though we're the same age. "She's a troublemaker," my grandfather said the first day he arrived on the island. "Stay away from that one. She's not gonna make it. She will let them catch her just to be defiant."

I blink at her a couple times. Then I scramble out onto the dirt path and take her hand. I jerk her into the thick jungle shrubbery and she fights me, so we end up tumbling down the embankment and splashing into the river.

"Let me go!" She screams it.

My heart thumps in my chest. Because the other rule was, "Don't say nothing, Nathan. Don't cry, or talk, or scream. Or they will find you." And then he shook me by the shoulders. "Do you hear me?"

I nodded.

But Indie must not've gotten this cheat. So I cup my hand over her mouth. Tight. She's a fighter. Real tough for a girl who is barely five. But I am taller. And heavier. And I like her. I would like her to live. Maybe my grandfather will take her home too?

So I wrestle her, pinning her underneath me in the cold river water. She gasps for air, and swallows water, and starts to cough.

But I do not take my hand away from her mouth.

I lean down in to her ear and whisper, "If you stay still and quiet, I'll help you cheat, Indie. I'm leaving. My grandfather is taking me away from here and if you stay still and quiet, I'll take you with me."

Then she went still and her eyes closed. And I knew something was wrong. So I let go of her. But she didn't move, or cry, or scream or do anything.

So I just stared down at her face as it turned blue.

And then I slapped her.

Because I'm scared. I don't want to do this. I don't want to be caught. And I don't want to be alone.

I slap her again and this time she coughs. Weakly. And water comes up out of her mouth. Her face isn't blue anymore. But she's still quiet, and her eyes are still closed.

I hear small feet crashing in the brush on the top of the embankment and I hunker down on top of Indie, trying to flatten myself into the water. It's a shallow river. But the water splashes up over Indie's face every now and then. I cup my hands around the side of her mouth so the water can't get in.

And I listen.

The little kid up above us is walking slowly now. Hardly making any noise. Then there's a great crashing through the underbrush and a scream.

A girl. It's a little girl, just like the one underneath me. Except that one up top doesn't have enough fight in her. She's not gonna make it.

The crack of the rifle makes me jump and I let out a whimper before I can stop myself.

Something thumps up top on the embankment. And then boots in the underbrush. Crashing through the leafy shrubs.

The little girl is dragged away. And then I hear the hunter call, "Number seven! Over here! I got number seven!"

I know who that voice belongs to.

But for some reason, even though my grandfather warned me not to leave the river because the river makes me cold and they can't see cold, they can only see heat, I need to see him. I need to burn that face into my brain.

I need to know who my enemies are.

So I leave Indie in the river and carefully crawl back up the embankment, slipping on the muddy earth. But there's a lot of commotion now. Lot of kids screaming in the jungle. More cracks of the rifles shooting darts at them. More running boots.

And when I get to the top I hide behind the broad leaves of a shrub until the boy comes into view.

He's not like the other hunters.

He's the worst of them.

His dark hair and dark eyes are a clear contrast to the rest of us who are all light.

Carter.

He is *Carter.*

My grandfather said, "If that dark one even gets close to you? You run, Nathan. You run and you do not stop until you get to the beach and have nowhere else to go."

373

So I wait for more kids to get caught. I wait for more noise to cover me.

And then, when I think it's safe, I *run*.

I'm standing in front of the house where the nest of girls live. Right by a stone structure that acts as a mailbox when the memory fades. I open the mailbox and shove my hand in, not expecting much, so I'm surprised when I pull out a stack of mail.

My truck is still down the road a piece, so I don't stop to look at it. Just take it with me. And when I reach the truck, I throw the mail on the passenger seat and leave, heading south towards Old Home.

Because even though I don't owe her, I still *owe* her.

I'm not leaving Indie Anna Accorsi in the fucking river while I run away like a coward.

I've come too far, I've done too much, I've lost so many people... it has to *mean* something.

I will *not* leave her behind again.

CHAPTER TWENTY-SEVEN

I dream of her funeral.

It was as unorthodox as a funeral can get, but it was fitting too. She wouldn't have wanted people to cry, she would've wanted them to celebrate. She really believed that this plane we were all living on was just a temporary phase before we transition into something else.

Something bigger.

Something better.

That's why I was wearing a tux when McKay's call came in.

The day Indie Anna Accorsi decided to come back into our lives I was at Ana Avery's funeral.

I know what I said. I know. I was there.

I told her, "No, thanks. I don't need the help. I need to do this myself."

Because I knew what would happen if she got my secrets. I knew.

This is what would happen.

Her funeral.

Which was a grand black and white affair up in the Ten Sleep, Wyoming, Healing Center. A charity event, because that's the kind of woman she was.

Ana Avery was the real fucking deal.

Kind. Pretty. Generous. Compassionate.

People like her don't *cheat*.

People like her *die*.

With *integrity*.

I don't realize I'm awake until Indie squirms on top of me and shifts position, sliding off the side of my chest and turning over. Her face pressed into the pillow. Her breathing deep and even.

We're in one of the bedrooms along the breezeway that leads to the great room. McKay and Adam are in the one next door.

Everything smells a little musty in here, but we didn't care. It had been a long day for everyone. I don't know what happened on McKay and Adam's trip. Something, obviously. Because Adam looked wrung out when we were in his office.

But I know what happened on my day.

There is no river town.

Those things Indie wrote in that journal about the river town never happened.

And if that didn't happen, what else didn't happen?

Was any of it real?

Hell, I'm starting to believe none of it was real. Not this house, not these people, not the swamp outside, or the boy who lived in a cottage across the duck lake that is no longer there.

And there was never a Carter, was there?

He wasn't real, was he?

Ana tried to tell me so many times that I just made him up. But it's not true. It would be very comforting and convenient to think that all this shit that has happened to us was just a dream or an illusion.

But it's not.

Indie really was bought at an auction. We really did send her on missions to clean things up for the Company. There really is a Company—still is a Company. And Adam is running it. Or maybe Nick? Or maybe someone else. Maybe Carter?

Carter *is* real. And he's close. I can *feel* him.

I slip my arms around Indie and hug her. But it's not Indie I'm hugging. It's Ana.

She was my world for four years. Four beautiful, peaceful, blissful years.

I never actually left her healing center. We settled down in that cabin and fucked. We ate. And laughed. And had afternoon tea.

Of course, I did go back to LA all the time. But LA was never my home. Old Home was never my home either. Hell, my actual home wasn't even my home.

That cabin in the woods with Ana Avery, that was the only place I ever felt at home.

I pet Indie's hair. But my eyes are closed, so I imagine I'm petting Ana instead.

I miss her so damn much. And if I could make a trade—come up with some… *sacrifice* to give to the fucked-up gods running this place—I would give anything. I would trade *anything* to be with Ana again.

Sometimes when I think about her, I want to cry.

But we don't cry.

That's what Ana's will said. *There will be no crying at my funeral.*

We don't ever cry.

We only *celebrate.*

I get up and go out into the great room, looking for my shorts. I'm not tired and I doubt I'll get any more sleep tonight. I'm just about to turn around and go into the kitchen to make a snack when I see a flash of movement through the long wall of French doors that open into the neglected back gardens.

Someone is here.

I can't go through these doors. The alarms will wake up the whole fucking forest. I go back to the other side of the house, disarm the security system with my master passcode, and slip outside, closing the door behind me.

I stand on the porch for a moment. Listening. Waiting.

And then I hear it. Someone is walking through the trees off to the right. "Hello?" I call. "If there's anyone out there, you better get the fuck out of here."

I walk down the porch steps, stop at the bottom to listen and look, and hear it again. "I'm fucking warning you. I have a gun and I will blow your fucking head off."

And then he steps out of the woods.

And I almost lose my breath. "*Carter?*"

CHAPTER TWENTY-EIGHT

I feel Donovan get out of bed, but I'm so comfortable, I don't care. My dreams are sweet for once. Filled with love and warmth. I half remember the night before. The sex, yes. But afterward too. Because we all sank into that couch like a heap of best friends, and then Donovan cracked a joke, and we were all laughing.

It felt like... finally. *Finally* this is right.

This is who we are and where we belong.

And it's real. It's something that *lasts*.

I let myself replay it all in my head again. The whole day. Even though it started out confusing, it ended just perfect. The whole afternoon on the river was fun. Sitting in the sun, and just enjoying each other.

We've never done that before. Life before today has always felt like a struggle.

And then, all of a sudden—it's easy.

Just easy.

I hear some noise coming from the other side of the house. The sound of the front door opening and closing.

379

I sigh, forcing my eyes open. I should go see what's bothering Donovan. He would do the same for me if I was the one wandering the halls of Old Home. So I get up, find my clothes in the great room, and walk quickly down the breezeway, stopping for a just a moment to push open the mostly closed door of the other bedroom where Adam and McKay fell asleep.

They are both face down. Hugging pillows. Bare backs and asses. Breathing heavy and deep. Which makes me stifle a laugh.

I close the door back up, leaving it slightly ajar, and pad down the breezeway to the living room. "Donovan?" I whisper-yell it. But there's no answer. I check the kitchen real fast and I'm just about to go upstairs when I glance out the living room window and see him disappearing into the woods.

"Donovan?" I say it, even though he obviously can't hear me.

I jog to the front door and go out onto the porch, jumping down the front steps as I scan the woods. "Donovan!" One more whisper-yell for good measure.

But he's gone.

I look back at the house. Should I go get Adam and McKay? But then I hear crackling in the woods. Like tree branches breaking. And it's not far off. I know these woods by heart, and I'm not afraid of the dark. But we do have a creepy stalker called Carter. So I duck back into the house real fast and grab a gun from the top shelf of the hall closet, and then leave the house and head towards the woods.

There are two paths over on this side. One of them is a winding, overgrown trail that will eventually lead you around the duck lake and the other is well-worn and follows the river a little way and then eventually ends on the embankment of a shallow canal.

I choose the well-worn one along the river, walking deeper and deeper into the forest. Then I pause, hearing some shuffling. Which is faint, but it's also far away. So it must actually be loud.

"Donovan!" I scream it. Not caring about stealth anymore. "Where are you? What are you doing?"

Then I hear a scream.

I stand there in shock, my feet stuck in place as I process that scream.

Because it's Maggie.

"Donovan!" I yell again. And then I'm running. Running fast and hard. Branches and leaves slapping me in the face as I push my way through them.

My toe hits a rock and I fall forward, reaching out with the palms of my hands to break my fall, but there's nothing there but air and I tumble, head-first, down the embankment and hit my head on a rock in the shallow river.

It's a hard hit. The kind that stuns you into a state of *unthinking.*

Dirty swamp water pours into my mouth and I cough and turn over, just as my eyes close and everything disappears.

CHAPTER TWENTY-NINE

I didn't stop driving until I reached the road that used to be my driveway once upon a time. And then I cut the engine and left the truck on the side of the road.

It was a long, three-hour drive to get here, and even though I haven't slept in days, my eyes are wide open. Literally and figuratively.

The pile of mail I stole was mostly junk. But there were two interesting pieces, neither of which solved any big mystery for me. I've always known what I was up against. But I'm sure Adam and McKay will both find this to be very interesting.

The first letter is an electric bill and the second is from Duke University Medical School Alumni Association.

Both of them are addressed to Dr. *Carter* Couture.

He has been running this show from the very beginning. And everyone but me fell for it.

I guess that's not really fair. I *knew* him. I *saw* him that night in the woods on the island. And if I didn't get picked up on the beach the following morning, and if I didn't get taken off that island and brought to the little cottage adjacent to Old Home, and if I *didn't* have a grandfather called Nikos Szabó who came from a long line of Company huntmasters and told me everything about Carter Couture the very day that Indie Anna Accorsi appeared on my river, then I would be just as *fucked* as Adam and McKay.

But I'm not.

I am running down my old driveway when I see Indie walk out of the house and head towards the woods. I want to scream her name. Make this stop. But he can't know I'm coming. This secret—it's the only thing I have left to hold over his head.

So I slow down. Be very quiet. And slip right back in to the boy I used to be.

I am not five years old anymore.

I am not afraid.

And I will make sure that Carter Couture never walks out of this forest alive.

And that's when I see *him*.

A bare-chested man carrying someone small in his arms as he makes his way through the woods in the direction of the firefly treehouse I built for Indie's first kiss all those years ago.

When I look back towards Old Home, Indie has disappeared inside the dark, swampy woods.

CHAPTER THIRTY

I roll over and sit straight up in bed, *knowing* something is wrong.

"What the fuck?" Adam turns over on his back. "What are you doing?"

"Shhh." We're both silent for a moment.

"What?" Adam whispers.

"Do you feel that?"

"Feel what?"

"Warm air." I look up at the AC vent. I can hear it. And I feel the cold air too. But there's another current in the house coming from the partly open door that leads to the breezeway. It's hot and humid.

"Shit." Adam and I do everything in sync. We say this word. We jump out of bed. I push the door open because I get there first, and we stand there, naked, in the breezeway.

Adam yells, "Where the fuck are my clothes?"

And then everything about him goes fast and everything about me slows down.

He's already in the great room as I stare down the breezeway at the open door that leads to the living room. The front door is open. That's where the heat is coming from.

Adam comes back wearing shorts. He thrusts mine at me, then pushes past. Heading towards the living room.

And that's when I see Nathan St. James running into our woods through the breezeway windows. It's like a bad case of *Groundhog Day*. Indie's twentieth birthday. Nathan St. James looking down at us with nothing but disgust on his face. Our worlds colliding and then spinning out of control.

No. Fuck that. No way. I'm not doing this again. I just got all my people back where I need them. Right here, next to me. And just... *fuck that*!

"Maggie!" I yell. "Find Maggie!"

I pull my shorts on and by the time I make it to the stairs, Adam is already standing at the top, looking down at me. "She's gone."

"Nathan has her! I saw him running into the woods!"

Adam practically jumps down the entire flight of stairs. Then he swings on the bannister to go around the little curve at the bottom and lands next to me as I reach for the gun we hide on the top shelf of the hallway closet.

It's not there.

"Fuck the gun. I'm gonna kill that little fucker with my bare hands right now."

We go outside together, jump down the porch steps barefoot, and then take off into the woods.

CHAPTER THIRTY-ONE

Indie

The sound of Carter's far-off laughter wakes me. I don't move. Just lie real still and wait for the screams. Because anytime anyone laughs on the island, screams always come next.

There they are, I say to myself when the screams echo through the jungle. And this makes me feel smart, even though they tell me every day that I'm too stupid to live.

But who's the stupid one now? Hmm? Not me. I'm smart because I'm still alive.

Then I remember the boy with the blond-blond hair and the light-light eyes and I lift my head up a little to look for him but all I see are blinking dots. It takes me a moment to realize they are fireflies. And then I allow myself a few more seconds to wonder how such pretty things could live in my nightmares.

The boy.

I don't know his name. He wouldn't tell me, even though I told him mine. He said someone smart ordered him to keep it a secret. That's probably a lie. Almost everything people say on the island is a lie.

Like what they told us before the hunt started. *Just run. Run as fast as you can and you'll be fine.*

Lie. Nothing was fine. And everybody ran. Even I ran. But not for the same reasons as the other kids. I did want to get away from the hunters, but I wanted to get away from the other kids more.

I know how to handle the hunters. The kids were the ones gonna get me killed.

But then I stopped. They like it when you run because it makes your blood pump chemicals. Donovan told me that. They want that chemical inside you when you die. That's why they like us to cry.

And that's why I don't cry.

That's why I'm not afraid of nothing.

Nothing.

So I stopped in the woods. I stopped running. And I screamed their ugly words back at them, daring them to kill me. Because I would show them. I would die unafraid and they would get *nothing* from me.

Then the boy with the blond-blond hair and the light-light eyes was there. Dragging me down into this little river.

Yup. Now I remember. That's how I got here in the river.

I think he was trying to be nice even though I couldn't breathe when his hand was on my mouth.

I'm shivering. Freezing cold. And I should get up and go somewhere else.

But I'm having second thoughts about staying alive.

Donovan said it only gets worse from here. He said, "Indie, it's gonna be bad." I like the way he talks.

It's a special way of talking. And his words make me want to believe him.

Not like Carter. He talks like me. His words are just regular and stupid. And he always lies. His words come out and I know right away who's speaking. The liar.

They look alike. Almost exactly alike. But they are nothing alike.

Donovan is good and sweet and brings me little cakes he steals from his grandfather's afternoon tea. He wraps them in pretty cloth napkins and sneaks them under my pillow so that after the house mother turns off the lights, I can eat them and no one even knows.

And he brought me a present for my birthday. I didn't even know it was my birthday. I didn't even know what a birthday was until Donovan told me. He said I was five. Five whole years old. And that was special because when the kids on the island turned five, we had to do new things like run in the woods. And Donovan said he was going to help me. He couldn't help everyone, he said. They would notice. So I was special because he picked me to help this year. I was his special friend, he said.

But I could not tell Carter. Not even one word of this could get back to Carter because he would tell and then Donovan might be killed too.

I didn't want to imagine life without Donovan. He was my only friend. And he told me all the secrets. If I didn't have Donovan then I would have no one.

But then that boy with the blond-blond hair and the light-light eyes was here. And maybe he would be my friend too?

I wonder where he is?

I sit up in the water and look for him. Really look this time.

Nope. He's gone.

And I can still hear Carter. Still laughing. Whoever he caught is still screaming too. He's not close, but he's not far, either.

So I just close my eyes and let the cold water flow over me.

Some time after that I stop shivering. Just go numb. And then the next thing I know, someone is picking me up. They carry me back to the bunkhouse and put me in my bed.

The shivering comes back. The pain too. But there are no screams so I sleep.

I sleep for a very long time.

And when I wake up, all the beds around me are empty. Stripped down to the bare mattress like it's sheet-changing day. Only there are no kids in here either.

It's just me.

Donovan never comes back. So neither does Carter.

I'm glad Carter is gone, but I miss Donovan terribly.

And even though I didn't like the other kids, I miss them.

And then I think about the little blond-blond boy and miss him too. He got out. He got away, just like he said he would.

Why didn't he take me with him?

"Indie?" Someone is shaking me. "Indie, can you hear me?"

These words are very soft.

And then I smile. Because I recognize his voice. "You came back."

"I came back." He pulls me up into him and that's when I realize he's not a little boy.

He's Nathan. *My* Nathan.

I open my eyes and almost scream, but his hand covers my mouth to stop it. "Shh," he says. "Carter's here."

I shake my head quick and fast, say, "No," into his tight palm.

"Carter. Is. Here." Nathan stares down into my eyes.

I grip his hand and pull it off my mouth with such force, I take him by surprise. "You're dead!" I hiss.

"I'm not dead."

"I killed you!"

"You didn't kill me. McKay saved me."

"What?"

He cups his hand over my mouth again. "Shhhhhhhhhhhh! Carter is here, Indie. He came for you. But I'm not gonna let him get you. Not this time."

I pry his hand off one more time. "You *left* me! You left me there! You left me in the freezing cold river and you got out!"

"I was five years old!"

I feel the tears welling up in my eyes, the pain in my heart as I think about how he got away and I didn't. About how he had five extra years here—right here! On this very river!—while I was taken and... "Oh, God. You have no idea what they did to me, Nathan. None! Did you know? Did you know it was me, all this time?"

"Indie—"

"Fuck you! Fuck you, Nathan! And then you left again! Where did you go? Where have you been for the last four years?" He looks very sad right now. But I don't care. "Answer me! Where have you been? What have you been doing? Why are you just coming here now?"

"Shh! For fuck's sake! You tried to kill me, Indie! If it wasn't for McKay, who knows? Maybe you'd come back to finish the job!"

"I didn't—"

"Know? Is that what you're gonna say? You didn't know what you were doing when you tried to kill me?"

His words echo in my head. And then I picture that day when everything went wrong.

And then, like I'm being hit with a bolt of lightning, I know *why* it went wrong.

"Carter was there," I whisper.

"He has always *been there*, Indie. You knew this." He shakes me. Hard. "You *knew* this. And you know he's here now, Indie!" He takes my face in his hands. Stares into me with those light-light eyes I would recognize in the darkness. "I'm sorry I left you when I was five. OK? Don't you think I fucking regretted it every single day when I had to see you here? In these woods? Losing your fucking mind, day, after day, after day?"

"What are you talking about?"

"Think!" He taps my head. "Remember! For once in your life, please! Just… make yourself face the fucking truth! Every day you came out to these woods and lost your mind. Every single fucking day you were living in some dream world where we had friends in other towns, and ate ice cream in drugstores, and… and had *fun*."

"What?"

"It wasn't *fun*, Indie. It wasn't fun watching you go crazy every day, then talking you out of it before I could send you home to Adam and McKay and that piece of fucking shit, Donovan!"

"No. That's… no. I remember everything now."

"Is that right?"

"It wasn't all fake. I didn't make it all up. We have a *child* together. I loved you. And you. Loved. *Me*."

His face softens now. "I *do* love you. The only reason I'm here right now is because of you. You wanna know what I've been doing? I've been working for Nick fucking Tate trying to stay one small step ahead of Carter Couture and his brood of little girl assassins all these years. But he caught up to me a few days ago. And he took the last two friends I had. I came here to get you and Maggie and get the fuck out of this place and away from these people once and for all! I'm sorry I left you when I was five. And I'm sorry I stopped trusting you four years ago. But you're all I have left, Indie. You and Maggie are all I have left. I'm not leaving you now. And you're not staying here. But we need to get Carter before we go or he will use all those little girls he made to hunt us down and—"

"Carter?" I gasp.

"We need to kill him, do you understand?"

"No!" I shake my head. "No! We *can't* kill Carter!"

"We have to, Indie. There is no other way."

I struggle against him. "No, no, no!"

And then I'm free.

On my feet.

393

Running.

But he grabs my ankle and I go down hard, hitting my head again.

And black out.

CHAPTER THIRTY-TWO

He's holding Maggie in his arms. She's… not awake.

Probably not sleeping, either.

Not dead, drugged.

And then the image of the little empty vial of Brevital starts to make sense.

"Well, there he is." My brother's accent was always different than mine. It's the one thing that really set us apart. "Finally. He shows."

"What the fuck are you doing here?"

"Come on, Donny!" His laugh scares a small animal in the thick underbrush near his feet and it goes scurrying.

When he uses that name—Donny—I get a really sick feeling in my stomach.

"Donny, Donny, Donny. I kinda like calling you that. Ana did too, didn't she?"

"Fuck you. You do not get to even say her name."

"No? But I thought we shared everything?"

"Give me Maggie. Right now."

"So you can do what? Take her back home?" He laughs again. "They're never going to let you back in that house after this, Donny. You're done here. It's over."

"No. You're giving me that little girl, I'm going to take her back home, put her to bed, and then you and I can sort this out."

"I'm afraid not, brother." He tsks his tongue. "That's not how it's going down at all. You and me?" He points at himself, then me, then himself again. "We've been apart way too long, don't think? You doing your thing. Me doing my thing. It's kind of a waste."

I don't know what to say to that. "You want... me... and..."

"Yes! Yes. That's exactly right. You've got it! I want us to be partners again."

Now it's my turn to laugh. "You're insane."

"If I'm insane, so are you."

"No. I'm not the one holding a drugged little girl in the middle of the woods in the dead of night."

Carter cocks his head at me. Smiles. "Are you *sure* about that, *Donny*?"

CHAPTER THIRTY-THREE

We slow down once we enter the woods. I don't know how familiar McKay is with the property these days, but my knowledge of this part of it was at its peak about ten years ago when he and I still had to round Indie up every night for dinner.

McKay slows. Then stops.

"What is it?"

He uses one of our familiar hand signals to tell me to be quiet.

Someone is up ahead.

I feel this person before I hear him. It's like a sixth sense.

McKay leans into me. "It's Nathan." I listen more carefully. Because it's not just Nathan. McKay adds, "I think he's got Indie."

"You mean *Maggie*."

"No. Listen."

I do. And he's right. There is whispering. Urgent whispering that doesn't come out of a kid's mouth. Not even my kid—who, let's face it, isn't really a kid. "Then where the fuck is Maggie?"

"Maybe she's unconscious?" McKay offers. "I saw him creeping into the woods, but he was alone."

"Maybe he drugged her, then came back to get Indie?"

"Speaking of drugs—where the fuck is Donovan?"

We both look back at the house at the same time, then look at each other. I say, "Donovan wasn't in the house when we left. I know we didn't check, but—"

McKay cuts me off. "I agree. He wasn't there. You can just feel when that house is empty."

"Yeah," I say, breathing out a sigh. "You can."

The whispering up ahead becomes yelling and then abruptly stops. And then it's just Nathan's whispers, no Indie.

McKay is still looking at me. And I don't need to say a word for him to know what I'm thinking. "We'll find her. And Donovan. But first, we need to save Indie. Come on."

We creep forward in stealth mode. McKay is leading, since he has always been better at this than me. It only takes a few minutes for the low whispers to become truly audible and we stop to pick out some words as we process the scene on the banks of the narrow creek that feeds into the river.

Nathan is sitting in the mud holding Indie in his arms. Rocking back and forth. Cradling her.

McKay bursts forward, all stealth gone now. "What the fuck—"

That's as far as he gets, because I pull him back. "Easy," I say. "Hold up."

"She hit her head, McKay! Twice!" Nathan is frantic to explain. "I didn't hurt her! I'm trying to save her!"

"From who?" I am seething with anger from the accusations in his voice.

"From Carter!"

McKay and I both go still. Then McKay says, "He's *here*?"

"Of course he's here! He's always been here! What the fuck—"

Indie begins to moan and McKay rushes over to her, bending down to hold her head in his hands. She's got a wound and it's bleeding pretty good. But head wounds do that. It's not always a sign of trauma. "Indie!" McKay is right down in her face now. "Indie, can you hear me?"

"Don't kill him," she grumbles. "Please, don't kill him."

I walk over to them and kneel down in the mud next to McKay. "Indie, we're not going to kill Nathan. Don't worry. As long as he cooperates—"

"Not Nathan!" She screams it. "Donovan, Adam! Don't let him kill *Donovan*!"

McKay is confused. "Indie, we're not gonna kill Donovan!"

At the same time I'm saying, "Why the fuck would we kill Donovan?"

And then Indie opens her eyes and looks up at Nathan. She's begging him with those eyes. "Please. Don't kill him. He's my friend. He's always been—"

"Indie!" Nathan yells it. "You *know* he's not your friend! You *know* this! You saw what he did to those kids on the island! You saw him! You were there.

399

We"—he pokes her in the chest, then pokes himself too—"*we* were there! And if you saw what I just saw on my way down here—if you even *knew* what he was doing all these years"—Nathan shakes his head—"you would not ask me to save him!"

"That wasn't *him*!" Indie is screaming now too.

And McKay is saying, "What the fuck is happening? What the fuck are you talking about? Why the hell are we talking about Donovan?"

But I know why.

Suddenly all those pieces I was missing to this puzzle fall right into their proper places.

And then an offhanded thought pops into my head:

Someone has to die at the end.

That's just how these stories go.

And that's when Maggie screams from somewhere deep inside the woods.

CHAPTER THIRTY-FOUR

Carter cocks his head at me. Smiles. "Are you *sure* about that, *Donny?*"

His accent is American. Always has been. I don't know where he picked it up, maybe some Company official? I have never understood how we could be so alike in every way and yet sound so different when we spoke.

And suddenly I'm not sure about anything.

"Well, are you?" Carter takes a step towards me and I take a step back. "Where you going, Donny?" He laughs. "Do you really think you're gonna get away this time? No, sir. This is what we psychiatrists call a *transformative moment*. Oftentimes goes hand in hand with its twin, *cognitive dissonance*."

"What the fuck are you talking about?"

He laughs. "Really? Come on, Donny. You're not *really* gonna stand here and refuse to see the fucking truth, are you? When it is literally staring you right in the face?"

I take a step back. He takes a step forward.

"No. Stay away from me, you psycho. Stay. The fuck. Away from me."

Carter is grinning like a boy. Then he leans forward just a little bit and says, "Look *down*, Donny."

And I do it. I don't want to, but I do it.

And then I drop to my knees and Maggie moans as she falls out of my arms and rolls on to her side in the mud.

3.5 MONTHS AGO
HYPNOSIS SESSION #89

Donovan Couture – Patient

Ana Avery, PhD, LMHC
Counselor In Attendance

ANA: OK, Mr. Couture. Tell me what we're doing.

Donovan: Jesus, Ana. I signed a stack of papers four years ago and we do this every time.

I can't risk it. You know that. I'm not a doctor.

Funny. Everyone calls you Doctor.

Just play along, please. Be a good boy, Donny. And I'll make it worth your while tonight.

You little tramp.

Are we going to flirt all afternoon, or do you want to have this session? Because I'd rather be having tea. We're not getting anywhere. We've been stuck for over six months now. I don't know why you even want to keep doing this.

Because I feel like something has changed.

What has changed?

I don't know. I can't put my finger on it. But it's been a long time since we had a session, so maybe that's what I need?

Alternatively... you could let it go. If you were one of my healing center clients that would be my advice. You haven't had a nightmare in almost a year. You're back at work in LA, doing surgery twice a week, and you're teaching a class at Duke. Everything is going great. Sometimes I wonder if you're just...

Just what?

Looking for reasons to...

Reasons to? What?

Not be happy? Sometimes people have guilt—

You don't need to lecture me. I understand this. But I really want this session. I can feel it. I'm approaching my transformative moment. One more good push and I'll be on my way. And I want you to put me under deep this time.

Drugs?

Yes. Use the drugs.

You're sure? Because you've spent the last four years insisting that we *not* use the drugs.

I hereby absolve you of all responsibility for questioning me under the drugs I have already prescribed myself.

Jesus Christ. You have the syringe ready?

I came prepared, Ana. This is it. This might be the last time we ever do one of these sessions. Now, are you ready? Because I'm gonna push these drugs in and if you're not going to do your part, then I'll just take a nice little nap and then we'll just argue about it all over again when I wake up.

Fine. If that's what you want. But let me check my notes real quick. I need to figure out a plan.

You do that. I'm just gonna tie the tourniquet.

Wow. You're really good at that. Doing it to yourself, I mean. Using your teeth and everything. You're such a clever little animal, Donny.

Funny.

OK. Shutting up. You go ahead. I'm right behind you.

...

How you feeling?

...

Donovan? Can you hear me?

Mmhh.

Good. I'd like to start with your childhood again because those sessions always felt... transformative. So... that island you lived on. Can you   go   there   now?

...

Donovan?

...

Donovan?

I'm here.

Where's here?

Home. My island.

Perfect. Can you describe it to me?

Tropical. Hot. Lots of kids. We like kids here.

Well, that's nice. Children always make a place more cheerful, don't they?

Not these kids.

What? And why are you talking in that accent, Donovan?

This is how I talk.

No... I've known you, quite intimately, for nearly ten years now. And you have never flashed an American accent at me.

You don't know me at all, Ana Avery.

...

What's wrong?

You're... sitting up.

So?

406

I just watched you push a whole lot of diazepam into your arm. You should be feeling a little sleepy right now. Donovan! *Donovan!* **I think you should sit down before you fall! Don't come any closer! Donovan!**

I'm not Donovan. I'm Carter. So nice to finally meet you, Ms. Avery. But I'm gonna have to cut this short now. The game has begun.

Maggie screams in front of me.

And at the same time, Ana screams in my memory as Carter's hands—*my* hands—wrap around her throat until she goes limp and quiet.

He killed her.

I. *Killed her.*

"Maggie!" I reach for her but she scrambles away from me. She's clearly still drugged because she's trying to get to her feet and can't.

"Stay away!" she yells. "You stay away from me or my daddies will kill you! Do you hear me? Kill you!"

She's screaming these words at me. They echo in my head. And then I hear myself say, "Maggie, if you

407

don't shut your fucking mouth, I'm gonna cut off your tongue just like I did to those kids on Snake Island. And then I'll use it as bait for the gators. Little snack before they eat you."

She screams again.

I grab my pistol from the back of my pants and then—

I stop.

Look at the gun. Then Maggie. "What the fuck is happening?"

"You know what's happening," Carter says.

Only it's not Carter. Or is it?

I don't know anymore.

His words feel like they're coming out of my mouth.

Maggie kicks at me just as I hear people thundering through the underbrush.

I grab her leg, pull her towards me, and then aim my gun at her head—just as Adam, McKay, Indie and... *Nathan?*—come rushing into the little clearing.

"Let her go!" Adam growls. "Let her go, Donovan."

I look down at Maggie again. And I'm about to do what Adam asks. I don't even know why I'm holding her or why I'm pointing the gun at her head.

But when I open my mouth, it's Carter who speaks. "I'm not Donovan."

CHAPTER THIRTY-FIVE

I want to smack him. Force the crazy out of his head with a punch to the teeth.

"Donovan." I *growl* out his name. "I don't care if there is some rogue personality living inside your brain. If you don't move that gun away from that little girl's head—"

"You'll *what?*" he growls back at me. "What are you gonna do, McKay? Put me in timeout? Take away my wireless password? Make me eat my vegetables?"

"Donovan."

He looks over at Indie and snarls. "I'm. Not. Donovan."

Indie is not convinced and she takes a step forward. "Oh, yes, you are. You are Donovan. And by the time we leave these woods here tonight, that's the only person you'll be."

Carter laughs and presses the gun he's holding to the side of Maggie's head just a little harder. "I remember you. You know that, Indie? I remember you." Then he looks at Nathan. Nods his head. "You too. Little fucking coward. Running away that night like a baby."

"Like a baby?" Nathan says. "I was five, you sick son of a bitch. I was a baby. But you weren't. You knew exactly what you were doing in those woods. You knew exactly why you were sent in to hunt kids. And you did it anyway."

"Hey," Carter laughs. "Perks of being Company, right?"

"Fuck you, Carter." Indie steps forward with a gun of her own. The one missing from the foyer closet, from the looks of it. "You need to leave. Donovan!" She yells it. Like Donovan is somewhere in the woods and not lost inside his own head. Like if she could just shout a little louder, he'd call back and we'd track him down and bring him home.

But that's not where Donovan is.

"Donovan," she yells again. "I know you're in there. And I know how much you love Maggie. You love to eat breakfast with her and make faces at her. You love us, Donovan—"

"Shut up!" Carter is the one yelling now.

I feel like I should be doing something. Rushing in like a hero, maybe? Saving Maggie. But both Adam and I are too far away and we're not armed. So I leave it to Indie.

"No, I will not shut up! I will not shut up! I want to talk to Donovan!"

And then it occurs to me that Indie knew.

She *knew*. Maybe not consciously, but she was with Donovan at least twice while she was missing those four years.

"Donovan!" She's still yelling. "Come out here and talk to me! Right now!"

At first, I think she's just trying to find the more reasonable personality to deal with, but that's not it.

Indie *loves* Donovan. Maybe not as much as she loves Nathan. But she never loved any of us the way she loves Nathan.

Carter begins to breathe hard and his gun hand gets a little too shaky for my comfort level. I watch his trigger finger, ready to rush in and take over if it gets any twitchier.

It's not gonna help. I'm not close enough.

We have made a wide circle around Donovan now. Both Indie and Nathan are facing him dead on. Like this is some predetermined showdown with the villain and they're the heroes.

And they are, aren't they?

I only had to see Nathan St. James's face for ten seconds yesterday morning for the truth to sink in.

He *is* Maggie's father. Maybe I could pretend that Maggie was the spitting image of her mother, but it's so clear now that she is the spitting image of them both, I look over at Adam—across from me, and on the other side of Donovan—to see if he's seeing too.

He is. He knows. And if he had a gun right now, I know how this would end.

And Indie would never forgive him for that.

That's why I let Nathan live four years ago and that's why Adam won't kill him tonight.

Maggie moans. Her eyes are open. She looked drowsy, like he drugged her, when we first got here. But she's blinking rapidly now. Squirming in Donovan's arms.

411

Carter's arms.

"Donovan!" Indie shouts again. "Talk to me! Right now! You come out here and talk to me or I swear to God, I will... I will..."

But what can she do? She is *not* gonna kill him. I can see that now. She is *not* going to shoot this man or he would already be dead.

"You know"—everyone looks over at Nathan, even Carter—"I never liked you."

Carter snarls at him, but doesn't say nothing. And then his face screws up. Like... something is happening inside his head and he can't quite control it.

"But," Nathan continues, "Indie does, Donovan." Carter moans a little. "She loves you, Donovan. And she begged me not to kill you tonight. Not kill Carter and let you become collateral damage. And at first—"

Carter starts to sob. And I look at Adam and find him just as disturbed as me.

"At first, Donovan, I didn't think it was possible. But you are stronger than him. You fought him all these years. Even after your father tried to kill you. Tried to make you go away. You were too nice for him. You wouldn't do the things that Carter would. That's why he was in the woods that night when we were kids, and not you. You could not be that monster. But he could." Nathan whispers that last part. "He *could*. That's why he's here. But you don't *need* him—"

"Shut up!" Carter is breathing hard. Panting like a fucking dog when he screams this. "Shut up! You don't know what you're talking about! I'm the strong one! I'm the smart one! I'm the fucking doctor! Not him!"

"You're wrong," Adam says. "You're plain wrong. Donovan Couture is the brains of this operation and

412

you know it. He's the one who went to medical school. He's the one who—"

"Fuck you!" Carter is grabbing his hair with one hand and his eyes are closed. "That's *my* name! *My name* on those diplomas! Not his! Everything he has is *mine*!

Carter is going to lose this game. I can feel it. He's so close.

"He was the kind one," I say, picking it up. "The good one. The one who loved and was loved back. Not you, Carter!"

And as soon as the words come out of my mouth I feel guilty. For not seeing this sooner.

Not his split personality, but his… *heart.*

"No, no, no…" Carter is moaning now. And then he tosses Maggie over to the side and she scrambles away on her hands and knees, then collapses into the mud just a little bit behind Donovan.

I want to go to her. Pull her out of this.

But Carter begins to scream. A chilling scream that is right at home in the Louisiana swamp.

He screams like a creature of this place. Like a wounded possum or a rabbit caught in the jaws of a gator.

And then he drops his head and just cries.

"Donovan!" Indie rushes forward, and I'm about to grab Maggie when Donovan looks up and points the gun at his own head. Indie stops in her tracks.

Maggie is squirming behind him. And at first I think she's trying to get away, but then she's pulling something out of the waistband of Donovan's shorts and I see the gun.

"Donovan!" Indie yells. "Donovan, you listen to me, you crazy son-of-a-bitch. You are not going to kill

413

yourself! Do you hear me?" He doesn't say anything and she screams it. "Do you. Fucking. Hear. Me? We do *not* kill ourselves. There are too many people out there trying to do that for us! We do not kill ourselves! You are stopping by a wood on a fucking snowy evening and that's all there is to this! Do you hear me! I don't care what anyone says, he was just stopping in the *fucking woods*!"

At first I don't even know what she's talking about. And I get a sick feeling that she's losing her mind right in front of my face. And then I remember her journal. And that poem by Robert Frost. And how she insisted, over the objection of just about everyone, that the man in the woods was *not* going to kill himself.

Donovan looks at her. Tears are streaming down his face as he presses the gun to the side of his head. "I can't do this anymore, Indie. I can't."

"You can," she says. "You *will*." And now she's crying too. "You will do this, Donovan. You will—"

And then Maggie has the gun in her hand and she's squirming backwards, pointing it at the back of Donovan's head.

Adam and I both yell, "No!"

Donovan *turns*.

Not around. He *turns*.

Back into Carter.

And he points the gun at Indie.

Three things happen in the same moment.

Maggie *shoots*.

Carter *shoots*.

And Indie *shoots*.

The kick from the gun makes Maggie fall to the left and Donovan fall to the right.

Indie's bullet grazes the side of Donovan's head just as Maggie's hits him true.

And Donovan's bullet passes right through the dark, dead air between Indie and Nathan.

TWO WEEKS LATER

We decided not to have a funeral for Donovan.

In the old days this would be a big deal. An Untouchable dying is always a big deal and usually we'd gather on some island and make it a production.

But there is no more Company like that. Oh, we're still here. Drifting around trying to figure where the fuck we fit into things. But there is no island to meet up at anymore.

So we don't have a funeral.

But we do make sure certain people who count hear about his death. Get the rumors started. Let them know, one small leftover group at a time, that he's gone now.

Of course, he's *not* gone.

Turns out that Donovan Couture—regardless of what I have thought about him in the past—is a true fuckin' fighter.

417

That gun in the waistband of his shorts? It was a tranq gun. I don't even know where it came from, but that's what Maggie shot him with.

However, when you get hit point blank to the back of the head, even with a tranq gun, there are severe consequences. And Indie's bullet did graze him too.

I saw the x-rays. There is a chip in the left side of Donovan's skull. Right above his ear. In fact, the top part of his ear was shot clean off.

Something ironic happened after the shootout was over. I recalled that I had a doctor on staff, a retired one who didn't really work anymore. The very same doctor who patched up Indie's slit wrists all those years ago. I had been paying him a pension for reasons I never fully articulated back when I made him the offer.

But I am one of those people who plans for the worst and fully expects it to happen.

If, at some point, some overly confident and motivated ex-Company kid decided he would like my job and tried to take me out, then I would need somewhere to go if I got hurt.

So that's who I called that night. He came with two nurses and they moved in to the spare bedrooms along the breezeway.

Donovan has been in a coma since the incident. The doctor tells me the drug Maggie shot him with was a psychotropic. And I spent a good day wondering what Carter was planning with that drug.

But it doesn't matter now. He literally got a dose of his own medicine.

That wasn't Donovan's only injury. You can't take out a part of a person's skull with a .357 Magnum and not expect some internal damage, even if the bullet just grazed him.

The doctor—his name is Bolton—came with an entire ICU setup and we put that in the great room.

So that's where Donovan is now. Still unconscious. Bolton says he might never come out of it. And if he does, we won't know for sure which personality survived, if any.

It's not an ideal situation, but I'm trying to fix that.

I press the green tab on my phone and listen to it ring on speaker.

"Helloooooo!" a teenage girl answers.

And for a moment I forget where I am in time and say, "Sasha?"

"No. It's Lauren. Who's this? Your number didn't come up."

"Adam."

Silence for a moment. Then, "Hmm." And, "Mom! It's Uncle Adam!"

Uncle?

There's some shuffling on the other end, then a breathless Sasha says, "Hey. Are you bringing the steaks today? Because if so, don't get none of those shit vegan ones, OK? You hear me? If you show up with vegan T-bones, I will—"

I cut her off. "It's the *other* Adam, Sasha." All I hear is breathing and the sound of some busy place in the background. "You still there?"

"I'm here." She whispers it. "What do you want?" Her tone is no longer light and happy. It's very, *very* dark.

"I'm looking for a guy—"

"Never heard of him."

419

"Don't be a bitch. This is a true fucking emergency, OK? Did you hear about Donovan?"

"I heard. Sorry for your loss."

"That's why I'm calling. I didn't lose anything. Yet. But I need some help here. He's not dead, but he's in a bad way and I need a certain type of guy to help him past this."

She pauses. "What kind of guy?"

"PSYOPS. He's been fucked with. Badly. And by someone who really knew what he was doing. He's in a coma right now, but he could wake up at any moment and then I'm gonna need this guy, Sasha. If I'm gonna save him."

"Maybe you shouldn't save him. I know what's going on. I know all about Carter. So maybe you should just let him die?"

Part of me hates her right now. And to be clear, I have never felt any kind of fondness for Sasha Cherlin. She was a weapon to be used and nothing more. But if she *knew*. If she *knew* that Donovan was Carter, she could've fucking spoke up and said something *ten years ago*.

Fighting with her now defeats the purpose of my call so I sigh and rub my temple with two fingers. "I can't. It's not fair. He helped me. I don't think anyone understands how *much* he helped me. I owe him this one last chance."

"You owe Carter Couture?"

"No. *Donovan*. I don't give a fuck about Carter. In fact, if this man you know can get rid of him when Donovan wakes up, all the better. But if not, then we need a way to control it, Sasha. Please. How do I contact *Merc*?"

She lets out a long breath. "He's retired. Has been for…hell, a decade almost. And so am I. I don't appreciate this phone call. My life is sorted. I have a family—a husband, two kids, and fucking dog. I don't need this."

"If I had anyone else to call, you know I would."

She snorts. "How could you possibly not have anyone else to call? You run the fucking Company."

"PSYOPS died out. Donovan was the last one."

"You mean *Carter* was the last one."

"Whatever. I would not ask you if I didn't have to. I swear. Please. One last favor. If you do this I'll tell you something I know. Something very secret."

"What secret?"

"Will you help me?"

"What. Fucking. Secret, Adam?"

"Before I say any more, you need to ask yourself if you really want to know this secret. Because like you said, you have a husband, and two kids, and a fucking dog. And if I tell you this, you might walk away from all of it."

She laughs. "Not fucking likely." But then she goes quiet. "What is it?"

"Will you call Merc for me? Talk him into giving me a hand?"

She pauses. For several long seconds. Which is good—for her, anyway. Bad for me, but good for her. Because she doesn't need this secret. It will rip her life apart. And if she was smart, she'd hang up on me right now and forget she ever knew a man called Adam Boucher.

She finally sighs. "Keep your secret. I'll make the call."

And then she's gone.

I stare out the dining room window.

How many times have I stood in this same spot and looked out across the duck lake at the cottage that used to be there?

Too many to count, for sure.

There are a lot of interesting things to see over there right now though. And that's what I'm looking at. I'm not thinking about the past or how many ways I might kill Nathan St. James.

No. I'm looking at McKay over there. He's in a front-loader tractor smoothing dirt as the concrete truck idles not far off. He's building a fucking house. Only Core McKay would wake up one day after we lived through Hell out in the Old Home woods and say, "I think I'll build a house."

But that's what he is doing.

I'm not sure who's gonna live over there. McKay and I sleep in my room now and Indie and Nathan have taken his. Maggie is right where she belongs in Indie's childhood bedroom.

So none of us need a house across the duck lake. I'm fairly certain Indie will not want to live there, even if Nathan does. So I'm equally as sure that it's not going to happen.

Maybe he's building it for Donovan?

Maybe he's just… keeping busy? Doing something to take his mind off the fact that our best friend is insane and in a coma. And if he ever recovers, he might try to kill us.

Maggie is over there 'helping him' and I recall all those days gone by when it was Indie out there giving McKay a hand.

Nathan and Indie are trying to figure out their past. They sit out there on her swing in the pavilion and go over it every day. She's still not sure what was real and what wasn't.

But only one thing really matters as far as I'm concerned.

Nathan St. James *is* Maggie's father. Bolton has a colleague at Ole Miss who runs the molecular biology department so he sent in a DNA test for Maggie and Nathan and it came back a match.

Two weeks ago, I'd have been upset about that. But now I think I might've lost my mind if he wasn't Maggie's father and Carter was.

I turn away from the window and walk back into my office. Take a seat at my desk and stare down at the packet of papers I found in my twin brother's grave.

It almost makes sense.

Most of it does.

I think my father was a friend to Nathan's grandfather. Otherwise known as Nikos Szabó.

I think my father helped save Nathan. I think... maybe... I regret getting him killed.

I think I would've liked to hear his real story. Hear about my twin, who is missing. There is no baby-boy body in our family mausoleum.

I think I would've liked to know why he took me out of the Zero Program. Why he bought McKay when it seems pretty clear to me now that he never really intended to go through with any of it.

I think I would've liked to know *him*, actually. The man behind the father. The one who did his best to protect me, even though I never felt particularly protected.

Then I chuckle a little under my breath. Because I'm fairly certain Indie would say the same thing about me.

I will never touch Indie again. Ever. Not even a kiss on the cheek. And neither will McKay. Maybe we're not biologically related to her, but it doesn't matter.

We are the only fathers she ever had.

I don't really know if Mallory Machette and Sidonia Ameci are important in the big picture. Not even sure it matters. Because I don't think these were my father's secrets to begin with. I think they were Nikos's.

So I put them to rest with all the other secrets I've come across in my life and just let them die.

But there was that envelope with Nick Tate's name on the front.

I read it. No way I couldn't. And it said a lot of things make sense and yet don't quite add up.

My phone rings on the desk. Right on time.

Nick Tate is nothing if not predictable.

I tab accept and say, "I'm glad you called."

"You knew I would."

"So you heard?"

"I heard."

"We're out."

"You're not out, Adam. There is no 'out'. There is a nest of little girls—

"Yes. I know. But they're gone."

"Gone. How? Nathan?"

"No. Not Nathan. We went up there to check it out and the entire house is empty. One can only assume Carter had a final back-up plan and they got swept up in it."

"Then they *aren't* gone. So no one is *out*."

"Well"—I sigh—"we're gonna have to agree to disagree on this one, Nick. Carter and Donovan are dead now, so whatever was going on, it's probably over."

"So you say. It's all pretty convenient."

"Which part?"

"All of it. But especially the part about Donovan and Carter. It's too bad they died."

"Why's that?"

"Because we're a little short on PSYOPS people these days."

"Still got you, right?"

I can hear him smile on the other end of the phone. "You are well aware that wasn't me. It was my double. He was the one who went through that training. And he was the one I needed to kill to make my escape."

"Sucks to be you, I guess."

"Tell me again how Donovan died?"

"Point-blank shot to the head."

"And that little girl, Maggie, did it?"

"Part of it. Indie took a shot too."

"Interesting."

He doesn't believe me. But I don't care. I'm gonna play this last card and leave it at that. He will walk away. He won't have a choice. "I know of another one."

"Another what?"

"PSYOPS specialist. Goes by the name of Merc. You ever hear of… *Merc,* Nick?"

He's silent on the other end of the phone.

"He's a good friend of Sasha Cherlin's." More silence. And I know I've got him. "You should give him a call. Oh. Wait. I forgot. You can't. Because you lied to Sasha when you made her kill your double. And you dropped your daughter off with her too, didn't you? Can't really come back from something like that. I get it though. If I had dropped Maggie off with my best friend ten years ago to protect her, and then she suddenly came back into my life… well. I'd have a hard time staying away after that. I'd ruin everything to be with her again, and I wouldn't even care. All my careful planning. All those tears Maggie would've cried when I left her behind. All that begging she would've done to keep us together."

He says nothing.

I lower my voice and whisper the next part. "You don't get to be the hero, *Nick.* Not then, not now, not *ever.* You don't get to drop little girls off with other people and make her an unwilling accomplice to your pretty nightmare of lies that *broke hearts*—and still hold on to your self-righteousness like it's a goddamned war medal. That's not how this is going to end, you hear me? You're not the good guy here."

"And you are?"

"I have never pretended to be good. Ever. I take full responsibility for what I've done and who I've hurt.

And if you think you're gonna use us the way you used Wendy, you better think again. Because I will hunt you down and kill you myself if I hear one small whisper that you're anywhere near my guys, or my family, or anyone else I hold dear."

"Kill me, huh?"

"We both know you're not the legend everyone thinks you are. That was your double. He was the mastermind. You were nothing."

"And yet… I'm still here and he's not."

"Stay the fuck away from us. And that includes Nathan. He's mine now. Do you understand me? *Mine*."

"You seem to think everyone is yours these days."

"They are. There is a new king of the Company now, *Nick*. And it's *not* you."

He's quiet for a long moment. And I'm just about to hang up when he says, "Whatever Wendy told you, it's not the whole story."

Wendy hasn't told me anything. She won't even answer my calls. But I'm not gonna tell Nick that. Nathan filled me in on this little Wendy and Nick situation. He didn't know much either, but it was enough to know that Nick fucked up with her. He did something to her that she can't forgive. And his final words are gonna be just that. The last thing he ever gets to say to me. "Well, it was good talking to you. Have a nice—"

Alarms start screaming through my house. Wailing, screaming alarms.

Not the security system. The ICU machines on the other side of the breezeway, which have been connected to the central sound system so we would

427

know, anywhere in the house, if Donovan's condition changed.

Then Bolton is in my office doorway and before I can put up a hand, he says, "He's awake! He's awake!"

Bolton leaves with a swish of his white coat and then it's just me and Nick.

He laughs on the other end of the phone. *Loud.* Loud enough for me to hear him over the screaming of the ICU machines.

The alarms cut off just as quickly as they started.

Nick is still laughing. "You almost had me, Adam. You sneaky little fuck. You *almost* had me."

And then the call ends with three quick beeps.

Welcome to the End of Book Shit. You know what this is so I'm just going to get to it. Quick reminder - this part is never edited so you will probably find typos.

I think we can all agree that 2020 has been a super-weird year so far and when I started this Company storyline back in 2013 with the book "Slack" (now part of the Ford book) never did I ever imagine that we'd be in the middle of a worldwide pandemic that had the fictional Company fingerprints all over it. I mean, who needs these books about these crazy Company people when we have real life, right?

Obviously I write books about the Company because I find the idea of a shadow government that controls, not just the United States, but the entire world, to be fascinating.

I remember liking that Bridget Fonda movie, Point of No Return back when I was a kid. And The Professional, with a very small, but formidable, Natalie Portman. There are a bunch of others out there. LOST comes to mind. I was really in to that show. And of course, every movie or TV show where the government and the corpos are in evil collusion together, Mr. Robot, anyone?

I just enjoy puzzle stories like that where you never quite know who the bad guy is and then, eventually, you figure it out, but he's really the good guy—at least as far as you're concerned.

But the thing that really intrigues me, and this is one of the reasons I started this storyline, was the idea that there are certain people in this world WHO LIVE OUTSIDE OF IT.

Maybe they are hackers or thieves?

Or soldiers who saw too much and have too many skills?

Or rich, powerful families that 99.999999% of us can't even TRY and relate to?

Or maybe they were just in the wrong place at the wrong time and saw more than they should?

Or perhaps they are like Nick Carraway in the Great Gatsby and just, by accident, know someone who is one of these people and they get caught up in the fever dream?

Or maybe they grew up in a cult and there is no fucking way in hell they will ever fit into society?

These are the people I like to write about. These "outsiders" who see the shadow. Who notice that it's not moving right. It doesn't *look* right. And they see this when others can't because, through some twist of fate or bad accident, they're *a part* of it.

Maybe a small part, maybe a big one. It doesn't matter. Once you look past the shadow and see the darkness underneath, you can't go back.

When I wrote Tragic I knew Rook was in some bad shit. The details would all come later. But I based the spine of the series plot on the movie Ocean's Eleven. A team of people who were so coordinated, and smart, and sneaky, and talented, and patient that they could pull off the heist of the century and get away with it.

Anyone can steal things, right?

But not everyone can get away with it.

That's what I set out to do when I wrote Rook & Ronin.

But then Sasha Cherlin and Merc showed up in Slack and the little world I had created in Fort Collins, Colorado suddenly went global. And that's when the Company was born.

Things kinda spun out of control after that. The story took on a life of its own and more and more characters appeared with even darker and more nefarious backgrounds to consider.

And it's fun, as a writer, to try and piece all these things together and come up with—wait for it—**a conspiracy theory**!

It's just fun.

So I was in to it.

But I didn't start *questioning* any of it until I wrote Meet Me in the Dark.

If you've read that EOBS you know how much research I did and you know I was disturbed by it all.

The reason it's so disturbing is because a lot of the mind control stuff I've written about is actually true. The US government admits it. This brainwashing shit—this *PSYOPS* shit—this actually happened. They destroyed most of the records in the Seventies—most likely all the of the really nasty shit—but the documents that survived—mostly financial statements and boring things like that—were enough to corroborate what that program was doing, and then, of course, they admitted it. And that program was brainwashing people. i.e.—they were being PSYOPS'ed.

When I started Merc's book I didn't even know what MK Ultra was. I mean, maybe I had heard of it? Maybe? In a movie—I did love that movie with Mel Gibson, Conspiracy Theory. But was I paying attention to the details? I will go ahead and admit to you right now, I rarely pay attention to *any* details. Just ask Johnathan McClain how often I forget shit. Even shit I write. It drives him crazy. But he has learned to live with, and maybe even love, my brand of insanity.

So no. Even if I had heard of MK Ultra, I was paying zero attention to it.

But of course, I have this really active, cool imagination and I've seen a lot of these "conspiracy" type movies, and I *did* read *The Da Vinci Code*, bitches! And fun fact, Ancient Aliens is my most favorite show of all time and I'm kinda jealous of Jason Bourne's hidden abilities that enable him to MacGyver his way out of pretty much any sticky situation in any country on Earth, all while speaking the native tongue!

Plus, I was a child of the Seventies so I was *there* for Watergate and the aftermath of the Vietnam War and my father was a golf-pro hippy living in Lake Tahoe with friends in Big Sur, and had books on his shelf called *Zen and the Art of Motorcycle Maintenance* and *In Watermelon Sugar* sooo… ya know. I was kind of born into this weird counter-culture, but at the same time didn't quite live in it because my mother is *totally* normal and boring and I lived with her most of the time after my parents divorced.

So HELLO!

I'm like… not a *newb* at this shit. This is Hollywood. This is the ramblings of crazy people. This is fiction.

But for fuck's sake… when I find out in 2018 that there's this cult of weird child sex traffickers hiding behind a "multi-level marketing" company called NXIVM who brand women like they are cattle, run by some sick fuck called Keith Allen Raniere, who—get this—goes by the supervillain name of *Vanguard*—and this plot is almost exactly what I wrote about in 321 in 2015… what the fuck am I supposed to do but admit that not all of it is fiction?

And of course, in 2019 we learn about another sick-fuck sex-trafficker named Jeffery Epstein who runs some kind of orgy island in the Caribbean and all kinds of people we thought we knew and respected were on said island with him at one point or another—some of them many times—and then he mysteriously "kills himself" while on suicide watch in prison before he goes to trial?

Are you fucking kidding me?

Come on—who's been reading my Company books?

Guys! Get your own plot! This one is **mine**!

Or not. lol

So anyway… yeah. It's crazy.

Truth is always stranger than fiction.

But I love this world I've created. And I love the antihero. I think most of you know that already. I love the idea that some jaded asshole who has seen too much, and done too much, and knows too much, finally—*FINALLY*—grows a pair of balls and takes a goddamned *stand*.

Just throws the fucking gauntlet down and says, "You and me, motherfucker! *Right now.* Let's go!"

We've taken lots of these stands on our little journey through the minds of the Company kids and their friends so far.

The list is long:

Rook

Ronin

Ford

Ashleigh

Spencer

Veronica

Merc

Sydney

Sasha

James

Harper

Nick

Jax

Blue
Ark
JD
Logan
AJ
Yvette
Jesse
Joey
Johnny
Alonzo
Tony
Vann

And now we're here. With Adam, McKay, Nathan, Indie, Nick, and (hopefully) Donovan. But one can't be too sure—I mean, Adam is right, after all. Someone *has* to die at the end.

All these people making all these stands adds up to one really long, amazing, web of beginnings and endings, and truths, and lies and good guys, and bad guys that, when put in the proper context, create synergy.

Something bigger together than they were alone.

I saw a review for Creeping that said it was too complicated.

I reject that characterization.

My books are not too complicated for the right readers. The people who enjoy these books like complicated and if you're not into the story the way they are, this book wasn't written for you. It was written for them.

And if you're one of them who is enjoying this ride, then I hope you're ready for who come next.

Not what.

Who.

Book three—titled Gorgeous Misery (no pre-order yet) will release in October 2020. There is a reason for the five-month gap and that reason is called Johnny Boston. (If you want to know where Johnny Boston fits into the story, read the cheat sheet after the EOBS).

We're going to move locations in Gorgeous Misery and we're going to get another point of view.

Nick Tate was right—there's always another side to the story.

Thank you for reading, thank you for reviewing, and I'll see you in the next book!

Julie

JA Huss

If you want the complete Company story you should read the books in the order below. I made some notes about which characters first show up where, if you're just looking for a specific Company storyline.

Rook and Ronin Series

The entire Company beginnings start in this series. But each series is its own entry point. You can jump in and read them out of order as long as you follow the specific series reading order.

Tragic
Manic – Vaughn Family and Sick Boyz appear here.
Panic – Vaughn Family and Sick Boyz appear here.
Ford – Sasha Cherlin (age 12) and Merc first appear here
Spencer – James Fenici first appears here – Five is born, Vaughn Family and Sick Boyz appear here.

The Company - Rook & Ronin Spin-off – new entry point into the series

The Company – James and Vincent Fenici age 28, Sasha Cherlin age 13, Nick and Harper Tate age 18. This is the **full story of the "Santa Barbara Incident"** where Adam and Donovan's fathers die.

Meet Me In The Dark – Merc, Sasha Cherlin age 21, Sydney Channing (Company Girl like Indie and Sasha)

Three, Two, One – STANDALONE BOOK – Jax Barlow first appears

Wasted Lust – Sasha Cherlin, age 24, with Jax Barlow.

Nick Tate, age 29, plays a major role and the rest of the Company characters also show back up.

First appearance of Angelica Fenici and "other Adam".

Wasted Lust takes place DURING Creeping Beautiful. Specifically when Indie is 15 years old and the "Company falls" and when Nick meets Adam in Daphne, Alabama.

Vaughn Family and Sick Boyz appear here.

The Mister Series – Rook & Ronin/Company Spin-off – new entry point into the series

Mr. Perfect
Mr. Romantic – First appearance of the Silver Society – i.e. The Company
Mr. Corporate – First appearance of "Five"
Mr. Mysterious – Spencer's daughters
Mr. Match – All the Rook & Ronin Kids come back to play.
Mr. Five (or just Five) – Ford's son and Spencer's daughter
Mr. & Mrs. – Ford and Spencer show back up with all the kids. – Vaughn Family appears here.

The Bossy Brothers Series
Rook & Ronin/Company Spin-off – new entry point into the series

In to Her – STANDALONE BOOK – Logan first appears
Bossy Brothers: Jesse – First appearance of The Way – i.e. The Company
Bossy Brothers: Joey
Bossy Brothers: Johnny – Logan shows back up Indie first appears at age 14, Chek's first appearance
Bossy Bride: Jesse and Emma – Chek and Wendy mentioned
Bossy Brothers: Alonzo – Chek and Wendy mentioned, Vaughn Family and Sick Boyz appear here.
Bossy Brothers: Tony – Vaughn Family and Sick Boyz appear here.

Creeping Beautiful – Rook & Ronin and Company Spin-off – new entry point into the series

The complete story of Nick Tate, James and Vincent Fenici, "Wendy", "Chek", Indie Anna Accorsi, Adam

439

Boucher, Donovan and Carter Couture, Core McKay, and Nathan St. James.

Creeping Beautiful (book 1)
Pretty Nightmare (book 2)
Gorgeous Misery (book 3)
Lovely Darkness (book 4)

ABOUT THE AUTHOR

JA Huss is the New York Times Bestselling author of 321 and has been on the *USA Today* Bestseller's list 21 times in the past five years. She writes characters with heart, plots with twists, and perfect endings.

Her new sexy sci-fi romance and paranormal romance pen name is KC Cross and she writes novels and teleplays collaboratively with actor and screenwriter, Johnathan McClain.

Her books have sold millions of copies all over the world, the audio version of her semi-autobiographical book, Eighteen, was nominated for a Voice Arts Award and an Audie Award in 2016 and 2017 respectively. Her audiobook, Mr. Perfect, was nominated for a Voice Arts Award in 2017. Her audiobook, Taking Turns, was nominated for an Audie Award in 2018. Five of her book were optioned for a TV series by MGM television in 2018. And her book, Total Exposure, was nominated for a RITA Award in 2019.

She lives on a ranch in Central Colorado with her family.